ALSO BY LUCY SCORE

Undercover Love
Pretend You're Mine
Finally Mine
Protecting What's Mine
Mr. Fixer Upper
The Christmas Fix
Heart of Hope
The Worst Best Man
Rock Bottom Girl
The Price of Scandal
By a Thread
Forever Never
Things We Never Got Over
Maggie Moves On

RILEY THORN

Riley Thorn and the Dead Guy Next Door
Riley Thorn and the Corpse in the Closet
Riley Thorn and the Blast from the Past

BLUE MOON SMALL-TOWN ROMANCE

No More Secrets
Fall into Temptation
The Last Second Chance
Not Part of the Plan
Holding on to Chaos
The Fine Art of Faking It
Where It All Began
The Mistletoe Kisser

BOOTLEG SPRINGS

Whiskey Chaser
Sidecar Crush
Moonshine Kiss
Bourbon Bliss
Gin Fling
Highball Rush

SINNER AND SAINT

Crossing the Line
Breaking the Rules

By a Thread

LUCY SCORE

Bloom books

Cover design by Kari March Designs
Cover image by taxiro/Adobe Stock
Internal design by Ashley Holstrom/Sourcebooks

Published by Bloom Books, an imprint of Sourcebooks
P.O. Box 4410, Naperville, Illinois 60567-4410
(630) 961-3900
sourcebooks.com

Originally self-published in 2020 by That's What She Said, Inc.

Cataloging-in-Publication Data is on file with the Library of Congress.

Printed and bound in Canada.
MBP 10 9

To you.
For trusting me with your heart
and your book budget.

1

DOMINIC

A junior editor chirped in my ear about canary-yellow sundresses and Cuban photo shoots while the January wind worked its icy fingers through my layers. I navigated the curb buried under foot-tall piles of what used to be snow. Now it was gray slush frozen into dirty, depressing clumps.

I identified with those frozen clumps.

There was a guy, homeless by the looks of his ripped-up sneakers and worn coat, huddled into the corner of an abandoned storefront. He had a dog wrapped in one of those cheap fleece blankets department stores practically gave away at Christmas.

Goddammit. I hated when they had dogs.

I'd never had one myself, but I had fond memories of my high school girlfriend's black Lab, Fonzie. My *only* fond memory from that particular relationship.

I tilted my head in the guy's direction, and my driver,

Nelson, gave me a nod. He knew the drill. It wasn't out of the kindness of my heart. I had neither kindness nor a heart.

I considered it atonement for being an asshole.

Nelson ducked behind the rear of the SUV and opened the hatch. He did the shopping and "distribution" while I funded the ongoing operation.

When I came back, the guy would have a new coat, a pocket full of gift cards, and directions to the nearest shelters and hotels that allowed animals. And that furry little mutt, looking up at his human with blind adoration, would be in some warm, ridiculous dog sweater.

I headed toward the damn pizza place that my mother had insisted upon. Coming all the way to the Village from Midtown on a bone-chilling Tuesday evening was not *my* idea of fun.

But making me do things I didn't want to do was my *mother's* idea of fun.

If there was anyone in the world for whom I'd willingly do shit I didn't want to do, it was Dalessandra Russo. She'd had a rough year. I could give her greasy pizza and my uninterrupted attention before having Nelson haul my ass home to the Upper West Side, where I most likely would glare at a computer screen for another three hours before calling it a night.

Alone.

Saving a family name and rescuing a family business didn't exactly leave a lot of time for extracurricular activities. I wondered if I should get a dog.

My coat flapped in the frigid wind as I stalked toward the restaurant's dingy orange sign, and the art director chimed in with her thoughts on designer pieces for the May cover.

Winter in Manhattan was depressing. I was not a sweaters-and-hot-chocolate kind of guy. I skied because that was what you did when you were born into a wealthy family. But instead of ski slopes, I preferred to spend two weeks in the Caribbean every January.

At least I had in my old life.

I yanked open the steamy glass door of George's Village Pizza. A little bell tinkled above me, announcing my arrival. The heat hit me first. Then the scents of garlic and fresh-baked bread, and maybe I didn't hate that Mom had dragged my ass down here.

"What are your thoughts, Mr. Russo?" the junior editor asked.

I hated being called Mr. Russo. I also hated the fact that I couldn't yell at anyone about it. That was the worst part. Not being able to let out the temper that had been building for over a year.

My attention was caught by curves and curls.

The woman straightened away from the table closest to the door, stuffing the cash tip into her flour-sprinkled apron. Her eyes locked on mine, and I felt something…interesting. Like the ghost of recognition. Like *she* was the one I was here to meet.

But we were strangers.

"That sounds fine," I hedged into the phone.

"I can put together a board for you," the junior editor offered helpfully.

"I'd appreciate that," I said, relieved that she'd offered and I hadn't had to ask this time.

They were all finally getting used to the idea that I needed to *see* things together before I could tell if they worked or not. I hoped that they were also getting used to the idea that I wasn't my fucking father.

Curves and curls was a server, according to the GVP polo she wore over a long sleeve thermal. Her jeans were generics.

Sneakers were at least two years out of functionality, but she'd done something artistic with Sharpies to the white space on them. She was inches shorter and miles curvier than most of the women I'd spent time with recently.

In the last year, I'd become immune to leggy, waiflike models in their early twenties. Which, to be honest, was about damn time considering that I was forty-four. There was something arresting about the woman eyeing me and now pointing to the No Cell Phones sign posted on the corkboard just inside the door.

Interesting face. Softer, rounder than those diamond-edge cheekbones that graced the pages of the magazine. Full lips, wide brown eyes that looked warm, like honey. Her hair, more brown and chestnut there, was jaw-length and styled in lazy, loose waves that made me think of putting my hands in it while she breathed my name under me.

I couldn't stop staring at her.

"I'll have it for you first thing in the morning," the junior editor promised.

I couldn't remember the editor's name—because I was an ass—but I did remember her earnest, eager-to-please face. She was the kind of employee who would stay at the office until midnight without complaining if asked.

"By noon tomorrow is fine," I told her, enjoying the glare Sex Hair was sending me as I continued to ignore the sign.

Sex Hair cleared her throat theatrically and, reaching around me, tapped the flyer fiercely. A trio of cheap, colorful beaded bracelets wrapped around her wrist. I smelled the bright, happy tang of lemons as she leaned in.

"Take it outside, buddy," she said in a throaty, no-nonsense voice.

Buddy?

Clearly, she wasn't intimidated by an asshole in Hugo Boss with a haircut that cost more than her entire outfit. I basked in her disdain. It was miles more comfortable for me than the terrified glances and "Right away, Mr. Russos" I got in the hallways at work.

I covered the mouthpiece of the phone—I hated those earbud things and staunchly refused to use them. "It's cold. I'll be a minute," I told her briskly, leaving no room for debate.

"I didn't create the weather or the phone policy. Out. Side." She said it like I was a truculent three-year-old and hooked her thumb toward the door.

"No." I didn't sound like a whiny toddler. I sounded like an annoyed, inconvenienced patron who had the right to expect respect.

I uncovered the phone and continued my conversation.

I was a spiteful son of a bitch.

"Get off the damn phone, or I'll make you wish you had," she warned.

People were starting to look at us. Neither one of us seemed to care.

"Don't you have tables to wait on?" I asked. "Or do you specialize in shrieking at customers?"

Her eyes were nearly gold under the fluorescent lighting, and I swear she almost smiled.

"Oh, you asked for it, buddy." She leaned in again, too close for New Yorkers who prized our personal space. The top of her head came to my shoulder. "Sir, are you here for STD panel results or hemorrhoids?" she shouted in the vicinity of my cell's microphone.

You shithead.

"I'll call you back," I said into the phone and disconnected the call.

Sex Hair beamed up at me, all faux charm. "Welcome to George's Village Pizza. Dining alone tonight, I presume?"

"That was a work call," I said icily.

"Isn't that nice that you can hold down a job *and* be that rude?"

It had been too long since I'd squashed a disrespectful underling. I itched to do it now. She looked not only like she could take it but like she might even enjoy it.

"Dominic."

I glanced over Sex Hair's shoulder and spotted my mother waving from a green vinyl booth in the corner. She looked amused.

Sex Hair looked back and forth between me and my mother. "Oh, she's way too good for you," she announced, slapping a menu to my chest and walking away.

"Mom," I greeted her, leaning in to kiss her on one flawless cheek before I slid into the booth opposite her.

"That was quite the entrance," she said, resting her chin on her palm.

She was the picture of confidence in an off-the-shoulder ivory sweater and red leather skirt. Her hair was its natural sterling silver, cut in a short, hip cap. The haircut—and the chunky emerald on her right middle finger—had been her gift to herself the day after she'd kicked my father out of their Upper East Side town house a few decades too late.

My mother was a beautiful woman. She always had been. She'd begun her career at fifteen as a doe-eyed, long-legged socialite-turned-model before deciding she preferred the business side of fashion. Now sixty-nine, she'd long ago abandoned doe eyes in favor of wielding her sharp mind and tongue. She was comfortable being both loved *and* feared in the industry.

"She was incredibly rude," I insisted, watching as Sex Hair made small talk with a table across the skinny restaurant.

"*You* were incredibly rude," my mother countered.

"It's what I do," I said, snapping open the menu and scanning. I tried to ignore the temper that was bubbling up inside me like a sleeping dragon awakened. I'd spent thirteen months locked down, on my best behavior, and I was starting to crack.

"Don't start the 'I'm an asshole' spiel again." She sighed and slid her reading glasses back on.

"Sooner or later, you're going to have to give up on the hope that I'm a human being with a heart of gold underneath it all."

"Never," she insisted with a saucy smile.

I gave up. "Why are we here?"

"Because I wanted to spend time with my only son—the light of my life—away from the office."

Our working relationship was as old as her new haircut.

It wasn't a coincidence.

"Sorry," I said and meant it. "I've been busy."

"Darling." She said it wryly, and it was warranted.

No one was busier than Dalessandra Russo, former model and current editor in chief of *Label*, a fashion magazine that had not only survived the onset of the digital age but spearheaded the transition. Every month, my mother oversaw hundreds of pages of fashion, advertising, interviews, and advice, not to mention online content, and delivered it all to readers around the world.

If she were photographed in a pair of shoes or sunglasses, they sold out within hours. If she sat front and center at a show, the designer's collection was picked up by every buyer in attendance. She made designers, models, writers, and photographers important, successful. She built careers. Or destroyed them when necessary.

And she hadn't asked for or earned the chaos of the past year.

For that, I had to atone as well.

"Sorry," I said again, reaching across the table to squeeze her hand. The emerald winked at me under the fluorescent lights.

"Can I get you a drink?" Rude Sex Hair was back.

"I don't know. *Can* you?" I shot back.

"We're fresh out of the blood of children, Satan. How about something that matches your personality?" She was saying the words nicely. Sweetly even.

"I'll have a—"

"Unsweetened iced tea," she filled in for me.

Bitter. Boring. Bland.

"Is this one of those places where you pay people to be assholes to you?" I asked my mother.

"Oh, honey. I'm doing this for free." Sex Hair batted thick lashes in my direction.

I opened my mouth to destroy her.

"He'll have water. Tap is fine," my mother cut in.

"Absolutely. Now, how about dinner?" Sex Hair flashed my mother a genuine grin.

"I've heard rumors of your pizza crusts far and wide," Mom said coyly.

Sex Hair leaned in, a friend sharing secrets. "Every word is true," she said. "It's perfection."

I smelled lemons again.

"In that case, I'll have the personal with green onions and black olives."

"You are a woman of excellent taste," the mouthy server announced. "How about for you, Prince Charming?" she asked.

"Pepperoni. Personal." I closed the menu and held it out without looking at her.

"Very creative," she quipped.

So maybe it wasn't fair of me. She obviously didn't know she was pushing a button. That I still wasn't confident in my ability to *be* creative, to be good at the job my mother needed me to do. But she said it. And I reacted.

"Shouldn't someone your age have a real job by now, Maleficent? Because obviously you're not good at this one."

The entire place went silent. The other patrons froze, gazes fixed on our table. Sex Hair met my eyes for one long beat. God, it felt good to let out some of the fight I'd been bottling up for so long.

"Since you asked *so* nicely, I'll be sure to give your order *extra* special attention," she promised. The wink she gave me was so insolent, I almost got out of the booth to chase her into the kitchen.

"Don't you dare," Mom said, grabbing my hand before I bolted.

"She can't get away with that. We're paying customers," I told her.

"You are to sit there. Be polite. And eat whatever she sees fit to bring you," Mom ordered.

"Fine. But if she poisons me, I'll sue her and her entire family. Her great-grandchildren will feel my wrath."

My mother sighed theatrically. "Who hurt you, darling?"

It was a joke. But we both knew the answer wasn't funny.

2

ALLY

Decorating Charming's pizza was the most fun I'd had in… Ugh. Never mind.

Let's just say life had been a shit show lately. And messing with a grumpy guy—what was it with assholes today anyway?—who looked like he'd waltzed right off the pages of some men's magazine was definitely a highlight. Which said a lot about my current situation.

I didn't have time to worry about the consequences of being stretched too thin. This was the kind of life crisis that you muscled through.

When it was all over, I would book myself a vacation on a beach where the only thing I had to worry about was if my straw was long enough to reach the bottom of my frozen cocktail.

"Table twelve wants their check, Ollie," George, my boss and the grumpiest Italian grandpa I'd ever met in my life, announced brusquely, as if I'd spent the last four hours ignoring diners instead of waiting on them. He hadn't bothered to learn my name when I started three weeks ago. I hadn't bothered to teach him. The guy went through servers like new parents went through baby wipes.

At least the checks were made out correctly by Mrs. George. That was what mattered.

"On it," I told him.

A mango margarita, I decided, hefting the plates and pushing through the swinging kitchen doors.

By the time I had that mango margarita in hand, I might be in my sixties instead of a ripe old thirty-nine—thanks for pointing that out, Charming—but I would fix what needed fixing. There was no other option.

The dining room, though in desperate need of a complete makeover and maybe an industrial scrubbing, was warm and cozy.

Maybe I could offer to do some after-hours cleaning for a couple extra bucks?

"Here you go," I said, sliding the pizzas in front of them.

The woman with the to-die-for leather skirt and I'm-a-badass haircut seemed to approve my topping smiley face on hers. She laughed in that way that born-rich people did. Not too loudly and with absolutely no snorting.

Charming, on the other hand, scowled down at his pizza. He had a face for scowling. That strong jaw was even more defined with his teeth clenching like that. Those icy eyes that couldn't decide if they were blue or gray narrowed.

Ugh. He had those yummy little crinkles at the corners of his eyes.

Was grumpy and rude suddenly the new hot? My vagina seemed to think so.

It hadn't been *that* long since I'd given her some action, but apparently she was into well-dressed douches now. Great. Thank

God I was working myself to death for the foreseeable future and wouldn't have time to explore her new inappropriate preferences.

"Can I get you two anything else right now?" I asked, a paragon of helpfulness.

"That's it," Charming said, tossing his napkin on the table and sliding out of the booth. "You and I are going to have a little screaming match about how to treat your customers with respect."

He stood and closed his long fingers around my wrist.

I knew he felt it too. That unexpected jolt. Like taking a shot of whiskey or sticking a finger in a light socket. Maybe both at the same time. For one moment of pure insanity, I wondered if he intended to take me over his knee and if I'd let him.

"Dominic, for the love of God. Behave yourself," the woman sighed in exasperation.

In answer, he spun his pizza around so his mother could read it.

FU spelled out in greasy pepperoni.

"Is there a problem, *sir*?" I asked with sugary politeness.

"Oh my," the woman said, pressing her fingers to her mouth and trying to stifle a laugh. A real one this time.

"It's not funny," he snapped.

"It is from where I stand," I said.

"You are a server. Your job is to act like one and serve," he said.

Ass. And. Hole.

"You're a human. Your job is to act like one," I countered. Any other day, I probably would have let it all go. I knew better than to jeopardize a paycheck. But I'd come in after the lunch shift to find the nineteen-year-old server sobbing into paper napkins in the back because a dick in a suit had unloaded his bad day on her.

Freaking George the jerk caught me trying to comfort her and screamed, "There's no crying in pizza."

"I want to speak to the manager," Dick 2 in the suit announced.

"Dominic, must you?" his date sighed.

"Oh, he must," I said.

I had him pegged. This guy was one of *those* people. He believed that everyone under him existed just to serve him. I bet he had a personal assistant and that he had no idea they were human. He probably called them at 3:00 a.m. and made them run to the convenience store for lube or eye of newt.

"I'm so glad you agree," he said dryly. He was still holding my wrist. That electrifying zing was still sizzling its way through my veins. His eyes narrowed as if he felt it too.

Table twelve, a couple of early twentysomethings, looked like they were thinking about dining and dashing. Shifty-eyed and uncomfortable.

"Let me get this table their check, and then we can continue our battle royale," I offered, yanking my hand free.

"Sit back down," Charming's lady friend insisted, pulling him back into the booth. "You're causing a scene."

I left them, grabbed the check for twelve, and made serious eye contact with them while I thanked them profusely for coming in. It wasn't going to be a good tip. I had an instinct about these things since waitressing and bartending had become my main source of income. But at least they weren't going to walk out on the check.

"I can take that for you now if you're ready," I offered.

The guy reluctantly pulled out a wallet on a chain and opened it. "Keep the change," he squeaked.

Two dollars. It was probably all they could afford, and I totally got that. But I needed to find real work, like six months ago.

"Thanks, guys," I said brightly and shoved the money in my apron.

Charming was sitting, arms folded, staring down at his untouched FU pizza while his date daintily cut hers into bite-sized pieces.

"George, table eight wants to talk to you."

"Now what the fuck did you do?" he snarled, dropping his fork in the double helping of pasta primavera he'd made himself. He acted as if I'd been nothing but a troublemaker, and I considered making him his own pizza. I wondered if the twelve-inch pie was big enough for "dumbass" spelled out in sausage.

"The guy was being a jerk," I told him, knowing full well George wouldn't care. He'd side with the ass. Asses liked other asses.

He hefted his bulk off the rickety stool that was going to give up the fight against his three hundred pounds any day now. At five and a half feet tall, he was a grumpy beach ball of a human being. "Let's go. Be fucking polite," he said, wiping his hands on the sauce-stained apron. George lumbered through the swinging doors, and I followed.

"Thank you for coming to George's Village Pizza. I'm George," he said, all olive-oily charm now. The guy was a dick to his employees, his vendors, hell, even his wife. But to a diner with a fat wallet? George was almost sort of friendly. "I understand there's a problem."

Without saying a word, Charming spun his pizza plate around.

George's eyes narrowed.

"Is this supposed to be some kinda joke, Ollie?"

Great. I could see the vein in his neck.

That wasn't a good sign. I'd seen it twice before. Once when he'd fired his delivery driver for stopping to help direct traffic at an accident scene and again when a server had slipped on a grease spill in the back and sprained her wrist. He fired her on the spot and said if she tried to collect workers' comp, he'd burn down her mother's house.

The server was his niece. Her mother was George's sister.

I shrugged. "Maybe that's just how the pepperonis arranged themselves."

"This kind of service is unacceptable," Charming insisted.

"Of course. Of course," George agreed, all apologies. "And I promise you the situation will be rectified."

"She should be fired," Charming said, leveling me with a cold look. "She's a detriment to your business. I'm never coming back here."

And there it was.

I knew I was out of a job.

"Good," I said. "You should stick to torturing servers uptown."

"Ay! Not in my restaurant," George bellowed. His third chin vibrated with rage. If I didn't get out now, I might cause a coronary, and I didn't really want that on my conscience. I also really didn't want to have to give this guy mouth-to-mouth. Wisely, I zipped my lips.

"I really think this is an overreaction," the woman said smoothly.

"No. It's not," George and Charming said together.

They could get Team Asshole jerseys.

"Ollie, get your things. You're fired."

The son of a bitch wasn't even going to let me close out my tables. I had at least another thirty bucks in tips coming. Maybe I should burn *his* mother's house down. But the woman made a hell of a cannoli and caught me up on *General Hospital w*hen she came in. I'd burn down George's house instead.

"I don't think that's necessary," the woman said.

"Yes, it is," Charming snapped.

"She's fired, and I'll bring you another pizza. On the house," George insisted. "Good?"

Charming, still looking at me but now with the slightest victorious curve to his snarly lips, nodded briskly. "Fine."

I already knew George would be taking the cost of the two pizzas out of my last paycheck. *Jackass.*

Without a word, I headed back into the kitchen. I grabbed my coat off the rack, scooped the money out of my apron, keeping my bank and the tips and throwing the rest on top of George's primavera. *Take that.*

"You fired?" the cook called from behind the stainless-steel worktop where he was rolling out dough.

"Yep," I said, shrugging into my coat.

He nodded. "Good for you."

I gave him a wry smirk. "Yeah. Fingers crossed, you'll be next. George would love to have to make and serve his own pizzas."

He gave me a floury two-finger salute as I slipped on my backpack and went back into the dining room. I could have gone out the back door into the alley, but I was already fired, so there was no harm in making a scene.

"You two could learn something about how to treat people," I said, pointing my finger in their direction.

Physically, they couldn't have been more different. George with his barrel-shaped body, greased hair, and too-small polo shirt. Charming with his tailored suit and fancy boots. He probably got manicures and facials and then accused the spa staff of looking him in the eye.

"This might come as a surprise to you both, but we're all people. We're not here *just* to serve you. We have lives and families and goals. And *your* lives might start looking a hell of a lot better if you remembered that."

"Get outta here, Ollie," George hissed. He made a shooing motion with his beefy hands.

Charming was smirking at me.

“Maybe I was wrong. Maybe there’s no hope for you,” I said to him. I knew his type. Well, not personally. But from a safe distance where I could armchair quarterback it. “Rich, miserable, empty. Nothing and nobody ever lives up to your expectations. Including yourself.”

That chiseled jaw clenched, and I knew I’d hit a bull’s-eye. *Good.*

“Get out!” George screeched. “And don’t come back!”

“Don’t even think about stiffing me for my paycheck, buddy,” I told him. “I know where your mother lives.”

He turned a worrying shade of purple, and I decided it was time to exit. I swept toward the door and felt pretty damn good about my speech.

“Here. You deserve this.” The girls at table two pressed a crisp twenty into my hands. “We used to work in food service.”

I wanted to not need it. I wanted to sweep out of here with my dignity intact and my head held high. But I needed every damn dime.

“Thank you,” I said quietly.

The young couple from table twelve held the door for me. “Here. We were going to the movies, but you earned it,” the guy said, holding up a few crumpled dollars.

“Take it,” his girlfriend insisted. She beamed at me. And I realized that them giving me their last seven bucks was going to make them feel better than me refusing it.

I couldn’t afford to have any pride.

“Thanks, guys.”

“Pay it forward,” the guy said.

I swallowed down the rage, the fear, and that bite of stromboli I’d managed an hour ago.

I would. Someday.

3

ALLY

I gave up my seat on the steel bus bench to a shaggy guy in a puffy red ski jacket with the size sticker still on it and a dog in a pink turtleneck sweater.

I had three hours to fill before my next shift. A night gig on the bar at a mediocre hot spot in Midtown. It was mostly tourists buying fifteen-dollar cosmos, but the tips were good. It wasn't enough time to run home to Jersey and take a nap like I wanted to, but I could hit the library and look for a new server gig or check the freelance site and see if I'd landed any projects.

Pretty please, sweet baby Jesus.

When I'd first arrived here, I thought landing a job as a graphic designer would be easy. I'd run my own small business back in Boulder and done well. But it turned out New York firms didn't enjoy taking a chance on a self-taught designer who needed a flexible schedule for "family emergencies."

Restaurants and bars, however, didn't give a shit what

hours you took as long as you showed up when you were on the schedule. I took freelance projects when I got them and held down five regular part-time gigs.

Make that four. Thanks, Charming. And George.

I indulged myself in a little fantasy.

Mogul Entrepreneurial Me storming into Charming's corner office, because of course he had one, and firing him on the spot because I'd just purchased the company after he pissed me off. If I were wildly wealthy, I'd do shit like that. Sure, I'd give back. Rescue dogs. Eradicate cancer. Take care of the elderly. Buy nice interview outfits for women who needed better jobs. I'd start a spa where women could get massages along with gynecological exams, mammograms, and dental cleanings. With a bar.

And for fun, I'd buy up corporations and fire assholes.

I'd wear a Satan-red dress and heels and have security drag him out of his chair. Then I'd give everyone an extra week of paid vacation just for dealing with him.

Fantasy complete, I put my mental energy into picking out the best bus route to the library. I needed to replace my pathetic pizza income ASAP.

The wind stabbed at my exposed skin like a thousand tiny daggers.

It was effing cold. My righteous anger kept me as warm as it could. But January in Manhattan was arctic. And depressing. The last snow had been pretty for all of five minutes. But the traffic snarls and gray slush defied whitewashing. Plus, it had made my commute into the city an even bigger nightmare.

I shifted the straps of my backpack, hiking it up higher. My ancient laptop had the dead weight of a sleeping toddler.

"Excuse me?"

I debated pretending like I hadn't heard her. New Yorkers didn't strike up conversations at bus stops. We ignored each other and pretended we lived in soundproof, eye contact–proof personal bubbles.

But I recognized the red leather under a very nice ivory wool winter coat.

"Ollie?" Charming's date asked tentatively. She was tall, and not just because she was in a pair of suede boots that I'd sell a kidney for.

Long-legged. High cheekbones. Killer haircut. Emerald the size of a postage stamp on her middle finger.

"Ally," I said warily.

"I'm Dalessandra," she said, reaching into an impossibly chic clutch. "Here."

It was a business card. *Dalessandra Russo, editor in chief, Label Magazine.*

Whoa. Even I'd read *Label* before.

"What's this for?" I asked, still staring at the linen card.

"You just lost a job. I've got one for you."

"You need a server?" I hedged, still not understanding.

"No. But I could use someone with your…personality. Show up at this address on Monday morning. Nine a.m. Ask for me. Full-time. Benefits."

My stupid, optimistic heart started to sing a diva-worthy aria. My father had always warned me I was just a little too Pollyanna and not enough Mr. Darcy.

"I just show up, and you give me a job?" I pressed, trying to squash the hope that bloomed inside me.

"Yes."

Well, that was vague.

"Hey, lady. You maybe got another job in there for me?" a burly guy in ripped cargo pants and a hunter-safety-orange ski cap asked hopefully. He had a spectacular beard and wind-reddened cheeks. His smile was oddly beguiling.

She looked him up and down. "Can you type?"

He winced, shook his head.

"How about sort packages? Deliver things?"

"Now *that I* can do! I worked in a mail room for two years in high school."

High school looked like it had been about thirty years ago for him. I recognized a fellow Pollyanna.

Dalessandra produced another card, and—using a ballpoint pen that looked like it was made from actual gold—scribbled something on the back. "Go here Monday and give them this card. Full-time. Benefits," she said again.

The man held it like it was a winning lottery ticket. "My wife ain't gonna believe this! I've been out of work for six months!" He celebrated by hugging every person at the bus stop, including our lovely benefactress and then me. He smelled like birthday cakes and granted wishes.

"See you Monday, Ally," she said before walking down the block and sliding into the back seat of an SUV with tinted windows.

"Ain't this the greatest day?" Guy Pollyanna asked, elbowing me in the ribs.

"The greatest," I repeated.

I didn't know if I'd just hit the lottery or if this was a setup. After all, the woman had been on a date with Charming the Douche Weasel.

But I literally couldn't afford to not take the chance.

4

DOMINIC

Morning, Greta," I said, handing my assistant her daily cappuccino.

"Good morning," she responded, doing her customary scan of me. She leaned back in her chair and crossed her arms. "What's wrong?" she demanded, raising a Nordic eyebrow. She was in her early sixties, suffered no fools, and was obstinately loyal. I was fully aware of the fact that I didn't deserve her.

The one and only time she'd mentioned the word *retirement*, I'd given her a raise so obnoxious she'd agreed to stay with me until she hit sixty-five. We'd cross that bridge in less than six months. And at that point, I was prepared to double my offer.

I didn't want to have to break in a new assistant. Get to *know* someone.

I kept my circle small, tight. Greta was a part of that circle and had stayed by my side through thick and thin. Scandal to stable.

She'd worked for me at my old firm, a carryover from my former life and the days when I'd assessed risks and enjoyed the freedom to yell at people. No one took it personally. There were no eggshells under my feet. I was me. They were…well, them. And everything worked just fine.

Now nothing worked, and the eggshells here were sharp enough to draw blood.

But Greta was here. And with that continuity, with someone I could trust implicitly, I was fumbling my way through my father's former job description. Doing my damn best to prove that Paul Russo's blood wasn't poisoning me from the inside out.

"Nothing is wrong," I hedged. Nothing besides my mother laying into me and filleting me over the incident at the pizza place. In her criticism, she hadn't said the words outright, but I knew she was thinking them.

It was something my father would have done. Abusing his position of power to have someone who dared stand up to him fired.

That made it worse.

I already hadn't felt great about it, but I couldn't seem to stop myself. A year's worth of pent-up frustration had finally boiled over. Not that the woman had been an innocent victim. There was nothing "victim" about the opinionated, curvy Maleficent.

Minus the firing, I thought we'd both enjoyed the sparring.

"Liar," Greta said fondly.

We were close but not *that* close. As a rule, I didn't spill my guts to anyone. Not to my mother. Not to Greta. Not even to my best friends. It was part of being a Russo. We did what was necessary to protect the family name.

Even if it meant never admitting anything was wrong.

A leggy woman in a fitted sheath dress trotted by, a tray of eye-searing juices in one hand and four Hermès shopping bags in her other. She was making a beeline for the conference room when she spotted me. Her eyes went wide in that deer-in-the-headlights, fearful adrenaline kind of way. She stumbled, the point of her shoe grazing the carpet.

I looked away as a putrid green juice tumbled into one of the bags.

She yelped and sprinted away.

Another day, another terrified employee.

I'd assumed they'd all get used to me. Apparently I'd assumed incorrectly. I was the beast to my mother's beauty. The monster to the heroine. When they looked at me, they saw my father.

"Maybe if you smiled once in a while," Greta suggested to me.

I rolled my eyes and pulled out my phone. "If I smile, they think I'm baring my teeth at them."

"Rawr," she teased.

"Drink your poison, woman," I said gruffly.

"Maybe someday you'll grow up to drink coffee too," she said, fluttering her eyelashes.

"When hell freezes over." I was a staunch tea drinker, and the preference had nothing to do with the beverage itself. It had been the first of my many rebellious stands.

She nodded in the direction of the windows. Outside, New York shivered and froze. "Looks like it already has."

I leaned against her desk, thumbing through my inbox on my phone. "What's up first today?"

"You've got advertising at ten, proofs for approval due by noon, Irvin asked if you could take his place in a budget meeting at two, and Shayla would like five minutes of your time right now."

Greta nodded behind me, and I knew the beauty editor was standing there. I felt her perpetual cloud of low-level annoyance.

I turned.

The terms *statuesque* and *stern* came to mind. Shayla Bruno had earned the Miss Teenage America title at age seventeen and enjoyed a brief career in modeling before moving behind the camera. She was a few years my senior, had exquisite taste in jewelry, mothered three children with her wife, and—in my opinion—her talents were being wasted as beauty editor.

Too bad for her that the position she wanted was the one I currently occupied.

"Good morning, Greta. Is now a good time, Mr. Russo?" she asked, her tone making it clear that she didn't care if it was or wasn't.

"Dominic," I reminded her for the one-hundredth time. "Of course." I gestured toward my office.

At least with Shayla I didn't have to pretend to be something I wasn't. Like kind or caring. Or interested in her life in any capacity. She recognized me as the uncaring bastard I was.

While I hung up my coat, Shayla crossed to the lightboards in the corner and clipped a page layout in place.

So it was going to be one of those meetings.

"These aren't right," she said, slapping a long-fingered, ebony hand to the board. Brushed gold rings glittered against the glowing glass.

"In what way?" I joined her in front of the board and crossed my arms. It was a series of product images organized around a shot of two models in a studio. Something did feel off, but I couldn't quite put my finger on it. And I certainly wasn't going to show off my ignorance by playing a guessing game.

"The model shot. It's too small. It needs to be the anchoring piece, not the cardigan and the belt. The people are always the point, even if it's the products we're talking about," she lectured. "The people are the story."

I made a noncommittal noise. I'd delegated—dumped—the artistic details to the page designer and let him run with it because I didn't know what the fuck I was doing.

If there was one thing I hated more in this life than being wrong, it was not knowing what the hell I was doing in the first place.

"It needs to be laid out again. Dalessandra won't okay it as is," she said.

"Do you have any other suggestions?" I ventured.

"I would think the creative director of the world's second-largest fashion magazine wouldn't need any input." She didn't say it snidely. Didn't have to. It was fact.

We glared at each other for a long beat.

"Say what you need to say," I told her.

"You shouldn't be in this office," she said. "You didn't earn it. You haven't spent years of your life working in this industry, reading these magazines, and living and breathing fashion. Now, someone else has to make it their job to babysit you."

"And that someone is you?" I ventured coolly. "It's in your job description to advise on fashion layouts?"

"No. But it's in yours. And if you can't do it, then it falls on someone who can."

I wished that she was wrong. Wished that she hadn't landed a direct hit to my already dented ego. I was struggling with this job, and it irked me that others could tell.

I hated not being good at something.

I hated failing.

And I *really* hated being called out on it.

"I do a thousand things a day that don't fall within my job

description. We all should," she continued, her words coming out at a fast clip, the cool finally giving way to the angry heat beneath. "We're a team with the goal of making every piece of content as valuable and as eye-catching as it can be. You shouldn't be making these decisions when you're not equipped to make them. You shouldn't be at that desk."

I met fire with ice. "I'll take that under advisement. Is there anything else?"

I got the feeling Shayla was fantasizing about pushing me into my chair and shoving it through the windows at my back.

Ambitious. And rightfully angry. But being pissed off didn't change what was. I was *Label*'s creative director. And I would find a way to do this job.

"Redesign this before your mother sees it." She'd added the "your mother" as a jab.

I knew it because I would have done the same.

I was about to press her for suggestions or at least a recommendation on a designer who would have better instincts than the first when there was a knock on my open door.

"Dominic, my boy. Have you got five minutes for an old man?"

Managing editor Irvin Harvey strolled into my office in suit and tie, a smile on his face. The man was the sole surviving crony from my father's unceremonious ousting. He'd been with *Label* for fifteen years after my mother—heavily influenced by my father—poached him from a fashion house. At sixty-five, he was the stereotypical Manhattan executive. Well-compensated, he excelled at schmoozing and golf and was a master at maintaining relationships. He knew everyone worth knowing in the industry, from designers to photographers to buyers and advertisers.

My father had been Irvin's best man in his third wedding.

The only reason he was still here was because there had never once been a complaint made against the man, and he'd sworn to my mother that he had no idea what his old pal Paul had been up to.

I wasn't as inclined to take him at his word. But I understood that replacing another title so high on the masthead would have only added to my mother's nightmare.

"Are we done here?" I asked.

"Sherry, get me a coffee, will you?"

"Shayla," she said crisply.

I felt the punch of anger that radiated off her.

The man probably snapped his fingers at servers in restaurants.

I flashed back to my pepperoni pizza and the woman who'd served it, then winced.

"Help yourself to the machine," I said to Irvin, nodding in the direction of the beverage bar just inside the door. Until recently, its primary function had been to display bottles of champagne and scotch. It was now home to a tea station and espresso machine. Though I still kept it stocked with my mother's favorite white wine and a bottle of bourbon for particularly frustrating days.

"Never could figure those monstrosities out," Irvin said cheerfully, winking at Shayla, then grinning at me.

"I'll speak with you later, Shayla," I said, dismissing her. I'd make the damn coffee if it meant I didn't have to figure out how to get bloodstains out of the carpet.

She gave us both a cool nod and left.

"What can I do for you, Irvin?" I asked, starting an espresso for the man.

"I had drinks with the buyers from Neiman Marcus last night. Catching up, gossiping like teenage girls." He wandered over to the windows to study the skyline. "You know how Larry is," he said conversationally.

I didn't know *who* Larry was. But this had been the hallmark of my relationship with Irvin since taking over the position. I was his stand-in for my father. I imagined the two of them had shared many a scotch in this very room.

But I wasn't my father, and I didn't have time for gossip. I handed him the coffee.

He seemed to recognize that I wasn't Paul. "Anyway, after a few gin martinis, Larry gets loose. Runs his mouth. He mentioned hearing some rumors about your mother, the divorce. Is she seeing someone new?" His silver-tufted eyebrows raised suggestively.

I had no idea. I wasn't sure if I should know if she was seeing someone or not.

"I see," I said, pointedly ignoring the question. Whether I should know if my mother was dating again was entirely different from whether Big-Mouthed Guess-What-I-Heard Irvin should know.

My mother, this magazine, didn't need the shadow of Paul Russo to cause further harm. Every inquiry, every interview question about the situation had been met with stoic silence. The Russo modus operandi. Protect the name at all costs.

Even if it meant sheltering a villain.

"Anyway. Thought you'd like to know. They're just rumors," Irvin said, taking a dainty sip of his coffee. "They'll blow over as soon as something more scandalous comes along."

"I'll take it under advisement," I said.

5

ALLY

Thank the goddess of Wi-Fi signals. There was internet in Foxwood today.

Triumphantly, I plucked my frozen fingers out of the sleeves of my two-layered sweatshirts and logged into FBI Surveillance Van 4.

It was Saturday morning, and I had three whole hours until I needed to catch the train into the city.

I'd already spent an hour throwing debris out of the second-floor window into the dumpster that took up the entirety of my dad's square inch of front yard. Then another hour working on a freelance logo design project. It was for a family-run butcher shop in Hoboken and it paid a grand total of $200.

But $200 meant I'd be able to bump up the thermostat a hedonistic degree or two for a few days. That's right, ladies and gentlemen, I might be able to strip down to just one layer of clothing! So Frances Brothers Butcher Shop would get the best damned logo I could design.

With my borrowed Wi-Fi, I typed "Dalessandra Russo" and "Label Magazine" into the internet search and scrolled past the results I'd already visited. Turns out *Label* had been going through a "transition" period recently. There was plenty of information on formidable and fabulous Dalessandra. Former model turned fashion industry mogul and editor in chief of one of the largest surviving fashion magazines in the country. Her husband of forty-five years, Paul, had "stepped down" as creative director for the magazine as of about thirteen months ago.

The official line was that they were parting ways personally and professionally. However, gossip blogs hinted at a more sinister scandal, citing the exodus of several other employees around the same time. Mostly women. The blogs were careful to tap-dance around it, but one or two of them hinted that Paul's extramarital affairs played a role in the demise of both the personal and professional relationships.

I found comfort in the fact that a woman as smart and sharp as Dalessandra could be hosed too.

My gaze flicked over the screen of the laptop to the forty-ton porcelain clawfoot tub still lodged in the living room floor. Then up to the gaping hole in the ceiling.

Yeah. Even smart and sharp got hosed on occasion.

"Knock knock!" A cheery woman with a thick Romanian accent chirped as she pushed her way in through the front door.

I really needed to replace the lock and actually use it.

"Mrs. Grosu," I said, snapping my laptop closed and mentally resigning myself to picking up the rest of my research after my two bartending shifts. If the Wi-Fi held.

"Hello, neighbor," she said, bustling inside, a yellow casserole dish in her hands.

Mrs. Grosu was a widow who lived next door in a tidy brick two-story with a hedgerow so precise it looked as though it had been trimmed with lasers. She had four children and seven grandkids who came for Sunday lunch every week.

I adored her.

"I brought you Amish country casserole," she said cheerily. My dear, adorable, elderly neighbor had two great loves in this life: feeding people and Pinterest. She'd deemed this year to be her cultural culinary exploration, and I was along for the ride.

"That's very sweet of you, Mrs. Grosu," I said.

As bad as literally everything else was in my life, I'd hit the lottery with my father's neighbors. They were delightfully entertaining and absurdly generous.

She clucked her tongue. "When are you going to get that tub out of your living room?"

"Soon," I promised. The thing had to weigh three hundred pounds. It was not a one-woman job.

"You say the word, and I have my sons come move it for you."

Mrs. Grosu's sons were in their late fifties and in no shape for heavy lifting.

"I'll figure it out," I insisted.

With an eye roll, she headed toward the kitchen. "I'll put this away. Instructions are on the sticky note," she called in her thick accent.

"Thank you," I yelled after her, tunneling my way out of my burrow of blankets.

"This is a thank *you*," she insisted, returning to the living room as I climbed off the couch. "You got my groceries when my feet were swollen like watermelons last week."

We were in an endless reciprocation of favors, and I kind of enjoyed it. It felt nice to be able to give something, *anything* really, when resources were depleted.

She tut-tutted when she looked at the thermostat. "It's colder than a snowman's balls in here," she complained.

"It's not so bad," I insisted, stirring the fire in the brick fireplace my father had rarely ever used. I had one more log allotted for the morning, and then I'd turn on the furnace to heat the house to a balmy fifty degrees while I was at work.

I'd never been poor before, but I felt like I was really getting the hang of it.

"Why do you not take my money?" the woman pouted, crossing her arms in front of her gigantic bosoms. Everything about Mrs. Grosu was soft, squishy. Except for her motherly tone.

"You already paid for the dumpster," I reminded her.

"Bah!" she said, waving her hand as if it had been nothing to shell out a few hundred dollars to cover the cost of an eyesore that was lowering her own property value.

"This is my mess. I'm going to fix it," I told her. "You need your money for your grandkids' Easter baskets and for your single lady cruise."

"Did I tell you that we're going to a male cabaret in Cozumel?" she asked, throwing her head back and roaring with laughter.

She had. And I still couldn't get the vision out of my head. Mrs. Grosu and five of her closest girlfriends took a girls' trip once a year. I was amazed they'd never been arrested yet. But there was always Cozumel.

"I think you mentioned it," I said, stuffing my hands into the pocket of my sweatshirt.

"Okay. Good. Let's go then," she said, hooking her arm through mine and towing me toward the door.

"Go? Where?" I asked. "I don't have shoes or money."

"Get shoes. You don't need money."

That was a laugh. I desperately needed money.

"I have some work to do," I said, trying again.

"No. You always have work. Your calendar on the refrigerator says you work at three. It takes you forty-five minutes to get to work. Therefore, you have time to come with me."

I'd argued with her before and always lost.

"What you are doing for your father is a very good, beautiful thing. We're not going to let you go through this alone," she said, shoving me into my winter coat.

I stuffed my feet into boots and fumbled for my purse.

"I don't know what that means," I admitted. "And who's we?"

"You start a new job on Monday. Mr. Mohammad and I are taking you shopping at that thrift store you like for some work-appropriate clothes."

I dug my heels into the ruined plywood, making sure to avoid the strip of carpet tacks. "No, you're not."

Mrs. Grosu often talked about her older brothers and their wrestling prowess. Apparently they'd taught her a thing or two, because I found myself outside. Mr. Mohammad, an Ethiopian immigrant who arrived in America several decades before I was born, waved from his twenty-year-old sedan.

"Oh, no. He has the car," I said.

"You see how important this is?" Mrs. Grosu said.

Very few things could convince Mr. Mohammad to actually take his car out of the garage. The car had somewhere in the neighborhood of eight hundred miles on it because its smiling, mustachioed owner loved to walk. Before he retired, he'd walked the two miles to his job as a grocery store supervisor. Since his retirement, he still walked. But now it was to church every Sunday and to bridge at the community center on Wednesdays.

My dad had been Mr. Mohammad's bridge partner. Together they had ruled the community center with subtle nods and indecipherable body language.

So many things had changed in such a short time. Now, instead of looking out for my dad, his neighbors were looking out for me.

"Don't fight us on this. We've got social security checks burning holes in our pockets, and it's Senior Citizens Day at the thrift store," Mrs. Grosu said, stuffing me into the back seat.

"Hello, Ally," Mr. Mohammad sang. He was the happiest person I knew.

"Mr. Mohammad, I can't let you two do this."

"You just relax, girly," he insisted. "We *want* to do this."

It was true. They really did. Dad's entire neighborhood seemed to thrive on the "love thy neighbor" principle. When I sold Dad's house, when this was all over, I'd pay them back. And I would miss them fiercely.

"Fine," I sighed. "But I'll pay you back."

Mr. Mohammad and Mrs. Grosu shared an eye roll in the front seat.

"Do not make this weird, Ally," Mr. Mohammad said and cranked up the Billy Joel cassette tape.

6

ALLY

Label's offices took up the forty-second and forty-third floors of a shiny metal tower in Midtown. It was a fancy building in which fancy people worked fancy jobs.

I was rocking a thrift store pencil skirt over bargain-buy lace leggings that made my legs itch. But I'd managed to add my own flair with the thick, colorful hair ties I'd stacked up both wrists. Functional and fashionable. Coincidentally also cheaper than a diamond tennis bracelet.

As the elevator zoomed skyward, nerves had my heart flip-flopping in my chest. I was a pro at starting new jobs. I was great at people-ing. But stepping into that elevator with women who were six inches taller than me and thirty pounds lighter was an eye-opening experience. So was the guy pushing a cart with two dozen Chanel gift bags.

The air smelled expensive in here like subtle brand-name perfumes, luxury creams, and lotions. Meanwhile, I smelled like bargain-brand lemon-scented shampoo.

The gazelle next to me bobbled the tray of coffee cups she was holding. She caught it, but her phone went flying.

I grabbed it off the floor since I was the closest one to it. It would probably take any one of the glamazons a full ten seconds to bend gracefully from their heights to reach the floor.

"Here," I said, handing the phone back to her.

"Thanks," she breathed. "I'm such a klutz, and they still make me do the coffee runs downstairs."

She was closing in on six feet in her suede ruby heels. Her heritage looked like it was somewhere in the Indigenous meets Japanese range. In any bar in the city, she'd be considered stunning. Here, she was a coffee getter. I wondered if I was about to learn that my new job involved scrubbing toilets.

I didn't care. I'd still take it.

Besides, clearly none of these people ate or drank. The bathrooms were probably unused and spotless.

"You're a model who does coffee runs?" I asked.

She looked at me, blinked, and then laughed. Until she bobbled the tray again.

As a safety precaution, I took it from her.

"That's adorable," she said, grinning at me. "I work in the admin pool for *Label*."

"But you look like…that," I said, waving my free hand in the direction of her face. "Does *Label* have a surplus of cover model–worthy women so they just redistribute them to other departments?"

"I'm a hella fast typist, and organization is my religion. And if someone put me in front of a camera, I'd fall on my face. Plus, I can't smile on command." She held up her company ID. In the grainy photo, she looked as if she were retracting her head into an invisible turtle shell. "Do you work in the building?" she asked.

"I'm about to. First day."

"Cool. What company?"

"*Label*," I said.

"Coworkers," she chirped. "I'm Gola, by the way. What department?"

"I'm Ally, and I'm not sure. Dalessandra just told me to show up and ask for her."

Gola blinked. "Dalessandra *Russo*?" She said the name with equal parts awe and fear.

"Yeah."

"I have so many questions," she confessed.

"That makes two of us."

The elevator dinged, and the doors opened on the forty-third floor. We both got out. "Here, I'll take you to the front desk," she offered, taking back the tray of coffees.

"Thanks. That's really nice of you."

I opened one of the glass doors for Gola.

"First lesson, we're not all models, and we're not all super mean. But some of us are both," Gola said, leading the way to a horseshoe-shaped counter of glowing white quartz. The woman standing behind it was an ivory-skinned redhead in a chic, plaid sheath dress.

I felt like I'd shown up to the prom in pajama pants.

"Ruth, this is Ally. She's here to see Dalessandra about a job," Gola said with an eyebrow wiggle.

"What kind of job?" Redheaded Ruth asked, cupping her chin in a dainty hand.

"That's the best part. She doesn't even know!"

"Pretty sure it's not a cover model gig," I joked. "She gave me this card and told me to ask for her." I fished Dalessandra's business card out of my coat pocket and handed it over.

"This is exciting!" Ruth insisted. "This is the second new

random hire today." She pointed to a small waiting area. Low, white leather chairs looked more fashion-forward than comfortable. Gold planters held glossy green ferns in front of windows that framed the gloomy Midtown skyline.

Bus Stop Guy was sitting gingerly on one of the artsy-fartsy chairs. His leg was jiggling to a nervous beat. He'd trimmed his hair and beard and was wearing an orange sweater that stretched tight over his belly, making it look a little like a pumpkin.

He looked so happy I was actually scared for him.

"Hey, bus stop buddy!" He waved at me.

"Hey," I waved back and sent every good vibe I could muster his way. Mean people ate sweethearts like him for breakfast.

"You two know each other?" Gola asked. "Even more intriguing."

I turned back to the women. "So what you're saying is this doesn't happen often?" I hadn't been sure if Dalessandra made a habit out of playing employment fairy to strangers.

"Never," Ruth said. "Maybe this is some kind of midlife crisis."

"The woman is sixty-nine," Gola reminded her.

"If anyone can live to 140-ish and still be fabulous, it's Dalessandra," Ruth insisted.

"I gotta go," Gola said, juggling the coffees. "But maybe we can do lunch today? You can give me all the deets on how you met Dalessandra."

"There aren't many details. Her dinner date got me fired."

Gola and Ruth exchanged another look.

"Dinner date?" Ruth whispered gleefully.

"My extension is on the company list. I'm the only Gola."

"Call me too," Ruth said. "I need to know about the dinner date!"

Lunch buddies. Okay. This wasn't so bad.

"Sounds good."

Gola backed through a second set of glass doors, and I breathed a sigh of relief when the coffee survived.

"Let me just call back to Dalessandra's office to let them know you're here," Ruth said, picking up the phone.

I watched a grim-looking woman in a dove-gray suit walk up to my bus stop buddy. He rose and beamed at her. She frowned at him.

"Follow me," I heard her say without enthusiasm.

My buddy gave me a thumbs-up with one hand and clutched his brown-bag lunch to his chest with the other.

"Please let the mail room be friendly," I whispered.

"Ally? Dalessandra is ready for you," Ruth said, hanging up the phone. "You're just going to go through those doors and follow the hallway all the way around. It's the last office on the left, and you'll see two terrified assistants sitting out front."

Oh, goodie.

"Thanks, Ruth."

"Good luck! I'll see you at lunch."

If I survived that long.

I found the office—and the two assistants, only one of whom looked terrified—without needing to ask for directions. Which was good because everyone I passed in the hallway looked like they were running off to war. There was an urgency that permeated the entire floor. People seemed on edge.

Or I was overanalyzing everything, and this was a typical office environment. *Label* was a big business, and that meant a lot of money, power, and influence. Also probably a high incidence of stomach ulcers.

"Hi. I'm Ally," I said, startling the closest assistant into nearly falling out of his chair. He caught himself but sent a pen cup flying.

He clutched at his chest. "Holy macaroni."

"Oh, for Pete's sake, Johan," the second assistant complained. "You knew the front desk was sending someone back here." She stood while Jumpy McJumperson scrambled to pick up his pens. "I'm Gina," she said. "You can come with me."

She led the way into the glass-walled inner sanctum behind her.

Dalessandra Russo stood behind a sleek worktable with bowed metal legs in a blue so deep it was almost black. The walls were papered in some exquisite fern and leaf pattern in soft creams and greens. Silver framed photos of the woman in question with celebrities and other important-looking people were hung in a pattern too pleasing to the eye to be accidental.

She and a thin, bespectacled man were studying something on her desk.

Dalessandra looked up over delicate reading glasses. Her dress was an ivory and sterling knit wrap dress with long sleeves that played off her gray hair. Her necklace was what someone more educated in fashion would probably call a statement piece, a thick gold bar with tiny gemstones sprinkled over it.

If I wore something like that, I'd chip a tooth hitting myself in the face the first time I bent over.

"Ally. So happy you could join us today," she said.

"I'm happy to be here," I said warily.

I was still waiting for the "I've changed my mind" conversation.

"Ally—what is your last name?" she asked.

That got the attention of the man beside her. He looked up, puzzled.

"Morales," I said.

"Ally Morales, meet our production manager, Linus Feldman."

Linus gave me the once-over, and I knew he was wondering what the chick in the thrift store skirt was doing in Dalessandra Russo's office.

"Hi," I said.

Linus was short, slight, Black, and—from the heights his cute, furry eyebrows climbed—a teensy bit on the judgmental side.

I couldn't fault him. I had no idea what I was doing here either.

"Hello." He drew out the word like he was waiting for an explanation.

"Ally is joining our admin pool," Dalessandra said.

Whew. Okay. There really is a job after all.

Linus looked relieved by that explanation too.

"Best of luck to you," he said, briskly stacking the papers. "I'll get these over to the editorial team."

"Thank you, Linus. Please close the door on your way out," Dalessandra said, sinking into the chair behind her desk.

She gestured at one of the ivory armchairs opposite her.

Linus's eyebrows were nearing his hairline again when he did as he was told. The look he shot me as he closed the glass doors was more "beware" than "good luck."

I sat, gluing my knees together. It had been a while since I'd donned a skirt. I felt like I was mid crash course relearning how to sit like an adult.

"So, Ally," Dalessandra said, interlacing her fingers. "Welcome to *Label*."

"Thank you," I said. "Why am I here?"

She didn't laugh, but her smile was warm.

"That is why," she said, pointing at me.

My hair? My charming confusion? Maybe I reminded her of a long-lost best friend from summer camp?

"I'm afraid you'll have to be more specific."

She did laugh then, and I could hear the assistants' chairs outside spinning in our direction.

"I'm hiring you for our admin pool. You'll have new administrative tasks every day. You might help with research or fact-checking. You might be called upon to take notes in meetings or run scheduling on a specific project. You could liaise with a designer's team to help coordinate photo shoots. You may fill in for personal assistants, or you may be asked to organize catering, pick up coffee, et cetera."

"Okay." That sounded reasonably doable.

"But." She let the word hang in the air between us.

I waited for the very luxurious stiletto that was about to impale me from above.

"I'm interested to know what you noticed about our offices so far," she said.

"You mean in the three minutes I've been here?"

"Yes."

Great. There was already a test. I knew there was an answer she was looking for. I just didn't know what it was.

"Everyone seems..." I trailed off, not sure how honest I should be.

"Say it," she said.

"Terrified. Like deer in headlights."

She sighed and tapped her pen on her desk. "We recently went through a...difficult transition."

"Mmm," I said, not ready to admit that I'd internet stalked her and her company.

"In the transition, we removed, lost, and replaced several key employees. The ones we removed were no longer the right…fit," she decided, "for our values. They had become liabilities of sorts. Unfortunately, we also lost several valuable team members."

There was a whole hell of a lot that she was dancing around behind the public relations vocabulary.

"My husband took advantage of my generosity and abused his power here. I was aware of some of his…flaws. But I was not aware of just how inappropriate he'd become." Her tone was steely, and anger all but crackled off her. I hoped she got the guy's balls in the divorce.

I stayed silent and forcibly choked down the kajillion questions I had.

"I was so focused on growing a brand, transitioning into digital-first, and enjoying the perks of being a powerful woman in an exciting industry that I didn't look closely within my own family, my own company. Maybe I didn't want to."

"But it's over now," I guessed.

She nodded. "Years too late. So much damage could have been avoided. But the past is in the past. It has no bearing on the present and future. I brought my son on to take his father's place and tasked him—perhaps unfairly—with cleaning up his father's mess. As you saw last week, the strain is getting to him."

I was busy wondering exactly what Dalessandra *wasn't* saying when that last bit of information landed.

Oh, shit.

"Charming is your *son*?"

She looked bewildered. "Who did you think he was?"

"I thought he was your date. I told him you could do better than him," I said.

Dalessandra laughed again.

Again, I heard the swivel of chairs from the other side of the glass.

"Dominic is my son."

Maybe I could empathize just a tiny bit with the man being called in to clean up a family mess. But still, I wasn't an asshole about my situation.

"So why, on my first day as an admin, am I in your office?" I asked. I felt like I was missing a few very large, important puzzle pieces.

"Because my son owes you a job, and Russos always pay their debts."

More mystery. The woman seemed like a vault of secrets.

"Okay," I said, drawing out the word Linus-style.

Dalessandra leaned on her elbows. "And if by some chance you manage to take the temperature of our staff and find out if there's something I can do to make our environment more stable..." She held up the palms of her hands. "Then I hope you'll feel inclined to discuss it with me."

And there was the ask.

A vague one.

I felt like we were communicating in code...and only one of us had the code...and the other one of us was me.

"I'll do what I can?" It came out more like a question. But it was the answer my new boss was looking for.

"Good. If there's anything you need, please tell me," she said, picking up her reading glasses and sliding them on.

"I do have a few questions."

She peered over the frames at me. "Yes?"

"Can Charm—your son fire me?" I asked.

Her smile was feline. "No. Dominic can't fire you."

"Okay, then. Do I have to be nice to him?"

She leaned back in her chair, considering. "I think you should have the relationship you feel most comfortable having with my son."

7

DOMINIC

My mother's assistants were glued to whatever was going on in her office and didn't see me approach.

I muttered a greeting, startling the guy so badly he sloshed water down the front of his checkered shirt.

"Oh, Mr. Russo, your mother is in a meeting," the less terrified assistant—Gina or Ginny—said, rising as I reached for the door handle.

My mother laughed at whoever was sitting across the desk from her.

I frowned. "Who's in there?"

"Uh, um, a new hire," the damp assistant squeaked, patting himself dry with napkins.

I hadn't heard Mom laugh like that in a long time.

They were standing now, and I decided it was as good a time as any to interrupt.

"Speak of the devil," Mom said when I stepped into her office.

The other woman turned around. She was smiling.

She was...*here?*

"No," I growled.

I heard a thud behind me and assumed the nervous assistant had fallen over trying to eavesdrop.

"Oh. Yeah," FU pizza girl said smugly.

"No," I said again, shaking my head.

"Dominic, meet Ally. Ally is joining our admin pool. Ally, Dominic is our creative director here at *Label*."

"A word, Mother," I said. She couldn't just dole out jobs to people who were too rude to keep them. She'd already hit her quota with me.

"I'm sorry, darling. I don't have time. Be a dear and show Ally to HR," she said, picking up the phone. "Get me Naomi."

We were dismissed. But I was going to have several words with my mother at her earliest convenience.

I stopped by the assistants' desk and took a stab at her name. "Gina, schedule me an appointment with my mother at her earliest convenience. Tell her it's a budgetary meeting so she doesn't try to cancel it."

She blinked at me. Her mouth opened and then closed.

Shit. I should have gone with Ginny.

"Is there a problem?" I asked.

"You know my name."

"Of course I know your name," I snapped, secretly relieved.

"You're a real man of the people, Charming," Ally said dryly behind me.

I turned on her. "Don't bother getting comfortable here," I warned her.

"Or what? You'll ruin another job for me?"

"You and I both know that you deserved to lose that job,"

I insisted. "You can't be that rude to customers and then be surprised when you're called out on it."

"And *you* can't be that rude to *people* and not get called out on it," she countered.

"You started it," I snarled.

"And you thought you were above the rules."

Okay. She may have had the thinnest, most microscopic point.

"It was an important call," I lied.

"Was it?" she asked, wrinkling her nose in theatrical disbelief. "Everyone else in that restaurant had no problem following the rules."

"The rule is bullshit."

"Of course it is!" She threw her hands in the air. "George also had rules like servers can only have half a slice of pizza per six-hour shift. Toppings were extra! And you could only take one pee break per shift!"

"If it was so miserable, why are you so upset he fired you?"

"*You* got me fired," she yelled. "And I need the money, you buffoon!"

No one in my entire life had ever called me a buffoon. At least not to my face. I would guess it hadn't been bandied about behind my back either. Asshole, yes. Motherfucking bastard, definitely.

"Buffoon?" I repeated, smirking.

"Shut up. I'm mad."

Good.

"You should be thanking me," I insisted, pushing the button I knew would set her off.

"Are you completely delusional, Charming?"

My mother's easily startled assistant whose name I definitely did not know gasped behind me, reminding me that we had an audience.

I gripped her by the elbow and pulled her away from the office and our audience into a small conference room. It was the same feeling as when I'd held her wrist in the restaurant. An awakening, a hum in my blood.

"Are you dragging me in here to dismember me?" she demanded, swatting at my hand.

Reluctantly, I let go.

We were toe-to-toe just like we'd been in the restaurant. I could smell lemons again. And as angry as I was, I realized it felt pretty damn good to have someone looking me in the eye even while they hurled insults my way.

If I had to have one more conversation with a woman in this office while she spent the entire time looking at her shoes or at some distant spot over my shoulder, I was going to freak the fuck out.

"Because of me," I explained, "you landed a full-time job with benefits that doesn't make you smell like garlic and allows you as many restroom breaks as you require."

"Gee, thanks, Charming." Her sarcasm was so thick I was surprised it didn't drip onto the floor.

"You're welcome," I shot back.

She leaned in. "I really don't like you."

"I'm not a fan of yours either."

We were too close. Much too close for boss and employee. And I wouldn't put it past her to produce a knife and stab me with it.

I took two self-preserving steps back.

"Good," she said.

"Great," I agreed. It looked like Ally, the disrespectful pain in my ass, was the only woman in the building besides my mother who was brave enough to make eye contact with me.

Lucky me. And what in the hell was my mother thinking?

"Listen, Charming. How about you try acting like a grown-up? It's a big company. We'll probably never see each other."

I tapped out a staccato rhythm with my thumb against my leg. "You're fired."

She smiled evilly at me, and I was taken aback by how attractive I found that. "That's something you're going to have to discuss with your mother. I don't believe you have the authority to fire me." She tapped a finger to her chin.

"That's something I will be remedying, Maleficent," I promised her.

"See how well we're getting along already?" she said. "We already have cute nicknames for each other. We're practically mani-pedi buds. Now, if you can point me in the direction of human resources, I'll get out of your hair, and if we're both very, very lucky, we'll never see each other again."

I would have liked to point her in the direction of an open window.

At least that was what I thought that urge was. I was confused by the fact that my dick seemed to be waking up.

"You stick to your ring of hell, and I'll stick to mine," I agreed.

"Perfect solution." She yanked the conference room door open. "HR?" she said in a much friendlier tone to my mother's assistants, who just happened to be lurking outside.

"I can show you," Gina volunteered. She ushered Ally away but not before the woman shot me a look of pure contempt over her shoulder.

8

ALLY

You need an emergency contact." The same woman who had glared her way through an introduction with my bus stop buddy was tapping an impatient fingernail on my screen as I scrolled through onboarding paperwork.

Label's HR department was made up of five very stylish women sitting behind neatly decorated desks arranged in what I assumed was an approved feng shui flow. None of the other reps looked nearly as pissed off as the short straw I'd drawn.

"Uh," I hesitated.

"No family in the city?" She sounded like it might actually kill her to care.

"None that I can count on in an emergency," I said flatly.

"Then pick a friend," she said in exasperation. "You *do* have one of those, don't you?"

I guessed she was projecting.

I entered my best friend Faith's contact information and

hoped to the gods of workplace emergencies that if HR ever needed to call her at work, this lovely flower would have the honor of hearing "Club Ladies and Gentlemen, we've got tits and dicks." Faith was part owner of one of the most over-the-top strip clubs on the island.

I completed the paperwork to the background music of Lady HR's annoyed sighs and fingernail tapping on her watch. The salary listed with the job description had me doing a little shimmy in my chair. It wasn't "I can afford a one-bedroom in Manhattan" money, but it was "I only need three part-time gigs on the side to almost make ends meet."

"Almost make ends meet" was way better than where I'd been when I woke up this morning.

I'd keep the dance class, the highest-paying bar shifts, and take one or two catering jobs a week, I decided, running through the calculations in my head. I still wouldn't have much time for doing the actual renovations, but this was a medium-sized step in the right direction.

If I could just hang in there until the renovations were done and the house was on the market…

"Look here."

I looked up in time to wince at the flash of a camera.

The picture loaded on to the computer screen next to her. It looked like I was mid sneeze. I suddenly had a good idea of who had shot Gola's company ID.

"You're seriously going to put that on my ID?" I asked, actually impressed with the woman's "I don't give a fuck" attitude.

"I don't have all day to orchestrate a photo shoot to please new admins," she snapped.

"Well, all right then. Let's go with the mid sneeze. It'll be a nice icebreaker." It was rather freeing to know that this was all temporary and I didn't have to worry about fitting in or making a good impression or staying on track for a promotion.

Finish the renovations. Sell the house. Mango margarita.

The printer spat out my badge, which doubled as a key card. HR lady smugly handed it over. It was even worse off-screen.

"Admin pool is on the forty-second floor. Ask for the supervisor."

And with that, I was unceremoniously dismissed.

I found my way to the stairs and went down a flight, using my spiffy new key card to enter the suite of offices. The mood here was similar to the forty-third floor. A lot frantic, a little distrustful.

On the blindingly bright side, I didn't have to deal with Grumpy HR Lady or Charming on this floor.

I asked the first beautiful, six-foot-tall woman I saw where to find the admin pool. It turned out that I was standing in the middle of it. *Label*'s second floor of offices opened into a sea of low-walled cubicles taking up some serious acreage surrounded on two sides by glassed-in offices.

Everyone was, if not breathtakingly beautiful, perfectly coiffed and tastefully accessorized.

I asked a stunning brunette who was frantically trying to fold some kind of silky chartreuse fabric into a white gift box to point me in the direction of the supervisor and caught the woman at her desk between rapid-fire phone calls.

The nameplate said Zara. Her long, black hair was tamed in a sleek braid. There were sticky notes of every color organized in neat little rows on her desk.

She eyed my outfit. "New hire? Grab an empty desk, dial the IT extension, and have them set you up with a log-in and an email."

"Thanks," I said, wondering what I'd do then.

But her phone was ringing, and her computer dinged six times in rapid succession with chat and email notifications. "For shit's sake," she muttered, grabbing one of two iPhones on her desk as they both started vibrating.

I ducked out of the office, leaving her to the beeping and vibrating, and did a quick lap searching for a clear flat surface. I found one in the back on the outer ring of cubicles and about as far away from the windows as you could get. But beggars couldn't be choosers. I wove my way through the desks and busy people and claimed my new territory with my purse, coat, and container of the last helping of Mrs. Grosu's Korean barbecue chicken.

"Okay," I whispered to myself.

I tried out the chair and found it reasonably comfortable. To be fair, every other job I'd had in the past six months didn't involve chairs or me sitting in them, so having any chair was a big step up.

The computer monitor was a sexy, state-of-the-art flat-screen, and the only other items on the desk were a thin white keyboard and a phone.

I picked up the receiver and skimmed the buttons looking for IT.

"You new?"

I peered around the jumbotron flashing the *Label* logo and found a woman looking back at me.

She had glossy hair the color of a wheat field with subtle silver-toned highlights. It was pulled back in a low ponytail that no strand dared escape. Her face was generic perfection with high cheekbones, expertly applied contouring, and a petite nose that other women probably took pictures of and presented to their plastic surgeons. She would have been downright beautiful if not for the pinched line of her overfilled lips and the mean girl vibe.

"Hi," I said. "Yes. I'm Ally. Just started today."

She gave a derisive snort that still somehow managed to sound ladylike. "Don't get in my way."

"You must be the welcoming committee," I said, cocking my head. I couldn't tell if she was twenty-eight or thirty-eight.

"Any assignments that come in for Dominic Russo are mine. Got it?"

I laughed. It was a perfect match as far as I was concerned. "You can keep him. I prefer my men with hearts."

Her lips got impossibly flatter, and I worried they might pop.

"Are you making new friends, Malina?" Gola strolled up and perched on the edge of my desk.

The woman in danger of a lip filler explosion turned her icy glare to my newest friend. "I'm filling her in on the ground rules."

"Her name is Ally, and no one is getting in the way of your delusions," Gola said.

Heads snapped up over cubicle walls around us like prairie dogs scenting danger.

Gola turned back to me. "Malina here has career aspirations of forcing at least one Russo into a prenup. It didn't quite work out the first time around. Did it?" she said, wrinkling her nose in fake sympathy.

Interesting.

"You'd be smart to watch your step, Gola," Malina hissed. "And your fat ass."

"Don't make me twerk up on you again, Mal." Gola's grin was wicked.

Without another word, Malina threw her ponytail over her shoulder and stormed off.

"So you already met the mean girl," Gola teased.

"She seems *lovely*."

"A *total* charmer. People are always saying, 'That Malina is the *nicest* human being in the entire department.'"

"I'm *so happy* I picked the desk behind hers," I sighed.

"Lunch in thirty?" Gola moved to tap the folder she was holding on my desk and ended up dumping its contents on the floor.

"Sounds good," I said, helping her pick up papers and fabric swatches.

It was the fanciest cafeteria I'd ever stepped foot in. Unlike my high school cafeteria with its vinyl stools and burnt, canned marinara smell, here the floors were some kind of white marble and huge urns filled with real greenery created a Zen, urban jungle feel.

There was definitely no canned marinara smell.

It was more of an atrium or a conservatory than a cafeteria. Even the food was fancy. I couldn't afford it, but that didn't stop me from glancing at the sushi chef's display and the Keto Korner.

Gola and I grabbed an empty table between a potted palm and another table full of tall, thin women picking at lettuce and animatedly discussing a fight between a photographer and a makeup artist.

Gola placed a glass of green juice and a bowl of clear broth on the table in front of her. "I'm doing a cleanse," she said, catching me eyeing her questionable "lunch." "You've got to try it. It makes your skin radiant."

"I'm more of an accidental fasting person," I joked.

"Intermittent fasting is so the rage," she nodded sagely.

"My situation is kind of 'ran out of food' and have to wait for my next paycheck fasting."

"You're broke?" Gola said with more interest than pity.

"More like newly and temporarily poor."

Gola spotted Ruth in the crowd and waved her over. The redhead plopped her kale salad down and planted herself in the chair across from me. "Did I miss the beginning of the inquisition?" she asked breathlessly.

"Nope. Inquisition starts now," Gola said.

"Tell us everything about you, including how you met Dalessandra, how you got this job, and if you really called Dominic Russo a megalomaniacal monster to his face," Ruth said. She took a bite of her salad and crunched with enthusiasm.

"Uhhhh."

"Okay. Start with meeting Dalessandra," Gola said.

"Hey, bus stop buddy!" My orange-sweatered pal popped up next to the table, clutching his wrinkled paper bag. He beamed hopefully. "Mind if I join you?"

"Have a seat," I said, gesturing at the open chairs. Turning back to Gola and Ruth, I explained, "We met at a bus stop when Dalessandra gave us both jobs on the spot."

"You absolutely need to join us," Ruth insisted, patting the chair next to her.

I breathed a sigh of relief.

"Thanks," he said. "I'm Buddy, by the way." He held out a beefy hand that Ruth and Gola took turns shaking.

"I'm Ally," I told him.

Gola wiggled in her chair. "Okay, spill it, kids. What was Dalessandra Russo doing at a bus stop?"

Buddy unrolled his paper bag and pulled out a cute little sub, a bag of chips, and a Fresca. "Well, I don't know what Ms. Russo was doing there, but I'd just finished one of those under-the-table painting jobs in the Village. And I'm sitting there at the bus stop, and I see Ally here talking to Ms. Russo. Ms. Russo is apologizing about something and then hands her a business card and is all 'come see me Monday for a job,'" he said, theatrically producing an invisible card.

Ruth and Gola were enthralled, so I dug into my chicken.

"I'm thinking, this is my chance. One of those once-in-a-lifetime jobbies. I gotta say something. If I don't, I'm gonna regret it forever. So I pipe up, and I say, 'You got any more of those jobs?' And when she looks at me, she isn't all hoity-toity. She says to me, 'What can you do?' I say, 'Whatever you need me to do.' So here I am. The newest clerk in the mail room. I have a desk. I don't gotta paint anything. And once the health insurance kicks in, I'm taking my wife straight to physical therapy."

"Why does your wife need PT?" Gola asked. Another point in my book. They were now more invested in Buddy's story than juicy office gossip.

"Got hurt on the job a year ago. She was one of those linemen—line lady, she liked to say. Anyway, she fell on the job. Seventeen feet and landed on her back on concrete."

I winced.

"Bad spinal injury. She's in a wheelchair. She couldn't work anymore. Company fought the workers' comp claim. I lost my job for missing so many days after the accident. Without good health insurance, we couldn't swing PT appointments anymore. And that was the only thing that made her feel like she had hope, you know."

"Buddy, that's awful," I said.

"It's been a tough time," he agreed. "But I always knew there was light at the end of the tunnel, and now look at me. Sitting here with three beautiful ladies with a job in a big-time office and brand-new health insurance."

I wanted to hug the guy and was deeply moved when Ruth actually did it.

"You're a great guy, Buddy," Gola said, reaching across the table to squeeze his hand.

He hooted with laughter. "Wait'll I tell my wife!"

9

ALLY

Buddy inhaled his lunch and raced back to the mail room, eager to prove his worth on the first day.

"That was, like, the most inspiring thing I've heard in my life," Ruth sighed. "I think I love him."

"Get in line," I said in unison with Gola.

"Okay, girl," Gola said. "Let's get *your* story. What was Dalessandra Russo doing with you at a bus stop?"

"She was apologizing for her son—who I thought was her date at the time—getting me fired," I said.

Gola knocked the remains of her green juice over.

"Mr. Ice Statue of Perfection did what now?" Ruth demanded, handing over a stack of napkins.

"Charming—I mean, Dominic—met Dalessandra for dinner at the pizza place I was working at. He was being rude, so I returned his rudeness, and I spelled out an immature message in toppings on his pizza. As one does."

Gola was gaping at me like I'd just turned into Tina Turner in front of her.

"Yeah, I'm going to need the immature message in its entirety," Ruth decided.

"FU."

"You said 'fuck you' to Dominic Russo?" Gola said slowly.

"Well, I spelled it with pepperonis. But yeah."

"What did he do?"

"Blew a gasket. Yelled."

Ruth and Gola exchanged an incredulous look. "He *yelled*?"

"Oh yeah. He yelled. We called each other names. He demanded to see the manager."

"I knew there was a volcano under that iceberg," Gola said, slapping the mound of sopping wet napkins. "Didn't I tell you?"

Ruth nodded. "You did. You called it."

Gola leaned in. "Dominic Russo has been Frosty the Fine Snowman to everyone since he got here over a year ago," she explained quietly. The palms probably had ears.

Interesting. My limited experience with Charming had been the exact opposite. I hadn't seen frigid. I'd seen hellfire.

"Who knew it would be a pepperoni pizza that pushed him over the line?" Ruth mused.

"Okay, so back to the story. FU, demands to see the manager," Gola recited, waving her hand dangerously close to Ruth's hot tea.

"So George waddles out of the kitchen, takes a look at Dalessandra's red leather skirt and Dom's fancy coat, and fires me on the spot."

"No!" they gasped.

I liked these two as an audience.

"Yes. I grabbed my coat and bag and went back out into the dining room, made a speech about how we're human and people like him shouldn't treat us like we're not. And then I left."

Gola and Ruth were hinged forward, hanging on my every word.

"So I'm at the bus stop trying to figure out what to do before my bartending shift—"

"Ally is poor," Gola explained to Ruth.

"Got it." Ruth nodded.

"And Dalessandra comes up and apologizes for Dominic and offers me a job on the spot. I didn't know who she was or what the job was. And here I am." I decided to leave out the whole vague "Hey, why don't you tell me what's wrong with morale" part.

"And here you are," Ruth repeated in wonder. "This is the most exciting Monday I've had in a long time."

"She has the desk behind Malina," Gola told Ruth.

"Oh, that sounds fun." Ruth winced.

"What's her story anyway?" I asked.

There was another one of those long, pointed looks.

"She was Dominic's dad's girlfriend." Gola whispered the word *girlfriend* and looked over her shoulder.

"You mean side piece," Ruth hissed.

"Ruth!"

"What? It's true." Ruth scooted her chair closer. "So Paul Russo, Dalessandra's husband and Dominic's father, used to be the creative director here. But rumor has it he tended to use his position to go fishing in the company pond, if you catch my drift."

I was an excellent drift catcher.

"Not all the fish were *willing* to be caught," Gola added.

This was news.

"Basically he was a big ol' perv," Ruth whispered. "It was

common knowledge with the staff, and according to the rumor mill, he'd fired a few of his less-willing victims. So if you wanted to keep your job, you let him grab your ass."

"That's bullshit," I gasped.

They nodded.

"Of course it was," Gola said.

"And Dalessandra didn't do anything about it?"

"We don't know if she knew. I don't think she would have let him get away with it," Ruth said. "But no one wanted to test the theory that she'd believe an intern or a junior editor over her own husband."

"And then there were the Malinas," Gola added. "She was happy to lock herself in his office for a quickie. He even took her out of the country for a few shoots and shows."

"She thought she was going to be the next Mrs. Russo," Ruth added.

"Poor little gold-digging dumbass," Gola scoffed.

"Anyway, we don't know for sure, but rumor has it that Paul finally grabbed the wrong girl. And all hell broke loose," Ruth continued.

"What happened?" I pressed.

"We came in one day, and there was no more Paul. No official announcement. Just Dominic with an assistant clearing out his father's office. Side note: Another rumor has it he found three boxes of condoms and a bottle of lube in the desk."

"He got all new furniture because ew," Gola chimed in.

"A week later, HR rolled out a shiny new harassment and fraternization policy, which pretty much confirmed the rumors."

"Paul immediately got a job with *Indulgence*," Ruth said, naming another fashion magazine. "All the executives here have noncompetes, so who knows how he pulled that off."

"What about the women?" I asked.

They both shrugged. "We're not really sure what went down. There was an exodus of almost a dozen people. Again, it was super hush-hush. A handful are still here, including Malina," Gola said. "None of them ever answered any direct questions."

"I heard from an acquaintance of a friend of a friend that there was some kind of settlement involving iron-clad NDAs," Ruth explained.

"Wow." I didn't know what else to say. No wonder the vibe was so off here. It didn't sound like a solution; it sounded like a cover-up.

"But things are better now," Ruth insisted. "The sexual harassment policy wasn't drafted in the 1950s. And a fraternization policy kind of sort of adds more protection."

"What's that?" I asked.

"Basically relationships can't exist between executives and underlings," Gola said.

"That's not *exactly* what it says," Ruth disagreed.

"It's the spirit of the rules. They're trying to prevent relationships with lopsided power dynamics. But it kind of comes across as 'we fucked up, and now we're holding the rest of you responsible,'" Gola sighed.

"She's touchy because she's in love with a junior VP in fashion," Ruth teased.

"Used to be. And I'd say it was more lust," Gola corrected her.

"He is really, really cute," Ruth mused. "But not cute enough for either of us to lose our jobs over."

I picked up my fork and cut my last bite of chicken in half, hoping to make it last. I was beginning to get a few ideas about where Dalessandra had gone wrong.

"So how come you're poor?" Ruth asked cheerfully.

"It's a long, long story," I sighed.

I felt an arctic breeze skim down my spine and looked up.

Two tables down, Charming was glaring at me while pulling up a chair next to the Linus guy I'd met in Dalessandra's office this morning. I returned his withering stare with a phony smile and a finger-wiggling wave.

"Girl, you are the bravest person I have ever met," Gola whispered without moving her lips.

"Your vagina must be made out of steel," Ruth guessed.

"Aren't they all?" My phone timer buzzed, and I sighed. "Okay, ladies. Back to work."

I was a planner by nature. Things got lost or went undone if there wasn't a plan in place. Commitment to me meant doing what I said I was going to do.

I just happened to have to commit to a lot of things. So I planned. Ruthlessly. There were dozens of daily alerts scheduled in my phone.

Plan out week.

Choreograph dance class.

Leave for dance class.

Teach dance class.

Buy more ramen.

Leave for bar shift.

Start bar shift.

End bar shift.

Catch train home.

Send design invoices.

Make payment on astronomical debt.

Go the fuck to bed.

Wake the fuck up.

Do it all over again…

If I didn't schedule every single task, it might fall off my plate and get kicked under some piece of metaphorical furniture only to be remembered months later in the middle of the night. And if someone was counting on me, I needed to deliver.

"Let's get drinks after work tonight," Ruth suggested. "I feel like we have so much more gossip to impart."

I grinned, standing. "I can't. There's that whole I'm poor thing, and I'm working tonight."

"You have a second job?" Gola asked.

"I have four second jobs."

"Girl, you need a vacation."

And a mango margarita.

10

DOMINIC

I *hated* these kinds of meetings.

This whole face-to-face brainstorming thing was bullshit. How the hell was I supposed to know what designer should dress our models for a fall office fashion shoot? Or what makeup products were at the center of a social media maelstrom?

Photo shoots and everything leading up to them were more politically fraught than a UN meeting. Designers who clashed with models. Photographers who wouldn't shoot certain designers. Inventory miscommunication. Too many editorial opinions. Sales reps who made promises they shouldn't. Last-minute location disasters.

And I was expected to make the most diplomatic decisions. *Ha. Some fucking joke.*

"You ready?" Linus, the snarky production manager, asked, joining me in the hallway. He adjusted his glasses.

"I'm ready."

I hated not being good at something. At the age of twelve, I'd been tossed out of a baseball game for hurling my bat over the fence when I'd struck out yet again. Baseball hadn't been my game.

My dad—a high school baseball star of his own time who, for some inexplicable reason, actually made it to the game that day—told me I should focus on something I was good at...like watching TV or whining.

We'd had a similar conversation when I'd told him I was taking his position here. He'd given me the same sneer of disdain and wished me luck filling his shoes. I'd told him I'd rather burn his shoes and everything that was in this office to the damn ground.

It wasn't a healthy sense of competition that drove me in this position. No, it was a pulsing need to prove to myself that I was better than the man who'd never earned the loyalty I'd once so freely given.

That was what I'd done with baseball. I practiced every damn night. Spent hours in batting cages and running drills. In the end, I'd gotten good enough to earn a scholarship offer to play in college, something my father hadn't managed in his own life.

That was a good enough measure of success for me. Challenge conquered, point proven, I'd quit and never picked up a glove again.

I'd do the same here. Force myself to rise above an innate inability, do my fucking best, and when it was all over, never ever look back.

"Remember what we talked about," Linus said, pausing outside the conference room door.

"Yeah," I said. Then for some stupid reason, I remembered Ally's passionate exit speech at the restaurant. About people deserving better treatment and all that garbage. "Thanks," I said.

Linus's eyes widened a fraction behind his tortoiseshell glasses. "You're welcome?" he said after a beat.

I called it proof of asshole. It was something I tallied up on occasion. When someone looks at you cross-eyed for saying thank you because apparently you'd never said it before? Definite proof of asshole.

I stopped abruptly inside the door.

She was there.

Arranging coffees and pastries—that no one was going to eat because carbs were evil—like it was her job and not some cosmic joke.

Everyone else was already settled around the table, and conversations came to a halt. I had that kind of effect on a room.

Ally looked up and didn't bother hiding the eye roll. "Oh great," she muttered under her breath.

Yeah, well, I wasn't happy about seeing her either.

I ignored her and took my seat at the head of the table. "Thanks for being here," I said gruffly. "Let's get started."

From the looks I got around the table, none of these people were used to the t-word coming out of my mouth either. I bit back a sigh.

Ally planted herself at the foot of the table behind some ancient dinosaur of a laptop. She was wearing a cropped mock-neck sweater in cheery fuchsia over black pants. She wore bracelets made out of some sort of fabric—maybe denim—wrapped up her right wrist.

"We're interested in your input on the fall makeup tutorials, *Mr. Russo.*" Beauty editor Shayla was baiting me again.

Ally lifted a questioning eyebrow as she typed. Our gazes met, and I knew she'd noted the tone too. The last thing I needed was two of them.

"Let's take a look," I announced.

Everyone scrambled through their handouts to the spread that was up for discussion. I didn't bother flipping to it. I'd been coached.

"I think the bones are good, but you're missing the mark not including some kind of bronzer. It's a transition season, and not all women are necessarily ready to let go of the sun-kissed look."

Both of my evil little notetaker's eyebrows winged up in surprise.

Shayla played it cooler. "Do you have any suggestions?"

"That's not my area of expertise," I reminded her. "I'm sure whatever you choose will be fine."

Fine. Not "good." These subtle little digs back and forth were boring, annoying. In my old job, we'd lock ourselves in an office, yell for twenty minutes, and move forward with a solution. Here, things just festered. The bottom line was it didn't really matter if Shayla wanted me here or not because I *was* here, I was in charge, and we all had to deal with it.

"Moving on," Linus said, smoothly steering the meeting back to the agenda.

I found myself watching Ally throughout the meeting. She seemed to find it impossible to hold still, typing while swaying side to side ever so slightly to a beat only she could hear.

Our eyes met and held over the gigantic laptop screen several times.

No messages passed between us. No "fuck yous." No thinly veiled insults. Just long, shared looks. Her eyes looked more brown than gold in this lighting. Her hair, even though it was tied back in a short tail, still had that just tousled by a man's hands look with the waves escaping around her face. And those lips seemed to be permanently quirked as if always ready to smirk or smile.

I didn't trust smilers.

She stuck her tongue out at me.

Ever so casually, I raised my hand and rubbed at my eye with my middle finger.

She was definitely smirking now.

"Excuse me a minute," I said, interrupting an editor. "Do you mind typing just a little quieter? It sounds like you're trying to stab your way through the table."

Everyone turned to stare open-mouthed at Ally.

She looked up. Smiled. And I suddenly couldn't wait to see what she'd do next.

"So sorry," she offered sweetly.

I was disappointed.

Momentarily.

As soon as the table returned to their debate whether peach or rose was a better background, Ally mashed her keyboard in an obnoxious crescendo.

Linus looked like he was about to swallow his tongue. Shayla cleared her throat and stared at the ceiling. The rest of the team around the table scooted their chairs as far away from Ally as possible, as if they didn't want to get caught in any crossfire.

"Would someone see about getting Sausage Fingers here a quieter way to take notes next time?" I said to the room in general.

There were actual audible intakes of breath.

"And if someone could see about getting Charming here a nicer personality that he could try on for meetings, that would be great," she shot back.

Linus choked on his gum, and the rest of the room was turning blue holding their breath.

"Moving on," I said, feeling marginally more cheerful.

Conversation began again. I wasn't sure if it was my imagination or not, but everyone seemed a little more relaxed.

Next on the agenda was a beauty brand that was jerking us

around, demanding prime product placement after backing out of an advertising deal.

I nearly fell out of my chair when a junior beauty editor asked me, "Do you have any suggestions, Mr. Russo?"

I took a breath and looked her dead in the eye. "Call me Dominic. Please."

She blinked rapidly several times, looking stunned.

As a matter of fact, I did have a suggestion. This was my area of expertise. Risk assessment. Managing inflated egos. Applying the right pressure at the right time. I had plenty of personal experience with that.

"Tell them we've decided to go in another direction. Name-drop Flawless," I said, mentioning another skin care company.

"We've had a relationship with La Sophia for years," Shayla reminded me. But she didn't sound like she hated the idea.

"Maybe it's time to break up," I said.

That got me an honest-to-God smile out of the woman. She'd looked at me with contempt, barely controlled her eye rolls when I made stupid suggestions, or just frowned outright when we passed in the halls.

But this was a look of approval.

"I've been wanting to do that for a long time," she confessed.

"Then I'll leave it in your hands," I said.

"Do you want me to reach out to Flawless or just say that I am?" she asked.

"If there's a brand you want to work with that you think would be a good fit for our readers, do it."

Shayla's smile got a millimeter wider, and I felt my proof of asshole score drop a few points. Not bad for a Tuesday.

A surprisingly spirited discussion broke out around the table about how best to illustrate the results of the magazine's online polls rating what readers looked for in spring jackets.

"Why don't you put them in motion?" an annoying voice from the far end of the table piped up.

"Because this is a print magazine. That means it's on *paper*," I said, heavy on the sarcasm.

Ally rolled her eyes. "Your sarcasm is noted, Dom. But I was talking about linking the print graphics to an animated one online. You want more crossover traffic between your print and digital content, right? You do something cutesy like this..." She stood up and walked to the whiteboard.

I divided my attention between two things: the way those pants hugged the curves of her ass and the competence with which she drew. She sketched out a rough trench coat with arrows pointing to parts of the construction and then another version mimicking motion.

It was fucking charming. That annoyed me.

"Then down here, you put a custom smart label that your reader can scan with their phone, and it takes them to the website. Link it to a cartoon or actual videos of models wearing each of the products, and break down the construction, best ways to wear them, where to buy at different price points."

Linus was pursing his lips and polishing his glasses, his tell that he liked an idea. "That's..."

"Not a horrible idea," I filled in.

"Thanks," she said dryly.

"Can you do a mock-up of the illustrations for me?" Shayla asked her. "Something in that style?"

Ally shrugged. "Yeah. Sure."

We wrapped ten minutes late. A first. Usually my meetings ended early because everyone was in a hurry to not be in the same room as me.

I took a moment to scroll through messages on my phone and purposely walked out behind Ally.

"Sausage Fingers?" she hissed at me.

I didn't like her. But sparring with her made an otherwise interminable meeting slightly more interesting. Plus, there was something enticing about that fresh lemon scent.

"You type like a Clydesdale."

"You know, you'd be a lot prettier if you smiled once in a while," she mused, fluttering her lashes.

No wonder women hated it when men said that.

"I don't have time to smile."

"I don't have time to smile," she mimicked in an annoying voice.

"Your maturity peaked in preschool."

"Aww, did Pouty Man Face get his feelings hurt?"

"You're fired, Maleficent."

"Good luck with that, Charming." She headed off in the direction of the stairs.

"Don't bother getting comfortable here," I called after her.

I didn't realize until a makeup artist gaped up at me and then walked straight into a glass door when I passed her that I was actually smiling.

11

DOMINIC

The admin pool was a place I generally avoided. It was loud and disorganized, and it had been my father's preferred hunting grounds for employees to harass. He'd most likely seen them as powerless and pretty. The perfect victims.

I saw it as a series of potential land mines. Busy women who did the dirty work for everything that happened inside and outside our offices. One false move and I could piss off the entire backbone of our company. It was safer to avoid them, to let them do their thing, rather than remind them that there was another male Russo in residence.

It was Ally's lunch break, but I hadn't seen her in the cafeteria. Not that I was looking. Or that I'd checked her calendar in the system for her schedule. Okay, so maybe I had.

I absolutely refused to think about my motives for personally dropping off a legitimate research request. I always had Greta email them, keeping the lines of communication clearly defined.

But if I dropped off this request in person, I reasoned, I could also see if Ally was ready to quit yet.

I tapped the folder in my hand and surveyed the space. Most of the cubicles were abandoned, but I spotted her and that pink sweater across the room. She had headphones on and was rhythmically shimmying her shoulders, lips moving to unheard lyrics.

I tapped the folder again, debating. What the hell. I had a few minutes for an argument.

She was still swaying in her chair when I walked up behind her. My dick inexplicably took notice of her proximity, which pissed me off. I was forty-four years old, not some pimple-faced teenager at a pool party. And unlike my father, I had self-control.

I peered over her shoulder, and she nearly jumped out of her skin. "Crap on a cracker, Charming!" She yanked her headphones off but got them stuck in her hair. "Ow!" She pulled harder.

"Stop it," I said, making a grab for the headgear and slapping her hand away. "You'll give yourself a bald spot."

I unwound her hair from the earpiece.

"I'd say thank you, but it's your fault I'm now balding."

"I see you're doing personal work on company time," I said, looking at the screen where she seemed to be in the middle of designing several versions of a logo for a butcher shop.

She picked up her phone—one of those knockoff smartphones that looked like it was ten seconds away from disintegrating—and showed me the countdown on the screen. "I'm on lunch, Mr. Sunshine. On my own laptop."

"You're on *my* Wi-Fi. And where did you get that poor excuse for a phone?"

She gave me a look that said *why don't you go kick yourself in the balls* before turning back to her dinosaur of a computer and disconnecting the internet. "Happy now?"

I was. I liked fighting with her. At least she didn't go cry in a corner if I looked at her wrong.

I glanced at her desk. There was a banana sitting next to the phone. "*That's* your lunch?"

"Yes, it is. Now, is there anything else you'd like to judge me on—maybe my outfit or perhaps I'm breathing too loudly—or can I get back to my lunch break?"

"A banana isn't lunch."

I'd been around the fashion industry long enough to know how rampant eating disorders were. But I'd seen the woman polish off two cranberry muffins during the meeting this morning.

"It is when you're newly and temporarily poor."

"Newly and temporarily poor," I repeated.

"Don't worry, Dom," she said dryly. "It's not contagious."

Dom. Not only had she used my first name, she'd given me a nickname...one that wasn't mean.

"Did you need something, or did you just decide to spread your cloud of doom to another floor?" she asked.

"Most new employees at least pretend to show a modicum of respect to management."

"Most new employees didn't already lose one job in the past week to management," she shot back.

"So you're blaming me for being newly and temporarily poor?"

"Don't flatter yourself. You just managed to make me a little poorer."

"Is that banana really all you have to eat?" I asked.

"Do I really need to converse with you when I'm off the clock?" she asked, reaching for the banana and peeling it.

As if the gods were smiling on me, her phone timer dinged, and I smirked. "Looks like you're back on the clock."

She sighed, hit Save on her laptop, and closed it.

"What can I do for you, *boss*?"

"Just keep being your belligerent self, and sooner or later, my mother will realize she made a terrible mistake."

"I don't know about that. She kept you around." Ally took a deliberate bite of banana, and I was instantly, stupidly aroused.

I was back to being pissed off. This was ridiculous. I'd never gotten a hard-on from a conversation with a coworker. Clearly my self-imposed celibacy had gone on a little too long if arguing with a woman while she ate fruit turned me on.

I leaned in. "Quit."

"Make me."

"I fully intend to."

"Great. Now that that's settled, how about you scamper off to whatever ring of hell you came from and let me earn my paycheck?"

I turned to leave and nearly ran into someone.

Malinda? Matilda? The blond with the *Real Housewives* lips was standing too close. She'd been one of the few who accepted the settlement and decided to stay. She'd also been one who had enjoyed my father's advances.

"Hi," she said, her voice all baby-doll breathy.

If she called me "daddy," I was going to puke.

"Excuse me," I said briskly, trying to step around her.

"Is there something I can…*do* for you?" M-something asked, planting herself directly in my way. Her gaze skimmed up my body, lingering on my crotch.

Ally mimed a creditable dry heave behind her desk, and I may have telegraphed a "please help me" in her direction.

"No," I said to…Melissa? Magenta?

She took a step closer. I was bent so far backward when her finger trailed down my tie that I could have won a limbo championship. "Anything at all. *Anything*," she repeated.

I backed into the cubicle divider, gritting my teeth. I was *not* my father, and the fact that she thought I was made me physically ill.

"Hey, Mal, why don't you try sexually harassing men on your own time?" Ally piped up, leaning over her wall. "Some of us are trying to eat here, and your praying mantis routine is nauseating."

Mal…inda shifted from "put a baby in me" to "dragon lady" in the blink of an eye. The look she shot Ally was so full of contempt I willingly put myself between them. Sure, Ally's mere existence pissed me the fuck off. But that didn't mean she should have to die by psychotic coworker while protecting me.

"I don't need anything," I said again. Colder this time.

She seemed to get the hint. Raising her chin, the woman sauntered away, a crocodile slithering into a swamp.

"That was a close one," Ally observed, taking another bite of banana. "She almost took your balls with her."

"Yeah. After ripping your face off to get to them."

She blinked at me and then snickered.

Fuck me. "That came out wrong. I didn't mean your face would be anywhere near…" I couldn't finish the sentence. Fuck. Five minutes in this room and I'd gotten a hard-on and suggested that an employee put her face near my balls. This was *not* who I was.

She laughed again, harder this time. "Relax, Dom. You might be an asshole, but you're not trying to get into my underwear."

I dropped the folder to cover what was now a raging erection because of course I was picturing her underwear. I hated myself.

"Now that Malina? She's going to try to crawl into yours. So you might want to consider a chastity belt or shark repellent," she suggested.

"Maybe you should get back to work," I muttered and then left the room as quickly as I could without running.

Back at my own desk, dick under control—mostly—I put in a request to HR.

While I waited for the paperwork, I buzzed Greta.

"Do me a favor and have some kind of snack sent to the admin pool this afternoon."

"Some kind of *snack*?" She repeated it like I was speaking a foreign language.

"Yes. Food. Something with protein maybe?"

"Enough for the whole department?" she asked. I could hear the curiosity.

"Enough for everyone. Use my card," I said. I spotted the research request on my desk. The one I hadn't bothered delivering. "Oh, and can you put a research request into the system for me?"

Five minutes later, I settled back in my chair to read everything there was in Ally Morales's file.

12

DOMINIC

I'd avoided her since Tuesday just to prove that I could.

Just to prove to my stupid cock that it did *not* run my life. That I wasn't a carbon copy of Paul Russo.

I didn't know exactly what the hell was going on, but I'd wasted more brainpower on Ally Morales in the week and a half since I'd met her in that stupid pizza shop than on anything that actually deserved my attention.

That was a problem.

And I was the smart guy who decided that since I'd proved I could leave her alone, I next needed to prove that I could be around her…and not want to fuck her.

I'd requested her.

It wasn't a big deal, I told myself as I glanced at my watch *again*. I'd requested admins before. Ones I knew would be less annoying or wouldn't make weird nervous humming noises if I asked them a direct question.

Requesting Ally didn't mean anything.

I wasn't interested. Not in *that* way. I didn't sleep with people who pissed me off and pushed my buttons. I was, however, curious about her.

What took a woman from being a semi-successful graphic designer in Colorado to a server living off bananas in New York? Her credit wasn't great. The credit report noted a shit ton of credit card debt in the last three months. But the street view of her home address—yeah, okay, so I'd looked up her address; I wasn't happy about that either—showed a family home in a nice neighborhood in a decent commuter town in Jersey.

She didn't own the house, but I'd stopped short of doing a totally legal property search to see who did.

I'd also stopped myself a dozen times from looking for her on social media.

I wasn't an impulsive guy. This itch to learn more about her annoyed me. I didn't even *like* her. But her company photo did make me laugh. I called up the picture again on my screen and smirked. Was she mid sneeze?

There was a knock on my open door, and I jolted in my chair.

Ally was standing in my doorway with a coat draped over her arm and a backpack slung over her shoulder. "Ready to go, Charming? Or do you need a few more minutes with your porn?"

I closed her picture and rose.

Those eyes went wide, and her lips formed an O.

I glanced down, wondering if I'd forgotten to zip my pants or something.

Nope. Zipped. "What?" I demanded.

Silently, she shook her head.

I looked back down. No stains. My tie was still tied, my vest still buttoned.

"Do you have a problem?" I asked, enunciating each word.

She shook her head. "Nope. No problem," she finally croaked. Now she was looking everywhere but me. The carpet appeared to be quite fascinating. Her neck was turning an interesting shade of pink.

"Try to pull yourself together before the meeting," I suggested, brushing past her.

Greta was waiting by her desk with my coat and briefcase. "Be nice," she ordered.

Ally snorted behind me.

"I'm *always* nice," I growled, shoving my arms through the sleeves of my coat.

Both women shared a laugh at my expense.

"You're a funny guy, Dom," Ally said, slapping me on the shoulder. She had apparently recovered from whatever seizure or psychotic break had rendered her mute. "Nice to meet you, Greta."

"Good luck, Ally," Greta said with a traitorous wink.

We didn't talk in the elevator, each doing our damnedest to pretend the other didn't exist. But as more people crowded in, I found myself pressed up against her in the corner. What was this annoying electric buzz every time we touched? Even through layers of clothing, I was still keenly aware of her shoulder pressing against my arm.

Hell, the guy from twenty-three was brushing my sleeve with his elbow as he played *Tetris* on his phone, but that contact barely drew my notice. There was a tension between Ally and me, wrapping itself around us and pinging back and forth.

I didn't like it.

The doors finally opened like a reprieve, and we stepped out into the lobby. I led the way, trying to get a few steps ahead of her so I could not smell that lemon scent that was messing with my head.

"Hey, Ally! How's it going?" A man wearing brown cargo pants and a cap that looked like it had once been a woodland creature shifted the half-dozen Dior bags he was carrying to wave.

Ally beamed.

I'd seen her smirk. I'd witnessed her annoyance. I'd even seen her laugh once or twice. But this was something else entirely.

Her face lit up with actual joy. Didn't she know joy had no place here? I wanted her to be as uncomfortable and annoyed by my presence as I was by hers. I wanted her unable to function.

"Buddy! Doing a little shopping?" she teased.

He laughed, a braying, donkey-like sound that was too loud to be dignified.

"Yeah, right! Doing a little pickup for a fancy photo shoot," he called. "You?"

"Heading off to a fancy meeting," she told him with a wink.

"See you at lunch tomorrow," he yelled as the elevator doors closed.

She was still grinning when we climbed into the SUV.

"Good afternoon," Nelson said when he slid behind the wheel. "I took the liberty of getting you each a protein shake for the drive."

Nelson's eyes met mine in the rearview mirror, and I felt his unasked question. Before today, I'd never once asked him to make a special trip for food or drink before a thirty-minute ride.

"Wow, thanks!" Ally said, making a grab for one of the shakes.

I picked up mine, pretending like I wanted it. "Who was that guy?" I asked her.

"Who? Buddy?" she asked, peering into the cup.

I saw the way her eyes lit up, and as annoying as I found her and as much as I enjoyed our back-and-forth, the hunger I saw there made my chest tight. I wanted to ask her why.

Why, when she had a full-time, decent-paying job, was she hungry?

"His name is Buddy?" I asked instead.

"I'm surprised you don't know. Your mother hired him at the same bus stop where she hired me. You know, after you got me fired."

"You got yourself fired." I peered out the window at cold, wet Manhattan and wished I were somewhere hot and tropical. Far away from everything else.

"Here's a thought. Since we're trapped working together," Ally began, "why don't we try this thing where we just agree to disagree?"

I shook my head. "That never works."

"Okay, fine. How about instead of mortal enemies, we make an effort to not be horrible to each other?"

"I don't feel comfortable making promises I can't keep."

Her lips quirked. It wasn't the full-on Buddy beam, but I still liked it.

"How long of a drive is this?" she asked with a sigh.

"About thirty minutes, miss," Nelson said from the front seat.

"It's Ally," she told him.

"Nice to meet you, Ally. I'm Nelson."

"Thirty minutes seems like a long time to be trapped in a car with a guy like Dom," she mused to my driver.

His eyes crinkled at the corners. "One gets used to it."

"So we can't pretend to be friends, and you can't promise not to be an ass," she recapped to me. "How about we clear the air? We can tell each other all the things we don't like about each other. I'll go first."

She was joking. But the idea had merit. I *didn't* like her. I *couldn't* like her. We both needed to remember that.

"Your attitude," I said, launching into my own list. "Your shoes. Your eyes are too big for your face. You have issues remembering that you're an employee and should act accordingly. And your hair constantly looks like you just rolled out of bed." *With a man.*

She blinked. Twice. And then her laugh filled the car. "You've put a lot of thought into that list for it to just roll off your tongue like that."

"I was just stating the obvious. I don't sit around thinking about you, Maleficent."

Lies.

She sent a cocky look in my direction. "Sure you don't, Dom."

"Not only are you not my type, you're so far in the opposite direction of my type, you rank next to my great-aunt Rose." *More lies.*

I did, however, have a great-aunt Rose on my father's side. She too was a horrible human being. There was something profoundly wrong with the DNA on that side of the family.

Ally laughed. "Don't start being funny, Charming. I like a man with a sense of humor," she warned.

"You'll need to fight your baser instincts and resist me," I grumbled.

She reached out and actually patted my hand where it rested on my thigh. "Don't worry, Dom. You're not my type either."

I snorted to let her know I knew she was bluffing.

She turned in the seat to look at me straight on. The movement made that stupid swingy skirt she had on slip a little higher on her thigh.

"You're callous, disrespectful, generally in a bad mood, and

I'd guess that you have trouble taking anyone else's feelings into consideration over your own."

Look at her hitting the nail on the head.

"You're a workaholic, which is fine. Work ethic is a good thing in my book. But you don't like your job, so that makes you either too stubborn or too scared to make a change. And I'm not a fan of either."

My eyes narrowed, and I could *feel* my nostrils flaring. "You don't know me."

"I know you're not my type," she said saucily.

She wished I wasn't her type.

"You're the type who waltzes into pizza shops and gets servers fired."

"I'd like to amend my list to add the fact that you're incapable of letting anything go," I said, pretending to be fascinated by the website traffic email that just came through.

"I was depending on that job, Dominic."

"And now you have a better one. You're welcome."

Ally growled. Actually physically growled. "There are consequences to our actions, Dominic Russo. And I'm going to make sure that one of your consequences is that you regret the day your mother hired me."

"Mission accomplished already. Why don't you quit and go ruin someone else's day?"

"Please," she scoffed. "I'm a tiny little fish in your very big pond. You don't even know I'm in the building."

Now *she* was the delusional one.

We sat in silence for a few minutes. I gave up on pretending to read emails and stared out the window at dreary, frozen Manhattan.

"Tell me what got you to shut up for five full minutes upstairs," I said finally.

The abrupt question threw her off-balance, and I noticed she skimmed her gaze over me again.

Then her slow smile had my cold, dead heart doing something odd in my chest.

She leaned in a little closer so Nelson wouldn't overhear her. I knew many things in that moment. I didn't like her. I didn't want to like her. I had no intention of treating her as anything but an annoyance. Yet none of that quelled my desire to be near her.

"I have this thing," she began tentatively.

My breath stopped. I didn't want the hammering of my heart to drown out her next words. When she didn't continue, I merely stared at her.

"For vests," she said, eyeing mine.

"But I'm not your type," I shot back.

She smirked. "You're only slightly less not my type in a vest. But don't worry, Dom. I promise to resist you."

13

ALLY

Friday afternoon traffic in Manhattan was stupid. Why anyone would choose to take a car rather than the subway was beyond me. Yet here I was, making money just for being stretched out in the back seat of a very nice SUV on some very supple leather.

I could almost enjoy myself. Almost.

The broody guy in the sexy vest next to me was short-circuiting my ability to relax.

"I didn't get much information from Zara. What's this meeting about?" I asked over the dueling horns of two cabs trying to get around a delivery truck. Middle fingers flew.

"You really should learn to do your own research," Dominic said. He was back to snarky, and I wished his crappy attitude would take his wow factor down a few notches. But my lady parts were steadfastly holding up their perfect ten scores.

"Humor me," I insisted.

"Christian James is a designer who's launching his own label. He was with one of the big fashion houses. Worked his way up the ranks. Put a new spin on the original designs that made them an industry name. And then he met my mother."

I perked up. "She's mentoring him?" I guessed.

Dominic nodded, glancing out the window like the conversation was boring him and he'd rather be anywhere but here. "She introduced him to the right people, the right suppliers, the right insiders. My mother believes in him. So *Label* is doing a spread about him, his career path, his designs."

"She sees potential in a lot of places," I mused.

"Not everywhere," he said, giving me a pointed look.

I laughed. "No, not everywhere. In my case, she saw righting a wrong. But she has wonderful instincts. Buddy, for example."

"I'm not convinced anyone named Buddy is cut out for high fashion. Even if it's the mail room of high fashion."

"You are such a snob," I sighed.

He didn't bother denying it.

"I suppose you're going to want to tell me why this Buddy is such a great addition to *Label*," he said.

"I suppose I am, even though I suppose you won't care," I said primly. I filled him in on the Buddy highlight reel. "Even Linus likes him."

"Linus doesn't like anyone," Dominic argued.

"He likes Buddy. It's impossible not to. I mean, for anyone who isn't you. I'm sure disliking people comes very naturally to you. Buddy is the opposite. He likes everyone instantly and without requiring them to prove anything. His attitude is incredible considering what's going on at home."

Dominic closed his eyes and tilted his head back against the seat. "I'm going to regret this, but what's going on in Buddy's home?"

I told him about Buddy's wife. Her accident. The insurance.

He didn't say anything.

"And your mother took a chance on him. A stranger at the bus stop. It gives me goose bumps," I admitted. "See?" I pushed up my sleeve and held my arm out to him.

His eyes skimmed my skin, and a new crop of goose bumps arose as if he'd actually touched me.

"You're annoyingly sentimental," he said.

"Are you adding that to your long list of my faults?"

"Maybe it would be a faster feat to start a list of things I like about you," he mused.

"Maybe you shouldn't be giving me so much thought," I told him. "You might accidentally start appreciating me and enjoying my company."

He snorted derisively and didn't deign to comment.

Christian James Designs was located in a trendy warehouse in the Meatpacking District.

We took a freight elevator up to the third floor, and the doors opened on glorious, colorful chaos.

"Please tell me we're shooting here," I breathed. It was an eye-catching mess of texture. The brick. The scarred wood floors. The light pouring through tall, arched windows. "It's so beautiful I want to barf."

"What is wrong with you?" Dominic demanded, shaking his head.

I guessed that all he saw was the chaos.

"Think about this. That dress right there," I said, pointing to a long, slinky cocktail dress that looked as if it had been dipped in gold. "A model, dark skin so the dress pops, standing in front of one of those worktables buried in red and orange fabrics. The rough brick in the back. The sun streaming in from the side."

He was looking at me like I'd grown a second head and asked him to make out with both of my faces.

"Oh, come on, Dom. Give me your phone so I can take some pictures." I held out my hand.

"I'm not giving you my phone," he said. "Use yours."

I held up my bargain basement, pay-as-you-go, not-so-smart phone.

"What the hell is that thing?" he asked. "A calculator?"

"Oh, shut up. Hand over your phone," I insisted.

He produced it from his pocket.

"Camera," I said.

He made a production of supreme annoyance, but he unlocked the phone and opened the camera.

I took it and snapped a few shots. "You'd want to time the lighting carefully," I said, snapping a few more. "I like the idea of fiery colors since it looks like he works in them a lot. And depending on when the article runs, you might want to play around with summer and fire and those themes. If it's a winter thing, you could shoot a bunch of soft grays and navies in front of that white stucco wall."

I scrolled through the pictures, nodding. I accidentally went too far, and instead of a design studio, I was looking at a selfie of Dominic wearing an expression of annoyance and flipping the bird. Why in the hell would chilly, callous Dominic Russo have a funny selfie on his phone? I couldn't quite cover the laugh that bubbled up.

He gave me the side-eye. Innocently, I pretended to be engrossed with a rack of pantsuits.

"Mr. Russo, Christian is just finishing up a phone call." A woman in cargo pants and a chunky turtleneck sweater approached. Her long, dark hair was yanked back in a lumpy ponytail, and her glasses kept sliding down the bridge of her nose. "I'm Agnes."

"Ally." I offered my hand.

She was holding an iPad open to a calendar app. "Christian has an hour set aside for your meeting today before he needs to take a call with a supplier."

"What calendar app is that?" I asked, peering over the screen. I loved a good calendar.

Agnes and I compared notes on organizational apps for a minute while Dominic ignored us both.

Her phone buzzed an alert, and she wrinkled her nose. "I'll show you two to the conference room," Agnes said, her brain already moving on to her next task. She led us to a glassed-in conference room. Framed black-and-white prints of models and dresses and presumably famous fashion people leaned against still bare walls. The long farmhouse table held a cluster of succulents in the center.

Dominic pulled out a chair for me, and I sat carefully, suspiciously, in case he thought it would be funny to pull it out from under me.

To my surprise, he sat next to me. For all his talk about being annoyed and inconvenienced by me, he didn't seem to be in any hurry to get away from me.

I unloaded my laptop and ignored his judgmental stare. Shame wasn't a feeling I harbored regarding my financial situation. It was an obstacle to overcome. A challenge. And I had no intention of failing.

"You really should consider the fact that you are representing *Label*," he said when Agnes left the room.

"I should, should I?" I challenged, keying in my log-in. This dinosaur took a good four minutes to lumber to life.

"Appearances are what drive this industry." His gaze skimmed my laptop and then my thrift store outfit.

"If *Label* is so concerned with appearances, they are welcome to accessorize me or—here's a thought—don't send me out in public," I said, exasperated. "There are plenty of more attractive admins capable of taking notes."

He opened his mouth to respond, but we were interrupted by pure, unadulterated handsome.

"Dominic, thanks for meeting me. And you must be Ally." The man who entered the room was quite frankly delicious. His smile was warm enough to heat up the January chill. Bright green eyes framed by thick lashes and dark, curling hair, cut short.

He wore low slung jeans and a tight long-sleeve tee. And a vest.

I beamed.

Dominic gave my leg a nudge under the table with his own. "Try to control yourself," he muttered dryly before standing and shaking the designer's hand.

Christian was an enthusiastic guy with big goals. As he personally escorted us on a tour of the facility, it became clear that everything he did came from a place of passion. Life to Christian James was color and texture and beauty and fun.

It was easy to see what Dalessandra had been drawn to.

I mean, besides the fact that he was abominably good-looking.

Where Dominic was frowny and broody, Christian was dimpled and friendly. Where Dominic was cold, Christian was warm.

"What's this?" I asked, pointing at a mannequin wearing a pair of still-under-construction wide-legged pants.

Christian grinned at me, and I gave myself permission to bask in that lovely warmth, ignoring Dominic's chilly glare.

Sure. Maybe my outside-this-building situation was a complete disaster, but right this second, enjoying the company of two very attractive men—in sexy vests no less—I could afford to feel pretty dang positive about life.

"Those are part of a pet project," he told me. "An inclusion line."

"I'm new to the industry," I explained apologetically.

"I'm sure he can guess that," Dominic said uncharitably.

I shot him a dirty look over my shoulder, and the man actually managed to crack the slightest of smiles. And there went those goose bumps again. I was an Ally sandwich with very handsome bread.

"An inclusion line is a series of designs created for individuals with disabilities," Christian explained, gesturing me forward. He demonstrated the hidden elastic waistband.

"Why is it a pet project?" I asked, intrigued.

"The demand isn't there," Dominic said, once again answering a question I hadn't intended for him.

"Yet," Christian and I said together.

It earned me another smile from the man and an eye roll from Dominic.

Christian held up one of the pant legs to me, and I ran my fingers over the material.

"Wow," I said. The material was soft and buttery, luxurious even.

"It started with my mother. Diabetic neuropathy robbed her of sensation in her fingers. It makes buttons and zippers difficult. But she still wants to look her best. So I dabble in garments that make it easy for someone with disabilities to dress themselves and look good doing it. We do hidden seams for people with sensory issues. Magnetic closures, extended sizing, wrap it all up in good fabrics and strong colors."

"She must be very proud of you," I guessed.

He grinned. "I tell her that every Sunday. She says she's holding out for me to get married and have babies before she's officially proud. It's the Cuban in her. Are you married, Ally?" he asked, giving me a sinfully flirtatious wink.

"Let's get back to what pieces you foresee using in the spread," Dominic announced, steering the conversation back on course. When Christian led the way into another room, Dominic handed me his phone again. "Maybe if you take some pictures, you'll be too busy to drool over the designer," he growled.

I smiled up at him just to annoy him. "Doubtful, Dom. Very doubtful."

14

DOMINIC

I hated to admit it, but Ally had an annoyingly excellent eye. I'd spent another hour getting schooled on color and texture by an ex-pizza server who had entirely too many opinions for an admin.

And Christian James seemed all too happy to eat it up. Smiling at her. Complimenting her taste. And I didn't like the way his gaze kept landing on the hem of her short knit skirt.

If I hadn't been there, I wouldn't have been surprised if the man had tried to talk her into drinks, dinner, and a quick fuck. Not that he'd have to coerce her. He was a charmer. Ally apparently enjoyed being charmed. And that set my teeth on edge.

I made a mental note to make sure not to include her in any further meetings with him. I didn't need that kind of distraction.

"Why isn't *Label* using the inclusion line in the story?" Ally wanted to know as soon as Nelson brought the SUV around.

Her skirt rose indecently high as she climbed into the back, and I tried not to notice. But the desire to push her facedown and flip that skirt up was so strong I had to wait a beat and take a bracing breath of winter air before joining her in the back seat.

"That's not our target demographic." I kept my answer short and terse, hoping she'd leave me the fuck alone.

"I get that," she said. "But what's the harm in including it?"

Her questions annoyed me. "Fashion isn't exactly known for being inclusive. It's more about being special, exclusive."

"But aren't things changing?" she pressed, clearly warming to the topic. "Other luxury labels are doing it. The population is aging. Wouldn't it follow that more people would be willing to buy clothing that allows them to keep their independence?"

"Have you ever read *Label*?"

"Don't be snippy. I'm asking the creative director a serious question. If the point of your magazine is to highlight what's special, you're missing the boat by ignoring Christian's inclusive line. It's human interest. It's highlighting the diverse buyer. And it gives you an opportunity to use a model or two who aren't the cookie-cutter, clothes-hanger type. It's real."

"People don't want real," I argued. "They want the fantasy. They want the dress that's going to change their life. They want clothing that makes them feel beautiful, sexy, special, one of a kind."

"And you can't feel that in a wheelchair?"

"Are you deliberately trying to annoy me?"

"Maybe. I'm also trying to figure out if you really believe what you're saying or you just like arguing with me."

"You have too many annoying opinions."

"Take it up with your mother," she said cheerfully.

"Why don't we play a game where we sit in silence for the entire ride back?"

She grinned and wrinkled her nose. "I'm just trying to make the point that *Label* has historically been at the forefront of change. You led the transition to digital without making a giant plummet out of the black. Why not consider inclusivity as your next history-making foray?"

"We sell a fantasy. Clothing that reminds readers about illness or disabilities isn't fantasy. It's real life, and they've got enough of that."

She frowned thoughtfully.

I didn't like defending *Label*'s brand. Not when I was still learning all the subtleties of it. Fantasy and image were essential to our brand. "Don't you have something else to do, like find a new victim's life to ruin?" I asked, changing the subject.

"You talk a good game, Charming, but I think you don't hate me nearly as much as you pretend to," Ally said airily.

"Wanna bet?" I sighed.

"Sorry. Broke."

A shrill ringing erupted from the depths of her backpack.

"Christ, what is that?" I asked as the sound pierced my eardrum.

She didn't answer. Instead, she frantically pawed through her bag.

"Hello?" she answered, breathlessly clutching her idiotic phone. Her entire body seemed to go rigid while she listened. "Is he okay?" she demanded. The hand gripping the phone to her ear went white-knuckled. She looked pale as she shoved a hand through her hair. "Okay. What hospital? Is it a precaution or…" she trailed off, nodding. "I can be there in—" She leaned over Nelson and glanced at the GPS display. "An hour. Two tops. Hello? Can you hear me?" She pulled the phone away from her ear and peered at the screen. "Dammit! Of course it goes dead."

"What's wrong? Where do you need to go?" I demanded.

She gripped the door handle like she was going to vault into traffic, and I clamped my hand over her knee to hold her in place. She was trembling, and it was killing me.

"Ally."

"Family emergency," she said, a catch in her voice. "Nelson, could you pull over? I need to catch a train."

"We're five blocks away from the closest subway station," I told her.

"I can walk. I need to walk." In short, jerky motions, she was zipping her backpack and then trying to shoulder it.

"Take the car, Ally," I said.

She stopped what she was doing and looked at me. Really looked at me. Her brown eyes were wide. She looked scared, and I decided I fucking hated that look on her.

I squeezed her knee, hard. "Breathe," I commanded.

She took a slow breath and let it out. "I can't take the car. I'm going to Jersey," she said, her voice calmer.

"Nelson loves Jersey," I told her.

"I live for it, sir," Nelson chimed in.

That got a shaky smile out of her.

"He'll take you to Jersey, and he can wait and drive you home," I said.

She started shaking again and reached for the handle. "I can't. The train will be faster. But thank you," she said.

"Ally," I said again. I couldn't let her just jump out of the car and disappear.

"It's fine. I'm fine." There was nothing in her tone that remotely reassured me.

Nelson signaled as he changed lanes, inching toward the subway station.

"Here. Take this," I said, yanking out my wallet. I threw a fifty at her. "Take a cab when you get to Jersey."

She looked at the money in her lap and started to shake her head. *Newly and temporarily poor but permanently, stupidly stubborn.*

"I c—"

"If the next word out of your mouth is 'can't,' I'm going to insist on personally seeing you to your destination," I threatened.

She looked at the bill in her lap again, then up at me. I dared her to defy me.

"I'll pay you back," she said. Her voice was tight, and those golden eyes looked a little watery to me. I didn't want her to go.

"I'll fire you if you do. Take the car. Please," I added, not liking how the word felt in my mouth.

"Train's faster."

Nelson roared up to the curb. He hopped out from behind the wheel.

"Are you sure you're okay?" I asked her.

"Everything's fine. I'm fine," she said. "Thank you, Dom."

I didn't expect the thank you. Or the chaste, friendly kiss she pressed to my cheek after.

Nelson opened my door, and Ally climbed right over me and hopped out.

I watched until she and that ridiculous backpack disappeared down the stairs.

"Back to the office, sir?" Nelson asked, sliding behind the wheel again.

I was still staring at the space that Ally and her backpack had occupied. "Actually, I have a stop to make."

15

ALLY

"Dad?"

I poked my head around the curtain that provided a sliver of privacy in the small room. It was like every other hospital room. Beige tile, industrial gray walls, and that stomach-turning smell of antiseptic and illness.

Dad's bed was next to the window, and he was staring listlessly at the gray world beyond while a nurse fussed over him. He was conscious, upright. And some of the knots in my stomach loosened.

An untouched tray sat in front of him.

His roommate on the other side of the curtain let out a tremulous snore over the *Judge Judy* episode he'd left on at full volume.

Thank God for health insurance. Judging from the IVs and the brace on my father's leg, we'd already be bankrupt otherwise.

"Mr. Morales?" the nurse tried. This time, my father glanced up.

His weight loss had slowed, thankfully. But he'd never be back to the pleasingly plump guy he'd been just a few years ago. The mustache he'd had forever was gone too. They shaved it for him weekly at the nursing home.

I missed the man my father had been even as I tried to build a new relationship with who he was now. It was mostly bitter and not enough sweet in this new dynamic.

"Do you recognize your visitor?" the nurse asked.

Dad gave me a cursory once-over and a careless shrug. "Should I?"

Logically, I knew it was a disease. But every time the man who raised me, the man who'd hand-sewn sequins on my jean jacket in fifth grade, the man who'd corralled six female neighbors in our living room the day I got my first period didn't recognize me, it felt like I lost another little piece of both of us.

The man who loved me most in this world was gone. And most days I was erased from his memories. Like *we'd* never existed. Like *I'd* never existed.

"Hi, Mr. Morales," I said, pasting on a bright smile that I didn't feel. "I just came to see if there's anything you needed from home."

"Home?" he harrumphed.

I nodded and waited.

He shrugged. "See if Bobby mowed the lawn. I pay the kid ten dollars a week, and he does a five-dollar job. Oh, and bring me my term papers. I can at least grade finals while I'm stuck here."

It was a C-plus day. Grumpy but not too agitated. In Dad's world, if there was an Ally Morales, she was eight years old, and it was almost summertime.

"Okay," I agreed. "Would you like any snacks? Your music?"

He didn't answer. He was back to staring out the window where a slow, icy drizzle had begun.

The nurse tilted her head in the direction of the hall, and I followed her out.

"How's he doing?" I asked.

"He suffered a broken tibia when he fell out of bed this morning," she explained.

"Did he break anything else?" I asked, leaning back against the wall.

Falls were especially dangerous with my father's diagnosis.

"Some bruising and swelling, but no other breaks," she said.

Thank you, goddesses of gravity. "How's his pain?"

"With dementia patients, it's hard to tell."

Everything was hard with dementia patients, I'd come to learn.

"We're administering low doses of pain medication every few hours and monitoring him. He's slept a bit since he got here, and we're doing our best to keep him in bed for now. Our PT and OT teams are coming in to evaluate him in the morning."

"How long will he be here?" I asked. At this point, unexpected hospital bills had the power to do more than bankrupt us.

"It's hard to say at this point. It depends on the therapy teams," she explained.

"Where's my wife?" my father demanded from inside the room.

I winced. I'd stopped wondering that decades ago.

"Will your mother be visiting?" the nurse asked me.

I shook my head. "No. She won't."

"I'll let you visit for a while. Try not to get discouraged if he's agitated," she said, patting me on the arm.

"Thanks." I returned to the room where I was a stranger. My father was back to glaring out the window, his food still untouched.

"That looks good," I said, pointing at the soup on his tray.

He grumbled under his breath.

I pulled out my phone and cued up my Dad playlist. There had always been music in our house. Dad's Latin roots combined with his love of B. B. King, Frank Sinatra, and Ella Fitzgerald created the soundtrack of my childhood. He played the piano well and the guitar a little less well. But his enthusiasm made up for it.

He'd given me the gift of music appreciation. And so much more.

Now I was failing him.

Dad's fingers drummed out a beat to Tito Puente's "Take Five." At least it was one thing the disease couldn't rob him of.

"Did you know that Tito Puente served in the navy during World War II and paid his way through Juilliard on the GI Bill?" Dad mused.

"Really?" I asked, pulling the chair up to his bedside.

"You look familiar. Are you Mrs. Vacula's daughter?" he asked.

"I am," I lied brightly and felt my neck flush red. Mrs. Vacula had lived across the street for twenty years—gracefully enduring hundreds of Dracula jokes—before moving to Mesa, Arizona. I'd learned quickly that correcting him, reminding him of the things he didn't know anymore, only hurt us both.

"Your mother makes the best beef vegetable soup, you know," he said.

"It's true," I said. "Let's see how this recipe measures up." I picked up the spoon and held it out to him.

It was late when I let myself into my father's house.

I nudged the thermostat down a degree or two and wandered into the kitchen, helping myself to a bowl of ramen and a stale bagel from yesterday's work snacks, emergency carbs that I'd snagged before they'd thrown out the leftovers. I'd thought a fashion magazine would have had nothing but juice cleanses being passed around. But the sheer amount of food in my department alone was the only thing standing between me and being too hungry at night to sleep.

I yawned. I'd get through this. I had no choice, and it was stupid to lament about it.

Heading upstairs, I stepped over the weak spot on the landing and continued into my childhood room. Too tired to worry about neatness, I left my clothes in a pile on the floor. My legs were red from the cold and itchy from the synthetic lace of the tights.

After bundling into a pair of sweatpants, a long-sleeve shirt, and a hooded sweatshirt, I climbed under the covers on my twin bed.

Wearily, I pulled out my phone and fired off a text to my catering boss, apologizing again for missing my shift that night. It was definitely going to hurt being out that money.

I should boot up my laptop. See if any invoices had been paid. Go through the bank account and see what I had to work with for next week. Not that I needed to. I knew down to the penny what was in there. It wasn't hard keeping track of three figures.

At least the hospital bills would take weeks before they started to trickle in. Because I wouldn't see a paycheck from *Label* for another week or two, I'd estimated low there just in case I'd calculated the taxes or the health insurance withholding wrong.

A full-time paycheck was going to make all the difference to me. I just had to hang on until payday, and then I could reassess everything and make a new plan.

For now, I'd just tighten the belt one more notch.

My phone buzz-clunked in my hand.

The text came from an unknown number.

Unknown: Did you make it home? By the way, this is Charming.

I stared at the text as I chewed stale bagel. What the hell was Dominic "I Hate Your Guts" Russo doing texting me at 11:00 p.m.?

Maybe it was an accident. Maybe the text was meant for someone else. Someone else who also happened to nickname him Prince Charming.

While I debated the possibilities, another message arrived.

Dominic: Nelson was crushed that you wouldn't let him go to Jersey with you. You owe him an apology.

Holy cheese and crackers. The man was texting me. On purpose.

I wondered if the cab he'd paid for had accidentally delivered me to a different time dimension where the Dominic Russos and Ally Moraleses of the world got along.

Me: Sorry to have dashed Nelson's dreams. I hope he'll forgive me.

I debated thanking Dominic for the cab money but decided it was safer to just pay him back instead. Ugh. Another unforeseen expense. But Dominic Russo wasn't the kind of man I wanted to be beholden to.

Dominic: How's the family emergency?

Me: Under control. Why are you being nice?

Dominic: I'm not being nice. I'm seeing if you decided to quit yet.

Finished with the bagel, I flopped back against my pillow.

Me: That sounds more realistic. I was worried you'd somehow managed to activate your soul.
Dominic: One must have a soul in order to activate it.

I worked up a smile as I stared at my screen. Was he being funny? On purpose?

Me: Are you drunk? Or do you only sprout a personality after dark? Or wait, is this Greta?
Dominic: You're annoying.
Me: Drunk Greta, is that you?
Dominic: Are you coming into work Monday or not?
Me: As long as you swear never to wear a vest again. Don't ruin this fetish for me, Charming. I'll hate you forever.
Dominic: Afraid you can't resist me, Maleficent?
Me: You're SO not my type...but just to be on the safe side. Ditch the vests.
Dominic: I'll think about it. Did you have dinner?

I rolled my eyes and scooped up a spoonful of ramen. The man had an obsession with food.

Me: Yes.
Dominic: Did you take a cab home?
Me: I did. Thanks. I have change for you.
Dominic: Shut up and go to sleep.

I had no idea what his game was, but I was tired enough to do as he demanded.

16

ALLY

I came into work Monday dragging ass. My mood was reflected in the head-to-toe black-on-black of my outfit. The only signs of Fun, Energetic Me were my gold hoop earrings with tiny colored beads, a Christmas gift from my father a few years ago.

"Hey, girl," Gola said, popping up in my cubicle, sucking down a green smoothie. "How was your weekend? How did that out of office meeting go with Mr. So Cold He's Hot?"

My weekend had been a mess. I squeezed in hospital visits between bar shifts, dance classes, and a sorry-for-flaking-on-you last-minute catering gig my boss had offered up. I hadn't so much as lifted a broom or watched a "How to Hang Drywall Yourself" YouTube tutorial.

I was so far behind on my plan that it made me want to hyperventilate into a paper bag just thinking about it.

To make matters worse, my last visit with my dad had

been an ugly one. I could handle him not knowing who I was. I could handle him calling me by my mother's name. Hell, I could even handle him listlessly staring into space.

But I couldn't handle it when the man I'd known and loved all my life became aggressive. It happened. Something would trigger him, sending him into an agitated state, and the happy, kindhearted, lovable man disappeared only to be replaced with a belligerent, violent stranger.

"The meeting was good. The designer was great. And I just worked all weekend," I told her. "You?"

"I met a guy," she said, trying to bring the straw to her lips but nearly taking out an eye instead.

"You did?" I wasn't in the market, but that didn't mean I couldn't live vicariously through friends' lives.

"Lunch. I'm definitely going to need more details about you sitting side by side in the back seat with a certain gorgeous grump in Midtown traffic," she warned me.

"And I want to know all about this guy," I told her.

She wiggled her fingers at me and headed toward her desk.

I booted up my desktop and was pulling my headphones out of my bag when Zara and her sticky notes appeared. "Don't get comfortable," she said blandly.

"Fired already?" *Damn that Dominic Russo.*

"New assignment," she said, peeling off a note and slapping it on my desk. "Linus needs extra hands this week. You're the lucky admin. You'll be stationed at a temp desk near his office on forty-three for the week."

"On it," I said, slipping my headphones back into the bag.

"On your way, hit up IT. They have something for you," she said.

I frowned. "What is it?"

"How the hell should I know? No one bothers to tell me

anything," she said. "Now go be productive and drop some hints that your supervisor has her eye on the new Marc Jacobs bag in case Linus needs to rehome it after the shoot tomorrow."

IT was a dungeon-y, cave-like room full of unhappy, casually dressed creatures.

I introduced myself to the closest one just across the countertop that protected the staff from human encounters.

The girl had jet-black hair tied in pigtails on top of her head and wore a baggy pink sweatshirt that said *Try Unplugging It*. Her jeans were name brand and distressed in all the right places.

"We can't help you with your personal electronic problems without a help desk ticket," she said flatly, her dark eyes boring soullessly into mine. She slid an iPad toward me. "Fill this out, and we'll get to you when we get to you."

If bored were a human, I was looking at her.

"Uh, yeah, actually, I'm here to pick something up," I told her.

She blinked in slow motion.

"I'm Ally Morales from the admin pool," I tried again. "My supervisor said I was supposed to stop in and pick something up."

"Oh." Pigtails wandered away, and I stood there, unsure if I should follow her or wait to catch the attention of a different robot. I was still debating when she returned with two boxes. "Here." She slid them across the skinny countertop.

"What's this?"

She slow blinked again. "It's a laptop and a phone. They are smaller, more portable versions of—"

I held up my hands, surrendering to her sarcasm. "I mean, why am I getting a laptop and a phone?" I asked, convinced there'd been a mistake. Especially since the laptop was the latest and greatest model that had bells and whistles for graphic design.

I'd secretly slobbered over a similar model in an electronics store a few weeks ago and added it to my Future Ally list. Right under a mango margarita with a long straw.

"You want *me* to tell *you* why you need a computer and a phone to do your job?"

I had a feeling Pigtails was one second away from unplugging me.

"Never mind," I said, taking the boxes and backing away. If it was a mistake, someone would tell me about it sooner or later. In the meantime, I could dabble with fun new technology. "Thanks."

Pigtails didn't respond.

Linus had an office down the hall from Dalessandra's and was unfortunately also two doors down from Dominic's frozen den of grumpiness. But I didn't have time to worry or fantasize about Dominic. Linus, in black trousers and another black turtleneck—I wisely swallowed the twinsies joke on the tip of my tongue—gave me a generous twenty seconds to stow my stuff at an empty desk before following him.

He flung instructions at me over his shoulder as we dodged assistants and makeup artists and delivery people.

There were models partially dressed in athletic wear pouting for makeup artists and working frantic thumbs over phone screens while stylists attacked their hair.

Still more people were organizing endless rolling racks of clothing.

"I need you to track down the size-eight Nikes because

Colossus over there lied about her shoe size," he said, waving a dismissive hand toward a barefoot model dressed in running tights and a crop top. Her hair was classified as wind-machine-Beyoncé fierce.

Size eight.

"Once you do that, get the crew's coffee order. We need these people caffeinated."

Coffee order. Easy.

From what I could tell, everyone present had already downed multiple espressos.

The photo studio was a circus. Busy worker bees unfurled white backdrops while photographers and assistants tested lighting and barked orders. Tables with every hair and makeup product known to humanity cut an L down the middle of the space. On the far wall was another table with sad-looking low-carb snacks.

"What about lunch?" I asked hopefully.

Linus stopped in his tracks, and I bumped into him. "Ally, these people don't *eat*. They drink, and they smoke, and they work very hard. Then they go home to drink and smoke some more."

"No lunch. Got it," I said.

He stormed on, weaving his way through a crowd of model assistants. I could tell they were assistants because they were dressed and made up to the nines but had their phones trained on their bosses.

"Then you need to go to this address, pick up four dogs, and bring them to the Balcony Bridge at Central Park no later than two p.m. We have a very tight window with the permits and the light. Do not, I repeat, do not fuck this up."

"Hang on," I said. "Dogs?"

Linus spun around and gave an elegant eye roll. "You are

not here to have all your life's questions answered. You are here to cross off items on my to-do list."

"Dogs. Linus, I don't have a car. What am I supposed to do? Take them on the subway?"

He retrieved a black silk handkerchief from a pocket and daintily dabbed at his forehead. "Try not to be completely useless, Admin Ally. You will take one of the company SUVs. Preferably one that won't need to be used tomorrow so the driver can get it cleaned before, God forbid, someone important gets dog hair on their gown. You will go to the address, pick up the dogs, and bring them to—"

"Central Park. Yeah, I got that part," I said dryly.

I spotted a Nike shoebox shoved under one of the makeup tables and ducked to scoop it up.

Size eight.

Triumphantly, I held the box toward Linus.

He held up his palms. "Don't give them to me. Give them to Colossus, along with a judgmental look for providing fake measurements. Then coffee. Then dogs."

"Is there anything else? How about a tasty little pastry to go with your coffee?"

"Be gone, woman."

I'd managed all of three steps before I heard Linus's stage whisper. "Blueberry scone."

I grinned and got to work.

17

ALLY

The behind the scenes of a *Label* editorial photo shoot was exciting enough, interesting enough, to pull me out of my funk.

In front of me, five models preened and posed for the photographer on a set constructed entirely out of white boxes. Music thudded from overhead speakers. The contributing editor in charge of the shoot gnawed nervously on a pen cap behind the photographer.

There was a bearded dude in stonewashed jeans whose sole job seemed to be flipping a large piece of cardboard at the models to make their hair look windblown.

Linus snuck his phone out of his pocket and snapped a few pictures in rapid succession.

"What's that for?" I asked.

He checked his watch and nudged me toward the door.

"We're doing high-level babysitting," he explained, firing off a text and tucking his phone back into his pocket.

"You're reporting to Dalessandra," I guessed, taking a slurp of the cappuccino I'd ordered myself on the company card. The caffeine and sugar made me giddy.

"That's right. I reassure her that everyone is doing their jobs so she can focus on doing hers. Usually it's all lies, and we're all just holding on by a thread."

I ducked as an assistant trundled a rolling rack between us.

When it passed, Linus was already halfway across the room. He snapped his fingers as he headed toward the door.

"Where are we going?" I asked, jogging to keep up.

He gave me a scornful head-to-toe look. "To do something with that God-awful footwear. And maybe the pants if we have time."

A Carolina Herrera skirt hit me in the face. I barely managed to catch the red, high-waisted pants that came next. We were in the area of the forty-second floor dubbed the Closet. It was a huge expanse of ruthlessly organized racks and shelves. Thousands of designer samples lived in this room.

My heart tapped out a happy little pitter-patter when I spotted the pair of leather moto leggings that I was positive Cher had been photographed in last year. I felt like the lead character in *The Devil Wears Prada*, except I'd never give up all these gorgeous clothes in a misguided attempt to prove I was a good person.

"This too." A gold corded belt flew in my direction. My arms were already full of luxury brand apparel, rained down on me by a man who'd apparently lost his mind.

Linus turned away from the rack and held up a creamy cable-knit sweater to my chest. "Eh, close enough," he muttered.

"What exactly is all this for?" I asked, spitting green silk out of my mouth.

"For you, Admin Ally with the wardrobe of a sad, poor teenager."

"I can't afford any of these," I squeaked as he dropped a pair of slobber-inducing pumps in purple suede on top of the pile. I was starting to tip backward.

"These are all seasons old. No one needs them. No one but you, Ms. Thrift Shop 1998."

"Linus, I have zero money. Like 'if I see a penny, I will pick it up' have no money."

"Don't be annoying. I'm gifting these to you like a black, crabby Santa."

"Are you kidding me?" Half of the items I was clutching fell to the floor.

He rolled his eyes and picked up a floral print dress. "Try to show Tracy Reese a modicum of respect."

"Are you messing with me right now? Because I have to be honest. If you tell me these are all mine for free, and then you turn around and say 'psych,' I will cry and very possibly burn down your house."

"Psych?" he repeated with disdain. "We'll worry about your vocabulary later. For now, let's focus on the more important. Your appearance."

A laptop. A smartphone. And a new designer wardrobe.

"Is it Christmas? Did I somehow stumble onto the set of *Oprah* during a favorite things segment?" I asked, still afraid to get my hopes up.

"These are not presents. I am not a benevolent lady billionaire. These are tools to do your job. I can't have you waltzing around Central Park photo shoots looking like fifty-percent-off day at the secondhand church sale."

"Your words wound me, Linus," I said, drooling over the pair of to-die-for caramel suede booties he pointed to.

I wanted to make out with them.

"I don't care. I just can't take this shapeless sweater thing for one more second. You're making my forehead veins throb."

"You don't have forehead veins."

"Thanks to Botox. Now don't make my forehead veins pop through the botulism barrier. Go put on anything other than that outfit, and grab one of the Burberry coats on your way out."

"You don't fool me," I told him over the armload of fashion.

"I don't know what you're talking about," he sniffed.

"You're being nice and covering it up with charming mean."

"Begone, Didn't Wear It Better."

"I'll make you proud," I promised as I headed in the direction of the closest restroom.

"I doubt that," he called after me. "Change fast. You have twenty-three minutes for lunch and then dogs."

I raced down to the cafeteria with my lunch—beef fried rice from Mrs. Grosu—and threw myself into a chair next to Ruth.

"I have three minutes before I have to leave to go pick up four purebred Afghan hounds."

"That sweater," Gola said.

"Those boots," Ruth breathed.

"I just told you I'm running a dog trafficking scheme, and you want to talk fashion?" I joked.

"Welcome to *Label*," Gola snickered. "I once had to wait five hours in an emergency department to pick up half a dozen sweaters that a bike messenger was carrying when he got hit by a cab. How's life on the forty-third floor?"

"Colorful. Chaotic. We need to catch up," I said as I ripped the lid off my meal. I didn't have time to heat it up.

"Let's grab drinks after work," Ruth suggested.

"Can't," I said through a mouthful of rice. "Teaching a dance class tonight."

"Where? We'll come," Gola said, perking up.

"It's not ballet," I warned them.

"Is it hip-hop?" Ruth wanted to know. "Can I wear leg warmers? I *live* for any excuse to wear leg warmers."

"Leg warmers are great. And it's pop and hip-hop and R and B. Kind of like dirty dancing for fitness."

"Yaaaaas!" Ruth clapped her hands. "This is the best thing I've heard all day."

"Wine after," Gola decided.

"Our treat," Ruth said before I could remind them of my poorness.

"One glass. I have to finish up a pitch on a freelance gig." One that would hopefully net me a few hundred dollars.

"Deal," Ruth said.

My lovely new phone made an angelic harp noise. My signal to hit the road. "Shit. I have to go." I gathered my new coat, my old backpack, and the last few bites of fried rice. "Later, ladies."

"You look great," Gola called after me.

I raised a hand in the air and plowed my way toward the front of the building.

I was delighted to find Nelson waiting for me at the curb.

"Mind if I sit up front?" I asked him.

"Not at all," he said, opening the door for me.

We chitchatted on the drive. Nelson had a wife, two daughters, and three granddaughters. He spent his weekends at soccer games and science fairs.

The traffic gods smiled upon us. We were fifteen minutes early. I hopped out in front of a three-story brownstone and jogged up the stairs, my fancy new coat swirling around me nicely like the cape of a superhero.

Had I done a better job with my hair and makeup this morning, I'd feel almost stylish.

Stylish, in control, and basically killing it at my new job.

I pressed the buzzer and smugly waited to succeed.

"Nelson, we have a problem," I said, pulling the door shut and rifling through my bag for my phone.

"I notice you returned without any four-legged passengers," he mused.

"There was a mix-up with the date. The dogs are at some fancy show in Connecticut."

"I hate when that happens," he said.

I found my phone and fired off a text to Linus.

Me: There's a problem.

Linus: Do not bother me with problems. Dazzle me with solutions.

Me: This is a big one.

Linus: I'm deadly serious. I'm up to my well-groomed eyebrows in disasters. How can three models have pink eye at the same time? Never mind. Don't answer. Just solve the problem or don't bother coming back.

I was pretty sure he was going to regret that one. I could solve problems. But the solutions might not be up to his standards.

Me: Fine. The photo shoot. What's the vibe?

Linus: Grey Gardens. Only less depressing and with more fashion. Now leave me alone.

I could work with that. "Nelson, we need to make a stop."

18

DOMINIC

"Where are my dogs?" Linus demanded. He clapped his hands at a wardrobe assistant. "You there. Tell me how exactly we're supposed to shoot this without any dogs."

The wardrobe assistant wisely tried to disappear into a hedgerow.

It was fucking cold. February was right around the corner, and if there was anything colder and damper than January in New York, it was fucking February.

Of course, fashion didn't heed below-freezing temperatures. No. Fashion made its own rules outside time and space and temperature. We descended upon Central Park with a team of forty people. It wasn't even for the magazine. It was digital content for our YouTube channel and website.

The models were huddled under blankets and coats around patio heaters staffers had hauled out here. There were cables and wires running everywhere except the fifteen feet of dreary, dead natural backdrop where we were supposed to be shooting models and dogs.

Everyone was decked out in parkas and knit hats and gloves that made doing their jobs impossible. The skies were a dull gray, and I bet there would be snow tonight.

A pretty whitewashing of snow was not the look we were going for here. We were shooting flower prints on a miserable, dead background. You know. Like the cavern in my chest where a heart should have been.

This had all sounded fine and not completely stupid five months ago when it was brought up in an editorial meeting. Back when we were indoors and not battling frostbite. I shook my to-go cup of now cold tea and longed fervently for the days when my main fashion concerns were which cuff links to wear and whether I should go with suspenders or a vest.

"Since I have you and absolutely nothing else is going right with this shoot, you'll do a one-on-one with the camera while I find and fire Ally," Linus said to me.

"No. I won't. And good luck with that."

The woman in question was the reason I was here. It wasn't that I *cared* about her emergency Friday; it was that I was *curious*. A very important and, okay, maybe slightly ambiguous designation.

"Yes," he insisted. "And watch me. Why are you here anyway?" he asked, pausing as if noticing me for the first time.

To check up on an annoyingly attractive admin. Fortunately, Linus wasn't in the mood to wait for answers.

"Never mind. I don't actually care." He snapped his fingers. "You there. Cameraperson. Get your tush over here and interview Mr. Russo on whatever the hell it is we're doing."

The woman with the video camera sprinted toward me, and I swore under my breath.

A guy from the media team with a scarf wrapped up to his eyeballs jogged after her.

I glared at the red light on the camera.

"We like to keep these informal, Mr. Russo." Scarf Guy's explanation was muffled by layers of blue and white stripes. "Just tell us what we're doing out here."

"We're freezing our collective asses off in Central Park," I said.

Scarf Guy laughed, mistaking my assholery for a sense of humor.

I'd rectify that and make sure Linus had serious second thoughts about putting me in front of the camera ever again.

I opened my mouth to deliver a scathing speech about whatever I felt like when someone shouted "Heel!" behind me.

"Oh my God," the camerawoman said, panning over my shoulder.

I turned around and beheld the spectacle.

Ally, in a tweed car coat that flapped in the wind behind her, was being dragged in my direction by four hulking dogs of questionable heritage.

I'd checked the shoot notes before I left the office. Those were not dignified, well-groomed Afghan hounds. Those were unruly, untrained mutts.

"Where are my hounds?" Linus shrieked.

"Scheduling conflict," Ally called out, fruitlessly trying to dig her skinny heels into the sidewalk and stop the team of dogs before it plowed into him. "Bruno, sit!"

The basset hound in a plaid sweater stopped abruptly and sat.

I made a grab for one of the leashes before Ally was ripped in half by bad-mannered dogs who seemed hell-bent on sniffing things on opposite sides of the park. I came away with a psychotic chocolate Lab that hurled himself at me. His front paws caught me in the gut, which apparently wasn't high enough, because the dog immediately leapt off the ground and into my arms. Long, pink dog tongue slathered my face.

"What the h—" My words were choked off by a dog-instigated French kiss. I dodged the next assault, and the Lab put his head on my shoulder and let out a sigh.

"Aww. He thinks you're his people," the camerawoman said.

"I'm nobody's people," I grumbled, wrestling away from joyful dog tongue. Dopey brown eyes looked into mine.

Ally shoved the remaining leashes at Linus. The long-legged one was an interesting mottled gray and looked like it had been bred with a greyhound that had chased the rabbit on the racetrack a few times. The last one was a big-ass brindle pit bull with shoulders like a tank.

"Where did you find these canine monstrosities?" Linus demanded, yanking a flask out of his jacket pocket with a free hand. "In a back-alley dumpster?"

"Midtown Fur Friends Rescue. I promised them credit. Rescue name, dog names, and a link to the adoptables," Ally answered, carefully reaching into her pocket.

"These things are adoptable?" I asked. They looked like they could destroy an apartment in under two minutes.

"They're not *that* bad," she insisted delusionally.

The basset hound was happily trotting around Linus as he screamed, effectively ensnaring the man's legs in leash.

I choked out a laugh. I had to admit, the dog I was holding might be ruining a perfectly good cashmere coat, but it was worth it seeing Linus lose his mind.

Ally smiled up at me, and I forgot about the coat and Linus and the cold and the dog tongue.

Scarf Guy hurried over and plucked the sixty pounds of dog out of my arms. "I'll just take this before…" he trailed off and scurried away.

Before what?

Did I look like the kind of person who would drop-kick a homeless dog? Christ.

"Here. Hold this one," Ally said, shoving a tiny, scruffy, shivering *thing* into my hands. At least *she* didn't seem to think I was going to devour it.

"What the fuck is this, a hamster?"

She pressed her lips together. "The shelter told me it's a dog. But I'm not buying it. He might just be something one of the bigger ones coughed up. His name is Mr. Frisky, and he's bonded to the one-eyed pit bull over there making time with your models."

The very large brindle dog was making moony eyes—correction, eye—at the women.

"Aren't you just the most handsomest boy in the whole world?" the Croatian, Kata, crooned to the beast.

"His name is Pirate," Ally whispered to me.

"We can't shoot with these mutants. Someone bring me a Xanax and a deep-dish pizza," Linus wailed.

"It's your turn for his pep talk," I said, nudging Ally forward. She grinned at me, and damned if I didn't feel my own mouth responding.

"You said solutions," Ally said, taking the man by the shoulders. "Here's your solution. Now show us how to make this work. Make it work, Linus, or a homeless dog just vomited in *Label*'s Escalade for no reason. Give us a reason."

The little blond ball shivered again, so I tucked it into my coat against my chest. "Your buddy is right there," I told Mr. Frisky, pointing toward Pirate the pit bull, who was curled up on one of the blankets belonging to a delighted model and showing the woman his belly. The hairball's ratlike tail tapped out a happy beat.

Linus pinched his eyebrows with his fingers. "This is impossible. This won't work. We'll be laughed out of the industry."

I waited for it.

"Unless," Linus said, lifting his head.

"Unless?" Ally repeated.

"I'm going to need sweaters, people. With flowers. And belts. Long, gold ones. Don't just stand there!"

19

ALLY

"Give it to me straight. Am I fired?" I asked Linus, collapsing against the leather seat.

He was slumped next to me as a car that hadn't escorted five dogs all over the city headed toward the office. "I don't have the energy to fire you," he sighed.

"I think it went well," I said. "I checked with the online content team, and they got video of Dominic getting French-kissed by the Lab."

That got the teensiest smile out of him.

"It wasn't the worst disaster in the history of my career," he said magnanimously.

"You managed to combine fashion, art, and good karma in one shoot. Face it, Linus. You're a genius."

The rescue director had personally arrived to escort the dogs back to the shelter, and I'd noticed the Croatian model cornering her and demanding a business card. I had a feeling

Pirate and Mr. Frisky were about to find the most amazing home.

"Genius? Ha. I'm just lucky." He produced the flask from his jacket and took a long pull before handing it to me.

"Thanks. I can't. I have a dance class to teach."

He wiggled the flask. "It's not alcohol. It's a super greens formula. It's the reason I look like I'm forty-five when I'm actually 107."

Curious, I sipped and winced.

"Beauty is pain," he quipped.

"And bitterness apparently," I said, handing the flask back.

"Speaking of bitter. You and Dominic seem to have a rapport."

"Do we?" I asked innocently, pretending not to notice his fishing expedition.

"Oh, come on, Admin Ally. The man *smiled.* His mouth lifted at the corners, and the clouds parted and angels sang as a sunbeam held him in a spotlight."

I laughed. "Are you sure there's no alcohol in that?"

"I'm saying the man has been a miserable bastard since joining *Label.* But when he looks at you…"

I wasn't biting. "He looks like he wants to commit murder. We don't get along. We don't like each other. However, I *do* like annoying him."

"Well, keep annoying him. It's nice to see him have a little fun for once."

"He is very serious," I said, annoyed with myself for wanting to fish for information.

"He was brought in to clean up a serious mess," he said. "He takes family and business very seriously."

"He also takes the arrangement of pepperonis very seriously."

Linus sat up straighter. "That *isn't* a rumor?"

I shook my head. "Nope. He was an ass. I spelled out FU

on his pizza. He had me fired. And Dalessandra offered me a job."

"You aren't nearly as boring as you look, Admin Ally."

"It's the coat," I joked, brushing a clump of dog hair off the lovely wool.

"You're the only one brave enough to yell at him, you know."

"I'm not brave," I told him. "He just can't fire me, and this is all temporary. Once everything is fixed, I don't plan on staying."

His eyes widened behind those owlish glasses. "This is a dream come true for a lot of girls out there."

"It's not my dream."

"Is that why handsome ogres like Dominic don't scare you?"

"Or sharp-toothed Medusas like Malina."

Linus shuddered. "She's one of the *worst* human beings I've ever met. And I work in fashion."

We rode in silence for a few minutes.

"Thanks for my phone and laptop, by the way," I said.

He squinted at me behind his glasses.

"Didn't you arrange it with IT? I mean, since I was assigned to you this week, I assumed these came from you."

"I didn't know that was a thing I could do," he mused. "I wonder if I could requisition a new Dior scarf?"

"If they're not from you, and Zara had nothing to do with it, where did they come from?"

"Maybe Dalessandra is playing Santa Claus," he guessed.

"Does she do that? With things other than jobs, I mean."

"Dalessandra does a lot of things that the rest of us don't know about."

It was almost six, and the forty-third floor was starting to clear out. A few panicked support staff sweated over emergency magazine tasks in cubicles and conference rooms. Some of the higher-ups were clustering near the elevator in gowns and black ties. Just another Monday night.

I changed into my standard dance uniform, high-waisted tights and a cropped tank, and plopped down at my desk to check my emails while listening to tonight's playlist before I left for class.

The pay from the studio wasn't great, but I loved dance enough that I allowed myself two classes a week instead of taking better paying shifts. I loved moving and sweating and feeling the music in my bones. It felt like a celebration of being alive.

The kinds of classes I taught were less about technique and more about moving in ways that made you feel strong and sexy.

Taylor Swift crooned in my ears as I shoulder shimmied and fired off an email.

My old, crappy phone vibrated in staccato on the desk. It was a text from my neighbor.

Mr. Mohammad: I visited your father. We ate Jell-O and watched Judge Judy.

He'd included a GIF of two women Jell-O wrestling. I had some regrets about installing the GIF keyboard on his phone.

I thanked him and gave him my new work phone number with explicit instructions that it was for emergencies only.

He responded with a GIF of cartoon thumbs.

"Working late?" Even muffled by Taylor Swift, I recognized the voice.

Dominic stood just outside my cubicle, hands in his pockets. His coat was covered in muddy paw prints of varying sizes. I liked the imperfection. It made him look less formidable. More human.

I pulled off my headphones. "Just catching up with work before I leave for more work."

He eyed my outfit, and I felt the heat of his gaze like it was an actual physical touch.

I really needed to go on a date. Or at least get a hug.

"Let me guess," he said, blue eyes lingering for a moment on the strip of exposed skin between the bottom of my shirt and the waistband of my pants. "Kickboxing?"

"Close," I said. My work phone chimed out its reminder for me to get my butt in gear, and I rose. "Dance class," I told him, pulling on my sweatshirt and tucking both phones into my backpack.

"Did your family emergency resolve itself?" he asked.

Surprised that he'd even given it another thought, I shot him a look. "Uh, not yet, but it's on the mend," I told him. "Everything is under control."

"Good."

He waited, and I wondered if he was hoping I'd open up and tell him everything. More likely, he was hoping that I would shut up and leave.

"New phone?" he asked.

I looked up. His face was unreadable.

"Did you have something to do with the IT fairies raining gifts on me today?"

"Do I look like the type of person who would do that?" he challenged.

"No. But the paw prints do soften you up a bit."

He glanced down at the ruined cashmere. "Remind me to have Linus fire you."

I clamped a hair tie between my lips and worked my hair into a short tail. "Nice try. But I think he likes me," I said around the hair tie. "You should give it a shot. Maybe give your blinding hatred a rest."

I wrapped the tie around my hair and gave it a tug.

"I don't hate you, Ally." His voice was quiet, gruff.

I wasn't sure how it had happened, but suddenly we were standing too close. Nothing good would come of this odd attraction. Yet I couldn't seem to help myself.

He was supposed to be cold. However, from where I stood, inches away, he seemed anything but.

"Good. Because frankly, I'm irresistible, and you might as well just give up the fight now."

"I can't afford to find you irresistible," he said.

We weren't touching. But it felt like the space between us was charged with something. It was acting like a defibrillator on my heart.

I don't like him, I reminded myself. *But clearly that doesn't mean I don't want him.*

Apparently I'd turned into a woman who would gladly rip her clothes off and jump a guy who didn't like her just because he was scary hot.

That thought led to an unfortunate fantasy montage of just how Dominic Russo would look if he were fucking me. On top. Under. Bent over me. Against a wall. Tangled in sheets.

"What?" he demanded.

The question had the effect of a record scratch.

I could only imagine the show my face was putting on right now.

"Nothing," I squeaked. "Gotta go." *Gotta go take a long walk in the frigid night air to cool the hell down and stop thinking dirty, dirty thoughts.*

But he didn't move when I did. And now we were almost touching. I could *feel* him. His hands were still tucked in the pockets of his coat. The heat that came off his body was extraordinary.

I could imagine just how it would feel if I slid my palms over his chest. I knew exactly how the texture of his crisp shirt would war with the body heat that seemed desperate to escape.

I could feel his breath on my hair. I would have bet money that he could hear the thrum of my heartbeat because I sure as hell could hear it. I could feel it everywhere in my body. An insistent pulsing of hot blood.

He leaned in and down, and for one split second, I thought that those firm lips were going to crush mine in the kind of kiss that no one survives. But he reached past me, then straightened. "Here," he said, handing me the headphones I'd left on the desk.

My fingers closed over them, but his didn't let go. We stood that way for another long beat. Looking at the headphones. At our fingers that were almost brushing.

He still wasn't touching me. But it felt like he'd stripped me down and spread me out to be admired.

Devoured.

Ruined.

Was he feeling this too? Or was I just the awkward woman who couldn't get out of her cubicle without making a mess?

I chanced a look up at him.

Those blue eyes bore into mine. He looked frustrated. Angry. Hungry.

"Did you have lunch today?" I asked.

He blinked like he was coming out of a trance. "Did I what?"

"Have lunch," I repeated. "You look hungry."

"You should go, Ally," he said, taking a deliberate step back.

And just like that, he took his heat with him.

I grabbed my coat off the back of the chair and swirled it around me like a protective cloak before leaving without a word.

I got off the subway one stop early just so I could suck in the cold air and calm my racing mind. I hadn't just had a moment with Dominic. Definitely not. He didn't have moments. And he'd made it abundantly clear that not only was I not his type, but he could barely stand to be civil to me.

I was tired. Distracted. I'd completely misread all the signs. He wasn't helplessly attracted to me. He was just being polite. Or annoying.

He hadn't touched me. Not even when he handed over my headphones, I reminded myself.

I was not about to enter a mooning downward spiral about the hot boy in school. I cranked up Beyoncé's "Single Ladies" and refused to let my brain replay the non-moment.

The studio was on the first floor of a well-kept building with fanciful arched windows in the Cast Iron Historic District. The windows were fogged from the last class. Students overlapped in the hall. Those leaving were sweaty and loose and smiling. Those arriving were tight and cold, ready to be guided out of their heads and into their bodies.

Gola and Ruth showed up in designer athletic apparel, and I ushered them to their spots on the glossy wood floor. We had a packed class, and I could already feel the energy rising as everyone began to shed their day.

This was what I loved most. The transformation from employee to person. From parent to dancer. From titles and responsibilities to a body that was ready to be used.

The small crowd squealed when I turned down the lights, cranked the music.

"Okay, ladies and gentlemen. Let's move!"

20

DOMINIC

Greta, I need some recommendations on dog walkers," I said, leaning against her desk and just so happening to find a direct line of sight to Ally at her new workstation. She'd been bumped upstairs temporarily to help keep Linus from losing his production managing mind for the week. And I was distracted by her presence.

Today, she was wearing a pair of high-waisted designer pants in fire engine red and some kind of black lacy blouse that looked Victorian except for the fact that I could see her bra straps. It was a conservative outfit compared to what usually strutted the halls of *Label*, but it was still enough to have me imagining everything else underneath it.

She'd added bracelets in turquoise and silver to one wrist and classic hoop earrings.

It bothered me that I felt compelled to take an inventory of every item she wore.

I felt compelled to do a lot of things where Ally was concerned.

Avoid her.

Ignore her.

Make up reasons to talk to her.

Pick a fight with her.

Touch her.

I'd been close enough to touch her Monday when I'd found her at her desk after work. It was much harder than it should have been to not reach out and trace a finger over her lower lip, over the strip of skin just below the hem of her tank.

It made no sense. I felt out of control around her. A feeling I loathed.

Every time I talked to her, passed her in the hall, sat across the table from her in a meeting, I wanted *more.*

I wanted more to blame her, but part of me was starting to wonder if this was in my blood. If my father had been a normal man until one day he'd snapped.

"Dog walkers?" Greta repeated. This was the third time I'd wandered out to her desk rather than calling, emailing, or just yelling through the open door like I usually did. Before the woman I couldn't stop thinking about had moved upstairs.

My admin not so subtly swiveled in her chair to see exactly what I was staring at. She spun back around and arched an eyebrow. I knew I wasn't fooling her.

I wasn't even fooling myself.

"Dog walkers. The sooner, the better," I told her briskly.

"I'll take care of it after lunch," she assured me. "Is there anything else you want?" She tilted her blond head not so subtly in Ally's direction.

Greta had managed my calendar for years. She knew the type of women I usually dated. I'd grown up around models and photographers and designers. It had been only natural to spend more…intimate time with the like.

But I'd taken a sabbatical from women since taking this job.

No dating.

No sex.

I'd needed to prove to myself that I wasn't anything like him. And yet here I was, lusting after a woman I didn't even like. Maybe it wasn't Ally that was getting under my skin. Maybe it was just a biological need to fuck.

That thought brightened my mood. I'd gone a year without sex. A year without feeling a woman under me. A year without touching soft, lovely skin.

It was too fucking long.

I wasn't a monk. Just a man intent on not committing his father's sins.

"Just the recommendations," I told her, pointedly ignoring the way Ally's shoulders slid side to side as she danced to music in her headphones. I wondered what was playing in those ears right now. "Thanks."

I returned to the refuge of my office. I hadn't bothered redecorating when I'd taken over the position. It hadn't been a priority. I'd come in on a Sunday and taken every framed photo, every memento, every shiny award, and thrown them all in the trash. The next morning, my new desk and chair—furniture that my father hadn't touched—had been delivered.

It hadn't been a fresh start so much as a hostile takeover.

I sat down behind my desk and pulled up the page layouts I was supposed to be approving. But Ally popped into my mind again.

Since my blindingly stupid moment with her Monday night—when I'd been so enamored with that peek of bare skin that I'd almost touched her—I'd thought of little else. I could imagine her. Moving to a hard-driving beat in those tights. Sweat glistening on her bare stomach.

And now I was hard again.

Fucking great.

I shifted in my seat, refusing to give in this time.

Yesterday, I'd run into her in the stairwell. I'd asked her *politely* to get the hell out of my way. She'd offered—less politely—to help me down the stairs, headfirst. All I could picture was bending her over the railing and dragging that flirty little skirt up to her waist. I'd made it back to my office, locked myself in the washroom, and masturbated violently while thinking about *her*.

In the middle of the day. In my own office.

I'd come so fucking hard my knees buckled.

When it was over, I couldn't look at myself in the mirror.

I was afraid it wouldn't be my reflection I'd see.

Today, I was keeping my fucking hands off my fucking cock and my fucking mind off fucking Ally. End of story.

I mustered every ounce of willpower I had and focused on the layouts on my desk.

Sheer stubbornness won out, and I didn't surface for another thirty minutes until there was a knock on my open door.

Harry Vandenberg, investment banker, snappy dresser, father of two, and the man who held the title of my best friend, lounged in my doorway. He was tall and rangy. I had inches and pounds on him, but he had the smile that women flocked to. He was charming. I was…less effusive.

"He *is* alive," Harry quipped, strolling into my office. He whipped out his phone and snapped a picture.

"What's that for?" I asked, standing to greet him.

We shook, then hugged.

"Proof of life for the rest of the guys," Harry explained, firing off a text. My phone pinged, and I knew it was a group text.

"It hasn't been *that* long," I argued, leaning against the desk.

He sank down in the chair in front of me. "I haven't seen you in a month. The last time you came out with the rest of us, the air-conditioning was still on."

I'd left a job I loved at Dorrance Capital thirteen months ago, baffling my investment banking coworkers with the decision.

"I've been busy," I told him.

"You're always busy. Hell, *I'm* always busy. But that's no excuse. We're going to lunch."

Lunch sounded good. Getting out of this office sounded good.

I reached for my phone, which was now buzzing at incessant intervals. I could only imagine the shit that was being dished out from my former coworkers.

"Not fair, Charming," Ally said as she stormed into my office. She held a clear plastic garment bag aloft.

I almost cracked a smile. *Almost.*

"What seems to be the problem, Maleficent?" I knew exactly what her problem was. That bag held four new vests that I'd ordered specifically with torturing her in mind.

Sue me. If her mere presence was torturing me, then I could at least make sure she was suffering too.

She turned to Harry. "I'm sorry. Is this an important meeting? Would you prefer if I come back to yell at this jerk later?" she asked him.

Harry grinned. "I'm an old friend of this jerk. Feel free to hurl insults at him in front of me."

"Great! Thanks," Ally said, tossing the bag on my desk. "I'll tell you what my problem is. His name is Dominic Russo, and he's a pain in my ass."

"I'm Harry, by the way," my idiot friend piped up. He was far too amused for my liking.

"No introductions," I said. "Ms. Morales won't be with us much longer. It's only a matter of time before my mother comes to her senses and fires her, since she seems incapable of behaving professionally."

Ally flipped me off.

I crossed my arms and looked bored. "Are you through?"

She jabbed a finger at the bag, then at me. "Make sure you know what you're doing, because this means war."

"Don't start something you can't win," I warned her quietly.

I get it. I'm an asshole. I don't want her around. But I can't leave her alone. Deal with it. It was worth the five figures those vests cost just to see her annoyed. Besides, I liked vests.

"I have no intention of losing, Charming." She turned her back on me, and I wanted to punch myself in the face for instantly noticing how well those fucking fire-engine-red pants accentuated the curves of her ass. "Harry, it's nice to meet you. I'm Ally," she said.

"Very nice to meet you, Ally," Harry said, all charm. He stood and offered his hand.

I clenched my jaw. He could touch her, and it meant nothing.

I, on the other hand, didn't trust myself to survive even basic contact. Ally was only safe, my soul was only safe, as long as I didn't touch her.

"Go away, Maleficent."

She turned her attention back to me, and I hated the relief I felt.

"Just remember, Dom. You started it."

She walked out, and Harry and I watched her go.

"Who was that?" he demanded.

"No one. Let's go."

"Why are you not chasing that woman around with a diamond ring?" Harry demanded the second the server walked away from our table.

"What woman?" I asked, pretending like I didn't know exactly who he was talking about.

"The Maleficent to your Charming. I thought you were gonna crack a filling or two."

"She's not my type," I said. "How's the debt market report looking?"

"Uh-uh," he said, shaking his head and ignoring my redirection. "Nope. No subject change. You and Ally. What's the story?"

"There's no story," I insisted, unrolling my silverware from the napkin to give me something to do.

Harry was silent, and I looked up. He was sniffing the air. "You smell that?" he asked.

I knew where this was going. "I do not."

"I do. It's strong. Here. Let me waft it toward you," he said, flicking his hands at me. "That's the smell of bullshit."

"It's nothing. She's just an admin at work. My mother hired her."

"The fashion icon and editor in chief Dalessandra Russo does not hire admins," he pointed out.

"She does when I get them fired from their jobs at pizza places in the Village."

Harry hooted in amusement. "Oh, this is good."

"Nothing is good. There's no story. There's no anything."

"Brother, the last time I saw sparks flying like that was when my father-in-law tried to microwave leftovers in tinfoil. You're either in deep denial, or you're trying to lie to my face right now."

"There's nothing there. Nothing has happened or will happen. We just get under each other's skin," I insisted.

"When's the last time a woman got under your skin?" he asked.

The server returned with our drinks, and I reached for mine with desperation.

The answer was never, and Harry knew it.

"The main requirement for me to be interested in a woman is that she doesn't annoy the shit out of me."

"There's a fine line between annoyance and 'damn, I really want to get that naked,'" he pointed out. "When I met Delaney, I spent fifty percent of the time wanting to murder her and fifty percent of the time wanting to get in her pants."

Delaney was Harry's wife. She was an attorney known for aggressive cross-examinations. They met at a bar and had spent the entire evening arguing over wine and football. Ten years and two kids later, they still considered a good argument to be the best kind of foreplay.

"Not all of us are as fucked up as you two," I said.

He ignored me. "I can't wait to tell Delaney that Dominic Russo finally met someone who bugs the shit out of him."

"You bug the shit out of me."

"Yeah, but I'm already taken. Is she?"

"Who?"

"Don't play me, Russo."

"She's single," I admitted.

"What a coincidence. So are you."

"Not happening. Besides the fact that she's annoying, has no professionalism, and pisses me off every time I see her, I don't date employees."

"Maybe you should look into changing that policy. Because she's definitely interested in you."

Was she? Or was she interested in what Dominic Russo represented?

It wouldn't be the first time a woman had been more interested in my name or family connections. After all, she'd already gotten a job out of just knowing me.

"Don't make me send you the middle finger selfie again," I told him.

21

ALLY

Wednesdays weren't the best bar shifts for making cash, but they were better than nothing. Plus I'd managed to finish up a design project for a client—a series of Facebook graphics for a product launch—between *Label* and my shift at Rooster's.

The invoice was sent, and my tip jar was half-full. My first paycheck from *Label* was slated for next week, and Dad had been discharged back to the nursing home this morning.

Things were moving in the right direction.

"Have a good night, guys," I called after two patrons who had warmed barstools for two hours, arguing seventeenth-century literature and flirting with me.

They'd left me a thirty percent tip that made my mercenary heart tap out a pitter-patter.

That pitter-patter turned into an aggressive timpani solo when Dominic Russo took one of the vacated stools.

We stared at each other while he shrugged out of his coat.

He was dressed more casually than he had been in the office. Jeans and a well-fitting gray sweater that made his blue eyes look more silver. His sleeves were shoved up, revealing tattoos on both forearms.

Yum.

What was it about this man that made me feel…whatever this was?

Wordlessly, I dropped a napkin on the bar in front of him.

The bar was still loud, still busy. But everything seemed to fade into a blurry background as we stared at each other.

What is this?

Why is he here?

Why do I want to climb over this bar and slide into his lap?

Well. Besides the obvious.

"What'll it be, boss?" I asked, going for light, blasé even. But when the words came out, they sounded like a proposition to me. *Beer? Bourbon? Me?*

He pointed to a craft beer on tap and leaned his forearms on the bar.

I poured his beer and set it in front of him.

"Yo, Al, got a round of bachelorette shots comin' up," one of the servers called from the end of the bar. I was old enough to be his very young aunt.

Relieved, I turned away from those eyes that were burning holes into me and yanked the ticket off the printer. I went to work, pretending that every fiber of my being wasn't focused on the man behind me.

I made six Screaming Orgasms, poured four more beers, and shook up two martinis before finding my way back to Dominic.

"Hungry?" I asked.

"Do you get a break?" He pushed his empty glass toward me. His gaze lingered on the beaded bracelets on my wrist.

"I get fifteen," I said, wondering what he could possibly want badly enough to come down here and sit at my bar.

"Will you eat with me?" he asked.

Now I was nervous. He was being nice. Polite. I trusted the grumpy, yelling version of him a hell of a lot more than this civilized one.

"Sure," I said.

He looked relieved.

"Another one?" I asked, taking his glass.

"Yes."

Twenty minutes later, I was seated across from my boss at a way-too-intimate high-top table tucked into a very dark corner.

Our differences were impossible to ignore. He was in designer duds. I was dressed like a cheap cowgirl. He'd ordered the filet, and I was dining on my employee discount hamburger.

"What's going on? You're not here to get me fired, are you?" I cut my burger in half so I could save one portion for lunch tomorrow.

He didn't crack a smile. If anything, he looked even more serious.

"How many jobs do you need?" he asked.

"As many as it takes."

"Does it have something to do with your family emergency?"

I chose to take a bite of burger rather than answer him. Dominic's nostrils flared, and he was back to glaring at me. This at least felt normal.

"Harry seemed to think that there's something between us." He said the words slowly and to the steak in front of him rather than to my face.

"Something besides a murderous rage?" I clarified.

He did look at me then. “He thinks that we’re attracted to each other.”

I didn’t say anything.

It was a self-preservation thing. There was no way in hell that I’d admit to being attracted to the man.

“I don’t know how to talk about this without putting you in an awkward position,” he admitted.

Since when was Dominic Russo worried about making me feel awkward?

“Okay. Now you’re starting to worry me,” I announced. “How about just be honest? Spit it out. Rip off the bandage. We’re adults here on our own time.”

“Fine.” He took a breath and then looked me dead in the eye. “Are you attracted to me?”

I laughed.

He frowned. Fiercely.

“What?” I asked. “That’s a ridiculous question.”

“Then give me a ridiculous answer,” he growled.

I rolled my eyes. “Yes, Dom. I’m physically attracted to you. I imagine most women and plenty of men are.”

He held up a bossy, obnoxious hand. “Don’t be flippant.”

“What’s the problem?” I asked.

“I’m your boss.”

“Technically, I have about a hundred bosses,” I corrected him.

“It doesn’t matter. There’s a policy—”

“I know there’s a policy. Are you accusing me of violating it?”

“What? No.” He closed his eyes for a beat and then opened them again. “What I’m trying to say is I’m not willing to violate the policy.”

“Wait a second. Dom, are you saying you’re attracted to me?” I asked incredulously.

He glared at me. "You're not stupid, Ally."

"Apparently, I might be. Are you attracted to me?"

I held his gaze, and for the first time, I saw the storm in those blue eyes. He was fighting some kind of internal battle.

"Dom?"

His jaw flexed twice before he answered. "I'm attracted to you, Ally. Very attracted," he said, his voice low and rough.

Oh, lord.

Sex hormones dumped into my bloodstream so quickly I felt light-headed.

"Oh." It was the only word I could get out as a wave of confusion and white-hot lust crushed me.

"Oh?" he repeated, looking annoyed.

"Give me a minute," I told him. "I'm processing. I thought you hated me."

"I told you before. I don't hate you," he said disdainfully. "I hate being attracted to you."

And just like that, those sex hormones turned into white-hot rage.

"You tracked me down *to my third job* to tell me you *hate* being attracted to me?" I said the words slowly, making sure I was reiterating his point with just the right amount of "you son of a bitch" in my tone.

"What I mean to say is nothing is going to happen between us."

"You're damn right nothing is going to happen, you cocky, imbecilic ass. You think I'm so desperate that I'd say yes to a quick hate fuck? That my self-respect is so low I'd throw myself at someone who doesn't *deserve* me?" I couldn't decide whether I wanted to smash my burger in his face or stab him in the hand with a fork.

"Ally, you're getting it wrong," he said dryly.

"I'm getting it wrong, or you're saying it wrong?"

He looked uncomfortable. Really uncomfortable.

"I just want to make it clear that I'm not going to get involved with you."

The arrogance of this guy was almost laughable. *Definitely go with the fork*, I decided.

"First of all, *boss*, I decide who I get involved with. Not you. And right now, I'd rather sleep with literally any human in this bar than you. Dead last. That's where you rank. Just because I *found* you physically attractive doesn't mean I'd want to sleep with you." I emphasized the past tense to drive my point home, ignoring the fact that that was exactly what it had meant up until forty-five seconds ago when he opened his big, stupid mouth.

"Eat your dinner, Ally," he said.

The look I shot him should have made his balls shrivel into raisins.

"Look," I said. "You don't get to be an asshole to my face when I'm on someone else's clock. You can do it forty-odd hours a week at the office but not here." I started to push my chair back, but he closed a hand over my wrist.

His grip felt like a shackle. A warm, hard, unbreakable shackle. And I *hated* the fact that I liked it.

I stared down at the fingers ensnaring my wrist and felt like I'd entered another dimension where casual physical touch from a man who'd just insulted me on the basest level could render me speechless.

"Ally," he said again. His voice was a rasp.

It was humiliating to know that the man could insult me to my face and my body would still want to see his naked. Had I lost my self-respect along with my life savings?

"This is coming out wrong," he said.

"I'm not sure there's a right way to tell someone that you're attracted to them but the actual thought of sex with them makes you nauseated," I shot back. "Are you the reincarnation of Mr. Darcy?"

His fingers squeezed harder.

"What I am fucking up over and over again is this: I want you to know that despite the fact that I find you interesting, intelligent, infuriating, and very, very attractive, I'm not going to pursue any kind of relationship with you. I want you to feel safe at work. I don't want you to think that I'm going to drag you into a copy room and fuck you against office equipment. I don't want coworkers whispering behind your back because you had the misfortune to catch my eye. I don't want your reputation torn to shreds just because I wonder what you look like naked. And yes, I do think about that. And no, I shouldn't be telling you that."

He said all this without lessening the pressure of his fingers. As if the physical touch and the words melded into one message. *Desire.*

Fuck me against office equipment? I'd put that in the "Obsess About This Later" folder.

We were both quiet for a long beat. Him still gripping my wrist. Me still staring at him as if he'd just announced he had four testicles and dreamed of someday raising miniature donkeys.

"I wanted to clear the air," he said, pressing on. "If Harry was picking up on something between us, then others will also. That's not the kind of environment *Label* is. Not anymore."

My brain was still wading through his speech. There was something real, something vulnerable in there, and I needed several uninterrupted days to process it all.

"Say something," he demanded gruffly.

"Well, the first thing that comes to mind is: I look great naked," I told him. The man put his head down on the table, and I almost laughed.

"Dammit. I knew it," he said mournfully.

"Did Dominic Russo just crack a joke?"

"Maybe. I don't know. Being around you feels like a never-ending boxing match, and I keep getting hit in the nuts."

I did laugh then. "You are really, really bad at this, by the way."

"Forgive me," he said dryly as he lifted his head. "I've never had this conversation before."

I flipped my hand over and wrapped my fingers around his wrist. "I think you're making this more complicated than it has to be."

"If anyone is overcomplicating things, it's you," he said, his tone grumpy.

"Stop being a baby. Just because we're attracted to each other doesn't mean we have to act on it. We're adults, not oversexed teens with no comprehension of consequences. I'm not your type. You're not my type, though in other circumstances, I'd be happy to broaden my horizons."

He growled at that. I grinned.

"But neither one of us wants to rock the boat at work. I like my job. And I don't fuck men who don't like me. I'm not going to lock your office door and show you that I'm not wearing underwear."

"Oh, for fuck's sake," he muttered, swiping his free hand over his face.

He looked tortured. I liked it.

"Never in the history of my adult life have I been so overcome with lust that I couldn't control myself. And I'm willing to bet the same is true for you," I guessed.

"Don't overestimate my control or underestimate your appeal, Ally."

And just like that, I was back in Put Your Dick in Me Town. "Geez, Dom."

"I'm serious," he said. "I'm not putting any responsibility on you. But I am infatuated with you, and I've spent a lot of time thinking about…things that I'm not going to repeat."

I really, really, really wanted to know what kinds of things.

I took a breath and let it out slowly. "We want the same thing."

His eyes narrowed, and I was overcome by a fantasy of him ripping open my cowgirl shirt and shoving my skirt up to my waist.

For one long second, I had the distinct feeling he was thinking the same thing. The temperature of the air between us rose to a smolder.

"What I mean to say," I said, clearing my throat, "is that neither one of us is up for a workplace affair. So we won't have one. It's as simple as that."

"What if I keep wearing vests?"

I leaned in and noticed his gaze dipped to the first closed snap on my shirt. "Then I'll just learn to control myself. Also, if you don't stop wearing vests, I'll stop wearing underwear to work."

He clenched his jaw and swallowed hard.

"Shut up and eat your dinner," he said gruffly, pulling his hand away.

I picked up my now-cold half burger. Not to be compliant but because, after the tips, the food was a highlight of the job.

"How do you get home from here?" he asked.

"Train," I said, taking a bite.

He reached for his wallet. "I'd rather you take a cab."

"No."

"No?" He sounded like he couldn't believe I was so stupid, so impertinent.

I rolled my eyes. "I'm not *yours*, Dom. You don't get to worry about me or play protector. You're my boss. I'm your employee. Unless you're forking up cab fare or Uber credits for all the admins on staff, the answer is no. No special treatment. No extracurricular sex. No seduction attempts. No flirting. The air is cleared."

He stared at me a long beat. Those eyes were impossibly sad.

It was what he wanted.

So why did the man look so damn miserable?

22

ALLY

It was early morning when I ducked in the side door to the Goodwin Childers Nursing Home as another family was exiting. I was on thin ice with the billing department, and I just didn't have it in me to have another conversation with Front Office Deena about the importance of being timely with my payments.

This nursing home had the best dementia ward in a fifty-mile radius, and my father deserved the best.

Even if I couldn't afford it.

Skirting the hallway that led to the front desk area, I snuck through the cheerful assisted living wing to the security doors of the memory ward.

Braden, one of my favorite nurses on the ward, waved through the glass as he buzzed me in.

"Ally! Good to see you back," he said. "We missed you and your dad around here."

"It's good to be back," I told him. "How's he doing?"

"It's a really good day," he said with a grin.

"Really?"

"So good, he's not in his room. He's in the lounge."

"You're kidding?"

Braden lifted a finger in the air. I stopped and listened. The faint notes of Hilton Ruiz's "Home Cookin'" reached me, tugging on the strings of my heart as a hundred memories flooded through me.

He grinned. "I'll take you back."

I followed Braden's defensive line–sized frame as he maneuvered past glass that opened into an internal courtyard of turf and concrete. The fountain had been drained for the season, and the colors of summer and fall were long gone, but the evergreens were decked in colorful Christmas lights for the duration of the winter, giving residents something to enjoy.

The piano got louder as we approached double doors propped open facing a nurses' station.

And there against a wall of windows, wheelchair parked nearby, was my father behind the piano.

"Ally, my girl!"

My father's gleeful pronouncement when I walked into the lounge room melted off the lingering cold. A rush of love so swift and fierce swamped me.

"Dad!" I crossed to him and hugged him hard, delighted when he hugged me back, rocking side to side in that way of his that had once been so familiar.

"Have a seat," he said, patting the bench next to him. "Tell me everything."

This tiny window of time was open, and I needed to savor every moment of it. Not willing to miss out on one second of this, I fired off a text to Zara.

Me: Running late. Family emergency. I promise I'll make it up.

I'd work till midnight every night if it meant I got to enjoy my dad being my dad.

"Let's take a selfie before I have to go to work," I insisted. I took one on every good day, knowing now how precious these moments truly were.

Dutifully, he slung his arm around my shoulders, and I clicked away as we hammed it up for the camera. He pressed a kiss to the top of my head before pulling back.

"Where are you working again?" he asked, a frown touching his lips as he bumped up against the hole in his memory.

I cleared my throat. "It's a new job. I'm working for a fashion magazine."

"Well, isn't that something. Do you love it?" he asked. My father was a firm believer in doing as much of what you loved as possible. A job was no exception.

I thought about it for a beat, then nodded. "I do. It's fun and fast-paced, and the people are…interesting."

"Is there a Miranda Priestly?" he asked, nudging my shoulder.

"When did you ever see *The Devil Wears Prada*?" I demanded with a laugh.

"I read the book."

"Smarty-pants," I said fondly. "The Miranda at my job is actually a Dalessandra, and she's pretty wonderful. Her son is another story though."

"Tell me everything," he said, noodling out a Sammy Davis Jr. tune.

"About what?"

"This son. Is he evil?" *Dun dun dun* went the piano keys.

I laughed and thought about Dominic. "Evil? No. A pain in my ass? Yes."

"Sometimes pains in the ass make life more interesting. Do you remember this one?" he asked, his fingers working the keys, teasing out another familiar favorite.

I smiled and rested my fingers on my end of the keys. I remembered everything. And now I treasured it.

I stayed another hour before leaving Dad at the piano when he volunteered to teach another resident a jazzy little tune on the piano. It was always a struggle knowing when to leave. If I left while he was still present, I was missing out on time with him. But if I stayed too long and the mood slipped, the ensuing disappearance of Dad was devastating.

Too in my own head, I didn't notice the danger until it was practically on top of me in a pink chenille sweater.

"Ms. Morales, I trust you're here to pay your late fees?"

Shit.

Front Desk Deena, harbinger of late fees, lurked just outside the memory ward. She had thin, flat lips that were always painted a bright pink. Her red hair reminded me of Ronald McDonald…if Ronald dabbled with a jewelry fetish. Today she was wearing four diamond rings, a pendant with several birthstones that suggested this woman actually had a family, and rather large diamond studs in her long ear lobes.

She terrified me.

"Uhh…" I hadn't even formed an actual word, but my neck was doing its best impression of a sunburn.

"$5,327.94." She rattled off the amount that I too knew by heart. It was exactly what stood between my father and another month in this facility.

"I'm aware," I said. "I believe it's due next Saturday." I'd memorized that too, from the thirty-day eviction notice she'd so helpfully sent me. It was the day after my first paycheck from the magazine. And I needed every dime of that paycheck to make this payment.

She pinched her lips together tighter, making the hot pink disappear completely. Her eyes narrowed behind purple-rimmed glasses. "I'd certainly hate to have to tell the nurses to start packing your father's things."

Her tone suggested otherwise.

"That won't be necessary," I assured her. My phone chimed. It was time to get back to the office and earn that paycheck.

23

ALLY

That afternoon, while Linus was out doing whatever Linus did, I was summoned for a meeting with the graphics team. I arrived early and was surprised to find coffee, tea, and muffins already neatly arranged on the impossibly hip glass conference table.

I was just reaching for a chocolate chip muffin when the door opened behind me and Dominic strolled into the room.

"Hi," I said, guiltily dropping the muffin.

After our bar shift confessional, I wasn't really sure where we stood.

"I heard you were late today," he said, slipping his hands into his pockets. "Another emergency."

"This one was a good one," I said. "Something I didn't want to miss out on."

He studied me silently, and I realized how that must have sounded. His thumb was tapping against his pant leg. A tiny little tic.

"I take my job seriously, Dom. Don't think that I was blowing off work for something frivolous."

"It must have been good for you to give up two hours of pay."

My spine stiffened, and my shoulders ratcheted up under my ears.

"Why don't you tell me what your problem is instead of beating around the bush, Charming?"

"I want to know what's going on."

"It's none of your business," I told him. "We're not friends. We're not lovers. I work for you. The only relationship that exists between us is a professional one. We both made the call, remember?"

"You missed work. I was concerned."

"Why? Lots of people miss work. I'm going to make up the hours."

"What do you want me to say, Ally? That I care?"

I shook my head vehemently. I most definitely did *not w*ant him to say that. And I certainly didn't want him to mean it. "I don't want to play games. Not today and certainly not with you."

"Then tell me what's going on."

"Why do you even care? I'm not some mystery to be solved. I'm a private person with a lot of shit happening right now that doesn't affect you."

"It does affect me when it keeps you from showing up for work." Frustration crackled off him like he was holding a live wire.

"This conversation is ridiculous."

"You're ridiculous," he shot back.

"I'm not sharing my personal life with you," I told him. "Don't take it personally. I have things going on that are easier to deal with than to talk about. And if you recall our conversation last night, we aren't going to pursue any kind of relationship outside work."

"We're at work right now," he stubbornly pointed out, crossing his arms.

"Malina missed half a day this week," I said. "Did you track her down to find out why?"

"Of course not."

"Why not?"

"Because I don't care about her," he shot back.

We both sat with that pronouncement for a minute.

"Dom," I started.

"Shut up. Forget it. I didn't mean it that way."

"Oh good. Mr. Darcy's back," I said dryly.

"What does that even mean?"

"Ugh. Another reason why I'd never let you get me naked. You haven't read or watched *Pride and Prejudice*."

Dominic collapsed in a chair across the table from me. Even with the entire expanse of glass and a mound of muffins between us, I could still *feel* his frustration.

"You annoy me on so many levels, it's incredible. What could *Pride and Prejudice* possibly have to do with us not pursuing whatever the hell this is?"

I sat opposite him. "Mr. Darcy pronounces his love for Elizabeth with an insulting speech about how he's into her even though she's incredibly unsuitable, poor, and ridiculous."

"I am not pronouncing my love for you," he said crisply.

"Did I not warn you that I'm irresistible?" I quipped.

He looked so angry I was worried he might rip the arms off his chair. I took pity on him.

"Look, Dom, since we're not pursuing anything—naked or otherwise—outside this building, I think it's best that we know as little about each other as possible."

He glared at me. "I disagree."

Of course he did.

"Okay. Why?"

"We're complete opposites. Wouldn't it follow that the better we get to know each other, the less we would be attracted to each other?"

It was stupid and yet... "Hmm."

"I thrive on challenges, Ally," he warned. "And right now, you and this mysterious background are demanding to be solved."

"What are you suggesting?" I asked with a laugh. "We become friends?"

"Not friends," he insisted. "Workplace acquaintances."

"That's what we are."

"No, we're workplace associates," he insisted.

"Are you drunk? Do you have a family history of stroke?"

"No and no," he said. "Think about it. The more you get to know me, the less attractive you'll find me, and the better I know you, the more repulsive you'll be."

I laughed. I couldn't help myself. Every once in a while, Funny Dominic snuck up on me to surprise and delight me. Thankfully the other ninety-eight percent of the time, he was an insufferable ass.

"Please. We both know the more you learn about me, the faster you'll be scampering off to pick out a diamond engagement ring big enough to lose an eye on."

He rolled his eyes. "You wish."

"I am a delightful person," I insisted.

"You're a delightful pain in my ass," he shot back.

I drummed my fingers on the table in front of me. "Are you purposely keeping the table between us?"

"Yes," he answered instantly.

"Is it for my protection or yours?"

"I haven't decided yet."

"You're acting like neither one of us has any control," I scoffed.

He scowled at me, then stood.

"What are you doing?" I asked as he rounded the table.

"Proving a point."

Hastily, I got to my feet, but I didn't get far because he was boxing me in against the table. So careful not to touch me. Yet there was no mistaking the buzz between us. My blood went hot, and I could hear my heartbeat ratcheting up the DEFCONs.

"Is DEFCON One or Five worse?" I asked in a squeak.

"One. Now tell me you don't see the problem, Ally," he said dryly.

I was more interested in feeling the problem…until I glanced down. I couldn't help myself. He was visibly hard. Like "stuck a kielbasa in his pants" visibly hard.

He was looking down too. But not at the outline of his cock. No, his gaze was locked on my stupid, lack-of-self-respect nipples that were saluting him through my shirt.

The door was closed, but the graphics team was due any minute. Anyone could walk in and see us like this.

"This is the problem," he insisted, his voice a rasp.

"That's a huge problem," I agreed, still looking at his erection. "It looks painful."

"That's not what I meant," he growled. "This is what happens when we're too close."

"So how do you propose we get to know each other without getting too close?" I asked. I sounded like I'd just climbed all forty-three floors at a dead run. One tiny step forward and my diamond-hard nipples would connect with his chest, his hard-on with my stomach.

He was looming over me, but rather than threatening, it

felt intimate, careful, almost safe. Like I wanted to be exactly here with exactly him.

I really needed to stop consuming dairy products. This had to be some kind of hormonal effect from too much glorious cheese.

I had a swift vision of Dominic placing me on the—hopefully reinforced—glass table at my back and sliding his hands under my skirt and slowly, slowly, peeling the underwear down my legs.

My vision started to go gray around the edges, and I took in a shaky breath. His eyes sharpened to a crystalline, icy blue. It felt as though a storm was brewing in the sliver of space between us.

"Completely inappropriate question," I said. "If you were going to touch me right now, where would you start?"

His exhale was a growl. "Your hair."

I blinked. "My hair?"

"I'd fist my fingers in it and pull so I could taste your mouth and then work my way down your throat."

"Gah." It wasn't a statement so much as a swallow getting tangled up with a moan.

"And this is exactly why we're not going to do this in person," he said softly.

"Gah," I croaked again.

His lips, that firm, mean line of them, lifted just a little, and I felt an explosion of dairy hormones in my core.

"Fine. Email then," I squeaked.

"On personal time from personal email accounts," he said.

The guy had given this a lot of thought.

"That's fair."

"Be honest. Brutally honest," Dominic said. "So we can get this—whatever it is—out of our systems."

I wanted to be offended by the idea that getting to know me would be a major turnoff to him. However, I was damn certain the more I knew about Dominic Russo, the less my lady parts would lust after him. What could possibly go wrong?

"Agreed."

He lifted a hand away from the table, and we both watched as it slowly moved toward my face, my hair.

Goddesses of secret lusty meetings, *please* let Dominic Russo fuck me on this conference table right now.

"Grab me a water, would you?" someone called outside the door. We jumped apart.

I shoved Dominic—and his magnificent fuck stick—into the chair I'd recently occupied before my sexual spiritual awakening and took a guilty step back.

The door opened.

"I don't care what you say. The *Game of Thrones* final season was not what fans were expecting," I announced emphatically.

He looked at me like I'd lost my damn mind.

"Oh, wow. I gotta agree with Ally, Mr. Russo," Shelly, a graphic designer with a penchant for facial piercings, agreed emphatically.

As the rest of the team filed in, a ten-minute discussion of the show and final season ensued while Dominic and I both tried to get our hormones under control.

24

DOMINIC AND ALLY

Maleficent,

Now that I know your feelings regarding *Game of Thrones*, let's move on. Why are you working so many jobs? Is the pay here really that bad?

Charming

Charming,

I wouldn't know. I'm still a week out from my first paycheck. What did you want to be when you grew up? Or are you living your dreams as a vest-wearing fashion mogul?

Maleficent

Maleficent,

This was *not* my dream. In the spirit of honesty, this is closer to a nightmare. When I was nine, I wanted to be a math teacher. How many jobs do you have?

Charming

Prince of Nightmares,

I am the current holder downer of four jobs. Five if you count freelance graphic design, which is feast or famine—mostly famine. Bar shifts, a sporadic catering gig, dance instructor, and my illustrious career as a jill-of-all-trades at *Label*.

I need to know more about this math teacher dream job.

For now, let's put the "why I need 700 jobs" in the Don't Talk About column.

Former Princess of Pizzas

Pizza Princess,

The mystery of why Ally Morales needs 700 jobs is annoying me.

I had a nice math teacher. His name was Mr. Meloy. He helped me with my homework after school sometimes. He loved math, and he loved teaching kids to love math. I thought being a math teacher would be cool.

What did you want to be when you grew up? I'm guessing pizza server wasn't high on the list.

Nerd Unveiled

Dear Nerd,

This isn't working. I'm imagining cute little Dominic looking up to his teacher with those baby blues asking for help.

Tell me the top five things you hate stat. (This is the secret to finding out just how bad a person is in case you need it for interviewing future wives or human sacrifices.)

I wanted to be a dancer from the time I was three. I realized early on that I didn't want a ballet career (hello, carbs and alcohol and sleeping in), but I also loved design and art. So I decided to do all of it.

Now hurry up and disgust me.

Rapidly Thawing Iceberg

P.S. Why was Mr. Meloy helping you with your homework and not your parents?

Dearest Climate Change,

So you're saying you knew what you wanted to do since you were a kid, and then you went out and did it? That's...unusual. Are you always so tenacious? Did you ever consider other lines of work?

If we can't talk about why you need 700 jobs, we will also not be discussing my parents.

Things I Hate:

1. People who litter
2. The rumor mill
3. Getting shit on by birds

4. Not being able to stop thinking about you

5. My father

I'm not asking you what you hate because you're annoyingly hate-less.

Hateful Boss

Boss,

Well, hell. That list wasn't hateful. Not even a little. And this experiment is not working. You're supposed to hate things like puppies and children with cute lisps, and then I'm supposed to finally be able to stop fantasizing about you naked.

I'm not tenacious. More like obnoxiously positive that things will go my way.

Pollyanna

Allyanna,

If I'm not hateful, then why is every woman at work terrified of me?

Hall Stalking Monster

Monster,

You're not actually serious, are you?

Incredulous

Deadly.

Dom

Dominic Russo,

You big, dumb lug of tattooed grumpiness. Have you really spent your entire year there thinking they hate you? You're playing with me right now, aren't you?

There's no way you can be so arrogant when you have me snuggled up against a conference table and then wander the halls of *Label* like a sad puppy because you assume everyone dislikes you.

Annoyed Ally

Annoyed Ally,

What the fuck are you blabbering on about?

Adding to my list. 6. People who never get to the point.

Also, are you obsessed with dogs?

Irritated Boss

Mr. Hot Bod Sexy Face,

The women of *Label* don't *hate* you. They're lusting after you. You're scary hot. Like "don't look directly in the eye" hot.

Baffled by You

Baffled,

That's *not* what is going on. They look at me and see a carbon copy of my father.

Dominic

Dom,

First of all, I want points for being respectful of your Do Not Discuss topic even though I really want to dig into why you'd assume that people see you and your father as one and the same. Lots of points!

That is absolutely the exact opposite of what everyone in that building is thinking. They rate your scary hotness on a scale of 1 to 10, and you've never been below a 13. They swoon down glass doors when you walk past them in the halls.

You held the door for Nina in advertising last week, and she got a standing ovation. I'm not making this up.

Ally

Ally,

This is stupid. I don't like getting to know you.

Dom

Dom,

Back at you. Let's go back to ignoring each other.

Ally

25

DOMINIC

I wanted to say that things changed after our talk and emails. That with the air cleared and her moving back downstairs to the admin pool, I was finally free to concentrate on work. And in a way, things had changed.

I'd shown her my cards.

Admitted my sins.

Confessed my fears.

But none of that stopped me from seeking her out. It didn't stop me from thinking about her. And it sure as fuck didn't stop me from wanting her.

My days began to organize themselves around her.

Emailing after hours. Verbally sparring over some bullshit in the office. One of us getting a rise out of the other.

It seemed innocent enough. Except for the undercurrent.

There was something addicting about our interactions now. As if every word had a double meaning. Every glance was a coded message. We were both attracted to each other. However, we were also both adults. It should have been an exercise in self-control.

But then I'd find myself locking the door of my private bathroom and jerking off while fantasizing about her on her knees in front of me, her on my desk with legs spread, demanding that I fuck her with my tongue.

Every. Fucking. Day.

Knowing that Ally was attracted to me made me feel both less guilty about the act *and* more frustrated by the fact that it was my fist I was fucking and not her.

Basically, I was becoming a complete disaster, and the woman had only been here… God. Less than three full weeks.

Some days, I held out until after everyone else had left for the night. Other days, I barely made it to lunch.

And then there was today.

At 9:05, she waltzed into my office in a pair of thigh-high boots and a Dolce & Gabbana dress. The dress was a garnet red. The front V wasn't scandalous by any standards, but to a man on a hair trigger of arousal, the hint of creamy white curves was dangerously seductive. The dress nipped in at the waist and flowed out again, ending just an inch or two above the soft suede boots.

"Sign these," she said, slapping a file down on my desk, and gave me a cheeky grin.

I dragged my gaze away from that inch of skin to the papers in front of me.

"You're welcome, by the way," she continued. "Malina was going to deliver this to you personally. I stole them off her desk."

"Thanks. What the hell are you wearing?"

She looked down at the dress and back at me. "Why are you so obsessed with my clothes?"

"It's Wednesday. On Wednesdays, you wear your navy pencil skirt." The one that hugged her ass. The one that I'd fantasized about shoving up over those smooth, round hips a few hundred times or so. And dammit, why couldn't I keep my mouth shut when this woman was in the room? Maybe I needed therapy. A twelve-step program.

"If I were a man and wore the same thing every Friday, you wouldn't have a comment. Karen from accounting wears the same black pants and black sweater every other day. Yet you insist on paying special attention to me?" She fluttered her eyelashes at me. "What did we say about special attention, Dominic?"

She was fucking teasing me, and I loved it. Almost as much as I hated it.

"You're annoying me. Go away," I said dismissively.

Instead, she perched on the edge of my desk, kicking her feet as if she had all the time in the world. If I rolled my chair a few inches to the right, I could push her knees apart and bury my face between her legs.

Any blood left circulating my body gave up and headed straight to my cock, which now throbbed like it had a migraine.

"Sign the paperwork, and I'll be gone from your life for the rest of the morning," she promised. "And if you must know, I have a date tonight."

"A date?" I was surprised the pen didn't snap in half in my hand. I felt something dark and oily spread through me. "Don't you have to work?"

I couldn't identify the feeling that grew inside me.

Rage? Fear? Blinding hate directed at a man I didn't even know?

"Just because I'm not *your* type doesn't mean every other man feels that way," she teased. "Payday is Friday, so I'm giving myself an actual night off."

I didn't trust myself to say anything. So I signed the contracts, pen tip scoring the paper. Her dress rode high on the thighs, and I couldn't help but notice. Inappropriate didn't even begin to describe the feelings stirring in me.

"You're wearing *that* on a date?" I hated myself for wanting her to feel insecure. Wanting her to change her mind so she wouldn't go.

She looked down, not remotely concerned with my opinion. "What's wrong with it? Linus approved."

Everything was wrong with it.

My chest felt tight, and why the hell was it so hot in this damn room?

"Depends. What kind of date is it?" To torture myself, I leaned back, changing the angle of my view. It was just a glimpse, and then I was averting my eyes. But it was long enough for me to know she was wearing underwear that matched that damn dress.

She raised an eyebrow at me. Like a silent challenge. *Go ahead and look. Tell me you're not interested. Lie to my beautiful, cocky face.*

Goddammit. I shouldn't have messed with her by wearing the vest yesterday. She'd outgunned me.

"First date. Drinks," she said.

"Drinks? That's it?" I was offended on her behalf. Nothing said "hookup" like just drinks. Not that I wanted her landing in a long-term relationship with someone. I also didn't want her enjoying a hookup.

I was not a good man, but as long as I wasn't dragging Ally down to the floor and fucking her, I was still better than my father.

"That's all I'm mentally prepared for at this point. I'm so rusty I feel bad for my next sex partner," she confessed.

Somewhere along the line, she'd started talking to me like we were *friends*. As if that moment of honesty in the bar, those emails exchanged, had somehow made us friendly. And while I craved her next confession, I also couldn't handle the intimacy. I was ripped down the middle, torn between wanting to know everything there was to know about this woman and wanting to forget she existed.

Something caught her eye, and she slid off my desk, wandering across the room.

I hated it when she walked away from me. It always felt like she took the light and heat with her.

I added that to my hate list.

Unable to help myself, I got up and followed her to the lightboard, where she studied the series of shots for an inside spread. I'd pulled two that I thought might work with the intent of dragging Linus in here to tell me which one made the most sense to show my mother.

"These are fun. I love that dress," she mused and pointed to a model in a gold silk gown. "Do you have one with her in motion?"

She scanned the subsequent shots, and I leaned in with her, just wanting to be closer to her. There was something about her that lured me in like a siren yet made me feel…safe. Comfortable. Fucking hard.

I tapped a shot that I'd pulled to the side. It had initially caught my eye, but the point of the shoot had been twofold: to showcase the vibrant red Galliano front and center and to subtly include a transgender model, the woman in gold.

"Oh, now that's a shot," she said, plucking it from the board and studying it.

The model in the gold gown twirled off to the side. The breeze from the fan had caught her hair and the skirt, lifting them both. She was the only one in motion. The red was still front and center, the model on the first rung of a ladder. The others were in varying traditional poses that in real life looked painful and contorted but through the lens showcased cuts and fabrics and colors.

"How did you meet?" I asked. *Please, for the love of my sanity, say a church group promoting abstinence.*

"Who?" she asked, rearranging the photos leading with the twirl.

"Your date."

"Oh. On a dating app," she said cheerfully.

Fuck.

"Here. Look at these. Now they tell a story. You're giving the eye an anchor point with the red. It'll land there, but it needs a secondary focus. You can't miss her: gold, twirl, smile. Her red lip plays off the focal dress and makes the whole piece visually satisfying. Headline goes here."

What she was saying made good sense, and I could have visualized it if I hadn't been so busy picturing her on some fuck buddy app shopping for a one-night stand.

"What kind of dating app?" I demanded.

She turned away from the lightboard and rolled her eyes. "I know. I know. Gola insisted on setting up a profile for me. By the way, from my sex to yours, a dick pic is *not* the right way to start a conversation."

I fantasized about hunting down every fucking weasel who'd sent her a cock and kicking them in the balls.

"Where's he taking you?" I asked, hating that I couldn't not ask. Hating that I needed to know.

"I'm meeting him at some bar called the Market. Have you been?"

Nicknamed the Meat Market, the lights were low, the

drinks were strong, and there were two hotels on the same damn block. I'd been.

"Yeah. Maybe I'll see you there," I said, pretending to scan the shots again. I couldn't forbid her from going. And as much as I wanted to, I couldn't make up a fake meeting that required her late-night presence. Not without her knowing it was a sham.

"You're going?" She sounded happy, and I wanted to ruin it. I wanted to make her feel as twisted up as I did.

"I'm meeting someone there myself. A date," I lied.

If I had to be tortured by thoughts of her hooking up with some random guy she met on a fucking app, then she could enjoy seeing me out on a date with real potential.

Her eyes narrowed, and I knew she could smell bullshit. "It's not on your calendar."

"I don't put my personal appointments on my work calendar." Another lie. I had no personal life. In fact, I couldn't even remember the last time I'd had sex. But I could remember every single fantasy I'd had about Ally.

"Then maybe I'll see you tonight," she said, grinning up at me.

I watched her leave.

And the second the door closed, I stalked into the bathroom. All I could see was that flash of red fabric between her legs. All I could think about was someone else getting to take them off her.

It was 9:30 in the morning, and I was fucking my fist, wishing it was her sweet, wet pussy clamped around my aching dick.

At this moment, I didn't like a single thing about Ally Morales.

26

ALLY

Austen was cute and smart and clearly in need of either a palate cleanser bang or some therapy.

But I couldn't take my eyes off the door of the bar long enough to decide if I was interested in him.

Because I was waiting for a man who didn't want to want me.

Ugh.

Purposefully, I turned my back to the door and my attention on the forty-two-year-old, divorced civil engineer. He'd ordered a glass of merlot and given the bartender a hard time about the pronunciation. I'd ordered a cheap, draft beer in case he insisted on splitting the check. He'd told me fifteen things about his ex-wife, and I'd mentioned Dominic's name twice.

As far as I was concerned, neither one of us was a catch.

I could feel it the moment *he* walked in. The air in the bar became electrically charged as if a bolt of lightning was about to strike the liquor bottles. I willed myself not to turn around, to focus on what Austen was saying.

"God, you must think I'm such a loser," he said, slumping his shoulders.

"What? Why?" I couldn't quite remember what he'd been saying. I was too busy trying to look like I was listening.

"I've told you more about my ex-wife than myself. I've asked you, like, one question, and that was just so I could lead in to another story about my ex. I'm so not ready for this."

"You and me both, pal," I said, raising my beer to his wineglass.

"My friends told me I needed a palate cleanser," he confessed, then blanched. "And I probably shouldn't have told you that. I'd find that really offensive if I were you. I am so bad at this. I'm not ready to date."

He was adorably bad at this.

"Don't feel bad," I said, bumping his shoulder companionably. "I'm not exactly in a healthy relationship space either."

"We're not going to hook up, are we?" Austen guessed.

I shook my head. "Nope. But you can tell me all about your ex and your divorce if you want."

He brightened.

The adorable man started at the beginning. Sophomore year of college.

I felt a tingle between my shoulder blades and *knew*. I didn't even jump when a familiar hand closed around my shoulder.

"Ally."

I turned and almost choked on my own damn tongue. Dominic had ditched his jacket and was rocking the rolled-up sleeves and suspender look. I finally felt like I understood what it was like to swoon. But there were no fainting couches in this place.

And then there was the other complication.

The stunning six-foot-tall woman who looked like she'd strutted off the cover of *Label* in a pearl pantsuit. She had flawless dark skin and the kind of short haircut that only really, really confident women with excellent bone structure could pull off. The only makeup she seemed to be wearing was a perfectly drawn red pout.

I was pretty sure I'd just fallen in insta lust with Dominic's date.

"Dom—Mr. Russo," I croaked.

His eyes narrowed.

It was a stupid game to be playing. I'd told him I'd be here. He'd told me he'd be here. And yet we were pretending to be surprised.

"Austen, this is—"

"Dominic Russo," Dominic said, offering his hand.

Poor unsuspecting Austen took it, and I thought I heard bone crunch.

"This is Delaney," Dominic said, introducing the unfairly beautiful woman. "Delaney, this is Ally."

Delaney not only had a flawless complexion, she also had a brilliant smile. I really, really wanted to hate her…or maybe make out with her.

"So nice to meet you, Ally," she said warmly.

Why couldn't she be a terrible person, I moaned internally.

Then I perked up. Maybe she was one of those closet bad people. Like one who parks in handicap spaces and throws fast-food bags out the window of her sports car at bike messengers.

"Ally and I work together," Dominic said. But the *way* he said it made it sound sinister. Like there was so much more to it than that. And if I were the beautiful Delaney, I'd be immediately suspicious.

"I work *for* Mr. Russo," I corrected.

Dominic clearly did not like me calling him that. Which made me want to do it more often.

Delaney and Austen introduced themselves to each other, since Dominic and I were too busy glaring at each other to do it.

"Get you something?" the bartender asked, interrupting awkward hour.

They ordered, and then Dominic took the freaking stool right freaking next to mine and pulled it out for Delaney.

She even *smelled* good.

The bar was busy. If Dominic Russo hadn't wedged himself in between me and his date, I would have been thinking about the tips the bartender was making. Instead, I was thinking about my boss's hand resting on the back of my stool. His leg pressing into my knee.

It was blindingly unfair that a man who didn't want to want me could get me in a sexual lather just by standing next to me. It had to be the cheese. I seriously needed to cut back. Everything Dominic did felt like foreplay.

Austen picked up the thread of the history of the greatest tragedy of all time with his proposal at their college graduation.

I tried to focus. But when Dominic picked up his drink, he kept his other hand on the back of my chair like he was claiming it. Claiming me.

The lightning feeling was back. Only now, it felt like the bolt was heading straight for me, and when it struck me, my head was going to explode. I didn't understand what this feeling was. All I knew was that I didn't have the time to explore it or the will to survive it. I *wanted* his hand there. I wanted him crowding me. I wanted those blue eyes locked on mine and those firm, stern lips moving against my ear as he told me he wanted to take me home.

I wanted to breathe.

"Would you excuse me for a minute?" I asked, cutting off Austen mid opine.

"Oh, uh, sure." He blinked his way out of his walk down memory lane.

I slid off my stool and had to press my entire body against Dominic's side to get out. I didn't bother apologizing, just made a beeline for the restroom. It was down a long hall, and at the end of it, just past the ladies' room, was an alcove that led to an emergency exit.

I'd made a logical claim: that I was capable of controlling myself around the man, that we could be friendly, not flirty. And yet here I was, trembling with sexual frustration in a bathroom hallway while the man I couldn't stop thinking about was on a date with the most beautiful human being in the entire universe.

What. The. Hell. Was. Wrong. With. Me?

Did I really just need to get laid? Would that uncoil this tightness in me? Would a few orgasms render me immune to him?

"Are you okay?"

I jumped and turned.

Dominic was staring at me like he couldn't decide whether to chop me into pieces or pull my hair and French-kiss me.

"No, I'm not okay!"

"What's wrong? Did that twerp say something? Do something?"

"Austen?" I laughed. "No. He's fine. He's still in love with his ex-wife."

"Then what's wrong?" he demanded, looking like he wanted to fix whatever it was.

"This is stupid, Dom."

"So it's Dom again?" He took a step closer, and that electricity fired up inside again.

"Shut up. I panicked."

"Why?" He had a ghost of a smile playing at the corners of his lips.

"For starters, I think I might be in love with your date. She's stunning."

"She is," he stupidly agreed. "She's a human rights lawyer."

So much for hurling fast-food bags at bikers.

"You should get back to your date," I said, crossing my arms over my chest.

"Not until you tell me what's wrong."

When I didn't answer, he took my arm and drew me into the alcove. The emergency sign burned red like a beacon. I felt like this situation qualified.

I was boxed in between the door and Dominic's broad chest. He rested his hands on either side of my head, caging me in between tattooed forearms.

"Talk."

"I'm not mentally prepared for another round of honesty with you," I confessed.

"Tough shit. Spill it, Maleficent, or I'm not letting you out of here."

He'd keep me there, boxed in without actually touching me, all weekend just to prove a point.

"Fine," I said. "I might be more attracted to you than I thought I was."

"And?" he said arrogantly.

"And I don't love seeing you on a date with a really, really, *really* beautiful, smart woman."

Those blue eyes weren't cold now. There was a victorious fire burning in them. And I was acutely aware that I was in immediate danger.

"I think I need to get laid. It's been too long," I confessed in a rush. "There's some kind of weird buildup of sexual energy, and if I don't let it out, I'm going to Mount St. Helens on you or some other innocent bystander."

He leaned in, waaaaaay too close for it to be anything but a come-on. I stood stock-still as he traced his nose over my cheek and jaw. "Good," he whispered.

"*Good?*" I gasped. I really wanted to hate him. But apparently my current priority was lusting after him.

"I want you to suffer the way I suffer," he said, his breath hot against my ear.

My heart was trying to blast its way out of my chest. I didn't know where the organ had gotten actual sticks of dynamite, but that was what was happening. My insides had turned to lava… or magma, whichever metaphor was most appropriate. And I could feel myself getting wetter and wetter between my legs. "That's not healthy, Charming. Friends don't want friends to explode."

"We're not friends," he said.

"What are we?" I asked. I was actually physically shaking from being so close and yet not close enough to the man.

"Feels more like enemies," he said. "One of us has to win, and one of us has to lose."

He didn't want to want me. But if he had to, he wanted me to suffer with him. *Ass.*

That felt accurate, but I was pheromone-drunk enough to wonder if we could both get what we wanted if we got naked once together. Enemies with benefits.

My skin was on fire. My little red thong was sopping wet. And my inner walls were having some kind of seizure. If he didn't back up or put some part of his body inside mine right now, I didn't think any court in the country would hold me responsible for my actions.

I reached up, and we both watched as I placed my palms on his chest. He was so warm, so solid. So obnoxiously sexy.

"You need to quit, Ally."

I dragged my eyes away from his chest. "Excuse me?"

"Quit your job," he said slowly. "If you don't work there, we can do something about this."

"You want me to quit my job so we can fuck each other out of our systems?"

So this was what an aneurysm felt like.

I'd always wondered.

His nostrils flared, and I swear his erection grew another half inch in diameter and flexed in his pants. "That's exactly what I want."

I was angry now. Incredibly turned on but very, very, *very* angry.

"We're both on dates, and you're telling me that if I quit my job—a job that is essential to my family's survival—that you'll be happy to fuck me," I summarized.

"I'll find you another job," he said, ignoring the being on dates part.

The smug, problem-solving balls on this guy. I wanted to kick him in them with the pointiest stilettos I could find.

"I can't afford to start over again." I kept my voice low, but it shook with emotion. I had *nothing* left in my account. I was hanging on by a thread until payday Friday. The beer on the bar? That was being paid for by lowering the thermostat to fifty degrees for the next two days. And Dominic Russo thought he had the right to demand that I give up *my* employment for *him*. "Besides, what makes you think you're worth it?" I seethed.

His blue eyes flashed, and he leaned in even closer.

I wanted to punch myself in the face for how much my stupid body *still* wanted him to touch me.

"We both know how it would be between us."

No. No. No. Nope. Never. Not gonna happen. No.

"Here's a thought. How about you go back to your date

before you say something even more incredibly offensive and stupid? Though I'm not sure you could if you tried." Fueled by feminine rage, I gave him a solid shove.

He took a step back, his gaze heated, hands fisted at his sides.

Oh. My. Lanta. That hard-on looked like it was determined to tunnel its way out of those very expensive trousers.

Dominic kept his gaze on me and reached down to adjust himself.

Holy baby goats in pajamas. I swear I almost blacked out. It was the most blatantly sexual thing he'd done in front of me.

And I wanted *more.*

I wanted to see him naked, spread out before me like a buffet.

I also never wanted to see him again.

He turned and started back toward the bar. Now I was staring at his very nice ass, wondering why I wanted to bite it *and* kick it. Then that unfairly fine ass was pausing.

"Oh, Ally?"

I made some kind of noise between a "huh" and a "murf."

"Delaney's not a date. She's Harry's wife."

"You smug son of a bitch. You brought her here to screw with me."

His smile was pure evil. "I'm not a good guy, Ally. Remember that."

"I've never forgotten it, you pompous jackass." He started toward me again, and I held up both hands. "This isn't fair, Dom. I don't like you playing with me like this."

His face hardened. "You think I *like* this? You think I like being the asshole who can't have you so I don't want anyone else to either? Do you know how I felt all day just knowing that you were dressing for someone else? That you were going out with someone? That another man was going to touch you tonight?"

I wanted to scream in frustration.

"This is so stupid. It's not that you *can't* have me. You *don't want* me. We could go home right now, get this out of our system, and be normal by tomorrow morning. But you don't want to."

"As long as we both work for *Label*, you are untouchable, Ally." He said it with an icy calm. "Quit."

I wanted to rearrange his stupid, sexy face. "No," I hissed. I needed a paycheck more than I needed a callous, condescending cock inside me.

"Then that means I'm not going to touch you. It also means that every time you have a date, I'll show up to ruin it because I am that asshole." It was his turn to show a flash of anger now. And for some reason—most likely cheese hormones—I didn't think it was directed at me.

No, Dominic Russo hated himself right now. For wanting me.

"That is a crock of shit, and you know it." I was losing my sanity. That was the only explanation for this night.

"I am aware. And I'm sorry. I am," he said, closing his eyes when I started to argue. "It's not fair. It's not remotely healthy. Believe me, I get that. It's not your fault. But I'm not a good guy, Ally. And life isn't fair. The sooner you understand that, the better."

"Oh, I get it loud and clear. And just what exactly will you be doing while I'm not dating? Fucking your way through every woman in Manhattan who doesn't work for you?"

He was back in my space again, and I could *feel* the pulse of his anger. It matched my own.

"I'll be doing what I've been doing since I met you," he rasped.

"What's that?"

"Fucking my goddamn hand and wishing it was you."

And there went my knees, buckling under me.

27

ALLY

It had not been my finest night.

After Dominic caught me when I all but swooned on him, I went back to the bar. Back to Austen. Back to the stool that my boss guarded like a gargoyle. And pretended like everything was just fine.

My neck hives had hives.

Dominic didn't touch me again, but his hand remained a firm presence on the back of my chair, a reminder of his claim.

I wished I had it in me to flirt with my "date" to knot Dominic up the way he did me, but I could only stare blankly at Austen while he talked about his wedding.

There I sat, debating my options.

Quit and get fucked.

Or stay and get fucked over.

I, of course, was taking the high road. My situation demanded that I keep this job. My circumstances would force me to keep my dignity when my body didn't seem capable of it.

Beside me, Dominic gave a rumble of a laugh in response to something Delaney said.

I was so tired. And sad. And angry. I'd wasted a night off. I could have had a visit with my father. I could have taken a catering shift or spent the entire evening figuring out how to patch the living room ceiling. Or, you know, making *actual* progress on a monumental task that was going to give me some breathing room.

Hell, I could have called my best friend, Faith, and caught up with her.

All these things were better than being sandwiched between a man who wasn't over his ex and one who was punishing me for not being stupid enough to quit my job to spend one night naked with him.

Because I was the one who had to compromise? Bullshit.

I fantasized about jabbing my elbow into his too-close torso, tossing my drink in his face, and then kneeing him in the balls.

Right now, I hated him. I loathed him.

The only thing I hated more was the fact that I *still wanted* Dominic Russo.

It was pathetic. My father hadn't raised pathetic. He'd instilled in me a deep and abiding faith in my inherent value. I was more than just some toy for a bored, horny executive to play with. I was better than a quick fuck.

But even as I told myself that, my underwear was getting damper and damper by the second. As if sex hormones had destroyed my brain so that nothing else mattered but being touched by the man next to me.

Every touch, no matter how innocent, how platonic, took on layers of meaning. Each one kicked off chain reactions in my body's chemistry. The brush of his pant leg against my calf right now was demanding more of my attention than Austen's story about… Oh, good God. His honeymoon.

Behind me, Dominic talked to Delaney easily, casually. They discussed everything from spring lines to kids to a humanitarian crisis her firm was following. But I *felt* the intensity he directed at me.

I'd had enough. I felt battered, exhausted, and sexually frustrated. The fact that I still wanted him to touch me made me doubt my decision-making abilities. Not since junior high had I been so hormonally compelled to make such a terrible decision.

That was what Dominic Russo was. A terrible fucking decision.

"Hey, do you want to split an order of cheese sticks?" Austen asked suddenly.

"You know what? I gave up cheese recently." Very recently. "And it was really nice meeting you, but I've got to get going," I told him.

He turned an adorable shade of pink. "I guess I really made a mess of this, didn't I?"

I slid off the stool, shoving Dominic out of the way with my ass. *Take that, jerk.*

"You just need time," I told Austen. And maybe some therapy. But didn't we all? "Don't feel bad about taking it."

"It was really nice to meet you, Ally," he said, rising. "Thanks for listening."

I laid my hand on his arm and pressed a kiss to his cheek. "I think you'll be just fine, Austen."

From behind, I felt a force field of disapproval slam into me.

I slid into my coat and turned to face him.

"Have a nice night, *boss*." To any innocent third party, the words sounded normal. But I pumped every ounce of venom I could muster into the look I shot him. We stared at each other for a long, hard moment.

"Aren't you staying for dinner?" he asked.

I blinked. That was a stupid, weird question.

"I'm not hungry," I said and pushed past him. "Delaney, it was nice meeting you," I called on my way to the door.

The bitter wind felt good compared to the fires of hell I'd left behind me.

It was still early, and I didn't want to head home to my cold, empty house to eat leftovers under the covers. I could go back to the office. If I finished up Shayla's changes to the graphics and sent them to her, I wouldn't have to come in early tomorrow. That meant more time with Dad.

There was just one thing I needed to do first. Decision made, I hunched my shoulders and headed into the wind.

The studio was closed for the night. Not many people in Midtown were interested in taking dance classes after eight on a weeknight. But I had a key and permission to use the space whenever I felt like it.

And tonight, I felt like it.

I changed into my dance clothes in the locker room, tied my hair back, and cranked my Fuck Off playlist on the speakers. I shut off all the lights except for the strands around the mirrors.

And I let go of it all.

Gretchen Wilson's "Her Strut" was all I needed to warm up. I paced toward the mirror, loosening up my shoulders with a shimmy. My hips had already found the beat and were working on making it their bitch.

I moved and spun and writhed around the studio's floor, pausing only to turn on the LED disco light.

A relentless beat from Nine Inch Nails washed over me, followed by Blondie. I was sweating now. My muscles were warm. My kicks higher. Backbends smoother. But that icy rage had yet to thaw in my chest.

Kid Rock's "So Hott" came blasting through the speakers, and I forgot about everything else but how it felt to move to music.

It had started with ballet class in elementary school. Even as a kid, it had been too rigid, too confining for me. I added tap. And then I'd fallen hard for Patrick Swayze in *Dirty Dancing*. I'd practiced MTV video routines in the living room while my father graded papers at the kitchen table. In high school, I'd made the trip into the city twice a week for a hip-hop dance class. There'd been dance classes in college. I'd even given ballroom a spin.

I'd learned the basics, the counts, the steps. And then I mashed them together in one celebration of movement.

Somewhere along the way, I'd started teaching. Dance made me feel like I was honoring my body, my life. It colored how I moved through this world.

I felt a tingle at the base of my spine. It worked its way up between my shoulder blades. If someone was watching me from outside, I couldn't see them through the windows. And it didn't fucking matter anyway.

I danced for myself.

The beat changed, and I melted down to the floor in a slow, muscle-stretching split. I crawled forward toward the mirrors, rocking and writhing on my hands and knees before climbing to my feet and kicking my leg into the air with violence.

Sweat ran in jagged rivers down my chest and back. My hair was escaping its confines in damp, sloppy curls.

Anderson East's gravelly voiced "All on My Mind" had me slowing down. I slipped into a familiar choreography I'd been working on and let myself pretend that nothing else existed on the other side of that glass.

28

DOMINIC

I hadn't thought it was possible to hate myself more.

And then I'd gone and out-assholed myself.

Ally had every right to want to murder me. Hell, I wasn't feeling too great about living with myself after tonight.

Delaney had tried to light into me after Ally and Austen had left—separately. I wasn't fooling her with the whole "she's just an employee" thing. So I'd gently shoved her in my car, directed Nelson to drive her home, and then decided to walk as many blocks as it took until my anger cooled or I got hypothermia.

I'd fucked up. I'd crossed so many boundaries in that hallway that I didn't think I'd ever be able to look at myself in the mirror again.

And then I'd gone and made it worse.

I hadn't known she'd be there. But I'd still gone.

When I got to the dance studio she'd listed on her employment application, well, I almost made a further fool of myself.

She was dancing in an empty studio, moving her body in ways that made me wish there was no glass between us, no barriers. I could hear the faint beat of her music as it pulsed inside.

Was this how my father had felt? Had he once been a normal man until something broke inside him and he couldn't stop himself?

Was I destined to follow in the footsteps of Paul Russo, predatory motherfucker and general dirtbag?

I couldn't stop watching her. She danced like it was a compulsion. Like she had to in order to keep breathing.

I understood it, recognized it even. But my compulsion wasn't this pure, beautiful art. Mine wasn't a celebration like Ally's.

Mine was dark. Dirty. And I was drowning in it.

I stood there watching her, aching for her, as the night chill slowly worked its way into my bones. Cold. I was a cold man. I wasn't capable of warmth. Of romance. Kindness. The woman on the other side of the glass deserved more than I could give her. But that didn't stop me from wanting her.

I'd taken things that weren't mine before. But not like my father. Never like my father.

My throat tightened, watching Ally slide to the floor and crawl toward the mirror.

I wanted what I couldn't have.

I wanted her to the point of desperation. And it made me hate myself just a little more.

The office was closer than home. I couldn't wait.

I gave a terse nod to building security and headed up to my office. The image of Ally crawling on her hands and knees was burned into my brain, distilled in my blood.

Tonight I'd done plenty of things to hate myself for. What was one more?

The forty-third floor was empty. And I fought my baser instincts by taking a slow lap. Daring myself not to do it. Willing myself to be strong enough not to.

But it was a losing battle.

I locked myself in my office, not bothering with the lights. By the time I crossed to the bathroom door behind my desk, I already had my cock out of my pants.

I kicked at the door, not bothering to close it all the way. It didn't matter. I had more pressing things to take care of.

Closing my eyes, I fisted my dick at the root, willing the pulsating need to slow or stop. I leaned against the vanity with my free hand and tried not to fucking come on the spot.

This was what she did to me. Every fucking day. I'd never wanted anyone with this gut-churning intensity before. I felt like my neurons were carving monuments to the woman in my brain.

"Fuck," I muttered under my breath, giving my shaft one violent stroke. "Ally."

I wished it was her. I wished I was pushing my way inside her while she wrapped her legs around me and breathed my name against my lips. I wished she was mine to take.

My vision was going black as I pumped into my hand. Hard, vicious strokes. I wouldn't last. I couldn't. Not when up against the imagined sighs from Ally's pretty, pink lips. Not when I could see her crawling to me, those brown eyes begging.

"Dom? Oh my God! I'm so sorry."

Fuck. Fuck. Fuck.

The bathroom door burst open, and there she was, back in her dress and those boots. Had I fucking conjured her? Was this some cruel joke?

"Get the fuck out, Ally," I growled.

"I'm sorry," she whispered. "I was dropping something off for Shayla, and there were papers for you to sign, and I used a key and…"

I chanced a glance at her in the mirror.

She was still there and she was staring at me, her mouth a perfect O. My throbbing dick jerked, and I held it in a choke hold.

I was so close to coming. And she was right there.

But this wasn't a fantasy. This was reality. There were rules.

And I was a goddamn monster.

Wanting her made me a monster.

"Dom," she said softly.

I squeezed my eyes shut. "Ally, you need to go." My voice shook.

"You said my name. Before," she said, then she took a step closer. She looked dazed.

She'd heard me say her name while I was stroking my own cock.

"Ally, I can't hold on. Get the fuck out of here," I said through clenched teeth. Desperation was bitter in my mouth.

She was next to me now. I could smell her goddamn lemon shampoo. "If you weren't worried about anything else," she began softly, "would you want me to stay?"

"Go. Now," I growled. I could feel my pulse in my head and the crown of my cock simultaneously.

She laid a hand on my shoulder, and it almost broke me. "Answer me, Dom."

"Jesus. Please, Ally." I was begging her now. If I released my hold on my dick, I'd come. And she'd stand there watching. I couldn't do anything but clamp my fist around my goddamn hard-on and look at her.

"Are you thinking about me?" she asked.

"Yes." I snapped out the confession through gritted teeth. "Happy? I'm always thinking of you."

"But you don't want me enough to bend the rules."

I chanced a look at her. Her lids were heavy, lips parted and wet as if she'd just licked them. "They are rules for a reason."

She stepped around me and slid between me and the vanity. The tip of my dick was centimeters away from her stomach. "So you can want to touch me, to fuck me. But the rule is more important."

Sweat was running down my back.

"Something like that," I breathed out. Right this second, my own logic didn't even make sense.

"I'm so pissed at you, Dom. But apparently that doesn't mean I don't want to know what it feels like to have you inside me. And I hate that," she confessed.

"Join the club," I rasped.

I tried to think about every unsexy thing in the universe, but nothing could tear my brain away from Ally. Not when she was stepping those fuck-me boots apart in front of me and reaching for the hem of her dress.

"Don't you fucking do it," I warned her.

"Can I show you? Please? I won't if you don't want me to."

I wanted it more than I wanted anything in the entire fucking universe. More than I wanted to go back to my old life. More than I wanted my father to not be a monster. More than I wanted to come. "God. Yes."

She lifted the hem of her dress, revealing those red panties I'd caught a glimpse of earlier. There was a wet spot on the front. She was fucking wet.

"Is that for me?" The words tore up my throat like they were made of glass.

"I think about you too, Dom. I like fighting with you,

flirting with you. And apparently, you being a high-handed alpha asshole is a turn-on too. And I don't like it any more than you do."

"I can't be with you, Ally. Not like you want. Not while you work here."

"And I can't quit," she whispered.

My dick was throbbing and turning an angry purple. I loosened my grip by a millimeter, relieved when I didn't explode right then and there all over her.

Watching me, she slipped her thumbs into the waistband of her panties and slid them down her legs. I didn't see a damn thing because the dress skimmed down, covering her goddamn promised land. Red cotton on smooth, milky skin. My dick spasmed. I resumed my choke hold.

She stepped out of them and handed them to me. They were warm. I barely restrained myself from holding them to my face and breathing them in like a fucking pervert. "Give me something to think about tonight, Dom. Please."

She was handing me a goddamn fantasy. And that "please." Those liquid honey eyes pleaded with me and had me taking an even firmer grip on my shaft.

Her petal-pink lips parted as she watched me, and I imagined her on her knees in front of me. I couldn't stop myself. Not even if I'd tried. Not even if the entire board of directors strolled through the door right now. Wrapping her underwear around my fist, I gave my abused shaft a long, hard stroke.

I groaned. But the whimper that tore its way out of her throat gave me the strength to hang on. I wanted more noises like that from her. And I wanted them all to myself.

We were inches apart in this bathroom, and I'd already crossed so many lines. What was one more? But this was *the* line. One my father would have crossed in a heartbeat without a second thought. Because it gratified him. Because he thought he deserved it.

I was different. I knew I didn't deserve it. I didn't deserve her.

"Ally. I can't." I shook my head, pinching my eyes closed. I couldn't be like him.

"Okay, Dom." She sounded so fucking disappointed, and it made me feel even worse. I was the bad guy, even when I was trying to be the good guy.

I heard the sound of the bathroom door closing softly. And when I opened my eyes, I was alone in the washroom.

Alone again.

I couldn't even go after her to apologize. Because I was too busy jerking off into those red panties. My balls ached as they drew up against me, and I felt it build at the base of my spine. In seconds, I was coming so hard it hurt. Watching in bitter, deviant fascination as my orgasm covered the wet spot that she said was for me. I kept coming, huge, wrenching spurts that couldn't be contained by a little swatch of cotton. But I didn't care.

"Ally." Her name scorched my throat. "Ally."

29

ALLY

The name of the game was avoidance.

After a long, sleepless night punctuated by not one but two icy showers, endless mental pep talks, and searching the internet for "distraction techniques," "how to stop picturing my boss naked"—don't Google that one, by the way—and "how to become a monk," I'd come to the conclusion that my only rational course of action was to pretend that Dominic Russo didn't exist.

I'd been furious with the man. And then one glimpse of the purple-headed sea monster in his pants, and I'd gone all pizza delivery porno on him.

The pain on his face when I'd walked in on him had burned into me. As had the vision of him fisting that magnificent fucking erection through his open trousers.

Me. He'd been thinking about *me*. And when I made it clear that I was available, that he could have the real thing, he'd shut me down. The man was masturbating to a fantasy about me, and he still didn't want the real thing.

The only thing that made any kind of sense was that he was hiding behind the rules, using them as an excuse. Because I was Elizabeth Bennet and so far beneath him, it made him sick to entertain the thought of actually being with me.

That pissed me off all over again.

The next morning, I slunk into the admin pool, surveying the room like a gentle woodland creature scenting the air for… whatever eats gentle woodland creatures.

"Nice of you to join us," Malina said snidely.

I was beginning to think she did everything snidely. Today, she was dressed in a winter-white sheath dress with her hair scraped back in a perfect platinum bun. Her mouth looked as if it had either had a run-in with some bees this weekend or she'd paid a visit to a syringe of fillers.

"You look nice," I observed.

She rolled thickly lashed eyes with contempt. "Ugh. Shut up."

I shrugged, then flopped down in my chair to boot up my computer. While it chugged to life, my nice new work phone signaled a text.

Dominic: We need to talk.

My brain screamed, *Oh hell no*, as my traitorous lady parts started an inappropriate celebration.

I was *not* putting myself in a situation where I could see, hear, smell, or be within fifteen feet of the man. I didn't know what was going on biologically with me, but I was an adult, gosh darn it. I was not a hormone-driven teenager with no respect for consequences.

The one thing that I'd managed to drill into my head

overnight was that this paycheck was the only thing keeping my father where he needed to be. And I wasn't going to do anything to jeopardize that. At least that was what I'd told my vagina last night.

Panic danced its way down my spine. If he walked in here and demanded to see me, I didn't trust myself not to do something stupid. It was fifty-fifty on whether I'd punch him in the face or just go straight for his zipper with eager hands.

Fortunately, salvation arrived in the form of my supervisor. Zara was hustling down the aisle between the rows of cubicles, sticky notes in one hand, Sharpie in the other. "I need a volunteer to go out and—"

"I'll do it!" I shot out of my seat like I was spring-loaded.

Zara looked at me like the weirdo I was. "You don't even know what the assignment is."

"Doesn't matter," I said desperately. "If it's out of the building, I'll take it. I'll take *all* the out-of-the-building tasks."

"It's ten degrees and sleeting outside," Gola said, appearing behind Zara. She looked concerned. I didn't blame her.

"I like the cold. Love it," I insisted. Words I'd never strung together in my entire life.

"Well, that makes my job easy," Zara said. "I didn't even have to bribe anyone with lunch." She handed me six sticky notes and then snatched her hand back when I ripped them out of her grasp.

"What's the hurry? Is there a sale at the soup kitchen?" Malina sniffed, giving my outfit a judgmental once-over.

I wasn't head to toe in designer labels, but I looked good. *You know, in case I accidentally ran into a certain someone who ceased to exist.*

I was wearing a swingy plaid skirt over ribbed tights. Solid thrift store finds. Linus had liberated my last-season thigh-high boots from the Closet for me. My turtleneck was a leftover from my Colorado life when I'd actually had more than thirty-two dollars in the bank after bills.

Come on, payday gods, and smile your blessings upon my bank account.

"Mal, soup kitchens are free," Gola sighed.

"What's the matter, Malina? Couldn't find any small children to kick on your way to work this morning?" Zara asked, rearranging the rest of her notes.

Malina made a hissing noise and primly returned to her chair.

I picked up the bag I'd dumped on the floor and started for the elevators. I didn't really think Dominic would come looking for me. He was more of a summoner. But I also wasn't willing to take that chance.

"What's going on with you?" Gola asked, her long legs eating up the distance between us as I yanked the glass door to the elevators open. "Everything okay?"

"Everything's great," I said. I felt the telltale red flush creep up my neck. I was a shit liar. "I'm great."

She looked unconvinced. "By 'great,' you clearly mean 'about to lose my damn mind.'"

I frantically stabbed the Down button on the elevator. Three times. "Ha! You look so pretty today," I said.

The stairwell door opened on the far end of the hallway, and the man who didn't exist stepped out. His eyes went straight to me.

I turned my back and stabbed the button again.

"Ally, I say this with love," Gola said. "You need a massage and a facial."

I could feel his gaze on me. It felt like wildfire licking its way over my skin. I had to get out. Now.

The merciful god of high-rise elevators shined his divine

love upon me, and the doors opened on a dignified ding. I stepped inside, hurling my body into the already crowded car. I couldn't afford to wait for another one.

"I'll call you later," I promised Gola frantically as I jabbed the Close button.

Stubbornly, the doors refused to close.

Dominic was closing in, stalking toward me with murder in his eyes and—was that a fucking vest? That son of a bitch!

I let go of the button, ready to take a stance against him, against the vest. Just then, the damn doors began to slide toward each other.

His blue eyes were icy and troubled. He looked the same as he had last night, except he wasn't, you know, violently masturbating and rasping out my name.

Was it weird that the sexiest moment of my life hadn't actually involved having sex?

I went weak in the knees with a desire so carnal I worried I might die on the spot.

"Can I help you with something, Mr. Russo?" Gola squeaked as he charged forward.

I glared at him, channeling all my angst and maybe a little bit of the heat emanating from my below-the-waist region through the sliver of space between the doors until they closed, severing our connection.

Everyone else in the elevator was staring at me, but I ignored them. A bead of sweat worked its way down my back as I let out a long breath. It felt like a victory. Like I'd just escaped a hungry lion. This dumbass gazelle would live to gazelle another day. The triumphant feeling stuck with me until I crossed the lobby and ducked out into the miserable cold, gray world.

My assignments were a mixed bag of pickups, drop-offs, and location snooping for various departments.

Halfway through my list, I broke down and ducked into a coffee shop. It was warm and cozy inside. It was also full of people who reminded me of the old me. Designers and writers, huddled over laptops, setting their own schedules, kicking back with foamy lattes they could afford.

I ordered a tall black coffee and looked longingly at the pastries in the case. Then I remembered the thirty-two dollars in the bank. Payday was tomorrow. I just had to hang in until then. I'd cut it too close. I was almost out of groceries. The gas bill was due. And I was as far behind as I could get on Dad's bills. I was holding my breath until that direct deposit landed at 12:01 a.m. Then, after writing those checks, I was going to buy myself a shot of whiskey. A bottom-shelf shot.

The music in my earbuds cut off as my text alert sounded. I knew before even looking at the screen who it was.

Dominic: You can't run forever. We will have this conversation sooner or later.

I grabbed my coffee off the counter and slid into a chair in the corner facing the steamy glass window.

Me: Nope.
Dominic: Where are you?
Me: You can't fire me.
Dominic: I'm not trying to fire you. I'm trying to apologize and promise it will never happen again. If anything, you could have me fired. You should have me fired.
Me: What is wrong with you?

Dominic: I don't know.

Dominic: It's safe to talk to HR. I wouldn't stop you from doing that.

I gave up trying to text through still-frozen fingers and dialed.

"Ally." The way he said my name had my lady parts clenching. "Where are you? Can we talk? It doesn't have to be alone. I can have an HR rep—"

"What the hell is wrong with you?" I demanded. The woman next to me carefully studying the Bible glared at me.

"You're going to have to be more specific," he said in my ear.

"Your office door was locked, Dom," I pointed out at a more modulated volume.

"It doesn't matter."

"Your office door was locked, and it was well after hours. You didn't lure me there, you idiot. I was dropping off files, and I used the key Greta keeps in her desk."

"My behavior was unconscionable," he said, his voice low and rough around the edges.

"Oh, please," I scoffed. "You should see what I get up to with a vibrator on Saturday nights."

"Ally." He bit out my name like he was in physical pain.

The guy in the lemon-yellow ski jacket texting on his phone like it was a full-time job shot me an interested look.

"Not gonna happen, buddy," I told him.

He went back to texting, and now I worried he was doing one of those live-tweet things. *Hey, Twitter, I'm sitting at a coffee shop minding my own business when the chick next to me starts talking about vibrators…*

"What?" Dominic asked.

"Not you. Well, also you. I'm not trying to harass you,

Dom. My point is that everyone acts unconscionably on their own time. I just happened to barge into your time. You didn't harass me. You didn't assault me. You *rejected* me."

"I think you're missing the bigger picture," he said dryly.

"Yeah, well, I think you missed the boat. You had a chance to get this out of your system, and you said no."

"I'm your *boss*. And you're being really stubborn about quitting."

"At this point, I don't really give a flying fucksicle, Dominic."

Bible study lady cleared her throat in a judgy kind of way and nodded her head toward the teenagers across from her.

"Sorry," I mouthed to them. "Look, you had your chance. You made it crystal clear that you have no desire to…get coffee with me," I said to Dominic.

"Coffee?"

"It's a euphemism. There's Bible studying happening here," I hissed into the phone. "Deal with it."

"Fine. I believe I made it clear that I've had nothing *but* desire to get into your fucking pants, Ally," he growled.

"Yeah, yeah. But you're not going to act on it, blah blah blah. And I'm not going to throw myself at you. You didn't harass me. I didn't harass you. As of this second, we have nothing to talk about ever again."

"So you're just going to avoid me for the rest of your life?"

"That's exactly what I'm going to do. Because I deserve better. I deserve a guy who isn't appalled at being physically attracted to me."

"That's not fair—"

"Shut up, Charming. Here's what we're going to do moving forward. Absolutely nothing. We will be polite at work. We won't text or email or chat or spar or fight. We won't ever be alone. We will never get coffee."

"Are you afraid of me, Ally?"

"I'm afraid that if I'm in a room alone with you, I won't be able to control myself."

I heard the intake of breath on his end and wondered if he was crushing the phone in his hand.

Bible study lady was now discussing a psalm at full volume, trying to drown me out.

"Control yourself?" Dominic's tone was deceptively neutral. But I knew, I *knew* he was anything but.

"Yeah, Dom. I'm afraid I might walk right up to you and break your damn nose."

His laugh was dry, humorless. "You're a hell of a woman, Ally."

"You're damn right I am. And you're the dumbass who missed out."

"I am," he agreed.

But I didn't want his pity agreement. I wanted to pretend he never existed. "Great. Now that we have that settled, get off my phone."

30

ALLY

Friday morning, I peeked into the payroll department, making sure the summons wasn't some kind of Dominic trap to get me to talk to him.

A never-ending loop of every mixed message and rejection from the man played in my head.

It should have been enough to overpower any carnal desire. But every time I thought about the man fisting his cock and *saying my name*, I went a little weak in the knees.

I chalked it up to cheese hormone withdrawals and doubled down on my decision.

There was officially no way in hell that I was going to (a) throw myself at any man too dumb or stubborn to enjoy it or (b) become some sexual-harassing subordinate. I needed this job. I needed this paycheck. I did not need my boss lusting after me and then making me feel like a fool.

I was going to buckle down, earn my paycheck, and dig my way out of the massive debt I'd managed to accumulate.

All I had to do was get through the rest of this day and I'd be boss-free for the entire weekend. I had two bartending shifts, a Saturday night catering gig, and a Sunday morning dance class, plus hours of home renovation glory to keep me occupied this weekend. I would come in Monday detoxed from Dominic and cheese and back on track.

Best of all, today was payday. I might be able to buy some actual groceries.

"Hi, I'm Ally Morales," I said, introducing myself to the woman at the first desk. "I had a message to come in this morning."

She gave me a sympathetic smile. *Uh-oh.*

"Ally, I'm afraid I have bad news. There was a mix-up with your direct deposit, and it's going to take until Monday to sort out."

My ears turned on their *whomp whomp whomp* filter as the woman in Marc Jacobs explained about transposed numbers on the routing number.

"So what does this mean?" I asked, blinking out of my stupor.

"It means your paycheck won't be deposited until Monday."

In my head, I ran through every swear word I knew. Even some I wasn't sure about.

"I can take a check. Or cash." Or one of those sparkling bracelets she was wearing that jangled when she moved her hand.

Desperation sweat steamed up my armpits. *Just so you know, folks, dollar store deodorant does* not *cut it in stressful situations.*

Marc Jacobs Lady flashed me another sympathetic look. "There's nothing I can do at this point. You'll just have to wait until Monday."

Wait until Monday.

I had stretched the nursing home's grace period as far as it would go without snapping it like a rubber band. Tomorrow morning at 9:00 a.m., the late fees plus a good-faith payment had to be made. I had to cough up $5,327.94. Or else.

I turned and walked out without another word. Into a hallway with beautiful people in beautiful clothes who had never been hungry, never had to choose between food and heat. Or food and their father's well-being.

It was amazing how many people didn't know what real desperation felt like. It was incredible that this was the first time in my thirty-nine years that I was feeling it. I'd had a life. A father who loved me. A career. Savings. God. That felt like ages ago rather than six short months.

I had almost $2,000 squirreled away. My paycheck was supposed to cover the rest.

What was I going to do between now and tomorrow to come up with more than $3,000 in less than twenty-four hours?

Maybe I could throw myself on Front Desk Deena's mercy and beg for more time?

On cue, my cell phone rang. It was the nursing home's office calling. Panic tickled at my throat.

"Hello?"

"Ms. Morales." Deena's wicked witch of New Jersey voice turned my blood to ice. "I was just calling to see if I needed to instruct the nursing staff to start packing your father's possessions today." She sounded downright cheerful.

"That won't be necessary." I choked out the words.

"Well, isn't that good news?" she said, her tone making it clear that she didn't believe me. "If it's more convenient for you, I'd be happy to accept your check today."

I gulped. "Tomorrow is good." I needed every second between now and then.

"I'll see you tomorrow at nine sharp," Deena said. It might have been my imagination, but I thought I heard her cackle just before she hung up.

Shit. Shit. Shit.

Reeling, blinded by unshed tears, I started to move.

I cut the corner short and bounced off a hard, vested chest like a pinball. But he didn't catch me. It was the other man next to him who steadied me.

"Ally, right? Are you okay?" he asked. Christian James. Designer. Dimples. I bet he wouldn't reject me if I handed over my panties. My brain was a roller coaster of confusion and then fear. I'd failed. Dad was going to lose his bed because of me.

"Fine," I lied, the word coming out like I was being strangled. Choking on my own failure. My neck felt hot and itchy.

"Ally, what's wrong?" Dominic was wrestling me out of Christian's gentle grip.

I couldn't catch my breath. *Label*'s classy walls were closing in on me. Dominic's blue, concerned eyes.

I wrenched free from him. "Nothing," I wheezed. He reached for me again, and I shook my head before fleeing for the door to the stairs.

Afraid he'd follow me, I went up instead of down at a run. By the time I hit the roof and burst through the door into the biting cold, I was on fumes. Mentally, emotionally, physically. This was it. Rock bottom. If rock bottom happened on top of a skyscraper in Midtown in February.

I dragged in an icy breath and let it out in a silvery cloud. Again and again until the tightness in my chest started to loosen.

"Panic attack. Not heart attack," I whispered to myself as I plastered myself against the wall and waited for it to pass.

There was no room for panic. No time to lament. I needed a solution. I needed help.

I gave it another minute, hoping for divine inspiration from the goddess of skyscraper meltdowns. When none came, I did the next best thing. I dragged my phone out and dialed Faith.

My best friend's face popped up on my screen, an eye mask sitting crookedly on her forehead.

"'Sup?" she rasped. Her natural jet-black hair was platinum blond with subtle streaks of violet shoved up into a lopsided knot.

"Late night?" I wheezed.

"I own forty percent of a strip club. What do you think?"

Club Ladies and Gentlemen was an equal-opportunity Miami-themed strip club with men, women, and a troupe of talented drag queens.

It was fabulous and even classy in a debauched, naked kind of way.

"Tonight's amateur night, right?"

She sat up in bed, bobbling the phone. I stared up at her ceiling for a few seconds and caught an accidental nip slip out of her hot pink negligee, because of course my best friend slept in lingerie.

"Are you coming?" she shrieked, picking the phone back up.

"How much did you say I can make?" I asked. Faith had been trying to convince me to come in on amateur night since I came back home.

"All participants get a hundred dollars plus two free drinks. Then the top three contenders split the prize money. You, with your ass-shaking abilities, are a shoo-in for first place, even without me as a judge. That's gonna be twenty-five hundred easy. Plus tips."

She had me at free drinks. And $2,500.

I wanted to cry. And all I had to do was shake my ass. Oh, yeah, and show a club full of strangers my boobs. How was this my life?

"I don't have to do any private dances or anything, right?" I clarified.

"Nope. Not unless you want to."

"Okay," I said, closing my eyes.

Ask her for the money. Ask her. Just say the words. Please help me, Faith.

But I'd made promises. And right now, those unbroken promises were the only thing I'd done right.

"You must need cash bad," she observed. She picked up an open can of soda on her nightstand and sipped through a Twizzler. Faith was one of those annoying people whose metabolism sped up in her thirties.

"Things are getting a little tight," I said lamely.

"Seriously, babe. If you need money—"

"I'm fine. Everything is fine. What time should I be there?"

She shot me an incredulous look.

"I'm serious," I insisted. "It'll be fun." *Lies. So many dirty, little lies.*

"Eleven."

Silver lining. At least I could squeeze in a few hours on the bar at Rooster's before my humiliation. Every dollar counted now.

"What should I wear?" It came out as a squeak, and I cleared my throat.

"Oh, honey. I've got you covered. Or uncovered. Wink!" Faith grinned.

My stomach lurched again. But I had no choice. I was out of options unless I wanted to realize my father's worst fears. I'd made this mess, and I'd clean it up no matter what it took.

"Okay." I fortified myself with another cold breath. "I'll see you at eleven."

"Can't wait! You're going to do great. Eleven p.m. backstage at Club Ladies and Gentlemen. Be there and ready to bare," she sang.

"Yeah. See you then," I said and disconnected.

I held the phone to my forehead in a lame attempt to ward off the headache that was starting to drill its way into my brain.

I gave myself another thirty seconds of fear and misery, of cursing the universe for its stupid plan for me. Then I straightened my shoulders and marched toward the door.

I would do what I had to. Just like my father had raising me. And someday, many, many, many years from now, I might look back and laugh at this disaster.

31

ALLY

Vance was a pale guy with a comfortable beer gut who dressed like a *Miami Vice* extra and talked like a Canadian Tony Soprano. He wore white pants and a red button-down with parrots and palm trees. A trio of gold chains tangled around his generous carpet of chest hair.

"Water and coffee are free. First aid kit's in the locker room in case you pinch yourself on the pole or get blisters from the shoes and whatnot," he explained as he led me along a long, mirrored wall that reflected the pink and purple stage lights. The bass was thumping, and there was a woman onstage wrapped around the pole like a koala. "On amateur nights, I spring for bagels for all the gals. You get a locker with a combination lock. Rule is no girl leaves the building alone. We got a big, beefy security staff that doesn't mind sendin' a message to patrons. No touching the dancers or the servers or the bartenders."

I nodded grimly and pretended not to see the sea of

men—and some women—who were crowded into booths and around round tables along the stage. All there to witness me giving up my last shred of dignity.

"You get two drinks from the bar per shift," Vance said, holding open an Employees Only door for me. "I wouldn't advise drinkin' 'em both at the same time, since Esther makes 'em pretty damn strong. You might fall offa the pole, eh?"

"Ha," I managed.

I followed his red-parroted shoulders down a long hallway.

"Boss told me to bring you straight back when you got here," he explained, tapping out a cursory knock before opening another door with a sign that said No Pants, No Problem. "Special delivery, boss."

"Boss" was Faith Vigoda, my best friend since fifth grade. She'd always reminded me of a tall, Black Gwen Stefani who couldn't sing. But Faith didn't need to sing. She'd been born with a genius business acumen.

The summer before sixth grade, her lemonade stand made so much money she got permits and two part-time employees. She paid for college with cash earned by running an illegal term paper–writing business for other schools. After college, she went legit, diversifying into property rentals and finally the entertainment business.

She'd been partner here for four years and had single-handedly doubled the club's revenue.

"I'm so excited you're here," she squealed, jumping up from behind her desk to grab me. She pulled me in for a hug that I desperately needed.

"It's so good to see you." And despite the circumstances, it really was.

"You've been a little busy lately," she said, forgiving me. "How's your dad? How's his leg? Tell me about work."

I flopped down in a pink velvet wingback chair and filled her in on everything but the financial situation and Dominic Russo, painting a picture of a dutiful daughter and diligent employee.

"None of that explains why you're suddenly here for amateur night."

"Things are just a little tight right now. My first paycheck from the magazine was late, so I figured..." I shrugged and trailed off lamely.

"Uh-huh. Well, we'll definitely be talking about all the things you're not saying after. But first, let's get you dressed. How do you feel about sexy cowgirl or professional cheerleader?"

Nauseous.

"What do you think?" I asked, stepping carefully out of the dressing area on five-inch, white patent leather stiletto platforms.

Faith was spinning slow circles in a salon chair parked in front of a kitschy makeup mirror while skimming profit reports. She stopped and put down the paperwork and made me do a twirl.

This was not like Fairy Godfather Linus's makeover. No. This particular transformation involved a checkered long-sleeve shirt with snaps knotted between my breasts, cheeky blue boy shorts that were already climbing their way up my ass, and sparkly blue pasties that I hoped no one else would see.

"Don't pick the wedgie. Wedgies get more tips," she insisted when I tried to do exactly that.

I sighed through gritted teeth and tried not to think about what I was going to be doing in about nine minutes. Gulp.

"You look great," she said. She stood and shoved her hands into my hair, ruffling it.

"Should I go heavier on the makeup?" *Maybe level it up to clown or mime so I could at least have part of my body disguised?*

"No. Wholesome is good on amateur night. You look like someone I'd take home to Mom if I were a man…or a lesbian."

"Tequila," I said weakly.

"Tequila, girl."

We both shuddered.

"Have a seat," she said, pointing to the makeup chair. "I'll get you some water. You're gonna sweat up there, so stay hydrated."

I was already breaking out in a cold sweat.

There was a closed-circuit TV in the dressing room that showed the tables around the stage and bar. It had gotten more crowded since I'd arrived. I tried not to calculate how many eyes would be seeing my boobs tonight.

The backstage area was cleaner and cheerier than I thought it would be. I'd unfairly pictured strung-out naked women slumped in metal chairs, chain-smoking cigarettes and dusting each other with body glitter.

There was definitely glitter, but the only dancer I'd seen had arrived in her minivan from her Pilates class with a fresh fruit smoothie. She wasn't even here to dance. She was MC-ing amateur night. The rest of the amateurs were corralled in a secondary locker room location so I could have my breakdown in peace.

There was a long, low sofa along one wall buried under a mound of furry pink pillows. Five vanities decorated with pictures and personal trinkets like high school lockers took up the opposite wall. There was an open wardrobe area, much smaller than *Label*'s Closet but just as neatly organized and containing just as many sequins. Soft, pink-toned lighting gave everyone a fresh, dewy-looking complexion, and oil diffusers filled the room with the delicate scents of peppermint and eucalyptus.

Faith returned with a glass of cucumber lemon water, and I guzzled half of it.

"I don't feel so good," I confessed.

She leaned down, putting her hands on the arms of the chair. "Listen here, Ally. Lots of people dance for money. Prima ballerinas, Jane Fonda, Laker Girls, backup dancers, Rockettes. All women who make money by moving their bodies. There's nothing remotely shameful about it," Faith insisted. "You aren't doing anything wrong. And anyone who tells you that you are is—"

"Part of the patriarchy," I finished for her. We'd had this discussion a few times before.

But never while I was already half-naked and planning to get more naked.

"That's my girl." She squared me off to face the mirror. "Do you love to dance?"

I nodded.

"Lemme hear you, babe. Do you love to dance?" she asked again.

"I love to dance," I said. I did. I really did. The only real difference, besides the hungry audience with fistfuls of cash and dirty fantasies, was that I'd be doing this dance with no bra on.

"You love the music, the lights, the dancing. And that's all you have to think about. You're going out there and you are celebrating your body. You're doing this for you. Not them. They're allowed to watch, but this is all about you."

"All about me," I said, more firmly this time. I wondered if Faith had ever considered a career in life coaching.

"Good girl. Now who has the power?" she asked.

"I do," I whispered.

"I can't hear you."

"I do," I said again.

"That's right. You do. So you're going to go out there and shake that talented ass of yours. And then you know what you're going to do?"

"Burn these clothes and get drunk?"

"No. Well, maybe. But first, you're going to collect the money you earned, and then you're going to come have a drink with me at the bar and explain to me just how bad things really are."

I winced.

I knew I could ask her for the money. And I knew she'd give it to me. No questions asked. No expectation of repayment. But I'd promised Dad. It was the only way I hadn't let him down yet.

I'd sworn that we would handle this the way we'd handled everything else: together. A two-man team against a disease that we both knew would eventually win.

My father was a proud man, and he'd instilled that particular value in me. If I accepted money from someone to help pay for his care, he wouldn't just be disappointed; he'd be devastated. I promised him he'd never be a burden, and I promised myself that he would never have the opportunity to feel like a burden.

Which was why I'd been lying to him on his good days, telling him his insurance was covering everything.

I made a promise.

And I'd do whatever it took to fix this on my own. Even if it involved pasties. My Morales pride would keep me warm on that stage.

"So what should my dancer name be?" I asked, changing the subject before Faith could demand a full accounting of my monthly bills.

"Hmm," she mused, popping a blue raspberry lollipop in her mouth and studying me. She grinned. "Candie Couture."

"Oh God," I groaned. "Can I at least spell it with a *y*?"

"Nope. It's *ie*." Faith smirked. "Now close your mouth."

"Wh—" My choking and gasping after eating the first spray of body glitter she aimed at me interrupted the question.

32

DOMINIC

I was going to fucking kill her. Drag her off the stage and into the alley and murder Little Miss Candie Fucking Couture with a Dirty Secret. But first, I was going to kill every son of a bitch in this room who dared to look at her. Starting with that greasy, gold-toothed dipshit in the corner who was grabbing his junk through his track pants. He'd be first.

When I overheard… Okay, fine. When I *eavesdropped* on her call on the roof, I thought I was hallucinating. My wholesome, untouchable admin wasn't really planning to take off her fucking clothes in front of a crowd of perverted strangers for money.

Yet here I was, sitting in a black vinyl booth with a table tent advertising two for one splits of champagne to share with your "favorite dancer." And there she was. On the stage in shorts so short I didn't think they qualified as clothing in front of at least a hundred and fifty assholes—myself included. She was squinting into the lights as a bunch of soon-to-be-dead men—and women—whistled and catcalled.

If I were feeling more charitable, I'd say I couldn't blame them. She looked unbelievably tempting.

But she also looked terrified.

I'd had enough. I started to slide out of the booth with the intent of getting her off that stage. She didn't belong there, and it was beyond fucking time that she came clean about everything.

But the music was starting, and the crowd was leaning closer. When she wrapped a hand around that brass pole, I forgot what I was doing and dropped back down into the booth.

The song was slow, dirty, tortured. I liked it. It reminded me of me.

She hooked a leg around the pole and spun, dropping lower and lower circling toward the stage. Her hair whipped out behind her, and when she stood again, it covered one smoky eye. My fingers itched to push it back, to hook it behind her ear, and drag her in for a kiss.

I wanted to scan the audience—and I used that term loosely—for any threats, but I couldn't tear my gaze away from the stubborn, desperate, delicious woman on the stage. I hoped to God security was up to the challenge tonight, because if anyone laid a hand on her, one single finger on her, I was going to lose my shit.

She moved her body as if a lover was touching it, her own hands slipping over those tempting breasts, coasting over her smooth stomach, thumbs hooking into the waistband of her shorts.

I held my breath along with the rest of the assholes in the crowd. And then she was peeling the shorts down her legs and kicking them off, revealing a plain black thong.

I'd buy her a thousand thongs if she were mine. I'd drown

her in lingerie and dresses and diamonds and fucking yoga pants. Anything she wanted, I would give her.

Her hips gyrated in a movement so unholy my cock flexed in my pants. I realized I'd been hard for her since the second she walked out onstage. I *hated* the hold she had on me.

The only thing that had kept her safe from me was the fact that my mother signed her paychecks.

That and the fact that she was clean, fresh, sweet. Not only was that not my type, the last shred of human decency in me didn't want to taint that, destroy that. I wasn't a complete monster. But the woman sliding down that goddamn pole, the goddess slithering across the stage like pure temptation, was not squeaky clean. She was deliciously dirty.

And I wanted to sink my teeth into her.

I wanted to get my hands on her and not let go.

My chest was tight. I couldn't breathe. Not while I watched her dance. Her eyes were closed like it didn't matter that there was an entire room full of men hard for her. Like she didn't care. Like she was untouchable.

It was raining money on stage. But I didn't want her to touch it. I wanted her to take from me and me alone.

She reached for the knot in her shirt. I felt the tension in the crowd rise as my dick turned to concrete.

"Don't fucking do it, Ally."

I wanted to see her breasts more than I wanted anything in this entire world, but not as one in a crowd. I wanted to be the only one. Panic clawed its way up my throat as her fingers toyed with the knot.

Every man in the room was holding his breath waiting for it. I held my breath and prayed for her to stop. The song was winding down. It was now or never. I picked up my drink, gripping the beer bottle like a weapon.

"Not like this," I whispered. "Please."

As if she'd heard me, as if the angel of strip clubs had passed my message along, Ally's fingers danced away from the knot. There was a collective groan from the crowd that seemed to crack the little bubble she'd built around herself. As though remembering there was a job to do, she grabbed the material over one breast and yanked it to the side.

"Fuck."

The blue pasty glittered under the stage lights, and the crowd went wild.

Cash littered the stage as she took another spin around the pole, arching her back and sliding lower and lower, one breast peeking out of her shirt.

She was going to pay for this. Tonight.

I flagged down a server with a hundred-dollar bill.

"Need something, handsome?" she asked.

"Yes," I said without taking my eyes off the girl onstage. "Her."

33

ALLY

The applause was ringing in my ears when I gingerly stepped offstage. I'd had to fight the urge to pick up the cash I'd basically rolled around in. But in Faith's club, dancers didn't touch the money. Walking away from the money was more badass and powerful than crawling around onstage, trying to pick it up. Shirtless guys with push brooms came onstage between each act and swept up each dancer's earnings.

My knees were shaking when I stumbled into the empty dressing room. Faith was off probably encouraging the audience to spend more money. I dropped into one of the spinning salon chairs and waited for my broom money. Even if it was all ones, there had to be at least $200 there. Add that to the $150 I made at Rooster's earlier, and I was getting closer to my goal.

"Please. Please. Please," I chanted.

There was a knock, and then the door opened. "Hey, New Girl, you got a private dance in the VIP room," Vance said, spreading his hands and then rubbing those big palms together. "Guy took a likin' to ya."

I shook my head vehemently. My stomach clenched. Even desperate, I wasn't *that* kind of girl.

"Not interested," I said, looking around for my clothes. I was going to take my money, drink as much free alcohol as I could get, and go home to set this outfit on fire.

"You didn't even hear the best part. Guy's offering five grand," he said.

I stopped in my tracks and slowly turned. *Five thousand dollars?*

"Club splits it fifty-fifty," he said. "Not so bad, right? No touching. There's a security button in the room and a bouncer right outside the door. He prepaid."

Twenty-five hundred dollars cash. On top of whatever I won tonight? That would cover the rest of the month. That would earn me two, maybe even three days off. I could buy the rest of the goddamn drywall *and* have those shots.

All I had to do was sell my soul to the perverted devil waiting in the VIP room.

I wanted to cry.

"It's only three minutes and twelve seconds," Vance said. "He picked the song."

"Twenty-five hundred?" I repeated.

He nodded. "Cash. Tonight. On top of those tips, and you're definitely placing in the top three. Some poor geology major cutie pie just fell offa the stage out there, so I'd say top two."

My sigh was so heavy, it moved the wispy strands of hair on his forehead.

Five grand. Five grand. Five grand. It wasn't even a choice at this point.

"Yeah. Okay," I said, swallowing hard. "But if I see a dick, I'm breaking his face."

He crooked his fingers for me to follow him. "You see a dick, sweetheart, you hit that security button and let Chauncey break his face for you."

I nodded rather than answering because I was two seconds away from barfing.

"Oh, hey," Vance said, stopping outside a red leather paneled door. "You want any special lights on in there? I can do disco ball, strobe. We got this pretty pink filter that makes everyone look ten years younger."

"Dark," I said grimly. "Make it as dark as possible."

"You got it, sweetie. And remember, he gets inappropriate, you push that button or just yell. The walls are thin."

Three minutes twelve seconds. Three minutes twelve seconds.

Vance fiddled with the lights and gave me a cheery thumbs-up.

I took a deep breath and stepped into the room.

Into hell.

Into Dominic Russo's personal ring of hell.

Humiliation burned my cheeks. Rage replaced the nausea.

He'd gone too far. Too damn far. My desperation wasn't a joke. This wasn't just playful teasing. Coming here to witness my damnation was cruel.

"What. The. Fuck, Dominic?"

"I paid for the dance." His voice was gruff and low.

I stalked toward him, ready to rearrange his face. I was going to take my half of his five grand and shove it down his throat until he choked on it.

And then I saw it. His face was hard, as always. That beautiful jaw in its perma-clench under the unfairly sexy five-o'clock shadow. But it was his eyes that stopped me. They weren't cold. They weren't mocking. They were fiery. Fierce. Hungry.

Had he finally snapped? Had I won?

I stopped a foot from him.

His intake of breath was audible.

I forgot about the money. The shame dissolved. I was here for one reason. To make Dominic Russo regret this night more than I did.

"No touching," I snapped.

"Do what I paid you to do," he demanded. His voice had a gravelly abrasion to it that gave me as much pleasure as dread. Even in the dim light, I could see he was hard. It was worse now that I knew what his cock looked like.

The music started, and I frowned when I recognized the song. It was a number from the dance studio. I wanted to ask him how he knew, but he flashed me that hard, smug look, and I made it my mission to wipe that expression off his perfect face.

I placed my palms on his thighs and thrilled when he stiffened at my touch.

"You said no touching," he rasped.

"You can't touch me." I sank between his knees, spreading my own wide. I used his legs for balance, for contact, to inflict misery. His jaw was so tense I hoped he'd need a dental appointment next week. I skimmed my hands higher, bouncing, twisting, gyrating. *Grinding.*

If he wanted a dance, I'd give him one he'd remember for the rest of his life. We both could remember the night I sold my soul with shame.

The music built.

I rose, snapping my hips back and bending forward into his space. My hair hung in a short curtain over one eye. I could feel his breath on my face. His gaze burned onto my breasts, just inches from that mouth. His lips parted just enough to draw in a thin stream of air.

I felt the beat pulsing in me. This was my fuck you to the cards I'd been dealt. I would survive. I would make ends meet. And eventually, I would go back to not giving a damn about money.

But first, I would make Dominic suffer like he made me suffer.

With a hand to his chest, I pushed him back against the tufted vinyl banquette, stepping over his legs to straddle him. I wasn't even settled on his lap yet, but his erection was doing its best to tear its way through his trousers. I could feel it flex through my embarrassingly thin underwear. The man was ruining more pairs of my underwear than I cared to think about.

His fingers flexed in the air, wanting to touch me. Needing to. But still that obnoxious self-control reigned supreme.

Undulating just above the ridge of his hard-on, I looked at him through my lowered lashes. He was wearing another goddamn vest. The sleeves of his dress shirt were rolled up to the elbows to reveal the tattoos on both forearms. So proper and polished on the outside, but underneath, ink and a hungry monster of a dick.

What did his denial get him? Or me?

Talk about life being unfair.

"Do you want me to stop?" I whispered in his ear.

"No."

I rose high on my knees, brushing the curve of my breast over the scruff on his jaw. Instinctively, he turned toward me, his mouth open.

"Uh-uh-uh. No touching." His hands clamped around the edge of the bench, and I was surprised it didn't rip in two.

I decided to make it much, much worse. I brought my fingers to the knot in my shirt and felt his breath catch. I loosened it, and he swallowed. Tugging it free, I held the material to my breasts, pushing them together before whipping the shirt open.

His groan was pained, eyes glued to my breasts. I felt his erection flex under me.

"Why are you here, Dom?" I breathed, leaning in and nipping at his ear.

The song. The dark. His mouth so close to mine. It was intoxicating.

"Because I can't fucking leave you alone." His breath was labored.

My heart rate was through the roof, my hormones careening through my system, making demands I couldn't meet.

"Why?"

I couldn't help myself. I swooped in and bit his lower lip, hard.

He growled, an unholy, inhuman sound, and I realized I'd finally pushed the man too far.

Those big hands of his released their grip on the cushion, and then his meaty fingers were sinking into my hips. He yanked me down against him, his erection spearing between my legs.

"I have no fucking control around you." To prove his point, he thrust against me.

"From where I sit, your control has been annoyingly admirable," I whispered breathlessly, gyrating against him. The song was reaching its crescendo, and it was now or never. As much as I regretted this entire night, I wasn't willing to add one more regret to it.

I shifted my hips, driving them forward, up his cock through his pants.

"Don't fucking do it, Ally," he warned.

But I didn't listen, and he didn't stop me.

"Tell me you don't want this. Tell me you don't want me in your lap riding you."

I was rocking my hips back and forth in time to the beat that I felt in my bones, in the pulse of my very empty, very needy pussy.

"Lie to me, Dom. Tell me you don't want me, and I'll stop right now."

Faster and faster. I was jerking him off with my still-covered lady parts. And I wasn't going to stop until either he said no or he was the humiliated one.

He grabbed my hair and pulled my head back, burying his face between my breasts. "I hate how much I want you," he whispered brokenly, nuzzling at the curves, nipping at the pasties. "I despise the fact that I can't think of anything else but you."

My breath was coming in shallow pants, and I was painfully close to an orgasm. But this wasn't about me. This was about him. We should both have something to be ashamed about from tonight. Some dark secret to keep hidden from the light.

I ground down on him harder, faster, and pulled his face into my breasts as I rode him.

"Ally," he rasped. "Baby." One hand in my hair, one on my hip, he gripped hard and grunted out a low, guttural sound. He went completely rigid under me, and I didn't know what had happened until I felt the warmth beneath me. The growing sticky wetness. He held me tight, bucking and shuddering against me, giving in to his shameful release. "Ally," he said again, thrusting against me. Using my body to ride out the orgasm.

I was on the edge of my own climax and held back on

principle. I wasn't going to give him that piece of me. He hadn't earned it. And if I had a first orgasm with Dominic, it sure as hell wasn't going to be in a strip club on amateur night.

I didn't need champagne and candlelight, but I did need to *not* be paid.

He was vulnerable, powerless. I'd won.

But it felt like just another loss. Because now I only wanted him more.

I'd just made Dominic Russo, my boss, come in his pants at a strip club.

I didn't know whether to go jump off a bridge or pat myself on the back. Maybe I'd do both. After those shots.

I decided a hasty retreat was required immediately. I slipped off his lap and out of his reach before he could reel me back in and make some crazy demand that made me think he cared.

"That's two you owe me, Dom."

And then I walked out.

34

ALLY

Here's a lesson, folks: Stripper shoes are impossible to run in.

I slipped out of the VIP room before Dominic could gather his wits—or a wad of tissues—and ran for the dressing room. Faith had thoughtfully left a shot of something that wasn't tequila for me that I knocked back while trying to drag on my pants. I gave up when I tripped and fell over a pink suede ottoman. So I opted for my coat. It was long enough to cover me to my knees.

Ally. Baby. Dominic's words as he came, as I made him come, hammered inside my head.

I'd heard a commotion outside the dressing room door and knew the shit was hitting the fan.

So I ran out the back and into the February night.

And now I was shuffle-jogging my way toward the closest bus stop, wondering if I'd lose my toes to frostbite or these damn shoes.

The list of how many stupid things I'd accomplished in the last hour ran like a silent home movie in my head.

1. I'd danced semi-topless for an audience.
2. I'd said yes to a private dance.
3. I'd ridden my boss to orgasm in the VIP room of a strip club. A classy one, but still.
4. I'd panicked and run out of the club, leaving my stage money and whatever winnings behind.
5. I hadn't stayed for my second free drink.
6. I'd placed my freaking pride ahead of my father's well-being. I should have just swallowed my stupid pride and asked Faith for a loan.
7. I hadn't gone with the cheerleader outfit with the cute little platform sneakers.

"Shit. Shit. Shit," I whispered, my teeth chattering. The February air was so cold it burned my bare legs. I was going to top this night off with hypothermia and frostbite. Tomorrow, I could go to the nursing home and help my father pack.

Because I couldn't stomach taking Dominic's money.

A tear formed in the corner of my eye and froze, binding the fake lashes to my lower real ones.

"Dammit." Shivering, I swiped at it with my sleeve and only made it worse.

"Ally!" I knew that voice and I knew that tone.

Dominic Russo was mad, and he was closing in.

"Oh, no, no, no," I chanted as I picked up the pace. I wasn't running so much as prancing briskly.

It took him all of four seconds to catch and capture me.

He grabbed my arm and whipped me around. I had no balance and fell into him. *Thank you, stripper shoes.*

He held me there against him. It was my first good look at his face, and I immediately regretted peeking. He. Was. Furious.

"Take your goddamn money, Ally," he said through clenched teeth.

"It's *your* goddamn money! I don't want a dime from you!"

"So you're willing to dance for a stranger and take his money, but mine is tainted? That's a murky moral ground, Ally."

"Fuck you, Dominic."

I tried to step around him on the sidewalk, but he wouldn't let me. His hands held tight on my arms, making it clear I wasn't slipping away from this conversation.

He was so angry and something else too. I saw it in those unfairly beautiful blue eyes. Hurt. I'd hurt Dominic Russo.

I'd wanted to hurt him. I'd wanted him to feel as ashamed as I felt. But there was no victory here. Just another defeat.

"Educate me," he said coldly. "Tell me why you'd take money from a stranger but not me."

"Because I don't have feelings for a stranger, you stupid, stubborn asshole!"

Great. Now both eyes were freezing with tears that this dumbass didn't deserve. That was the worst part. I had stupid feelings for a stupid man who was too stupid to be anything but disgusted by his attraction to me.

Dominic looked stunned.

His grip loosened on me, and I took advantage by stomping my stiletto into his foot and wrenching free. I took off at a slightly faster prance.

Nothing said pathetic like a clothing-optional dancer running down a dark street after amateur night. My life had reached a new low.

I didn't even hear him coming. The thunder of my heartbeat drowned out everything else as I tottered for my life. Away from the man who made me feel things when I had no business or time to feel anything.

Hands caught me, stopping me in my tracks, and then pushed me up against the brick of a building. A church. Oh, how appropriate. He pinned me there with his hips, crowding me. I was trapped between a building and my furious boss.

Jesus—sorry, church—cheese and crackers, the man was *still* hard. Maybe it was just his natural state. His pants were still wet from the orgasm I'd given him.

"If you think I'm going to let you wait for a bus or a train wearing nothing but a coat and a thong at this time of night, then you're the stupid, stubborn asshole," he growled.

I said nothing. Dominic was vibrating with rage. And for once, I felt like we were both on the same page.

"Why do you even care? I don't get you. I don't get this. Why can't you just leave me alone?"

He clamped a hand over my mouth. "I would love nothing more than to leave you alone. But I don't know how. So this is what is going to happen. You're going to get in my car, and I'm going to drive you home. And then we're going to have a long talk." Every word sounded like a threat.

My insolent eye roll was apparently *not* the response he was looking for. He gave me a little shake and then undermined it by rubbing his hands up and down my arms. Once again, mixed messages from Prince Charming.

"Do you understand?" he asked with a frigid calm. "I'll stand out here as long as it takes the come to freeze my balls to my dick if that's what it takes."

Heh. He had to be pretty uncomfortable running around with that in his pants.

I nodded slowly but let my watery, half-frozen eyes telegraph "I hate you" loud and clear.

He hauled me the block and a half to his car, a sinister-looking Range Rover, and shoved me into the passenger seat. I wondered if I was leaving a trail of body glitter behind me like I was a questionable life choices Tinker Bell. When I shivered on the leather, he pinned me with a glare and stripped out of his coat. "Here," he said, spreading it over me, tucking it in under my legs. "And if you even think about running again, I will make you regret it."

Running was out of the question, so I waited while he rounded the vehicle and climbed behind the wheel.

"Am I fired? Or are you taking me somewhere to murder me?" I asked.

"I haven't decided," he said, stabbing the button for my seat warmer. The leather beneath me heated instantly, and I shifted the coats to protect my practically exposed hoo-ha.

Those were the only words spoken during the drive. Until I realized we weren't heading toward New Jersey.

"Where are you taking me?"

The monosyllabic answer was delivered on a growl. "Home."

35

DOMINIC

I was a dirtbag of the highest order. I'd basically abducted an employee with the intent of holding her prisoner until she finally told me what the hell was going on. But I was too full of righteous anger to care about the consequences.

Ally was glued to the passenger side window, as far away from me as possible. I snagged an open parking spot just down the block and shut off the engine. She swung away from the window and glared at me, her jaw set in a tight line.

The fact that she was pissed off at me pissed me off even more.

"Don't give me that look. I'm the one who's mad," I said, stabbing my thumb in my chest. "We don't get to both be mad."

"You kidnapped me!"

"You're an adult. It's called abduction. And you tried to turn my foot into a kebab with your footwear weaponry," I snapped, getting out of the car. Stubbornly, she stayed put inside until I yanked her door open. "Out. Now."

"Where are we?" she asked, still not moving.

I half pulled, half dragged her off the seat and held her steady when she wobbled on those ridiculous heels.

"My neighborhood."

She swung her head around. "Where are the soulless skyscrapers and creepy dungeons? This is a neighborhood. You know, where actual *people* live."

"Very funny." I took her arm and none too gently propelled her down the sidewalk.

"If you seriously live here, your neighbors are going to think you brought a prostitute home," she hissed. She looked more concerned about my reputation than hers.

I realized then that I was never going to understand this woman.

She was limping now, and I was torn between parading her around the block a few times so she'd learn her lesson and getting her inside as quickly as possible.

She tripped and yelped and made the decision for me. I scooped her up in my arms and marched toward my town house. She went completely rigid against me. "You can't carry me around like a bride," she insisted.

"Yeah, well, a few hours ago, I would have said you couldn't jack me off in a strip club. I guess we're both wrong."

I took the steps to my front door and set her down more gently than I felt like doing.

Patting my pockets for my keys, I realized they were in my coat. I shoved my hands in her pockets. "Hey! No touching," Ally snapped.

"I think it's a little late for that," I said dryly.

"Bite me."

I found the keys and unlocked the door and pulled her into the foyer vestibule room thing that my real estate agent had been so excited about when I bought the place five years ago. "You can leave at any time, but if you try to go before we're done talking, I'll just keep bringing you back," I warned her.

"This is beyond fucked up," she said, crossing her arms. My coat billowed around her like a cape, enveloping her. She was raining body glitter on the black-and-white tile. Hell, so was I. The cleaning crew was going to think I'd either hosted a Girl Scout craft jamboree or an orgy.

"At least we both agree on that." I took my coat off her and hung it in the closet. I left her coat on, knowing there was very little beneath it.

There was a sad whine coming from behind the main door.

"Is that another exotic dancer you kidnapped?" she snipped.

"I'm starting a harem," I said and then opened the door.

Sixty pounds of chocolate Lab rocketed into my arms. Brownie—hey, he came with the name, okay?—and I were still getting to know each other, and I was still trying to figure out dog discipline.

"Oh my God, you kidnapped a dog too."

I put Brownie down and gave him a full-body scruffing before smushing his face and kissing the top of his head. This was the best unanticipated part of spontaneously adopting a dog: the greeting after a long day. Brownie didn't care if I abducted an employee. He still loved me.

"I didn't kidnap him, idiot. I adopted him."

My dog trotted over to her, oblivious to the tension. He wagged his tail and gave a happy bark.

"Shut up, Brownie. It's after one a.m. You'll wake the neighbors."

Ally sank down to greet him.

"Who's the most handsome boy in the world? Did you get adopted? Did you?"

His tail was a blur of happiness.

"Come on," I said, gesturing toward the main door. "And take off those stupid shoes."

"Fine. But I'm only doing it because I think I lost a few toenails, not because you told me," she said. Her groan when she slipped them off was sinful enough that the situation in my pants became a more complicated matter.

I kept my shoes on—in case she tried to make a barefoot run for it—and headed into the house.

Either curiosity or the need to finally hash this all out propelled her in behind me.

"Wow," she said.

"What?"

She gestured around the hall, the stairs. Off to the right was a den with a fireplace and wood-paneled walls. "I didn't expect this. I just assumed you lived in some…"

"Soulless high-rise with a dungeon?"

She shrugged.

"Yeah, well, I assumed you were financially responsible enough to not have to take your clothes off for strangers," I shot back.

"Why do you even care, Dom? I don't understand. I mean, talk about mixed messages. You say you don't want me—"

"Correction. I don't *want* to *want* you."

"You are such an ass. You don't want to want me, yet you eavesdrop on a private call, follow me to a strip club, and hire me to do a private dance. And then get so angry you abduct me and take me home with you."

"Wrong. I was angry before I got to the club," I shot back.

"I'm not yours to care about, Dom."

I snapped my fingers for Brownie, and he followed me into the kitchen.

Ally came along at a more leisurely pace. I fished out a treat from the puppy jar Greta got me and made Brownie sit. It was the one command we'd both mastered. "Take it nicely, buddy. Do not take my hand off," I said, holding the paw-shaped cookie high.

But Brownie had that single-minded gleam in his eye. He nearly swallowed my entire hand.

"Okay, we need to work on that."

Ally sighed like a good little martyr and stomped over to the jar. "Here," she said. She demonstrated holding the treat in a closed fist with part of it peeking out over her thumb. "Sit," she told Brownie.

He plopped his ass on the floor, thrilled at the prospect of two cookies.

"Nicely," Ally warned him. When he made an excited alligator lunge, she pulled back. "Uh-uh. Nice boy."

This time, she held her hand out, and Brownie carefully extracted the treat from her fist.

"Good boy!" she cheered.

Brownie snarfed it down and dissolved into happy wiggles at the praise.

She turned back to me smugly. "What? I had dogs growing up. I'd offer to help you with him, but I hate you."

Yes. There was that.

"Come on," I said wearily.

"Where?"

"Upstairs so I can get out of these fucking pants."

"We're not having sex," she said, looking appalled.

I brought my hands to my face and shoved them through my hair. "You are driving me in-fucking-sane, Ally. I just want to talk, but I need to get out of these pants."

"Why do I have to go with you?"

"Because the second I turn my back on you, you're going to

make a run for it. And it's cold, and I'm tired, and I don't want to have to chase you down the block in the middle of the night."

"Fine. Lead the way, boss," she said. She was trying to be snide and sarcastic, but it was the exhaustion and resignation that came through.

I poured two glasses of water and handed her one. "Come on."

My bedroom was on the third floor. Brownie raced past us on the stairs only to zoom back down twice to make sure we were still coming as we plodded along.

I noticed Ally peering over the railing at the second floor. "That's the main living space," I told her. "TV, fireplace, library."

We arrived on the third floor, and I led the way into my bedroom at the back of the house.

There was a king-size four-poster bed in the center of the room facing a fireplace I'd never used. The bed certainly hadn't seen any creative entertainment in the last year.

"Sit," I said, gesturing to the bed. Brownie jumped up and arranged himself on the pillows.

It got a smile out of both of us.

Ally perched gingerly on the edge of the mattress, her gaze taking in the room. Something on the nightstand caught her attention, and she leaned over to pick it up. She held up the copy of *Pride and Prejudice* accusingly.

I shrugged. "It's for decoration."

"There's a receipt for a green tea dated last week being used as a bookmark," she challenged.

"I'm not the one who owes answers tonight." I ducked into the dressing room and grabbed two pairs of sweats and two T-shirts. "Here," I said, handing her one set.

Her eyes went wide. "I'm not staying here, Dom."

We'd see about that. "Fine. But wouldn't you be more comfortable yelling at me in these rather than a thong and pasties?"

"You have a point." She took the clothes.

I pointed toward the door. "Bathroom's through there. You can shower if you want."

She glanced down at the glitter halo she'd shed on my bed, then longingly toward the bathroom. "You don't mind?"

"As long as you wait around long enough after I shower to have this out."

"You won't come in while I'm in there?" she asked softly.

Something twisted in my gut. I hated that she felt like she had to ask me. "I won't come in," I said quietly.

"Okay." She nodded.

"There's a lock on the door," I told her.

She nodded again and got up. When she closed the bathroom door, I waited to hear the snick of the lock, but it never came.

At least she didn't think I was that big of a monster.

I sighed and headed back into the dressing room. I stripped out of my vest and shirt and shucked off the ruined underwear, the pants with the half-frozen jizz explosion in the crotch.

The water in my shower turned on, and I tried not to imagine what was happening in there. But being a gentleman didn't come naturally to me. And instead of thinking about anything but the naked woman in my shower, I was thinking about how she'd looked as she'd ridden me to climax in the club. Her eyes hooded, lips parted. The stupid, primitive part of me wanted to see just how hard I'd come inside her, raw and bare. Pumping away until...

And now I was fucking hard again.

I needed to see a doctor. This wasn't normal.

I dragged on my sweatpants, shoved my head and arms through the T-shirt, and returned to the bed where I sprawled out and waited for her.

She came out a few minutes later, fresh-faced, hair damp.

My clothes hung on her frame. The urge to pull her to me and hold her was overwhelming and pissed me off all over again.

So I picked a fight instead.

"How did you get into a financial mess bad enough that tonight was your only option?" I asked. "Are you that irresponsible with money?"

"Oh good. I'd worried you'd turned human on me while I was in there," she snapped. She climbed onto the mattress and sat cross-legged in the corner farthest from me.

I wanted her closer. I wanted to hold her and run my fingers through those wet curls and promise her that I'd fix everything. And I couldn't do any of that.

"I saw your face on the roof and on that stage. You didn't want to be there. You didn't want to do it, but you did it anyway."

"I had to."

"Why?" My frustration was loud and clear.

"*Label* messed up my paycheck. It didn't get deposited, and it couldn't be fixed until Monday. I needed the money now."

"What's the money for?"

She gave me a long, stony look. "Bills."

"What kind of bills?"

Ally said nothing for a long beat. Bored, Brownie belly-crawled over to her on the bed.

"Why does it matter to you?" she asked me finally. She stroked a hand over Brownie's head and down his back. Long, slow strokes. I wished it was me she was touching.

"I care about you."

"You're so lucky I'm exhausted, because I would love to tell you how absolutely stupid you're being right now," she said.

"Tell me what's going on," I insisted.

She shook her head. "You don't get it, do you?"

"Get what?"

"You say you care about me. You're obviously attracted to me. And as much as you bitch and moan about me ruining your life, I think you actually like me. But not enough to want to be with me. And because of that, I can't trust you, Dominic. I'm not going to open up and share my life story with you. You haven't earned that access."

I pinched my nose between my finger and thumb. "I'm trying to do the right thing here, Ally."

"I don't understand what right thing you're going for."

"There are rules," I said. My frustration was rising again. Why couldn't she just give me what I wanted?

"I know, Dom," she said gently. "What I don't know is why those rules mean so much to you. Because from where I sit, you don't seem like the kind of guy who would let a piece of paper tell you how to live your life."

"Those rules are there for your protection," I snapped.

"I don't need to be protected!"

Brownie lifted his head up and gave her a goofy, confused look.

"Sorry, buddy," she said gently.

Appeased, he flopped back down on a groan.

"I'm saying I can't take these games anymore, Dom. I don't want to play. I have too much going on, and it's not good for me to let you toy with me. It hurts me."

I closed my eyes. "I don't mean to hurt you, Ally."

"You showed up on my date. You showed up at the club. You say you don't want to want me, yet it was your idea to get to know each other better. You wear vests just to mess with me. Then you tell me to quit the job that I desperately need so you can feel better about wanting to fuck me."

"I'm an asshole." There was no other way to cut it. I was a selfish, out-of-control monster.

She scooted closer, and when she took my hand, I felt like the worst human being in the world.

"Listen to me before you go into some shame spiral. You didn't force me onto that stage, and you didn't force me into that room with you. I wanted to dance for you. I wanted to make you feel the frustration you make me feel. I wanted to make you come and feel bad about it. You didn't make me do any of that. The only thing you forced me to do was not wait for a bus in freezing temperatures. Okay?"

I squeezed her hand and closed my eyes. "I can't seem to leave you alone."

"You're fighting this mutual attraction really hard without giving me a real reason. And if you can't trust me with your why, then I can't trust you with mine."

I hated that. I hated myself. I wanted to tell her why. To tell her everything. How it was all my fault that my father had free rein to inflict the damage he'd done. But I couldn't unpack that. Not to her. Not to anyone. Russos didn't air their dirty laundry.

I could only try to atone for it.

As if sensing my dip into self-loathing, Brownie crawled over to me and rested his head on my stomach. Having a dog was pretty great. However, having Ally in my bed was too much of a temptation. I needed to get her out of here before I broke.

"How much do you need?" I asked briskly, pulling my hand free from hers.

"How much what?" she asked, confused.

"Money. Tell me how much money you need." I swung my legs over the side of the bed. I had cash in the safe and a checkbook in my desk. I'd make it go away.

"I'm not taking your money," she said.

"You were willing to take money from strangers. You didn't know it was me in that room, and you walked in there willingly. You were going to take that money from someone. Why not me?"

She rose up on her knees on the mattress, looking like the goddess of war. I was mildly surprised when flames didn't shoot out of her eyes to incinerate me.

"Because I'm not going to owe you a damn thing. Not now. And not ever."

"Yeah, well, I owe you for the dance. You earned it." Offense was my default defense.

"Consider it a parting gift from me," she said, getting off the bed.

I stood up, and we met halfway to the door. "What do you want from me, Ally?" I asked coldly.

"The truth," she spat out.

"The truth? Fine. I've never not wanted you. I *only* want you. I'm no better than that dickhead you went out with. I don't want a relationship with you. I want a quick, dirty fuck to get you out of my system. But we both know it won't be enough. You'll get your hooks into my soul and—"

"Oh, shut up! I'm not some magical siren, you jackass! I'm not casting a spell and seducing you."

I grabbed her by the arms and squeezed. "Yes, you fucking are," I said through clenched teeth. "You dry-humped me in a strip club until I fucking came in my goddamn pants. I have no control around you, and you think it would be nice to have a fun little off-the-books fling? Then what?"

"How the *hell* should I know?"

I was grateful for the soundproofing in the walls.

"What does it matter now? I'm not on the table anymore," she said, quieter now.

"You mean the pole," I said bitterly.

Her brown eyes filled with fire.

"What in the hell possessed you to do that? If you need an advance on your paycheck, just ask. I'll give you whatever you want. Don't get up onstage and take your clothes off. Have some goddamn self-respect."

Oh, shit.

I'd said something so irresponsibly stupid I wanted to punch myself in the face. For a moment, Ally looked like she'd do it for me. But I still had her arms, so the best she'd be able to manage is a gut shot, which I deserved.

"I have *nothing* but self-respect," she said, her voice low and shaking. "Nothing."

"Why is that? Why don't you have anything? Why were you so desperate for money that you'd dance for strangers?"

With shaking hands, she peeled my fingers away from her skin. "Just like everything else regarding me from now on, that's none of your business," she said coldly.

"Ally—"

"Here's what happens now. I don't want you to ever speak to me again. I don't want my name to *ever* pass your lips again. If you need something from the admin pool, you call every other person in that room. Because we're done. No more flirting. No more getting to know you. No more 'I want you, but I can't have you' games. It's finished. When you see me in the hall, you will avert your eyes and walk in the opposite direction."

"And if I don't?" Cold licks of dread settled in my gut.

"I'll tell Malina that you had a sex dream about her. Now I'm going home. So if you have anything to say to me, this is your last chance."

All the things I should say, the whys she deserved to know, the feelings I had for her, the way I thought about her at night when I was alone…it all hovered on the tip of my tongue.

"I'll call you a car," I said.

36

ALLY

Front Desk Deena pounced on me the second the automatic doors whirred open.

The woman had an entire wardrobe of holiday-themed catalog wear. Today was a Valentine's Day sweater with lopsided hearts placed directly over her generous breasts.

"Ms. Morales, a word," she said sternly.

Reluctantly, I followed her buxom figure into the Pepto-Bismol pink office she shared with the much nicer, much flatter-chested Sandy, the nursing supervisor.

I thought about running. I thought about that lap dance and Dominic hauling me into his car, his home. I thought about the gigantic diamond rings on Deena's left hand. Mr. Deena must be a boob man to put that kind of hardware on her hand. I thought about a lot of things in the twenty seconds it took for Deena to settle herself behind her desk and take a judgmental sip of tea.

"Your father's account is past due," she said, assuming the role of Four-Star General Obvious.

"I realize that," I said, reaching into my backpack.

"Now what are we going to do about it?" she asked with a smile so phony her lips didn't even curve.

Nursing supervisor Sandy, the woman unlucky enough to share an office with Deena, rolled her brown eyes heavenward at her desk.

"If you can't produce exactly…" Deena swiveled to her computer monitor. The screen saver was of alternate-universe Deena beaming at her lap full of grandchildren, who weren't regarding her as an evil, shrewish monster. "$5,327.94 today, then I'm sorry, but we'll be forced to begin the eviction proceedings against your father."

She didn't sound sorry at all.

Sandy shot me a sympathetic look, and I wondered how many of these meetings she'd sat in on.

"I understand," I said. Sending up a prayer to the goddess of lotteries and cash windfalls, I reached into my bag and pulled out a check for every cent I had in my bank account and a stack of crumpled, glittery bills.

Faith had dropped off my first-place winnings—was it weird to be proud about that?—along with two bottles of really good red wine and hot wings that we reheated in the oven at four in the morning.

She also brought a check for the private dance. I didn't accept it. But I did accept the loan. Because of course my best friend walked around with a few hundred dollars in cash.

Between the rehashing of my scene with Dominic and my half-drunken declarations of "I love you" and "I'll pay you back," Faith had dragged the story out of me. And then told me I was a stupid, stubborn, prideful idiot.

"I've got it all here."

Deena's eyes narrowed at the stack of cash I pushed onto her desk. It couldn't be more obvious where it had come from. Plus, I was still wearing half my eye makeup from the night before. Faith's club makeup was industrial grade, sweat-proof, shower-proof, and grind-proof product.

"What?" I asked. "It's not like I robbed a liquor store for it."

Deena's laugh was mirthless. I took the time to rudely notice that one of her canine teeth was crooked.

"We don't accept cash, Ms. Morales. We're not *that kind* of business. Just because your father is a favorite among the staff"—she sent a withering glare in Sandy's direction, as if it were a crime to treat their residents well—"doesn't mean we're running a charity home."

"I don't expect charity. It wasn't my fault that there was a problem with my direct deposit. I have cash. Enough cash." I pushed it closer to her.

She steepled her fingers like a Bond villain.

"Well, it's certainly not *my fault*. If you can't pay all your late fees in an appropriate manner right now *and* make a good-faith payment on this month's bill, I'll have the staff start packing your father's things."

"You have got to be kidding me."

But Mean Deena didn't kid. She threatened. She ruined. She destroyed. But she didn't kid. "I am not responsible for your inability to read the intake forms and contract. We do not accept cash payments."

"Then I'll go to the bank and deposit it. I'll write you a check now, and you can cash it Monday."

"That's not how this works," she said with evil glee.

It was then that I realized this woman did not want my father here.

"Where will you send him?" I asked, trying to buy time. Trying to come up with some solution. Trying to decide between bursting into tears and grabbing one of Deena's solid gold bracelets and shoving it up her nose.

What was the annual salary for an evil accounts receivable rep these days anyway?

"The state has facilities for patients who didn't plan for their futures."

"None of this is my father's fault," I insisted. I'd definitely go for the nose bracelet.

"It doesn't really matter now, does it? Without the full amount due right now, your father must leave the property today. Our waiting list is full of patients who are willing to pay their bills on time."

And there it was.

"Do you get something for harassing patients' families? Is there some kind of incentive system for avoiding late payments?"

Deena blinked owlishly and then adjusted her gold bracelets. Busted.

"I don't know what you're talking about," she lied primly. "Now if you don't feel like taking him home, we'll transfer him to a state facility outside Trenton."

There were so many things I should have done differently leading up to this exact moment. So many decisions I'd made based on pride when in reality I couldn't afford to have any.

And now my father was going to pay the price for it all.

Fuck. Fuck. Fuuuuuuuck.

I wanted to throw up. Or throw a temper tantrum. I wanted to record Front Desk Deena behaving like a soulless banshee and then personally show her grandchildren what an asshole Grandma was.

Everything was falling apart, and now it was the worst-case scenario. My poor dad. I'd failed him when he needed me the most.

My work cell phone buzzed in my hand. The little pop-up alert on the screen caught my eye. I blinked rapidly. It was an email from the HR department with the subject "Temporary promotion and signing bonus."

Hope aggressively took flight.

"Excuse me a moment," I said, holding up a finger—not the one I wanted—at the woman gleefully telling me she had no problem shipping my father off to a nursing home that had been cited by the health department three times in the last eighteen months.

> Ms. Morales,
>
> You've been chosen from our admin pool for a sixty-day placement as a personal assistant to one of our executives. This move within the company includes a pay raise as well as a $5,000 signing bonus, which has been wired into your account. Stop by on Monday for the details of your new assignment. Congratulations!

"Sweet and sour chicken," I breathed. My eyes closed in a relief so palpable, the heartless robot across the desk from me asked if I was all right. *Five thousand dollars? Five THOUSAND dollars? Five thousand DOLLARS?*

I ignored Deena and toggled over to my bank app. Well, holy mother of last-minute saves. There was $5,000 sitting there in my checking account.

I shot out of my chair and pumped my fist into the air. "I have the money! I'll write you a check."

"A check?" Deena snorted ungraciously. "Ha! You expect me to accept a check from you?"

I shoved the phone in her face. "Is this good enough for you?"

She harrumphed while I triumphantly dug out my checkbook.

Sometimes good things happened to pretty okay people. My father was safe for another month. And with a raise, maybe I could take a few weeknights and weekends off to fix up the house. My eyes were swimming in unshed tears. This anonymous executive had just saved everything that was important to me in this life.

I was going to do this. I was going to make it through. I was going to be okay.

I signed the check with a violent flourish, spent an hour having breakfast with my dad, who thought I was one of his high school students, and then cried for ten minutes in the parking lot, letting the February wind freeze tears and industrial strip club eye makeup to my cheeks.

Fate had just saved me from a downward spiral from which I had no way of recovering on my own.

I was going to be the best damn PA she or he had ever had.

37

ALLY

"There has to be a mistake," I croaked, looking at the nondisclosure agreement the HR rep—a nicer, more pleasant one than the first—handed me.

"Oh no, Ms. Morales. It's all there. You'll be stepping in for Mr. Russo's admin, Greta. She's taking a two-month European tour. Isn't that exciting?"

"Exciting," I parroted as my head spun.

Pride warred with poor.

As soon as I woke up this morning, I'd checked my bank balance and danced a boogie in bed when I saw my paycheck had officially landed. There was money in my account. Enough to actually catch up on some bills, buy another box of drywall screws, and maybe even get myself some *real* groceries.

I'd already spent all of the signing bonus on Dad's late fees and the good faith payment. I couldn't afford to turn down the job and give it back.

But I could afford to be a complete ass to Dominic Russo.

He manipulated me into this. He hadn't been able to force me out of the company from a safe distance, so now he was going to try it up close and personal.

Well, Charming had another thing coming. I had staying power. A stubborn streak wider and deeper than the Pacific fucking Ocean. I'd sink my claws into this job and him. Maybe I'd make *him* quit.

"You're so lucky," she whispered conspiratorially. "He's so good-looking it hurts to look directly at him."

Yeah? Try looking at him after getting him off and then replaying those primitive grunts and growls for forty-eight hours straight without busting out the vibrator because you suddenly have principles.

I wisely chose not to share that sentiment.

See? I had self-control. I could do this. I could do my job, ruin this man's life, and finish the renovations on my dad's house, and when it was sold, when Dad was safe for several years, I'd get that gosh darn mango margarita. Or at this point, maybe it was better to just go straight for an entire bottle of tequila.

"And here's the employment contract," she said, cheerfully handing over another piece of paper that would require part of my soul. "You can read it if you like. It's pretty straightforward. The only new requirement is Section J."

I flipped to Section J.

"The employee will not pursue outside employment during the term of the contract."

That sneaky motherfucker.

I had a brief but entertaining fantasy of taking these papers and shoving them up Charming's ass, making sure he got paper cuts. But then I started thinking about his ass. Fortunately for all involved, the compensation section of the contract caught my eye and convinced me that my dignity could indeed be purchased.

I signed the papers, my hand gripping the pen so hard it cramped, and then forced a cheery smile as HR Lady gave me directions I didn't need to my new personal hell. I already knew the way.

My first instinct was to go in blazing hot. But that would give him the satisfaction of knowing he got under my skin. If mystery bothered him so much, this son of a bitch—wait, no. His mother was a lovely human being. This *alphahole* was going to suffer. I'd make sure of it.

Mr. Alphahole was not currently in residence.

But just looking through the open door into his domain had me feeling a little light-headed. I guessed it was a combination of righteousness and lack of cheese.

I stood there, glaring at Greta's empty desk for a long minute. I would be mere feet from the man I wanted to avoid for the rest of my life. All day, every day, for two months. One of us was bound to crack, and I really, *really* didn't want it to be me.

"Admin Ally moving up in the world." Linus appeared, slapping a stack of red-inked proofs against his palm.

I resisted the urge to grab Greta's trash can and vomit into it.

"It appears so. I didn't know Greta was planning a trip."

He shrugged personal trainer–sculpted shoulders. "Sounds like it was a surprise anniversary trip," he said.

"Some anniversary."

"Are you all right?" He peered at me through his tortoiseshell glasses. "You look even pastier than usual."

"Fine," I croaked. "Everything is fine."

And then it wasn't. Because Dominic Russo was striding

toward me in a goddamn vest with his shirtsleeves rolled up, looking like he owned half the world. I might need that trash can after all.

"Ally," he said gruffly.

I just stared dumbly and cursed my lady parts for bursting into an angels' chorus as they recalled Friday night in vivid detail. The feel of his fingers as they dug mercilessly into my hip. The sound he made, that long, drawn-out groan when he came. The warm, wet spread of his orgasm under me. The sandalwood scent of his body wash.

"Linus," Dominic said, nodding at the man next to me.

Record scratch.

"Good morning?" I said. It came out like a question because Linus was looking back and forth between us as if there was an invisible tennis match going on. If tennis were played with a ball of loathing that was slapped by rackets of angst, then we were in the middle of Wimbledon.

"These are for you from on high," Linus said, handing over the proofs.

Dominic dragged his evil, alpha, stupid, blue-eyed gaze away from me and glanced down at the papers.

"Much fewer red marks this time. Consider it a win," Linus said.

Dominic nodded but didn't say anything.

"Well, I'll just let you two get back to...whatever hot mess this is," Linus said before hurrying away.

We were back to staring at each other. The air between us vibrated with all the things we weren't saying. I had so many conflicting feelings that I wondered if I could actually implode from them. Then I spent an obscene amount of time pondering how long it would take to clean imploded body parts out of the carpet.

It would probably be easier to just redo the entire floor, I guessed.

"Come inside, Ally," Dominic said, leading the way into his office.

I nearly bit my tongue in half but did as the shithead commanded. *See? I could pretend.*

He gestured toward one of the chairs in front of his desk. I expected him to sit behind his desk. Keeping large objects between us had been his MO to date. So I knew I was in trouble when he leaned against the front of his desk instead.

No barriers.

In a defensive move, I stepped behind the wingback chair.

His lips quirked, and he crossed his arms.

I tried not to look at the sexy ink on his forearms. Dressed up and classy on the outside, but dig down a few layers, and Dominic Russo was a primal, rough-around-the-edges sex god.

"Thank you for filling in," he said.

I blinked and shook my head, certain I hadn't heard him correctly.

"Filling in?" I repeated.

"She speaks."

The man just couldn't go five seconds without pushing my buttons.

"It's not going to work," I told him haughtily.

"What's not going to work?" He had the sheer stupidity to look amused.

"I'm not quitting. Do your worst, Charming. But I'm sticking it out. No matter what strings you pulled to get me here when I expressly told you I never wanted to see your stupid face again—"

"You think I just what? Sent Greta off for a two-month vacation?" he scoffed.

"You handpicked me for this ridiculous farce of a job."

"I did," he admitted.

I'd expected more of a denial and had to scramble for the next point in my argument. I came up dry.

"You're the only one I trust." He said it as if it were a normal thing to say.

"You trust me? What kind of fucked-up relationships do you have, Dom?"

"We've shared several intimate…moments," he said, choosing his words carefully. "And you've never once divulged that information or used it to gain an advantage over me."

I was suddenly and overwhelmingly exhausted. My shoulders slumped as gravity increased its pull on me.

The observant bastard caught it and pushed away from his desk. "Sit down. You're dead on your feet, and it's only Monday morning."

He manhandled me into one of the chairs. I put my face in my hands and focused my energy on slow, calming breaths while he made some kind of a racket in the corner of the room.

"I'm not doing this to make you quit," he said quietly.

"You're doing it to control me. I saw the outside employment clause in the contract. If I work a bar shift or decide to take another stab at amateur night, I'm fired for breach of contract." I wanted to believe in my bones that he was doing this as some stupid mind game, that he got off on playing puppet master with my life. But deep down, I was worried that it was something much, much worse.

Dominic Russo was trying to take care of me.

"You can still teach dance," he said.

That controlling, caring, manipulative son of a bitch.

"I can, can I? How magnanimous of you."

"Do you want the job or not?" He was in front of me again

and pushing a cup and saucer into my hands. The man made me tea and was paying me an astronomical amount of money to manage his calendar and pick up his damn dry cleaning. And all I had to do was sign over my soul.

"The job? Yes. Your pity? No. Your thanks for dry humping you to orgasm? Definitely no. Being at the mercy of your whims to fire me? Hell no."

"It's your choice, Ally." He wasn't joking. He was leaving it up to me. I could take the job and leave my pride at the door. Or I could walk out of here with my head held high…and go pack my father's things because no admin salary, number of bar shifts, and dance classes were going to keep him where he needed to be.

And then the worst thing that could possibly happen happened.

My eyes got hot and wet. I forced a sip of tea down my tight throat.

"Don't," he said harshly.

"Don't what?" I rasped.

"Don't fucking do it, Ally."

"What? Cry? Why the hell not? I've done nothing but humiliate myself in front of you up to this point. I don't see why either one of us should expect anything else." I gave a pathetic, watery laugh.

Though my vision was blurred like a downpour on a windshield, I could tell Dominic was on the verge of panic.

He reached for me, then thought better of it and stuffed his hands into his pockets. One immediately freed itself and swiped over his face.

"You're stronger than this, Ally. Act like it."

That douchey, high-handed reminder was enough for me to heroically rein in my emotions. It took a long minute of staring at the ceiling and not blinking to reabsorb the moisture into my eyes. But I did it.

Dominic looked relieved.

I stood, still clutching the teacup because the tea was annoyingly fabulous and he wasn't getting it back. "Don't fuck me over, Charming," I warned.

He made no promises. Just gave me a brisk nod.

"I will be the second-best assistant you've ever had. But there's no going back to the way it was. You can trust me to keep your secrets, but I'll never trust you with mine."

His eyes were stormy. More gray than blue now. He looked like he wanted to say something. "About Friday night," he began.

I held up a hand. "Never bring up that night. As far as either one of us goes, Friday night never happened."

"And it will never happen again," he said sternly. "Your contract doesn't allow it."

I swore an imaginary blood oath on the spot that I would make this high-handed asshat rue the day he ever walked into George's Village Pizza.

"Order me some breakfast. Get yourself something too. You look pale. We have a meeting at ten."

38

DOMINIC

She ordered me plain, steel-cut oatmeal for breakfast.

On Tuesday, she instituted an email-only communication rule. When I handed her a bagel from the bakery down the block on Wednesday, she dropped it straight into the trash. Thursday she had a barista spell out "ass" in the foam of my chai latte when we were out of the building for a meeting.

As the days wore on, it was both a relief and a horrific kind of torture to only have to look through my open door and see Ally. We'd made accidental eye contact so many times the first day that she moved her computer monitor to the opposite side of her desk and sat with her back to me.

On Valentine's Day, I got every assistant on the floor a flower arrangement just so I could give her something. I signed her card "From Linus" so she'd keep the fucking flowers.

As the first week wore on and bled into the second, she remained icily professional toward me. We avoided each other as much as possible. There were no antagonistic emails or flirty texts. If I needed to sign something, she sent an intern into my office. If I needed to ask her a question, I cc'd half the team.

I kept my hands off my damn cock. It felt wrong with her right outside my office. Every night, I relived the lap dance, but I still didn't touch myself. Nothing but Ally was going to cut it. Not after she undulated and ground her way up my dick like it was her personal sex toy.

I was ruined and found a certain relief in accepting it.

But it was the silence, her complete withdrawal from me, that started to put the cracks in my facade. By the third week, I was a fucking wreck. I couldn't work with this kind of tension. I needed to develop a drinking problem stat.

The only thing that kept me hanging on was the fact that the dark circles beneath those honey-colored eyes were fading. The hollows in those cheeks weren't as noticeable either. Ally still packed her lunches, but they passed for actual food now. However, there was a new mystery to be solved. She was showing up to work with odd bruises and bandages.

What was she doing in her time off? My brain obsessively turned the problem over and over. Was she a submissive? Was she taking care of a large, clumsy dog? Had she taken up totem carving as a new hobby?

I wasted hours of my day thinking up questions that I was never going to get to ask her. I made up excuses to linger near her desk. Every night, I watched her leave without a word and wished she were going home with me. I didn't know what was worse, seeing her all day every day and not speaking to her or watching her leave and not knowing what she was doing.

I had no idea how I was going to get through the event tonight.

Christian James, the designer who dared flirt with Ally, was launching his new line, and we, as in a very large part of the *Label* team, were invited to the show and after-party.

I'd rather gouge my eyes out with a spoon than watch Ally, dressed to the nines, parade around a party. But I also wasn't going to let her go by herself. Not with a playboy designer toasting himself with champagne and flashing ridiculous dimples at her.

Speak of the devil. The woman who haunted my every waking moment hovered in the doorway.

"Yes?" I snapped.

My temper didn't seem to have the right effect on her. It only emboldened her.

She strode into the office on new gray suede stilettos that peeked out from under the wide cuffs of her red pants. I was grateful that she was facing me, so I didn't have to pretend not to admire her ass.

"These are from Dalessandra," she said, dropping a stack of proofs on my desk.

They looked as though they'd been massacred by a very sharp red pen. There was a note in the margin of the first page.

See me.

I'd been summoned.

Any progress I'd been making before moving Ally up here had vanished because I was too busy trying not to lust after my assistant to focus on the job at hand.

I swore quietly.

"Problem?" Ally asked.

She hadn't bolted for the door yet. I assumed she was hoping for a front-row seat to my meltdown, and I was happy to oblige.

"Problem as in singular? No, Maleficent. I have several. Including the fact that I can't stop thinking about my Frosty the

Snowass PA or seem to do my job anywhere near the standard my asshole father set."

She stared at me for a long, heated moment, then rolled her eyes. "Ugh. Stay there."

Ally left the room and fuck it, I stared at her ass.

She stomped back in, holding a folder and scowling. "I'm pissed off that you're making me do this, by the way."

"Do what?" I was so pathetically happy that she was speaking to me in multisyllabic words, I would have let her slap me across the face with the folder.

"This is an inside spread on incredibly hideous winter coats from two years ago. Your father signed off on it."

I glanced at the layout. They looked like sleeping bags in beiges and grays. Models slumping oddly inside them on a dingy gray background.

"Here's one of yours," she said, pulling the next layout from the folder. Similar to the first, this was winter boots. The models were in the studio on a set built out of square, wooden platforms. It was one of the first layouts I'd spearheaded after taking my father's position.

"What's your point?"

"Don't play dumb. You're not pretty enough for that," she shot back. "You can tell that yours is better."

"I had Linus and Shayla in my ear," I insisted.

"Did you have them in your ear when you got dressed this morning or when you decorated your town house?"

"No," I muttered.

"Look at how much better you, Linus, and Shayla made this," she said, tapping the spread I did. "You've *been* doing the job, Dominic. Your father had shit taste and thought he was great. You have great taste and think you're shit."

"I'm relying on the opinions of others to do my job."

"Who said it was supposed to be a dictatorship? You *should* be relying on the experience of others. You're making it a team effort rather than an ego trip. And it works. Look at the next page."

It was a spreadsheet tracking brand sales of the featured products.

"Your layout outsold your father's by more than double."

"Our readership grew since he was in charge," I argued.

"Look, if you want to have a pity party, have a pity party. But sooner or later, you might as well get used to the idea that you can do this job. Your father ruled with poor taste and an iron fist. Your mother let him. Just because you're doing the job differently doesn't mean you're not as good, if not better."

I flipped to another page. It was traffic stats on some of the web content I'd been in charge of. The video of Brownie French-kissing me was one of the most popular videos we'd posted in the last twelve months.

"Why do you have these compiled and ready to go?" I asked, baffled.

"I told you I was going to be the second-best assistant you ever had. What kind of an assistant would I be if I didn't have a 'Stop Freaking Out, Boss' file?"

She started for the door.

"Does this mean you're speaking to me again?" I asked.

She didn't even stop. Simply raised a bandaged middle finger over her shoulder. "Nope. Get back to work. Your pouty time is cutting into my to-do list."

39

ALLY

"How do we want to look tonight?" Linus mused, tapping a finger to his chin.

We were staring into the depths of *Label*'s Closet. Usually, I would be willing to take whatever would zip and hold in my boobs. But tonight I wanted something more.

"We want to feel beautiful and fierce," I decided. "Have any miracles up your sleeve to accomplish that?" It would take one. A bright, shiny miracle given how I'd spent the past few months feeling like a garbage bag of a human being.

First I'd been a stripper, then I'd almost let my father get evicted from his nursing home, and finally I'd made a deal with the devil just to keep my little family afloat.

Linus looked me up and down and raised a skeptical, well-groomed eyebrow. "Would you settle for reasonably attractive and moderately assertive?"

"I would not."

"Hmm."

"Don't do your hummy 'it would take a miracle' thing with me, Linus. I know you've got something up that fabulous sleeve of yours."

With a wicked gleam in his eyes, he yanked a garment bag off a rack.

"Well, since you mentioned it…"

"What is it?"

"Don't ask questions. Go get dressed, because you know we're going to need at least an hour on your makeup and that rat's nest you call hair."

Rolling my eyes, I took the bag and the criticism and headed into the restroom.

All uncharitable thoughts about how Linus must have been a mean sorority cheerleader kicked out of school for hazing in a past life evaporated when I unzipped the bag.

"Well, holy hell." It was a miracle in a bag, and Linus Feldman was my fairy godfather.

I walked back into the room feeling like Cinder-freaking-ella. If Cinderella's fairy godmother had given her a sexy, skin-hugging gown the color of crimson or, as I liked to think of it, Dominic Russo's crushed heart.

"Not entirely hideous," Linus said when I made a slow circle for him. He held out his hand. A pair of gold-dusted stilettos dangled by their straps from his fingers. "You'll wear these, and you won't whine about how much they hurt."

I nodded dutifully. I was an obedient Cinderella.

A quick spin through the makeup lab, half an hour in the chair of a miracle worker with a curling iron, and I looked like someone brand new. No more sad, poor, new girl lusting over her boss.

Nope. I was a breathtaking goddess deserving of tasteful lusting.

The dress. Oh, that damn dress. It was soft on my skin and a bold red. The skirt fell away from a split up my right leg. The fabric was light, airy layers of chiffon that billowed behind me like a cape when I walked—or stalked, as Linus instructed. The top ended an inch above my belly button, offering a peek of stomach and pale, New York–winter skin. It had cap sleeves and zero cleavage, but the way it hugged my breasts was almost sinful. There was a silk tie at the back of my top that kept it cinched in under my breasts, and when I moved, it felt like a caress.

And it wasn't just the clothes. Or the sleek, smoky eyes. Or the bold lips and sex-tousled hair. I was remembering who I was underneath it all. Beneath the stress and the broken fingernails, the cheap clothes, and the just starting to catch up on sleep again. I was Ally Morales, and I had a value that went way deeper than what one man accepted or rejected.

"Well, hot damn," Linus said.

Hot damn indeed. I nodded at my reflection.

"Where in the hell did you find this dress?" I asked.

He plucked a stray piece of fuzz off the cap sleeve. "It was a leftover from a shoot last year. We didn't end up using it. None of the models could be pinned into it since it was made for someone with…" He gestured at my boobs. The dress had been made for them. "It's Christian's. He'll like seeing you in it tonight."

I thought I detected a hint of mischief in his tone.

"What are you up to, Linus?"

He spread his hands, the picture of innocence except for the smirk that played over his lips. "Your fairy godfather doesn't need to have an ulterior motive."

"Now I'm very suspicious."

"Just go and don't fall on your face," he instructed.

"Aren't you going?" I asked.

"Like this?" he scoffed, waving a hand over his impeccable black-on-black suit.

"Uh, yeah."

"Can't. Kids have a school thing."

"*Kids?* You have *children?*"

"Why is everyone so surprised by that?"

He pulled out his phone and gave me a five-minute slideshow of little Jasper, Adelaide, and Jean-Charles.

I was still reeling by the time I got downstairs. One thing that I *really* liked about this job was the car service. It wasn't Nelson but a female driver who opened the back door for me. And the back seat was occupied by a very stylish Dalessandra.

"I thought we'd ride together and we could chat," she said, patting the seat.

There are moments in everyone's life when they stop, breathe, and wonder who the hell's life they're actually living. Cruising through Midtown in a limo with one of the fashion industry's most influential icons next to me in a design that had obviously been made just for her was one of those moments.

"You look lovely," she said. "That dress."

"*Me?* Look at your dress." Even seated and in the dim interior light, she stunned. The gown was layers and layers of silver and gray and cream arranged like swan feathers. Slouchy suede boots that I would have sold an ovary for peeked out from the hem.

"Perks of the job," she said, waving away the compliment. "Now, how are things?"

"Things are fine," I fibbed. My neck started to itch.

"Fine? Everyone you've met. Everyone you've talked to on staff. They're all fine?"

I was not mentally prepared for this conversation. No, what I'd spent all day girding my loins for was seeing Dominic outside work.

I will not inappropriately touch my boss tonight.

I will not inappropriately touch my boss tonight.

I'd repeated the mantra all damn day.

The past few weeks had been an exquisite kind of torture. Every morning when he arrived and walked past my desk, I smelled that body wash of his and was immediately transported back to his home, his shower, *the reason* I'd been in his shower.

And then I had to remind myself why I was barely speaking to the man.

"What about Dominic?" Dalessandra asked, pursing her red, red lips together.

"What about him?" I hedged.

She slid a knowing gaze to me. "You two are close."

I shook my head vehemently enough to have a hairpin fly out and land in my lap. "We're really not."

"You are," she insisted. "Is he happy? Does he hate me for what I've asked of him?"

I cleared my throat and felt disloyal to a man who hadn't officially earned my loyalty. "I don't think anyone would say that Dominic is a happy man," I ventured.

"But you see beneath all that bluster." Dalessandra made the statement like it was a fact. "Is he really unhappy? Did I ask too much of him in stepping in to clean up his father's mess?"

I considered gnawing my lipstick off but then decided it wasn't worth the tongue-lashing I'd get from Linus if he saw the pictures.

"I don't know exactly what happened last year," I said with a sigh. "Hell, nobody seems to except for you and Dom. And maybe that's part of the problem. But no, he doesn't hate you.

Beneath all those sexy vests and grumpy snarls, he's a caretaker. He wants you to be happy. He wants to make you happy. And I think you know that. I also think you should be having this conversation with him."

"We Russos don't have conversations," Dalessandra said with a sad smile.

Tell me about it.

"Maybe you should give it a shot. Especially if you're proud of the work your son is doing for you."

"Dominic knows I'm proud of him," she said stiffly.

"Just like everyone in the office knows that whatever mysterious thing went down last year will never happen again because you have their backs and will never let anyone take advantage of position and power again?"

The emerald on Dalessandra's hand winked as she tightened her fingers into a fist in her skirt.

"I have a reputation to protect," she said coolly. "Airing dirty laundry isn't how one survives in this world."

"Reputations can't be built on sweeping things under the rug," I reminded her. "They're built on stories. You're in control of your story and how it's told…or not told."

"You're not seriously suggesting that I bare my soul to the world about how I was stupid enough, blinded by ambition enough, to not notice what was going on in my own office, my own marriage?"

"Even if you were stupid or blind—which I certainly don't think you were—you aren't anymore. And that's what your people deserve to know."

"My people," she repeated to herself. "What if my story isn't only mine to tell? What if there are others who might not want their parts shared?"

"I think that's where those conversations come in to play,"

I said, patting myself on the back for the callback. I was nailing this sage advisor thing tonight. It was probably the dress.

"You certainly have a lot of opinions," Dalessandra mused.

"So I've been told. By your son. On multiple occasions."

"Speaking of my son, he likes you very much."

"I feel like it's more accurate to say I infuriate him very much," I corrected her.

"I've asked a lot of him," she said.

"You have."

"I hope he doesn't assume I'm asking him to put his life on hold for me, for this job."

Tread carefully, I warned myself.

"I don't think you're the Russo who's keeping Dom from living his best life," I said cagily.

Dalessandra studied me quietly in the dark.

"Have you spelled out any more messages for him with his food?" she asked, changing the subject.

"As a matter of fact..." I pulled out my phone to show her the ass foam.

40

ALLY

Dalessandra and I parted ways so she could walk the red carpet at the trendy gallery while I ducked in behind the action.

I'd been in this neighborhood a few times. It was funny how a few feet of sidewalk could be dotted with old chewing gum and discarded fast-food bags by day and transformed by night with a broom, a few sawhorses, and some red fabric.

Money could temporarily transform anything.

I checked my coat, thrilled that I no longer had to cringe at the thought of tipping later, and followed my nose to the bar.

The gallery was a wide expanse of concrete floors, high, industrial ceilings, and temporary walls. The current exhibit was some kind of modern art that I didn't get. Slashes of color, silly string glued to canvas, and a particularly confusing sculpture that looked as though it had been created by a day care class on Play-Doh day.

But the music thrummed at a seductive throb, the lights

were low, and a buzz of excitement circulated among the well-dressed attendees.

Hello, open bar.

"What can I get you?" The bartender was unintimidatingly cute. I needed to get back to finding that attractive instead of the brooding dominance of Mr. Created by Angels Until the Devil Took Over.

The bartender's eyes took a leisurely journey over me, and I remembered the dress.

"White wine. No, wait. Champagne," I decided. If I spilled it, it wouldn't stain, and the bubbles would keep me from mainlining it.

"You got it," he said.

"That dress on you," I heard a familiar voice say.

I turned and found Christian James, designer extraordinaire, behind me, a wicked grin on his handsome face. He pressed a palm above his heart, letting his fingers mimic a beat.

"It would appear the designer is a genius."

"Clearly," he said with a blinding grin. And there was the dimple. Yum.

From a detached, purely scientific distance, I weighed my reaction to the man. Charming. Funny. A damn genius with a needle and thread. He was flirting with me, and I was enjoying it.

And then there was a lightning strike of awareness a second later when I caught a glimpse of Dominic across the room. He was in conversation with a mix of beautiful people, but he was looking at me.

One look at the man in his jeans and boots and that fucking vest that I knew he was wearing just to piss me off and my heart rate accelerated into cycling class territory.

Did I somehow get off on the rejection? I took a hasty gulp of champagne.

Well, there would be no more rejections, because I was done where Dominic was concerned. He couldn't have been clearer, and neither could I. Plus, if I were stupid enough to offer myself up to him one more time, I'd lose the last piece of my self-respect.

If only I could just erase him from my brain. Even now, I could feel him glowering at me. A tickle of discomfort between my shoulder blades, a shiver of awareness up my spine. It almost felt…exciting. And that made me want to barf.

Maybe it wasn't the cheese hormones. Maybe it was something much, much worse.

"Do you mind?" Christian asked, offering me his hand. "So I can see how the fabric moves? Also, I just really like looking at you."

"It's your party," I said, putting a little more effort into the flirtation.

He put my drink on the bar and took my hand.

"Beautiful. I could see you in this in white. A beach wedding. Flowers in your hair. Very bohemian. After the ceremony, you'd jump into the ocean with your very lucky groom."

I was blushing.

"The beautiful, blushing bride," he mused. "What are your thoughts?"

"I don't have the time or prospects for marriage."

He grinned again. "I meant the dress. If this were your wedding gown, what would you add? Take away?"

"Shimmer."

"Ah yes," he said approvingly. "Something subtle that would catch the sunlight and make you look—"

"Magic."

"Exactly." The eyebrow he arched was elegant. "Turn for me?"

I shrugged. He pulled me in like we were on the dance floor and then gently pushed me away. I twirled like that faceless ballerina in the jewelry box my dad got me for my fifth birthday to store all my plastic rings and bracelets.

Then he was playfully pulling me back in. On a devilish grin, he used my momentum and leaned me back over his leg in an extravagant dip.

The guests around us broke into spontaneous applause, and I came up laughing. God, it felt good to laugh.

Someone at the bar behind us slammed a crystal glass down hard enough to crack it.

"Let me help you with that, sir," the bartender said, taking the broken glass from Dominic. That glower was a whole lot warmer up close. I felt like my dress was going to catch fire, burn off my body, and leave me standing here naked. Maybe I should have worn pasties again.

"Dominic." Christian turned his wattage on my boss and offered him that friendly manshake with the shoulder slap. "Good to see you. I'm hearing a lot of good things about you at *Label*."

Dominic's eyes blazed with something unrecognizable. He was looking at me.

"Do you have a minute? I'd like to discuss some logistics." The question was for Christian, but Dominic's eyes burned into my flesh like a brand. The hand he clamped on Christian's shoulder didn't look friendly as he steered my dance partner away from me.

"Honey, I don't know what that was about," the bartender said, staring after the men. "But Vest Guy looks like he can't decide if he wants to spank you or devour you."

I blinked. "So I'm not imagining it?"

"That was a code nuclear. If I had lady parts and took him to bed, I'd be concerned about my vagina spontaneously exploding."

It was a real concern.

"I think I need another drink."

"I think you do too," he said, placing another flute of

champagne on the bar and then pouring a shot. "This is to take the edge off Vagina Exploding Vest Guy."

"Thanks."

"Cheers, doll."

I made a few rounds, checking in on Dalessandra, and landed with a few of the ad sales reps near the kitchen. We'd astutely discovered we got first dibs on trayed appetizers if we actively stalked the waitstaff.

I kept tabs on Dominic as he circulated the room. Every time it looked as if he were heading in my direction, I made a hasty exit and went somewhere else. I'd even hidden in the restroom for twenty minutes trying to calm down. He was prowling. We were circling each other, and I just didn't have it in me for another argument or another ten reasons why I wasn't good enough for him.

"Can we just talk about how delicious Dominic Russo looks tonight?" Nina from advertising sighed into her wineglass. She was tall and slim with untamable curly hair and blue eyes that always seemed to twinkle.

"Yes, please," Ruth said, feigning a swoon.

"I don't think it's fair that someone that attractive isn't dating. Me. Dating me," copywriter Missie said. Missie was a petite little thing who had a tendency to burst into song when she was nervous.

"What's his deal?" asked Gola, who was looking entirely too fabulous in a navy slip dress that highlighted her truly fantastic shoulders.

"Yeah, Ally. What's his deal?" Ruth asked.

All eyes turned in my direction.

"Uh, how should I know?"

"You work five feet from the man. How is your brain still functioning?" Nina asked. "Mine would have turned to hormonal mush by now."

"Have you tried giving up cheese?" I offered.

"Ally is immune to the guy," Gola insisted.

"Immune? I wouldn't go that far," I said, pretending not to remember that I'd recently put new batteries for my vibrator on my shopping list.

"He's so different from his dad. Like, besides the looks, I can't believe they're related," Missie said.

"Yeah, Dominic Russo wouldn't corner someone in the copy room and show them his dick," Gola agreed.

No, he wouldn't. Not even if she—I—wanted him to.

"Isn't that a pity?" Missie said.

We all laughed. Some champagne made its way up my nose.

"It's a little ironic, isn't it, that what's harassment from one douche would be welcome coming from someone else?" Gola mused.

"Consent makes everything sexy," Ruth said.

"To consent," I said, raising my glass.

"I'd consent all over Dominic Russo if he'd let me," the adorably drunk Missie said to the bottom of her cocktail.

"Did that really happen? In the copy room, I mean?" I asked, swinging the conversation back in the direction from whence it had come.

"Girl, Paul Russo was a straight-up creeper," Nina said. "The day he left, a bunch of us went out at lunch and bought cheap-ass champagne and drank a toast to never having to get our asses groped again."

"And then we did it again when Dominic came on board," Missie added dreamily. "Because he's so beautiful."

"You guys ever think about telling Dominic that?" I asked.

"What? That we think he's crazy hot? Like 'the devil created him, he's that hot' hot?" Nina frowned.

"Uh, no. The part about you're glad he's here and you like working with him."

"You mean actually speak to that fine man fillet? Nope. No thanks. I once ran into him coming out of a conference room, and rather than apologize, I sprinted into the bathroom. The men's bathroom," Missie confessed. "He's so beautiful and broody, and I just want to be the one to tame him and show him love." She sang the last few words Broadway-style.

"But he's so ungettable. I think that's what I like about him best. If I could get him, I'd be beautiful and special and obviously really good in bed because he's not the type of man to settle for anything less." Ruth sighed.

I covered my laugh with another sip of champagne. Dominic would literally die if he could hear this conversation.

"What's it like being his assistant?" Gola demanded.

"Yes, spill. All the details."

Why was everyone pumping me for information on the man tonight? "Uh. I don't know. He likes tea. He's crotchety on the outside, but he's mostly an okay human being."

They waited raptly for more Dominic tidbits.

"He listens when I talk. He's careful, conscientious. He cares about what he's doing. He is definitely not his father. Overall, he's a good boss."

"You guys fight a lot. Not gonna lie, it's totally hot. I want to be you when I grow up," Missie trilled.

"We just rub each other the wrong way. And I'm only with him until his admin Greta comes back. Here's hoping I end up with a husband who surprises me with a two-month European tour next, right?"

They exchanged glances.

"What?"

"Her husband didn't surprise her," Nina said. "Dominic sent her away."

41

ALLY

I was blinking so rapidly, my eyelashes felt like hummingbird wings.

"Dominic sent Greta away?" I asked Nina, going for nonchalance.

"Would any of you lovely ladies like to try—"

"Not now, Carl!" I yelled at the approaching server with his tray of butterflied shrimp. The man ran off with his appetizers.

"Oh yeah," Nina said, waving a hand. "I heard it from a friend of a friend of a friend. Dominic personally arranged the vacation time with HR. He called Jasmine—the grumpy one with zero camera skills—at home at two a.m. on a Friday night and said he needed the deal done that weekend."

"Technically, she wasn't at home. She was out clubbing with a super cute jazz singer she met on a pub crawl," Missie chimed in.

"Wait a second. Grumpy HR Jasmine, the mid-sneeze

immortalizer, goes clubbing with jazz singers?" I asked. "You know what? Never mind. Please continue."

"Anyway, he said it was a thank-you for putting up with his bullshit for so long. He paid out of pocket for her time off *and* her travel. Can you imagine?" Nina gushed.

"Two a.m. on a Friday?" I asked.

"What would he have been doing at that time of night that he decided he needed to send his assistant away for two months?" Gola asked.

"Maybe she witnessed him committing a murder," I said nervously.

I knew exactly what he'd been doing that Friday night. It would have been about ten minutes after I stormed out of his town house.

I needed another shot from potentially bisexual bartender guy.

By the next morning, I'd had the promotion and "signing bonus." I knew he'd puppet-mastered me into it. I just hadn't realized how diabolical he'd been. I thought he'd taken advantage of a situation, not manipulated his admin into a sixty-day paid vacation.

"Not to stir up the rumor mill, Ally," Nina said, pulling me out of my bitter fugue state, "but I think he likes you. Like really likes you."

"Or hates you," Missie added. "We honestly can't decide. We go back and forth about it. I personally hope he hates you because he's saving all his love for me. But he looks at you like he wants to throttle you or throw you out of a moving vehicle or—"

"Fuck your brains out," Nina filled in helpfully.

I choked on my own spit. "Guys, I'm not, like, sleeping my way to the top. I assure you. And Dominic has no interest in me whatsoever."

"First of all, you're no Malina. You wouldn't bang your boss to get ahead. You'd bang him because he's so hot I bet he can make scrambled eggs on his abs," Gola insisted. "He's said that though? About not being interested in you?"

I closed my eyes. "On multiple occasions."

"He's lying. He's totally lying," Ruth squealed.

"I've never seen a man look at a woman like that. Like he's a kid looking in the window of a candy store and he's deciding if he's willing to break the glass to get to the candy and devour it," Missie said, glassy-eyed.

"Well, that's an uncomfortable description," I said.

I felt a thrill of heat work its way down my spine.

"He's looking at you right now," Nina said without moving her lips, which made it all the more suspicious. Everyone but me whipped around to zero in on Dominic.

"Definitely wants to throw her off a roof."

"After he gives her, like, ten orgasms."

"Can I please be you when I grow up?" Missie whisper-sang.

"Why wouldn't you two just get together?" Ruth asked, fanning herself with a cocktail napkin.

"Besides the fact that I'm not his type, he's not my type, he's not interested in me, and sleeping with coworkers is a bad idea?"

"Yeah. Besides all that," Ruth said.

"His dad," I said.

I faced four confused-looking women. "We're not picking up what you're putting down," Gola said.

"He takes your inability to stare directly into his beauty and your mad escapes to the men's room to mean you're afraid of him. You know, like you think he's another pervert."

Their resounding chorus of "Are you fucking kidding me?" was instantaneous and loud enough that half the room turned to see what all the fuss was about.

"Oh my God! Pull yourselves together," I said, shushing them.

"You know, if we lowered some of the barriers, maybe he'd make his move on Ally?" Ruth said.

"Lowered barriers? Guys, I don't think we should be conspiring against management."

"We're conspiring *for* him. Not against him," Gola mused. "If Dominic understood that we thought he was a good boss, that we weren't comparing him to his dad, maybe he'd break the glass and eat the candy."

"No, no, no. Nope. Nope. Uh-uh. No one is conspiring against or for anything. No one is eating any candy."

"Ally, you're the kind of fairy tale we all need," Nina insisted. "Poor country bumpkin—"

"Hey, I'm from Jersey, jerk."

Nina waved me off. "Shh! I'm telling a story here. Poor Jersey bumpkin comes to the big city and catches the eye of the gorgeous, grumpy boss who refuses to fall for anyone. But there's something special about her. Something he's never seen before in a woman."

"I want to be special," Missie whined.

"You are special. We are all special," I insisted.

I felt the frisson again. This time, it started at my toes and spread through my entire body.

"He's coming this way," Missie sang.

"Be cool, guys. For the love of God, be cool," I hissed.

"He's practically pushing people out of the way," Ruth observed.

I hoped to God she was exaggerating.

"Hey, beautiful. Feel like causing a stir?" Christian appeared at my side and gave me a heart attack.

I clutched my heart. "Jiminy Crickets! Where did you come from?"

"Uh, the bar." He grinned at me and wiggled a rocks glass. "I have an idea. Come with me."

He was safer than whatever torpedo of sexy was headed my way. I took the hand he offered and let him drag me away.

Five minutes later, an up-and-coming designer was on his knees in front of me backstage, and his hands were on my breast.

"Ouch. That's boob," I hissed. "Are you tattooing me?"

"Sorry," Christian said through the pins in his mouth. "Try to hold still, and I won't stab you as much."

"You know, usually I wait until at least dinner and drinks before I let a guy feel me up."

"This is completely professional. I promise," he insisted with a lecherous wink. "Not that you're not built to perfection, of course."

"Oh, of course." I rolled my eyes.

"I just only have room for so many obsessions. I've got a limited amount of bandwidth. Right now, mine is this line. What's yours?" He sat back on his heels and admired his handiwork.

"Oh, I don't think you have the time. Besides, tonight's your night."

He picked up the top layer of my skirt and fluffed it. "You know what I see when there's a pile of fabric in front of me and a beautiful woman?"

"I'm guessing not just a pile of fabric and a beautiful woman?"

He shot his pointer finger at me. "Bingo, smart-ass."

I helped him to his feet.

"I see a story, and I try to tell that story with cut and color, thread and accessories."

"I like that," I mused into my now warm and mostly flat champagne. I'd clung to the idea of using it as a prop. Also I didn't want to get shit-faced at a work function and throw myself at Dominic or throw him off a rooftop.

"Do you want to know what I see in you?"

"Definitely not."

"I see sexiness. Struggle. Someone who isn't living the life she set out to build," he mused.

"Are you like one of those fortune tellers who spouts generic crap until they hit the mark?" I joked.

He grinned, then continued. "I see a woman who would do anything for the people who have earned her loyalty. Someone who'll stand up for those who can't. I see someone who is fighting tooth and nail for something…or someone."

I frowned into my champagne.

"And I see that you have a very complicated relationship with Dominic Russo."

"Oh, come on. Not you too. Is it a full moon tonight? This entire city is obsessed with the guy."

"From where I stand, the guy is obsessed with you," Christian insisted.

"Okay, enough of this artistic babble. You're starting to freak me out."

"Don't be embarrassed. You're amazing. Own it."

"I can't afford to own anything right now."

"Then that's where this dress comes in," he said. "You're stunning. And bold. And your boss is going to have a coronary in about half an hour."

"I don't care if Dominic ever looks at me again," I lied. My neck immediately started itching.

Christian's smirk told me he wasn't buying it.

"I don't," I doubled down. "He had his chance, and I have

too much self-respect. I just want to make him suffer. Like a lot. But not enough for me to lose my job. It's a fine line to walk."

He flashed those dimples at me. "Then let's make the man suffer."

"Are you sure this is okay? I'm a nobody in the fashion world, and I don't look anything like the rest of these women." I looked around at the models in the midst of hair and makeup and fittings. They were all half-naked and looked bored. *Just another day at the office.*

"That's the point. Besides, I've never walked the end of a show with anyone. It'll get the press talking. You don't mind, do you?"

"I might wreck your entire show and ruin your launch, your career, and then your life. I'm not very lucky right now."

"I'll take my chances. Maybe you should take a couple of your own."

God willing, in a few short months, the house would be sold, Dad's bills would be covered, and I could afford to take a few chances. Maybe start a new life somewhere nowhere near Dominic Russo. Perhaps the West Coast. Or, I don't know, Thailand? Although I wouldn't feel comfortable leaving my dad. Not now. Maybe I'd just vacation in Thailand?

Bottom line. A little fashion industry speculation would have zero effect on my life.

"Eh. It's fine. Let's go stir up some shit," I decided.

"Good. It'll be fun," he promised.

42

DOMINIC

The show was finally about to start, and I was beyond grateful, because it meant that in thirty minutes, I (a) could give up the pretense of small talk and schmoozing, (b) had time for one more drink, and (c) could go home and forget about Ally and that goddamn red dress.

Lying to myself was my new favorite hobby.

Of course she'd look like that in fucking couture. Half angel, half devil in siren red. But I'd still be compelled to watch her from across the room if she'd showed up in sweatpants and an I Heart NYC sweatshirt.

I was drawn to her. Inexplicably. Unfairly. Stupidly.

And I had to do something to get her out of my head. It was unhealthy. This week, I'd actually looked up the dance studio schedule where she taught and thought about having Nelson cruise by after her class. Then I thought about how stalkers probably felt about their victims, and I had him take me to a bar instead.

I was drinking too much tonight, but I could blame that on my mother. Apparently, Drunk Me was nicer than Sober Me. My mother always encouraged me to have a few drinks before social events so I wouldn't scare away advertisers.

If I had too much—breaking news: hell yeah, I had too much—I'd Uber home, leave my car for an intern to pick up.

I ditched my empty glass on the bar and waited. The bartender in a gold lamé vest shot me a knowing look. "Rough night?" he asked, pouring me another.

"You speak the truth," I said. Dammit, the niceness was kicking in already. I picked up the fresh drink and turned to scan the ballroom. *Where is she?*

I didn't see a goddess in red. She'd camped out in front of the kitchen to snag more appetizers, which immediately made me worry that she wasn't using her new paycheck to buy actual food. I spent a lot of time worrying and wondering about her.

What she ate on the weekends.

What she did late at night when she couldn't sleep.

If she thought about me half as much as I thought about her.

I hadn't seen her since I'd worked up the nerve to go over and strike up a conversation with the women she'd been talking to. It was reasonable that I could ask the ad rep about the new online ad sizes we'd be rolling out. And I could have looked at Ally. Maybe even smiled?

But she'd disappeared. Whisked away by that goddamn designer who should have been more worried about the success of his line than one woman in a dress.

Even if it was Ally. Especially if it was Ally.

This cold, professional thing with her was killing me. I missed her sitting on my desk and fighting with me. I missed the sparks that ignited when we argued. I missed her.

The lights began to dim in the room. A buzz of excitement

rose as people moved to take their seats next to the runway on white linen-covered chairs.

I still didn't see Ally, and I was beyond the point of trying to hide the fact that I was looking for her. I stopped Irvin on his way to the front row. "Have you seen Ally?" I asked.

"Who?"

"My assistant," I said dryly. I lived in a world where everyone should know her.

"I think I saw her in a little United Nations circle." He chuckled.

Another comment that rubbed me the wrong way. I was going to revisit the topic of Irvin with my mother and soon. "I meant recently."

"In that dress? If she's smart, probably off enjoying a tryst in a dark corner."

I suddenly wanted to throw up the three or four scotches that were hitting my empty gut like a stomach bug. And then punch someone. Or maybe vice versa. My plan was a little muddled.

"Dominic!" My mother waved us both over, and we took our seats in the front row. "Are you all right?" she asked.

I had been better. "Great," I muttered.

"You smell like a distillery," she whispered.

"You smell really nice," I said sullenly.

Her lips curved in amusement. "Thank you."

At least my mom thought I was being a dutiful employee and not an obsessive, creepy stalker.

I didn't think she could afford to have both men in her immediate family disappoint her.

The show began, and I maintained a modicum of interest while carefully searching the faces of the audience on the other side of the elevated runway. No red dress. No Ally.

The thing about fashion shows is it's a lot of buildup, a lot of invested time, money, and energy for a few minutes of payoff. The models made their way past me one by one. Beautiful women in beautiful clothes. And not a damn one of them held a candle to my missing-in-action personal assistant.

Finally, the lights came up, and that was when I found her.

On the arm of Christian "About to Be a Dead Man" James.

They strolled down the runway arm in arm, laughing at an inside joke that they shouldn't have. There was a stir around me. I don't know if it was the dress, the designer, or the girl. *My* girl.

He pirouetted her like a fucking ballerina at the end of the aisle to the delighted applause of the crowd.

My mother elbowed me. "Start clapping, you clod," she said out of the side of her mouth.

I clapped with a decisive lack of enthusiasm, imagining smashing Christian's face between my palms. They were coming back now, still laughing, the crowd still applauding, trailed by the rest of the models that I didn't even see now. Because my attention was focused entirely on the small, white pearlescent heart sewn onto the dress's bodice.

Right over Ally's breast.

It was cracked down the middle.

Just like Christian's face would be if he'd sewn it on her personally.

43

ALLY

Okay, so it had been pretty damn cool to strut down the runway in a beautiful dress on the arm of a very attractive man in front of the guy who'd rejected me repeatedly.

When I returned to the party, I felt almost cheerful.

And suddenly exhausted. I wanted to go home, curl up in bed, and relive Dominic's shock over and over again in my head. I'd give it another twenty minutes, say my goodbyes, and be in bed within an hour.

"Oh. My. God. That was amazing. *You* were amazing," Gola squealed.

"I'm considering murdering you and assuming your identity," Missie trilled. I got the feeling she was only half kidding.

"Not creepy at all," I told her.

"That was incredible," Ruth said, throwing her arms around me and hugging me tight.

"Thanks. Now I could use a drink."

We moved en masse toward the bar. When I ordered a water, the bartender shot me a sly smile and leaned in. "Someone in a vest almost as sexy as mine was frantically scanning the crowd looking for you earlier."

I grinned. Victory was mine. It was a good night.

A very young woman I didn't know popped up next to me and squealed. "Girl, you are already trending." She held up her phone to my face. A fashion blogger had tweeted a photo of the end of the show, me and Christian laughing at the end of the runway.

Christian James ends show with mystery woman in #heartbreakerdress on arm.

I felt almost euphoric.

And then I wondered where Dominic was.

And then I wanted to slap myself for wondering.

I was going to need to start wearing a rubber band on my wrist and snap it every time I thought of him. At this rate, I'd amputate my hand inside twenty minutes.

The runway was disassembled into artsy cubes and rearranged for uncomfortable perching. Everyone was hitting the open bar like it was last call, and those little appetizers were doing nothing to soak up the liquor. It was entertaining, but I had a feeling this was how bad things happened at office Christmas parties.

Inhibitions lowered, tongues loosened, and shit went down.

I wanted to be out of here before that part happened. I'd rubbed my awesomeness in Dominic's face, and now it was time to go the hell home and eat some leftovers in bed.

Fifteen more minutes and I could slip out of here and fall asleep looking impossibly glamorous on the subway.

I limped toward one of the cubes with my water, wondering how the hell I was going to make it to the nearest subway station in these shoes. I didn't quite make it.

A set of keys dangled in front of my face so close they bounced off my nose.

A hard listing Dominic was attached to them. He had both of our coats draped over one shoulder.

"Are you playing Oprah? Did I win a car?" I asked warily.

"You won the honor of driving me home." He was tilting his head, making his grin lopsided. "You're so pretty, Malef—uh…Malcifa… Ally. Is your real name Ally, or are you Allison?"

Oh boy. I'd heard rumors of Drunk Dominic, but they hadn't prepared me for the reality of him. He was adorable… and in no way capable of functioning as creative director right now. I needed to get him home.

"Let's go, boss," I said, snatching the keys from his hand.

"Yay!" he said goofily. His smile was so sweet it made my teeth hurt.

Oh no. Nope. Nope. Nope. Not happening. I was not going to fall for sweet, drunk Dominic. No! I would remain steadfast in my resolve and other fancy words.

"Come on, big guy," I said, guiding him away from the party and toward the side entrance.

It was hell-froze-over cold outside, and Drunk Dominic insisted on wearing my coat draped over his shoulders because "It smells nice." So once again, I shoved my arms through his wool trench and towed the man toward the parking garage. At least this time I was wearing more than pasties and a thong under it.

"Why didn't you use a driver?" I asked.

"First, Nelson is at a science fair tonight for his granddaughter. And third, if I did, you wouldn't be going home with me," he said, throwing a heavy arm over my shoulder and nuzzling into my ear.

"I'm driving you home, not going home with you," I corrected.

The keys belonged to the Range Rover, and thanks to the *beep-boop* of the remote—which Dominic helpfully recreated a dozen times—I found the SUV on the second level.

I opened the passenger door for him since he seemed incapable. But he didn't get in. Instead, he wrapped his arms around me.

"What are you doing?" My words were muffled against his chest.

He stroked a big hand through my hair a little harder than he probably intended. His fingers snagged clumsily on bobby pins. "Hugging you."

"I can see that. Why?"

"I've always wanted to," he confessed.

My heart melted like full-fat, salted butter. Drunk Dominic was Tell All the Truth Dominic. *Oh, this drive is going to be fun.*

I weighed my options but finally gave in and wrapped my arms around his waist. He rested his face on the top of my head. "This is really nice," he slurred happily.

Dammit. It was.

He was transferring more and more of his weight onto me until I was the only thing holding up his 220-some muscled pounds. "Okay, buddy. Let's get you in the car."

"I'm not Buddy. Buddy is Buddy," he insisted. "Dr. Chopra loves Buddy."

"She does, does she?" I said, guiding him toward the passenger seat.

"Yep." He nodded forcefully. "She says his wife is doing great."

"That's nice. Don't hit your head."

He smacked his head getting in. "Ow."

"Are you okay?" I asked, cupping his face in my hands, looking for blood.

His eyes were almost indigo in this light.

"Can I hug you in the car?" he whispered.

"Probably better not. I'll be driving."

He looked so sad my heart cracked right down the middle.

"Oh," he said. Then he brightened. "Can I have a milkshake?"

I sighed. My dairy hiatus hadn't solved my problems. And a milkshake sounded really good right now. "Sure. Why not?"

I buckled him in, accidentally discovering that the man was ticklish, and then got behind the wheel. I mashed the push-button start and fired up the seat warmers. Then froze.

"Dominic Russo."

His head lolled to the side so he could stare lovingly at me. "That's me."

"How do you know Buddy's wife's physical therapist?" I asked.

He leaned forward. "How do you know I know her?" he asked.

"You just told me."

"I did?"

"You're drunk, not stupid. Spill it, Charming."

"I'm not supposed to tell."

"Says who?"

"Me. It's a secret."

"Did you hire Dr. Chopra for Buddy?"

"Absolutely not," he said very seriously. Then he started laughing. "I hired her for his wife because you were all 'Oh, Buddy is the greatest human being in the history of the world!'"

Dominic emphasized his relatively accurate impression of me with a sweeping gesture that nearly put his fist through the window. "Ow."

"Dom, maybe try not to flail around so much."

"'Kay."

"Why did you do that for Buddy? Do you even know him?"

"I did it for you," he insisted.

My wall was tumbling down one brick at a time, and I didn't want to let it go. I backed out of the space and found my way out of the parking garage.

"Don't tell Buddy about my secret," he said when we pulled onto the street.

"Why don't you want him to know? You're doing something amazing for his wife."

"Shh!" He slapped a finger over my lips and slid it partially up my nose. "He can't know. This way, *he* earned it. *He's* the hero."

"Oh, Dom." Damn it. My shattered broken heart was trying to knit itself back together just so it could fall for him all over again.

"Pinkie promise me," he said, jabbing his pinkie in the vicinity of my eye.

"Ah!" I jerked to avoid losing my cornea. The Range Rover followed suit and swerved into the other lane. I answered the cab's angry horn with a middle finger. "Yeah, okay. I'm losing an eye here, and you had to use your brakes. Big freaking deal."

"Ally," Dominic whispered.

"Dom, I'm a little busy trying not to kill us."

"You didn't pinkie promise me yet."

"Oh, for fuck's sake." I hooked my pinkie around his and tried not to fall in love with the idiot when he pressed his lips to our joined fingers.

44

DOMINIC

I felt warm and cozy and safe and happy. And very, very drunk.

I couldn't hug Ally because she was driving, but I could wrap up in her coat. So I shoved my arms through the sleeves and wore it like a blanket.

"What kind of a milkshake do you want?" she asked, double-parking and throwing the hazards on in front of the golden arches. She was so pretty.

"Pfft," I snorted. "The only kind there is."

She raised an eyebrow. "Chocolate?"

"Duh. Don't say the v-word in my presence," I warned. She gave me a "you're so stupid" smile, and in my drunken state, I decided to treasure it always. "I love it when you smile at me." The smile faded from those lips, and I realized I'd said the words out loud. "Oops. I'm not supposed to say that stuff."

"What other stuff aren't you supposed to say?" she asked.

"That I think about you all the time and I really want to see you naked." Somewhere deep in my brain, where the obscene amount of scotch I'd consumed hadn't yet penetrated, I was yelling at myself, pushing alarm buttons, and tapping out Morse code. *Shut. The. Fuck. Up. Man.*

"Oh boy," Ally sighed. "Wait here. I'll be back with your milkshake."

She slid out of the vehicle and jogged around the hood. I pushed all the buttons on my door before the window went down. "Get us burgers too. Those spoon thing appetizers were stupid," I called after her.

She waved over her shoulder, and I watched her disappear into McDonald's. I entertained myself by making up songs about her.

"Ally in the red dress makes me feel like a mess," I crooned through the open window.

A guy in a yellow ski jacket threw a buck at me.

I was working on the second verse when Ally came back with a greasy fast-food bag and two chocolate milkshakes. She looked tiny, dwarfed by my coat.

"Look!" I held up the dollar triumphantly. "I was singing, and a guy gave me this."

"Wow, Dom. Maybe you can quit your day job." She thrust the bag and one of the cups at me through the open window and then climbed behind the wheel.

"If I quit my day job, I wouldn't get to see you," I reminded her.

"Gee, darn."

"You'd miss me. Like a lot." I knew she would. At this point, I couldn't imagine not seeing her five days a week. At this point, five days a week wasn't enough.

"Did you pay Greta to leave for two months?" she asked.

Those warning bells were clanging loud and clear in my head. But I was too drunk to pay attention. "Yep. She deserved it after all those years of putting up with me."

"So you sent your admin away to give me the job?"

Danger, Dominic Dumbass. Danger.

"Uh-huh."

"Was it because I needed money or because you wanted to pull my strings?"

"Pfft. You don't have strings. You're a person, not a Pin… pinochle puppet. You were so tired. And scared. And I have money. But you wouldn't take it. So I made you take it."

"I want to be so mad at you right now," she said.

"Let's go home. You can be mad at me at home. Brownie's there, and he loves me," I sighed, grabbing a fistful of French fries and shoving them into my mouth.

She looked at me and shook her head.

"Wha?" I asked, and a French fry fell out of my mouth into my lap.

"Nothing."

"Hey, do you see all this glitter in here?" I asked.

"Shut. Up. Dom."

She sounded serious, so I kept quiet. I drank my entire milkshake and ate fries—all of mine and accidentally half of hers—until she turned onto my street.

She found a space at the end of the block, and I climbed—or, more accurately, fell—out of the SUV. Ally, carrying the rest of our food and her milkshake, hurried around and picked me up.

She started laughing and then couldn't seem to stop.

"What?" I asked.

She shook her head. "I can't handle how cute you are right now."

"Cute? Me?" I frowned. "That's not right. I am very sexy and handsome all the time."

She guided me up the steps to the front door. "You sure are. And right now, you're super cute. I think it's because you're still wearing my coat."

"Can I keep it?" I asked.

"No. It's winter. I need it."

"We could just swa-swa-swapsies. No one would have to know. You could wear my coat, and I could wear your coat, and it'll be a secret. We could pinkie promise again."

"I think someone might notice you wearing a wool women's trench backward."

"You think?" I was disappointed.

"Dom, did someone put something in your drink tonight? Did Malina show up in disguise with a pocket full of roofies? Keys, please."

I dug through both of Ally's coat pockets and then my own pants before producing the key ring. "Found them," I sang. But no one gave me a dollar this time.

"Good job, Charming," she said, taking the keys from me. I leaned heavily against her while she opened the door.

"Hang on there, big guy. I think these heels have a weight limit," Ally said, propping me against the doorframe. She slipped off her stilettos and managed to wrestle me and the food into the vestibule before shutting and locking the door.

There was a ruckus on the other side of the main door to my house.

"Brownie!" I had temporarily forgotten I had a dog. This was an excellent reminder. I yanked the door open, and a brown blur of fur hurled himself at me. "Hi, buddy! Hi! Did you miss me?"

I miscalculated the wind speed of an excited chocolate Lab and ended up on my ass as Brownie devoured my face.

"Ouch! What did we say about stepping on my balls?" Ally made a choking noise, and I looked up. "Are you okay?" I asked, closing one eye to bring her into focus.

She cleared her throat and looked everywhere but me and Brownie. "Stay strong, Ally," she was chanting.

Brownie, sensing a human being who wasn't currently giving him all her love, danced over to her and plopped his ass on the floor.

"Who's the most handsome boy?" Ally crooned, ruffling his ears.

"I am," I insisted. "But Brownie's okay too."

My dog shot me a "he-he" look and went back to seducing my girl with his big, dumb brown eyes.

"Get your own girl, dog."

"Don't you listen to your daddy," she said, smushing Brownie's ecstatic face between her hands.

I had the sudden, intense urge to tell all the women in my life how much I appreciated them putting up with me.

"What are you doing, Dom?" Ally asked when I wrestled my phone out of my pants pocket.

"First, I'm going to email Shayla—the one who hates me—to tell her she does a really great job. Then I'm going to record a song for my mom and send it to her." My phone's screen seemed unusually small and out of focus.

"Okay. Let's put that on hold before you damage a retina," Ally said, taking my phone from me. "Here's a free TED Talk. Drunk texting never does what you want it to."

"But I need to say good job!"

"You need to get to bed," she countered.

Bed sounded really good. Especially with Ally. But I was still the aforementioned super drunk and wasn't too confident in my performance abilities.

"I might need a few minutes and some tea and maybe a shower before I can…you know…"

Both Allys were staring at me like I'd started speaking Swahili.

"We're not having sex, Dominic. I'm putting you to bed so you can sleep this off."

"Will you sleep it off with me?" I tried to wink and show her my underused flirtatious side.

"Are your eyes bothering you?" she asked.

I tried the wink again. "No."

"You're blinking weird."

"I'm not blinking. I'm winking."

Brownie drew our attention with a whimpering noise.

"Hafta go out, boy?" I climbed to my feet and grandly opened the door for dog and woman.

"I can take him for a walk," Ally volunteered.

"Why are you so nice to me?" I wondered out loud. "I'm an asshole, and you're all like 'I'll walk your dog.'"

"Brownie isn't responsible for his father's personality," she pointed out.

I felt like there was a deeper truth ringing around in those words, but I was distracted by her red dress and that light lemony scent that followed her everywhere.

I led the way into the kitchen and brushed off Ally's concerns about me falling and hitting my head in the backyard. "Pfft. I have perfect balance," I scoffed.

I tripped over a table leg and barely managed to stop myself from taking a header off the deck.

My backyard was a neatly landscaped scrap of—now dead—grass enclosed by a fence tall enough that my enthusiastic dog couldn't vault over. He'd certainly tried since the Vargases next door got their beagle, Cornelius. Brownie trotted out to the middle of the grass to do his good dog business, and since I was here and a man, I joined him in a communal pissing.

Back inside, I found Ally plating up burgers in the kitchen.

"You've got a nice place here, Dom," she said, sliding a tall glass of water in my direction.

Of course I did.

"You're so beautiful," I sighed, sinking down on a stool. "Not just because you're in that dumb guy's dress, but, like, all the time. You just light up every room you walk into. It's like the sun coming up. Every time I see you, I feel better. I love it when you walk into a room."

"Dom."

"I'm super drunk, Ally. You can't hold any of this against me."

"I know," she said and stroked a hand through my hair. "We'll never speak of this again."

She took the stool next to me, and we ate greasy burgers in companionable silence in my kitchen. It might have been the scotch talking, but it felt right. I wanted more of this. More of Ally Morales in my home.

Finished, she put our plates in the sink, topped off Brownie's water, and returned to me.

"Let's get you upstairs," she said.

"'Kay."

She helped me up two flights of stairs and put up with me stopping to rest with my face in her hair every few steps. I was in excellent condition, but being embarrassingly intoxicated provided the perfect excuse for me to sniff her hair.

She didn't need directions to my room. And I hoped that meant she'd spent as much time thinking about that night that she'd been here as I had.

"Stay?" I breathed when I flopped down on the bed. My eyelids were so heavy.

She flicked on the bedside lamp, and I felt her move around the mattress.

She untied one of my shoes. "Dom, I can't do that. And you don't want me to do that."

But I really, really did. "This bed is so big. And Jersey is so far."

"Yeah, well, I'm taking your car," she said.

"You can have anything you want," I offered. I was a magnanimous drunk guy. Especially when it came to the woman I couldn't stop thinking about.

"Just not you," she said. I was too drunk to tell if she was teasing or serious.

"Just not me," I agreed. "I can't be like him. I mean, not more than I already am."

"Who?" she asked.

"My dad. He sucks. Hate 'im."

"I know," she said, and I felt the shoe slide off my foot.

"I'm my father's son," I slurred.

My other shoe disappeared.

"You're also your mother's son. And last time I checked, you happen to be your own man. You make your own decisions."

"Yeah, well, I decided I don't want to be anything like him. I can't sleep with you, Ally. No matter how much I want to. No matter how much I like you. No matter how many times I pictured you spread out right here under me. I want you so much, but I can't have you."

"Why not, Dom?" Her voice was so soft, and she was playing with my hair again. I decided that was my new favorite physical sensation. Ally's fingers in my hair.

"'Cause he would have taken you. Take take take. Whatever he wanted. I don't want to be him."

"Oh, honey. You're not." I liked her voice. Liked how she called me honey.

"You say that. But I'm 'zactly like him. I jerk off in the bathroom thinking about you. Well, not anymore."

She was quiet for a beat, and then her fingers were on my necktie. "Why not?"

"Doesn't seem right. You're right outside the door. It's disrep—disruh—dis-re-spect-ful," I enunciated clearly. I was so fucking tired.

"You're not responsible for your father's actions. What he did isn't your fault."

I covered my face with my hands. "Yes, it is. It's my fault he was there to do the things he did."

"Why?"

"Never mind. Forget I said anything," I told her. I didn't want to talk about it anymore. It made me sad and sick, and I just wanted to feel good. Even if I didn't deserve it. "'Sides, I don't deserve you anyway."

My tie loosened, then vanished, and those glorious fingers were working the buttons on my shirt free. I really liked that.

"Dom?"

"Yeah?"

"Open your eyes for a second."

I did as my Angel Ally asked.

"You're nothing like your father. You never have been, and you never will be. You're a good man. You take care of people who need it. You protect them and build them up. You're going to make some woman very lucky someday."

"Wish it was you."

She cupped my face in her cool hand, and I rubbed my jaw

shamelessly against it. That easy, physical affection Ally gave was something I had no idea I needed. And I was going to have to go back to living without it.

"Get some sleep, honey," she said softly.

My eyes wouldn't open anymore. I felt the weight of the blanket she pulled over me, the bounce of Brownie jumping onto the bed.

"Thanks for taking care of me, Ally."

"Back at you, Dom."

45

ALLY

My feet and my brain were numb.

Prancing around on pinching stilettos had probably permanently damaged the nerves in my toes. And as for my brain, my boss had rendered it useless.

I eased his Range Rover into the driveway and sat in the dark. Images from the night flashed on a loop through my mind.

The dress.

The runway.

Dominic "Alcohol as Truth Serum" Russo.

I had a lot of confusing, conflicting thoughts. But it all came back to one thing. He didn't want to be like his father. It was as simple and complex as that.

Nights like these changed lives and were retold as stories for years to come. But I didn't know what my story would be. Would it be the time the up-and-coming designer made me temporarily semi-famous? Or would it be the night I finally realized my heart belonged to a man I was never going to be with?

I got it now. I got *him* now.

He wanted me but not enough to do something that—in his mind—would put him in his father's league. I had experience in that department and could respect Dominic's decision.

I wanted that revelation to free me from whatever attraction I had to the man. I wanted to feel relieved. Instead, I just felt sad. Bone-deep, soul-deep sad.

My old phone cheerfully clunked out a facsimile of a ring.

Faith. My late-night checker-inner.

"Hey," I said.

"Oh. My. God. I'm so glad you're up!" she squealed. "Girl. You are all over social media as Christian James's mystery heartbreaker! Tell me you're out partying with fancy people. Are you in a limo on your way to some celebrity's penthouse after-party?"

Faith's life was significantly more glamorous than my own. It was a special treat to have a story finally worthy of sharing.

I laughed. "I'm sitting in my driveway in my boss's Range Rover that I may or may not have stolen."

"I knew you had an inner badass! Is this the same boss who chased you out of the club after you refused to take his sexy money?"

"That's the one. It's been a weird night."

"I absolutely need every detail," she insisted. I heard her crack open a can of what was probably Mountain Dew, her post-one a.m. beverage of choice because she was immune to calories, sugar, and caffeine.

Since the SUV was warmer than my house, I stayed put and told her about the dress and the preview and party.

Faith swooned appropriately. "Are you totally into this Christian guy?"

"He's super smart and sweet and sexy," I hedged.

"But?"

I smiled. She was an expert people reader. "But the chemistry isn't right."

"Bummer. He's gorgeous, and he'd shower you in designer goodies for all the days of your life until you had a dramatic divorce. Maybe you should introduce me to him," Faith teased.

Huh. That could be interesting, I thought. Two creative free spirits with nothing but hotness in common?

"So since you're not into Hot Fashion Guy, does this mean you and Grumpy Grump Face Lap Dance Guy are on?"

I wasn't one to kiss and tell. Or drive and tell. Or help strip a man down to just his pants, listen to his confession, leave him drunk in his bed, and tell. I was a good person, gosh darn it. And it was Dominic's story to tell. Not mine.

"Definitely and irrevocably not on." I sighed, picturing that bare chest with just the right amount of hair, those arms with just the right amount of ink.

"Disappointed!" she groaned.

You and me both, sister.

"Only you can be surrounded by hot guys who clearly want to tear your clothes off yet still end up fully clothed and home alone on a Friday night."

"I think it's the universe telling me I have too much shit going on to worry about men right now," I told her. It was also probably a kick in the teeth from said universe, reminding me that a man whose most important relationship in life was the hatred he had for his father would not make a good frenemy with benefits.

The universe was right. Focusing on my dad, the house,

and my job was all I had room for. Until I could fix up and sell this house, until my dad's bills were settled, I had no right to spread my focus around.

"You know, babe, sometimes it's up to us to tell the universe what we want. Not the other way around."

"My friend, the strip-club-owning sage."

"Spend enough time around naked people and you learn to see beneath the surface real quick," she said. "How is your dad?"

I perked up. "We had a good day this week. We had dinner together, and he remembered me. We talked about the neighbors—current, not deceased or moved away twenty years ago," I told her.

"Babe, that's awesome."

"The good days are getting fewer and farther between." I sighed, then pushed back at the melancholy that was trying to smother me. "But I'm going to hang on tight to every single one."

"It blows," she said succinctly.

"It really does."

"Hey, so besides interrogating you about your newfound social media fame, I was calling to tell you I've got a free day tomorrow and some muscle that could use a workout. Want some help around the house? I figure we could get that tub out to the curb and tackle patching the floor. I've been watching DIY videos."

This was a relationship I could count on. Faith had always been there for me, and I was grateful beyond words for her. Maybe I didn't have Dominic Russo down on one knee in front of me, but I had Faith. "I love you."

"Love you back. Even if you're carelessly discarding gorgeous, virile men left and right."

"I'll see you tomorrow."

"I'll bring coffee," she chirped.

We disconnected, and I saw that I had a new text on my work phone.

Dominic: You're beautiful. And not just tonight.

My stupid, stupid heart gave a pathetic limp.

It turned out that Faith's muscle was not actually attached to her own body. She brought a short, six-packed dancer named Rocco and a long-legged bartender who went by Rick during the week and Peaches Von Titz on the weekends.

"If I get hemorrhoids from this, I'm gonna be pissed," Faith gritted out.

"Why are bathtubs so heavy?" I wheezed.

Rocco and Peaches had muscled the cast iron tub out of the living room onto the porch and were dragging the new tub enclosure upstairs where it would live in the hallway until I patched the floor and could afford a reputable plumber.

Meanwhile, Faith and I were trying not to rupture our spleens carrying the tub down the front steps.

Faith was decked out in her winter weekend warrior best: a pair of carpenter jeans worn low enough to show off the skull and crossbones belly button ring beneath the cropped hem of her long-sleeve thermal. She'd tailored the shirt herself, adding a hot-pink lace-up corset closure. Her sleek, pink-tipped ponytail bobbed on top of her head.

With a cacophony of sound effects and several breaks, we were finally able to deposit the tub at the curb where Mr. Mohammad's antiquing friend with a pickup truck and strong nephews would retrieve it later today. Trying to catch my breath, I slid into the tub and hung my legs over the edge.

"Whatcha gonna do with the Range Rover?" Faith asked, climbing in next to me.

I eyed the SUV. "Return it without telling him."

She got the glint that always appeared in her pretty, devious eyes when she had a truly sneaky idea.

"You know, I bet we could fit a lot more drywall supplies in the back of that bad boy than my car." She hooked her thumb toward her flashy two-seater Mercedes parked at the curb.

I chewed on my lip, considering. "It would save the delivery fee." The man had chosen his vendetta against his father over his feelings for me. I could use his luxury SUV to haul supplies.

"Coincidentally, did you know that my favorite hardware store is right across the street from my favorite taco shop?" she mused.

"Did someone say tacos?" Rocco poked his head out of the second-floor window.

Tacos and home renovation supplies with an entrepreneur, a male exotic dancer, and a drag queen on her day off. Just another glamorous day in the life.

46

DOMINIC

The thing about being over forty is hangovers last about as long as a case of the flu.

Saturday morning, I skipped my usual workout in favor of walking two blocks to a diner to shamefully eat two greasy breakfast sandwiches while guzzling electrolytes and tea behind sunglasses.

Back home, my doorbell rang just as I was heading back upstairs to sleep off my poor life choices.

"Hey, Dominic." My chipper neighbor Sascha was bundled up in a lime-green, puffy parka and grinning at me over a wrapped platter. Her six-year-old son, Jace, stood next to her dressed in Spider-Man pajamas and a winter coat. His grin revealed a gap in his smile that hadn't been there when I saw him last weekend.

I was familiar with this drill.

"Sascha," I rasped. Pretending not to be hungover was about as effective as pretending not to be drunk.

"I'm coming to hang out with you, Mr. Dominic," Jace announced gleefully.

His mother elbowed him in the shoulder. "Not before we ask politely, remember?" she said out of the side of her mouth while still smiling maniacally at me.

"Mr. Dominic, we made you your favorite cookies. Can I come play with Brownie?"

Sascha held up the platter. "Cinnamon butterscotch. And it would only be for forty minutes. An hour tops."

Cinnamon butterscotch cookies were *not* my favorite. In fact, I hated butterscotch anything. But the day I'd moved in, Sascha, her husband Elton, and their then newly adopted baby Jace "dropped by" with a plate of cookies and the hopes that their new neighbor wasn't going to be the grumpy asshole their old one was.

For some reason, I wasn't eager to disappoint them and had been living a lie ever since, pretending to be a decent human being with a love of cinnamon butterscotch cookies. Sometimes I pulled their recycling bin back from the curb on trash day. Sometimes I shared a backyard scotch with Elton. And sometimes I watched Jace when he didn't feel like getting out of his pajamas and his parents didn't feel like fighting him.

"As long as you don't feel like moving around much or talking above a whisper," I told Jace.

"One of those nights, eh?" Sascha asked.

I nodded, then winced.

"Don't worry about it. Believe me, I understand. That's why we never speak of Christmas Day 2015. I can take Jace to Great-Aunt Alma's," Sascha said.

But that was a problem with knowing things about your neighbors. Jace hated Great-Aunt Alma's house. It smelled like cat pee, and she made him eat steamed carrots. The last time she'd babysat, the woman made Jace sweep the kitchen floor and called it a game. When he "won," he was "allowed" to sweep the front hallway.

"Do you have a bad decision flu?" he asked, his big eyes sad and solemn.

"It's fine," I lied. "I'm fine. Jace can hang out with me."

"Yay!" He punched his mittened fist in the air.

"Shh. Celebrate quieter, bud," Sascha warned him, clamping a hand over his mouth.

"Sorry," he stage-whispered through his mom's hand.

"An hour tops," she promised. "I'm just picking up a dress for our surprise anniversary dinner, which I promise we *won't* be asking you for your babysitting services for." Every year, Elton commemorated their wedding anniversary by surprising Sascha with dinner out at a new swanky restaurant. This year, in a continuance of my role as a good neighbor, I'd suggested he hire a chef to come to their house and recreate their favorite meal from their honeymoon. Apparently it hadn't been a totally stupid idea, because Elton tracked down a chef who specialized in Caribbean cuisine and had been texting me updates on recipes and wine pairings for two weeks.

I took the cookies and the kid, and after ten minutes of delighted dog and boy greetings, I hooked Jace up with headphones and the Xbox that I'd bought for just such an occasion.

I lounged on the couch next to him, reading *Pride and Prejudice* and identifying with poor, misunderstood Darcy.

For lunch, I made us fancy grilled cheese sandwiches with roast beef and three kinds of cheese—Jace's favorite. The kid ate two. I ate one. And Brownie ate six slices of roast beef before I caught him counter surfing. Sascha came back fifty-nine minutes after she'd left and collected her son and her empty cookie plate. Maybe I didn't hate butterscotch as much as I thought.

I spent the rest of the day on the couch, which delighted

Brownie. We watched the entire first season of *The Great British Baking Show* and then three episodes of *Queer Eye*. I was inspired to order and eat an entire sponge cake from the bakery three blocks over and pondered growing a beard.

Then I pondered what Ally thought about beards.

And the shame spiral began again.

Brownie dragged me out of the house for a walk early that evening, and I found my Range Rover keys tucked in the mail slot with a note that said, "Thanks for the ride."

My SUV was parked down the street, and there was a six-pack of sports drinks on the passenger seat with a leftover Christmas bow stuck to it. There was also a small bag of dog treats in the cup holder.

I was both touched and annoyed.

Ally had yet to respond to any of my texts since Drunk Me made an ass of myself. After a quick scroll through my phone, I could at least understand why. They ran the gamut from intoxicated adoration like "your hair looks like a sexy bird's nest" to "let's never speak of this again."

The bits and pieces that I remembered from last night gelled into one unflattering, inappropriate picture of a boss stepping over the line with his employee.

Once again, I'd proven that it was my father's blood running through my veins.

I let Brownie pick the course around the neighborhood, and when he paused at his favorite tree, I pulled out my phone.

Me: Thanks for returning the car and not driving it to Mexico.

Ally: I did the Mexico run for authentic tacos before bringing it back. BTW, you're low on gas, and you got seventeen traffic violations in Tijuana.

Me: You could have come inside.

Ally: I really couldn't have.

Me: I'm sorry.

Ally: Don't be. It's for the best. Besides, now we can try something new.

To me, "something new" meant stripping every article of clothing off her and licking, kissing, and biting my way over every inch of her body. I had a feeling this wasn't what she had in mind.

Me: New?

Ally: Friends.

Me: I'm sure what you meant to type was "frenemies."

Ally: Look at you, being down with the lingo. Good job, ol' buddy, ol' pal.

Me: I already don't like this.

Ally: Have a good weekend. Remember to hydrate!

"Friends? How the hell is that supposed to work?" I asked Brownie.

He dug his face out of the snow he'd been sniffing and looked at me. Apparently my dog didn't have the answer either.

I did us both a favor and didn't text or email her for the rest of the weekend. Sure, I picked up my phone seven hundred times to do exactly that, but I managed to stop myself every time. I'd crossed so many fucking lines with her. She deserved a break.

By Monday morning, mostly recovered from the scotch poisoning, I'd convinced myself that I could do this. I could be her boss, her friend. I could keep my fucking hands to my fucking self.

I'd find that self-control I'd once been so proud of and actually utilize it. And in another hundred years or so, I'd even be able to survive the idea of her meeting someone else. Dating. Fucking. Falling in love.

My still mildly unsettled gut rolled at the idea when I stepped onto the elevator and hurtled toward the forty-third floor.

Yeah. That day was not today.

I decided to focus instead on figuring out the strange scent that lingered in my car. Tacos and…what the hell was that? Concrete? Drywall?

"Morning." Ally's greeting was gratingly cheerful. She was wearing a—thank the fucking gods of winter—turtleneck. It hugged all the right places, but at least I couldn't *see* a damn thing. Her hair was partially pulled back into a tiny knot on top of her head. She wore brushed gold hoop earrings with crystals that kept catching my eye.

She'd painted her lips a classic, fuck-me red, and I wanted to kiss her until the lipstick smeared all over both of us.

When she cocked her head, I wondered how long I'd been standing there assessing how much I liked the way she looked.

"Morning," I said, belatedly handing over the coffee and breakfast wrap I'd brought her.

Her eyes lit up in that way that always made my cold, dead insides spark to life.

"Thanks! You don't have to do that, you know." She beamed up at me, the picture of platonic affection. She was entirely too enthusiastic about this "friend" thing.

I grunted a response. Maybe I wasn't allowed to bring the woman to orgasm, but I sure as hell could bring her food until I was convinced she was out of whatever stupid financial situation she'd gotten herself into.

She had a new bandage on her left ring finger but looked well rested.

"How was the rest of your weekend?" she asked.

In no hurry to leave her, I put my tea on her desk and shrugged out of my coat. I noticed that her eyes lingered on it and had a vague recollection of suggesting "swapsies."

Goddammit, I was a fucking idiot.

"Did you know scotch hangovers can last three days?" I asked conversationally.

She shuddered, closing those dark-lashed eyes. "Try tequila sometime. Last time Faith and I had a 'men suck, let's explore lesbianism' drink fest, it involved tequila. I was sick for five days straight."

I blinked and, of course, pictured it. *Whatever. Cut me some slack. I'm a man whose last two-party action had been a lap dance at…*

Abort! Abort! Abort! Do not get a fucking hard-on on day one of Let's Be Friends.

I gritted my teeth in what I hoped looked like a smile and pretended I wasn't picturing Ally making out with another woman. And then I knew I had it bad when some girl-on-girl fantasy only made me feel jealous. *Yes, Ms. Morales, here's a breakfast wrap with a side of my balls. You can keep them forever.*

Ally winced. "Sorry. I'm kind of nervous about this friend thing and trying to play it cool."

"By bringing up lesbianism?" I asked in exasperation. "Maybe we should take this a little slower and not speak."

She buried her face in her hands, and I admired her ringless fingers like the fucking sex-starved moron I was.

"Let's start over," she suggested, dropping her hands. "How was your weekend?"

"Fine," I lied. "How was yours?"

"Fine," she parroted back.

"Good."

"Great."

"Okay then." I was still standing there nodding at her and screaming at myself to walk the fuck away when a delivery guy hustled up, cracking his gum and giving Ally a once-over that was a little too thorough for my liking.

"Can I help you?" I asked him coldly. This guy was trespassing on my territory, and I had no problems letting him know it.

Ally shot me a "WTF is your problem, Crazy Pants?" look.

"Got a package here for Ally Morales," he said.

The old "got a package" come-on. Jackass.

"That's me," she said perkily.

"Here you go." With a stupid wink, the guy handed over a large box with a bold red bow on it. "Later," he said, walking away backward like a cocky motherfucker. I wished I was behind him so I could shove him into a trash can…or down a flight of stairs.

"What's with the glare, Grumpy Grump Face?" Ally wanted to know.

"That guy was flirting with you," I snapped.

The smart-ass coughed the word "friends" into her hand.

I glared at her.

"Buddies," she coughed again.

"Do you have bronchitis?" I asked.

"No, but I *do* have a mystery present," she said, slipping a white envelope from under the ridiculous bow. "You didn't do this, did you?"

I shook my head and immediately wished I had.

I shouldn't care what was in the box or who sent it to her. But shouldn'ts didn't seem to have a place in my reality. I wasn't moving from this spot until I found out. Friends cared when other friends got gifts, right?

Fuck it. I was staying.

She opened the card, and I didn't care for the way her lips curved. It was a female smile of pleasure and satisfaction. One that I knew a human being with a dick and designs on her attention had put there.

Wordlessly, she set the card aside and worked the attention-seeking bow off the box.

"Whatcha got there, Al?"

Ruth popped her red head around the corner. She stutter-stepped for a minute, noticing me, and then pasted a brave smile on her face and approached.

"I'm not sure," Ally said, slipping her fingers under the lid.

"Hi, Dominic," Ruth said.

An unprompted first name out of a staffer. It was about damn time. "Hi, Ruth. How was your weekend?"

She beamed at me. "It was great. How was yours?"

An explosion of fabric saved me from having a second go at the scotch hangover and lesbianism conversation.

It was pink and shiny, and to my eternal damnation, I noticed that it was the exact shade of Ally's lips when they weren't painted fuck-me red.

The women crooned and stroked the fabric as Ally pulled it free.

I snatched the card off her desk while she held the cocktail dress to her chest.

Ally,

Made this and thought of you.
Christian

Oh, I fucking hated that guy.

Meanwhile, *my friend* was doing a delighted twirl. If I'd been a generous guy, I would have had to hand it to the assface. The dress screamed Ally. The full, silky skirt nipped in to a tight waist with a gold, braided belt. The top was snowy white and draped over one shoulder, leaving the other bare. Colorful, soft, sexy. Just like the woman.

"Oh my God. There's pockets!" Ruth screeched.

They were drawing a crowd. Women—and Linus—were coming out of the woodwork to swoon over the dress.

"Who sent it?"

"Who made it?"

"Good morning, Dominic."

"You need to put it on!"

"This is better than flowers. Are you going to marry him?"

I headed into my office and slammed the door behind me.

"Just fucking friends," I muttered to the empty room. But the rationalization didn't help. I wanted to be more. And I couldn't have it as long as she worked for this company.

I heard a ripple of laughter coming from Ally's desk, and my inner asshole caveman came out of hibernation. Plan in place, I sat down at my computer and found the document I was looking for.

I was putting the finishing touches on my masterpiece on the screen when there was a jaunty knock, and my door opened.

"Irvin," I said, glancing up.

He strolled into the room in that not-a-care-in-the-world way he had when he'd come across a particularly juicy tidbit of gossip. Still trying to mold me into a version of my father.

He shut the door behind him and gave me a smug smile. "Quite the excitement out there," he mused.

"It would appear so," I said dryly, skimming over the changes I'd made to the document. Unlike the managing editor,

I didn't have time for idle chitchat. I had a budding relationship to ruin and a lengthy actual work-related to-do list for the day.

"It's always smart to reward a girl for her good deeds," Irvin said, taking an uninvited seat across from me.

Disinterested, I lifted an eyebrow.

"Your assistant," he clarified. "I heard she 'drove the boss home' Friday night." The man made air quotes as he said the words.

My stomach plummeted and was replaced with the raging fires of hell. "Is that what they're saying?" I asked, keeping my voice mild.

"Oh, nothing to worry about. A few of the gossip blogs picked it up this weekend and ran it as a blind item. Good for you, son. It's about time you had a little fun on the job."

I wanted to grab the man by his fucking Gucci tie, haul him out of the chair, and make him apologize to Ally. Then I wanted to toss him off the roof and burn down every blog that dared hint that I was anything like my father or that Ally was sleeping her way to the top.

"The apple doesn't fall far from the tree, does it?" Irvin crowed his approval. He slapped his knee. "Well, I'd better get back to it."

"I'd appreciate it if you were a little more careful with the reputation of our employees here, Irv," I told him. My tone should have frozen the man's balls.

But he waved dismissively. "Russo secrets are always safe with me." He gave a cheery wink and heaved himself out of the chair.

I watched him go, drumming my fingers on the desk. Irvin Harvey was rubbing me the wrong way and needed to be dealt with. He was shrewd and slimy, and I was certain he'd known exactly what my father had been up to behind locked doors here.

I'd speak to my mother about him soon.

But first, I took a red pen and underlined the new text I'd added under the fraternization policy.

Employees will not pursue relationships with designers or other vendors.

I was already standing when Ally stuck her head in the door. "Dom? Ten-minute warning for your meeting across town. Dalessandra is heading down to the car now."

I nodded briskly, sliding my arms into my coat.

"Here," I said, slapping the paper into her hands.

"You're such an ass, Charming," she called after me as I headed in the direction of the elevators.

I was. And the sooner she accepted that, the better.

47

ALLY

I was up to my elbows in drywall spackle and feeling like a DIY badass when the ringtone I'd assigned to the nursing home cut off Maren Morris's voice singing about bones and foundations.

I answered the call with my elbow and rested my face against the phone on the lid of the toilet. The last time I'd been in this position had been the infamous tequila lesbian night. I focused on that fact rather than the instinctive fear that gripped me every time the home called.

"Ally?"

"Yes?"

"It's Braden. Hey, no emergency or anything. We're having some trouble settling your father down for the night. We were wondering if you'd mind stopping in?"

"Of course," I said, checking the time. "Is he okay?"

"He's all right. Just agitated."

"I'll be there in half an hour." My father, the man who had only raised his voice when the Mets were playing or when he was shouting "Bravo" in a concert hall, suffered states of agitation where nothing short of strong sleeping meds could calm him.

The nursing home was a mile from me. The buses didn't run as often this late on weeknights, and it was too late to call Mr. Mohammad and ask to borrow his car. Walking it was. I bundled up in Dad's old ski jacket, pulled on the thickest socks I could manage inside my sneakers, and hit the sidewalk.

It was cold enough, windy enough, for my face to sting.

At least Dad hadn't fallen. At least he wasn't sick. At least I had a job, temporarily, that could handle a lot of the expenses. At least I was finally making progress on the house. I counted my blessings as I power walked my way through Foxwood.

So much had changed here since childhood. This street was one eighth-grade me had peered at through the school bus window while I planned my grown-up future. Spoiler alert: My imaginings had never looked like this.

My life in Boulder was one my eighth-grade self would have approved of. I had friends. Boyfriends. I worked jobs that I loved and took time off to live.

I spotted the big house all aglow on the corner behind its brick pillars and greenery and felt the familiar tug of longing. I'd loved this house and what it had represented my entire life. A family lived there. Two parents, kids who played outside and climbed trees and sold lemonade on the sidewalk. The Christmas light display drew crowds every year.

Now there were grandkids and Sunday brunches and holiday celebrations.

I paused on the sidewalk.

They were hosting tonight. A weeknight dinner party

probably running late because everyone was having too much fun to leave. Glasses of wine. Candles. The faint notes of a jazz record spilled outside to me.

A fierce longing hit me hard enough to have me turning away. I wanted a home and a family and friends who didn't mind a wine hangover on a Tuesday morning because we weren't ready to end the fun.

I missed my old life. Missed the comfort of believing my father was happy and healthy. Missed being able to breathe, to be selfish. I missed being able to go out for drinks on a Wednesday or take a friend out to dinner. I missed cooking for a cute date who I was excited about. God, I missed sex. I missed not having to know my checking account balance down to the penny.

I turned my back on the big house and followed the sidewalk away from someone else's perfect life.

Thirty-nine-year-old me didn't have a future.

There was only now. And I'd be grateful for every minute I had here with him.

The lights of the nursing home glowed ahead of me. Part of me hoped that the nurses had been able to get Dad settled, that I could just sit quietly with him while he slept. But Braden was waiting for me and buzzed me in the front entrance.

"Thanks for coming down," he said, briskly leading the way toward the memory wing. "Usually he doesn't give us much trouble, but he's pretty stirred up tonight. He took a swing at the nurse when she came by with meds."

"I'm so sorry," I breathed, trying to catch up to his long-legged strides.

"Not your fault or his," Braden assured me.

Fault, no. But responsibility was different. Violent patients could be removed from the facility and placed in secure mental wards. Deena was just looking for an excuse to give him the boot. There wouldn't be knitting lessons and dance classes and chair yoga and comfort foods in a secure facility. There wouldn't be a piano for Dad to play on his good days. Or staff who filled his Christmas stocking with his favorite treats.

It was late, and the lights were low in the hallway, making the crash that came from my father's room even more jarring. I pushed past Braden and hurried into the room.

Dad was on his feet in his cast, dumping his clothing out of the dresser into a pile on the floor. The pile already included everything that had lived on top of the dresser, including his Bluetooth speaker, a digital picture frame with a lifetime of memories, and a framed photo of the two of us on my high school graduation day.

The glass was broken, and there was a jagged tear over my beaming face. I'd had a world of beginnings in front of me then. Now it was just one more erasure of the only thing I'd ever been completely sure of in life: my father's love.

"Get out of here, Claudia!" Dad limped toward me, crushing the photo under his cast. "Haven't you taken enough from me?"

"Dad." I held up my hands. "I'm not Mom. I'm Ally. Your daughter."

"You stole it, didn't you?" he demanded. The sound of crushed glass under his feet made me wince.

"Dad, come over here so I can clean that up," I begged.

"You took my father's pocket watch! I had it in that drawer, and now it's gone. I want it back, Claudia. I want it all back!"

"Mr. Morales, why don't we check your nightstand for your watch?" Braden suggested, trying to coax my dad away from the glass.

But Dad wasn't open to suggestions. "You think you can just leave and take everything from me? I want it all back. You ruined everything!"

I felt hot tears cutting tracks down my still-cold cheeks.

"Dad, please."

He took another step in my direction and stumbled.

I reached out to steady him, but in his eyes, it wasn't me, the girl who had loved him her entire life. It was the woman who had built a family and a future on lies and then abandoned it all.

I saw his hand pull back and registered the sound of the crack before I ever felt the pain blooming bright and white-hot.

The man who had insisted on trapping spiders and setting them free in the backyard backhanded me with every ounce of strength he could muster from his frail body.

Stunned, I stumbled backward.

Braden hustled in, another night nurse on his heels.

"No! Wait," I insisted, stepping between them. Restraining him would only make it worse. My eye and cheek felt like they were on fire. Shame and sadness made an ugly brew in my stomach. It was selfish, but I knew that seeing them restrain him would very possibly break me into a thousand pieces.

I reached for my work phone and, with shaking hands, cued up the song.

The battered speaker on the floor picked up the piano tune and began to play over tiny slivers of glass.

Dad's breath was coming in heaves. The anger was still in his eyes, and I bumped the volume higher. We stared at each other for a long minute while the familiar song wove its way around us. His shoulders slumped, the violence and agitation slowly leaving his body as if he recognized that it didn't belong inside him.

His fingers began to move rhythmically against his pajama pants. Tears slipped from the corners of his eyes, and I felt my heart break yet again into more microscopic shards.

I glanced over my shoulder at the nurses. "It's him playing," I explained.

Carefully, I reached for his arm again. This time, he didn't fight me as I guided him out of the glass and over to the bed. I took off his slippers, his glasses. The nurse helped me tuck him under the quilt his mother had made decades ago.

His hands continued to follow the song on top of the worn blue and brown patches.

"I think I'd like to play piano tomorrow," he said softly.

"You can absolutely play tomorrow," the nurse promised him, brushing a wisp of hair off his forehead.

But promises didn't mean much these days.

I sat with him for another hour to make sure his sleep was sound.

While he snored softly, I put down the ice pack that Braden gave me and pulled out my phone.

The urge to call Dominic was overwhelming and disconcerting. It made no sense. He didn't know about my father. We weren't together in any sense of the word. But just thinking about hearing his voice pushed the urge into compulsion territory.

Biting my lip, I debated for another minute before settling on a text.

> **Me:** Hey. Do you want me to pick up breakfast for you on the way into work?

I hit Send and immediately felt like an idiot. He was my boss. Not my boyfriend.

My heart gave a kick when his response lit up my screen.

Dominic: That depends. Can you spell "fuck off" with Danish?

The smile tugged at the corners of my mouth, and my chest felt a little looser.

Me: You'd be amazed at what I can spell with breakfast foods.

Dominic: Your talents know no bounds. But I already have our breakfast planned. Just bring your annoying self.

Me: Okay. Hugs to Brownie.

He responded with a photo of Brownie sprawled across his legs on the couch. Dominic was wearing sweatpants, and there was a fire in the fireplace. It looked so cozy. So safe. I had to swallow around the lump in my throat. There was no cozy and safe for me. Just a long walk home on a winter night.

I left the ice pack at the empty front desk and headed for the front doors with Dad's laundry in a bag.

It was bitterly cold and almost midnight. Fat clouds blotted out the night sky.

The doors closed behind me, cutting me off from the warmth, and I took a deep breath of lung-shocking cold.

"Yo, Ally."

Braden was leaning against a sedan in the parking lot. He held up a bottle.

I hunched my shoulders against the cold and shuffled over.

"We keep this in the locker room for after tough shifts," he said, pouring a shot of Fireball into a little Dixie cup.

"I will accept this emergency Fireball," I told him.

"That was tough in there."

"Yeah." It came out as a gasp. The yummy burn in my throat was an improvement over the choking sensation of six months of suppressed tears lodged in there. "He thought I was my mom, his ex-wife…or wife."

"I noticed she's never come to see him," Braden said in that nice, nonpushy way of his.

"She left us about a hundred years ago. It's always been just him and me."

We were quiet for a long beat. Lazy snow flurries drifted silently down from that midnight sky.

"Do you have to write up a report about tonight?" I didn't want to ask the man to not do his job, but I also didn't think I could face another layer of jeopardy to my father's residency.

"We're not writing anything up," he promised.

I slumped in relief.

"Look, I know this is a shit situation," he said. "And I know you're doing your very best to keep it all together. But we all want you to know that when you're not here, we've got your dad. We're his family, yours too. And we'll do whatever it takes to keep him happy and safe."

"Thank you," I whispered.

Tears blurred my vision and battled the cold for supremacy. My eyelashes were going to freeze shut, and I was going to have to stumble home blindly. But my father had people who had his back, and that made any temporarily frozen corneas worth it.

"The rest of the staff want you to know that no matter what Deena the Bad Witch says, we want your dad here. No missed payments or late fees are going to make us treat him less than the best."

"Aw, crap, Braden," I said, swiping an errant tear away with my mitten.

"And one more thing," he said.

"I don't know if I can take one more thing."

"Give me the damn laundry."

"It saves me money to do it myself," I insisted.

"Do you have a washing machine and dryer at home?" he asked.

I considered lying, but just the thought of it had my neck flushing bright red. "No. But there's a laundromat with Wi-Fi just a couple blocks away—"

"You have better things to do than sit in a laundromat. We're taking care of your dad's laundry from now on. No charge."

"I can't ask you to—"

"You didn't ask. And we didn't offer. We're telling you. Leave the damn laundry alone."

I bumped his shoulder with mine. "You're kind of my hero right now," I told him.

He glanced down at his pants. "You think a cape would look good with scrubs?"

"Definitely."

"Cool. Now get in the car so I can drive you home before you freeze to death out here."

48

ALLY

"I look like I ran face-first into a bar fight," I complained to my reflection. My face hurt. Worse, it *looked* like it hurt.

The movies where the heroine gets backhanded and jumps back up to badassedly wipe the blood off her lips before grinning at the villain were total bullshit.

I'd tried makeup. All the foundation and concealer I had still couldn't disguise the swelling and the darker bruises. There was no way Dominic would (a) not notice that half my face was bigger and more purple than the other half or (b) let me get out of explaining what had happened.

I winced at the thought and then again at the pain the audacity of having facial expressions caused.

As much as I hated to do it, I had to call in sick. There was no way around it.

It was early enough that he wouldn't be at the office for at least another hour. I wasn't being a big ol' chicken, I reminded myself as I dialed his desk extension instead of his cell phone. I just didn't want to bother him with something as insignificant as my absence today.

My neck flushed hot and splotchy in the mirror.

"Hi, Charming. It's…uh…me. Ally. I'm sick. I can't come in today. But I swear I'll make up the time. I can work late tomorrow or on the weekend or…whatever." I remembered to cough, but it came out more like the honk of a wounded goose. My neck was on fire with lies. I bobbled my phone, dropping it into the sink. "Damn it!" I hissed, making a grab for it and disconnecting the call.

I really needed to work on my lies. But for now, I had moisture-resistant Sheetrock to hang.

I spent the day hanging and taping Sheetrock in the bathroom and not answering my phone. Dominic called three times, and I let it go to voicemail each time. And, of course, listened to the messages immediately afterward.

He sounded concerned, asking if I needed soup, then annoyed because who the hell was supposed to do all the work I was supposed to do? Very on-brand for Dominic Russo.

I didn't respond. But guilt at missing a full day of work started to eat away at me. I tried to stuff it down with a turkey sandwich, made just the way my dad liked—with thin slices of apple topped with sharp cheddar. It was nice to have cheese back in my life.

According to the nurse at the desk, it was a good day for Dad, which meant I couldn't see him.

Not with my face looking like this.

Not if there was a chance that he'd realize the bruises came from him.

By early evening, I couldn't take it anymore. I'd watched

my inbox overflow with its usual frenetic energy all day, but I hadn't been there to take care of anything. Looming responsibilities made me feel itchy. I decided I'd put in a few hours of work tonight and start fresh tomorrow…if my face cooperated.

I showered, dressed, and headed into the city. The night air was cold and crisp and felt like snow. It was after nine by the time I let myself into the office with my key card. The floor was dark and quiet, a ghost town compared to the daytime productivity.

In a nod to the overwhelming quiet—and, okay, to make sure Dominic wasn't pulling an all-nighter in his office—I tiptoed to my desk.

The office was empty, and I was alone. I breathed a sigh of relief and flopped down in my chair. My desk had a stack of new files. My email inbox was demanding my attention, and I had nothing but a few uninterrupted hours to make some headway.

I put in my earbuds, cranked up one of my favorite dance playlists, and dug into the work.

The hand that clamped down on my shoulder half an hour later scared the ever-living shit out of me.

"Oh, sweet Jesus!"

"Who the hell did this to you?"

The demand, growled over the volume of my music, nearly shocked me out of my chair and onto the floor.

But he caught me.

I was staring into the eyes of one furious Dominic Russo.

I clutched at my heart to make sure it was still functioning. He yanked my earbuds free.

"Who the fuck hit you, Ally?" He enunciated each word with a burning fury that was both terrifying and touching. None of that rage transferred to the fingertips that gently tilted my chin so he could get a better look.

"No one," I lied, trying to slip out of his hold. My neck was *en fuego*. This was so stupid. I should have just stayed home. "I had a little home renovation mishap. Not that it's any of your concern."

"That's a fucking hand mark on your face, Ally. Don't lie to me." He sounded pained.

My neck was a pulsing beacon of hives proclaiming my lies.

"Dom, it's none of your business," I said, trying to wheel back to put some distance between us, but he held my chair by the arms, and my feet skittered uselessly on the carpet.

"Don't pull that shit with me, Ally," he said darkly.

"Don't ask questions about things that don't concern you."

"You're my employee. You concern me. Are you dancing again?"

I rolled my eyes. Which was a mistake because (a) it hurt my face, and (b) it really pissed Dominic off.

"Again. None of your business. And no, I'm not dancing. It was an accident. He—" I choked on the word and immediately shut up.

"*He.*" His voice simmered with rage on the pronoun.

"Dominic, stop. It's nothing to worry about. It's my responsibility," I said, my voice breaking.

I realized with horror that my eyes were going hot and glassy. I thought I'd gotten a hold on the waterworks, but it was like someone had turned on a freaking geyser.

"Ally." He whispered my name. It was like a caress.

I shook my head. "Don't do this, Dom. Don't be nice. Don't ask me questions. I'm hanging on by a thread here."

He pulled me out of the chair and into his arms.

It was a hug. A hard, breathless hug.

And that was what broke me. The unyielding contact of his body pressed against mine, his arms wrapped around me tight enough that the only thing I knew for certain was that I was safe.

"I can't take this anymore, Ally," he breathed against my hair. "I can't just watch from the sidelines and pretend it doesn't fucking kill me that I can't touch you."

I didn't trust my voice. Didn't have any words worth saying anyway. I just wanted to be held like this.

The tears I'd been holding back for so long burst through the dam. Those defensive walls trembled once before crumbling to dust beneath the weight of relief. I was going to ruin his very nice shirt with my silent but dramatic waterworks.

"Baby," he whispered against the top of my head. "Talk to me. Please."

I shook my head.

His arms tightened around me. "Why do you have to be so fucking stubborn?"

Again, I shook my head. "Not *won't* talk. *Can't* talk," I managed between shaky breaths.

"You're killing me, Ally. Right now, I just want to murder whoever put that mark on your face without letting go of you."

That only made me cry harder.

In a moment that would have been incredibly romantic had I not been squirting liquid from both eyes and nostrils, Dominic picked me up, tucking my face under his chin, and carried me into his office. He kicked the door shut, threw the lock, and crossed to the couch.

He settled with me in his lap. Which was a much different feeling from the last time I'd been in it. Though, despite my hiccupping sobs, I still managed to engage my Dominic dick radar to notice that he was indeed hard. Definitely a permanent condition.

"You can't murder him," I told him mournfully.

"Give me one good reason why not."

"He's my father."

He stiffened against me.

More tears poured forth. An entire six months' worth of banked hurt, angst, and fear flowed down my cheeks and onto Dominic's crisp, white shirt.

He clutched me tighter to him. Murmured softly in my ear. Making promises we both knew he couldn't keep. Through it all, he stroked my hair, my back, in long, comforting sweeps. The sweetness, the gentleness of his touch when I could still feel him vibrating with anger beneath me steadied me.

"Tell me, baby," he demanded.

So I did. In fits and starts while silent tears slipped down my cheeks.

"Once I sell the house, that money will go to the nursing home, and he'll be safe for at least a couple of years. It'll buy me time to figure out how to make it work. I don't want to have to move him to another facility if I can help it. But it's so expensive. I'm not going to have a choice if I can't get the house on the market."

He said nothing, but I felt his arms band tighter around me.

Shifting in his lap, I sat up.

He cupped my face, then brushed my hair back from my eyes. His expression was so very serious. "Thank you for telling me," he said finally.

"My dad isn't violent," I said earnestly, wanting him to understand. "It's his disease. He's not who he was. There are still glimpses of him here and there. But for the most part, my dad is gone."

"I'm so sorry, baby," he whispered, wiping the fresh tears from my cheeks with his thumbs.

"Stop being nice to me, Dom."

"Not this time."

We stared at each other for a long moment. The night skyline of Manhattan glowed outside the windows across the room as the predicted snow fell steadily. I took a few slow, deep breaths, selfishly stealing Dominic's heat and claiming it for myself.

"I should go," I said. "I have some work to catch up on, and I need to get home before the snow gets worse."

"No."

"No?" I laughed. "It's adorable that you still believe you have a say in what I do."

"It's adorable that you think I would let you walk out of here tonight," he countered.

I made a move to get out of his lap, but he tightened his grip.

"Dominic."

"Kiss me, Ally. Let me make you feel better."

I hesitated, balancing on a very dangerous precipice. I'd already crossed lines tonight. I'd shared too much, been too vulnerable.

"I don't think that's a good idea," I said softly. If he kissed me now, when my heart was already in a million little pieces, I was going to do something really stupid…like fall in love with the man.

"Let me," he said, his voice grave.

Of all the ways we'd been intimate to this point, we had never kissed. I'd never had his mouth on mine.

"I don't know if I can walk away when I need to," I confessed, the panic rising up in me.

"We're past walking away, Ally."

A statement of fact, as if my fate were already sealed by his words.

"I'm not looking for anything," I insisted, nerves getting the best of me.

"I wasn't looking for you. But I still found you."

"What are you saying?" I squeaked.

"I'm saying I found you. And I'm not fighting it anymore. You're mine."

He shifted me in his lap so I was straddling him, just as I had at the club. Only this time, I was the vulnerable one.

"You're scaring the hell out of me, Dom," I admitted, digging my fingers into his shoulders, into the heat under that damn vest and shirt.

"I'm scaring me too," he said, nuzzling my jaw and down my neck. Moving his lips against my flesh. "I'm fucking terrified."

Goose bumps exploded on my skin. I was suddenly hot and cold and dizzy and rooted to the spot. His mouth moved ever so gently over the bruise on my face, erasing the hurt as it went.

I was spread wide over his crotch, his cock nestled up against where I ached for him the most.

"I don't want anything serious," I whispered on a shiver when he brushed a kiss to the corner of my mouth. My lips burned with the need to feel his.

His laugh was gentle, but I still heard the sound of prison doors slamming shut. "Oh, sweetheart, you no longer have a choice."

He kissed me then. Mouth firm and demanding, he devoured me until I lost the battle and opened for him. His tongue thrust home, invading me, taking from me any breath, any words, any sense that wasn't already completely wrapped up in and around him.

I was flying and yet anchored to this spot by his body, his arms. His hands settled on my hips, and he dragged me over his erection. Back and forth.

"Let me make you feel good, Ally," he demanded again, roughly.

"Yes."

And with one little word, I set us both free.

49

DOMINIC

I slid the sweater over her head, and when I realized there was nothing between Ally's perfect breasts and my mouth but a flimsy white tank top, I felt a primal growl work its way up my throat.

Her nipples were hard and pointed beneath the simple cotton. I cupped those breasts in my hands, loving the feel of those buds going even harder.

She attacked my tie, the buttons of my shirt, but lost her train of focus when I yanked the scoop neck down, baring one breast. I paused just long enough that she could feel my hot breath on her skin before sucking that pink, pert nipple into my mouth.

Her gasp of pleasure, the feel of that delicious rosette puckering against my tongue, made every torturous second in the last two months worth it. This moment of heaven was worth a lifetime of misery. I sucked harder, holding her to me.

She bucked her hips against me, driving my dick wild with the friction. She was in leggings, and judging by the wet heat I could feel through them, she didn't have a damn thing on underneath.

I needed her naked. Nothing between us.

"Why do you wear so many damn layers," she demanded, her voice shaking as she shoved my vest off my shoulders.

"Never again," I promised, moving my attention to her other breast and suckling hard.

"Please don't stop wearing vests," she begged.

"Anything you want, Ally. All you have to do is ask." I gave her nipple another resounding suck and had to tamp back the wolf inside me when she whimpered.

I helped her strip my shirt away and then reluctantly abandoned her breasts to pull the tank over her head. I tossed it on the floor in the direction of the growing pile of clothes.

"Come here," I whispered darkly, pulling her against me and reveling at the feel of her hard, wet nipples against my chest.

She hissed in a breath. "Chest hair. So good."

I wanted to laugh. But every cell of my being was entirely focused on her body and the endless list of things I wanted to do to her. The litany of ways I wanted to make her come.

Finally. Finally. Finally.

"Baby, we're going to have to stand up and get rid of the rest of these clothes," I warned her.

"I don't want to stop touching you," she confessed. Her hands were stroking over my chest and shoulders, down my arms, across my abs. I felt…worshipped. Loved.

"Just for a second," I promised. Despite my protesting cock, I lifted her off my lap.

"Strip faster," she demanded, peeling her leggings off in one swift motion.

She was spectacular. Naked in the city lights with snow falling behind her. Ally Morales was the most beautiful thing I'd ever seen in my entire life.

Humbled and stunned, I fumbled with my belt. She stepped in and loosened it for me. Together, we shoved my pants to the floor. She was trembling, shaking as she stared at me. It was the distance. Everything made sense when we were touching. Anything seemed possible then.

She started to sink to her knees, but I stopped her. I wouldn't be able to withstand that mouth on my cock. Not this first time. I'd had too many fantasies burned into my brain. Besides, I owed her. Two.

"No. It's your turn, sweetheart." I pulled her to me. Her skin was so soft and smooth against my own. My cock was pinned between us and demanding more.

She cupped my face in her hands and stared into my eyes. "I don't want your tongue. I don't want your fingers. The first thing you put inside me is going to be your cock, Dom."

My dick jerked its agreement between us.

Holy motherfucking shit.

"I don't have a condom," I confessed. I had no need to stock condoms in this office. I wasn't my father.

Ally's eyes closed, then opened again. "You don't need one tonight," she whispered. "I'm on birth control, and I'm clean."

I was struck by two things. Permission for my darkest fantasy. Of fucking her until her pussy closed around my shaft and milked my own orgasm out of me, making me pour myself into her. Making her mine.

And then there was the caveat she tried to slip past me.

"This isn't for just one night, Ally. So get used to it. Once I'm inside you, there's no going back." *Ever.*

I wished we were in a bed. My bed where I could spread her

out and look my fill, take my time tasting her. But I wouldn't survive waiting another minute and settled for the couch. I laid her out on it and slid a knee between her legs.

Before giving in to her greedy demands, I dipped my head and helped myself to her breasts again. They were rapidly becoming my newest obsession. My erection hung heavily, its tip painting Ally's stomach with precum as it leaked shamelessly from the slit.

This was what she did to me. Reduced my body to a series of biological and chemical chain reactions.

Her breath was coming in short, sharp pants as I nuzzled at her perfect fucking tits. I wanted to die with this nipple throbbing in my mouth.

She wrapped her legs around my waist, trying to pull me down to her.

"Are you ready for me, baby?" I whispered, fisting my cock at the root.

She nodded wordlessly, eyes wide. I felt so many things. Powerful. Vulnerable. Ready. Terrified. And the rage that simmered low in my gut every time I looked at that bruise. I was never going to get over seeing that mark on her face.

"Are you sure?" I asked, part of me wishing she'd change her mind. Because it was all going to change. "You trust me?"

"Yes. Dom, please!"

I lined the weeping head of my cock up against her pussy. She was so fucking wet I thought I might die. I wanted to tease her a bit, prepare her for me. But I couldn't help myself. I gave a shallow pump, force-feeding the first two thick inches into her.

Her gasp echoed inside my blood.

Gritting my teeth, I held on to my sanity as she squeezed the head of my dick. "Tell me you understand me, Ally. Tell me you know this makes you mine."

She was trembling around my throbbing tip, and if she didn't say it in the next five seconds, I was going to plow into her anyway and make her say it after. I could only hang on for so long. I was only human.

"Dom," she whispered brokenly.

"Say it. Tell me, Ally." I knew it didn't make sense. I'd spent the past two months telling her, telling myself, that we would never happen. Now I was claiming her. I didn't know what it meant or what it would cost, but I knew I was willing to pay any price.

She squeezed her eyes closed tight. "I'm yours," she whimpered.

The knot in my chest loosened, and as soon as she opened her eyes again, I fucked into her tight sheath on one long, hard thrust. I held there as she scrambled under me, managing to open just a little wider, and my last inch slid into her. I hit bottom and stalled.

I could feel her fucking quivering around me. Bare. Nothing between us. She was impaled on me, her beautiful whiskey eyes open now. Wide and glassy.

"Breathe," I gritted out. "Just breathe for a second." Her breasts were smashed against my bare chest.

She was so tight, clamped around my erection, and I was so damn hard, I was seeing stars. She sucked in a breath, and I swear to God, I felt it in my cock.

Sweat broke out on my forehead. "Are you okay?" I asked, trying to hold on to the reins and not just mindlessly fuck my way in and out of her body.

"If you move, I'm going to come," she warned me.

"That's my girl." I kissed her again, teasing her with my tongue, and when she started to relax, I pulled out and thrust back in.

"Oh, God."

"Dom, baby," I corrected. She lasted four glorious pumps before the quivering clamped down on my dick like a velvet vice.

"Dominic!" Her fingers bit into my back, and I fucking loved that nip of pain. I kept driving into her, biting my lip until I tasted blood, pushing off the armrest with my foot to power into her harder and harder. Determined to hold on through the most in-fucking-credible experience my cock had ever had inside a woman.

She undulated beneath me like she had when she danced for me, and in that moment, I counted myself the luckiest man on the planet. I felt every squeeze, every wave, and rode out her orgasm with her.

I was sweating. My balls were sending out an SOS. I couldn't hold on much longer, but right now, I was her fucking superhero.

I kissed her, and when she dreamily sighed against my tongue, I bit her bottom lip. "Mine. Ally."

"Yours," she agreed.

It gave me another dose of superpowers. I beat back the threat of my own orgasm, picked her up, and sat with her on my lap.

"I've been thinking about this since that night," she moaned, bringing her hands to my shoulders.

"I want to watch you while you ride my cock. I want to see your eyes go glassy and that pulse in your throat flutter. I want to watch your tits bounce while I tell you I'm never leaving you."

"Dominic," she whispered.

"I'm never leaving you, Ally."

"You can't say things like that," she argued.

I gave her ass a little slap and then another one because I liked the sound of it.

She liked it too. Because she was writhing on me just like she had in the club that I still wanted to burn to the ground. But this time, my cock was where it belonged. Buried deep inside her.

Wet didn't begin to describe Ally. She was a goddamn rain forest, and I couldn't get enough. I wanted to throw her down and eat her out. To flip her over and slam into her from behind. I wanted her in missionary and up against a wall. In every conceivable position. I wanted to take years discovering all the ways I could make her come. My own personal treasure hunt.

She was working my dick like there was nothing else in the world she wanted more. Like she didn't have a sick father. Or crushing medical bills. Or the man who'd rejected her too many times suddenly claiming rights to her.

I felt it again. That electric quivering as her muscles trembled around my dick. It was magic. A miracle. She was my fucking miracle.

"I feel you, Ally. I know you want to come again. Give it to me, sweetheart."

Because I could, I took her nipple in my mouth again and sucked hard. My world was glowing, bright and hot, and I was kicking myself for almost missing out on knowing what it felt like to have Ally Morales climax on my dick.

I held on to her hips, checking her speed, and started thrusting. Every damn time, I bottomed out in her. I got harder as she got wetter.

Reaching around, I gripped her ass cheeks in both hands and drove into her.

She came like that, with my cock buried in her, my tongue lathing her nipple, and my hands spreading her open from behind.

She bucked, rocking back and forth as those delicate miracles of muscle clamped around me greedily. And then my own orgasm was racing up my balls, drawing them up tight.

"Ally!" This time, when I came saying her name, she was here. She was all around me. It speared through me, gutting me as I poured rope after rope of my hot climax into her. *Finally.*

It was a religious experience, a spiritual awakening as I filled this woman with my seed.

Fulfilling my destiny and branding her as mine just as she'd carved her initials into my heart.

My life would never be the same. I was never letting her go. No matter what.

She writhed against me, still coming, still sobbing my name, holding my face to her breast.

We stayed like that long after the waves stopped coming. Sweat gave her skin a honey-like sheen in the soft glow of the light. I didn't want to pull out. I didn't want to ever not be inside her again. I felt her clench around me once, twice, as if she'd read my mind.

I gave her nipple one last stroke with my tongue before dropping my head back against the sofa. "Three-two," I gasped.

"Jesus, we're still not even?" Her laugh was breathless, and I felt that too in my still-hard cock.

"Give me a couple of minutes."

And the rest of your life.

50

ALLY

He took me home. Brownie was waiting not so patiently for us inside. I stayed in the kitchen, helping myself to a glass of water and hopping up on the edge of the counter while Dominic let the dog out into the backyard.

Minutes later, man and dog returned in a burst of energy. They'd clearly been playing in the dark. Brownie stuck his face in his dish, sloshing water everywhere. But Dominic set his sights on me.

He stalked toward me, a gleam in his eyes, and I felt a delicious cocktail of nerves and excitement mix inside me. He looked positively devilish, and I was pretty sure I looked debauched.

Stepping between my legs, he put those big hands on my thighs and ran them up to my hips, squeezing and kneading. My breath caught in my throat because apparently the two most volatile, explosive, violent, world-ending orgasms I'd ever had were not enough.

Judging by the subtle tightening in his jaw, I wasn't alone.

"I've fantasized about you just like this." His voice was a honeyed rasp that I wanted to bathe myself in.

Orgasms? What orgasms? My vagina's short-term memory was clearly impaired.

His hands slipped around my hips to my ass, and he yanked me against him. His mammoth penis definitely had a case of amnesia, because he was stone hard.

We needed to talk.

Needed to have a conversation about what the hell this all meant.

Discuss why he'd suddenly thrown his principles out the window and crossed a line that, for him, took him too close to his father.

Instead, I hooked my heels at his back and draped my arms over his shoulders. His strong, steady shoulders.

"I hate that someone hurt you, Ally," he confessed, bringing up a hand to tenderly trace the bruising on my face.

"Everybody gets hurt sooner or later," I said lightly.

"Not you. Not anymore. I can't take it."

I rested my forehead against his. "Some things are out of even your control, Charming."

"I refuse to believe that."

I was aware of the fact that he was only half joking.

"Your father," he began.

I leaned back to study his face. So strong, so serious. The cut of his jaw, the furrowed brow. I lusted after the subtle hollows in his cheeks. It was the face of a warrior, a god. And those blue eyes were anything but icy now. As if a fire had been lit deep within him.

"Does it bother you to talk about him?" he asked.

I shook my head. "No. It's the situation, the disease, that are hard to…" Talk about. Deal with. Face.

"I can't begin to imagine," he said quietly. He tucked me back into him, those hands stroking paths up and down my back. Comforting. Soothing. Turning me the eff on.

"He was the one person who never let me down," I told him. "The one person whose love for me I was always absolutely certain of. To have that taken away? To have the man still here but to lose everything that made him Dad? It's a devastation I didn't know could exist."

Dominic held me, and Brownie decided to get in on the action too. The dog danced on his hind legs to give my knee a slobbery lick.

"How did you end up being responsible for him?" Dominic asked. His lips brushed their way down my neck.

"I lived in Boulder for a few years and didn't notice the early signs for a while. He'd always been absentminded, forgetful. But things were getting worse. Dad's neighbors kept an eye on him for me. None of us realized just how quickly things were deteriorating until he went missing last summer."

Dominic stiffened, but his hands stayed gentle.

"I was on a plane home when the cops found him in a park ten blocks from his house. He couldn't remember where he lived. They dumped him in this horrible state-run facility." A shudder rolled through me just remembering the dirty linens, the stench, the windowless rooms. "Every day there was a special kind of torture, knowing that your loved one is suffering and ignored. I moved him out of it as soon as I could get him in a spot in a nicer place. But it was so expensive."

"Doesn't he have insurance? Retirement savings?" he asked.

I stroked a hand over Brownie's soft fur and sighed.

"Normal health insurance doesn't cover nursing homes. He's got a pension and Social Security, which go directly to the home. Which, did I mention, is astronomically expensive? Medicaid's skilled nursing coverage is tricky and limited. And, as it turns out, my parents are still married. Something I didn't know until I started digging through the paperwork."

"What does that mean?" he asked.

"Her finances, if she would bother responding to my emails, count against my father, and I can't complete the paperwork without them. Plus, here's the kicker, about a year before all this happened, my mother—and I use that term in the loosest possible definition—realized she still had access to all Dad's accounts."

Dominic's fingers flexed into my back.

"She helped herself to everything he'd saved. She took it all," I said.

"What the hell kind of monster is she?"

My laugh was humorless. "That's just it. On paper, she's a saint. She's been gallivanting the world, building wells, raising money for vaccines, giving speeches. I haven't talked to her since the day she left when I was eleven. But every once in a while, usually when tequila is involved, I'll Google her."

"She abandoned you," he said.

"She did. She left me and my father, saying the world had a bigger calling for her than wife and mother."

"Fuck her."

His unwillingness to cut the woman who gave birth to me any slack was sweet and satisfying. "The irony is she's doing good things."

"Probably because she gets off on the attention," he guessed.

I rewarded him with a smile. "She got an honorary doctorate for her fundraising work for Sudan. She goes by Dr.

Morales now. She gave a TEDx Talk about worldwide empathy. Nonprofits pay her as a consultant so she can tell them how to make people care."

"Why did she take the money?" Dominic asked.

I shrugged. "She's a virtual stranger to me. But I did some sober sleuthing and discovered she founded her consulting business right around the same time she helped herself to Dad's accounts. Oh, and I also found out her boyfriend won the United Nations Public Service Award."

"While her husband is on the verge of being kicked out of a nursing home for nonpayment. What are you going to do about her?"

"I can't afford to do anything about her. Not yet. First order of business is to get Dad's house ready to be put on the market. Once it sells, the money will be enough to keep him in the home for years. He'll be safe. If there's enough money left, I'll hire a lawyer. I don't care to see her or speak to her or listen to an impassioned speech about how she deserved the money more. I just want every dime of my father's savings back."

"How bad is the house?" he asked.

I winced. "Not terrible," I said, feeling the heat flare up on my neck. "I mean, it's nowhere near ready for sale. There was a little plumbing mishap. I'm doing as much of the work as I can myself."

"Ally," he said. And I knew that Caretaker Charming was dying to be let off his leash to fix everything.

"It's fine. This job saved me, saved my dad. The salary helps a lot, and your stupid no-outside-employment clause is giving me the time to actually do more than half an hour of sanding floors and mudding drywall at a time. Everything is going to be fine."

"I want to see the house," he insisted.

To distract us both, I squeezed Dominic's hips between my legs and felt the answering pulse of his cock against me.

"I'd rather see some other things right now, Dom. Please?" It was unfair, and I knew it. If I asked, he would deliver.

In answer, he shucked my sweater over my head and hurled it over his shoulder. The laugh that bubbled up inside me disappeared on a gasp when he sucked one of my nipples through my tank.

"Yes," I hissed. This was what I needed most right now. The physical sensations of lust and want and desire drowning out everything else.

He hooked his fingers in the waistband of my leggings and swiftly dragged them down my legs, adding them to the pile on the floor.

I chose to worry about lady juices on prep surfaces later and made a grab for his belt. Together, we fumbled his pants open.

When he freed and fisted his cock, lining up the velvet-smooth crown with my slick folds, a tremor made its way through my body.

Brownie, sensing he wasn't going to have our undivided attention anytime soon, tip-tapped out of the room, his tail wagging. He took my sweater with him. But like the lady juices and everything else that was wrong in my life, I'd worry about it later.

Dominic kissed me like he was starving for my lips, my tongue.

"I want to taste you," I whispered into our open-mouthed kiss. "I want to be on my knees in front of you."

"Is that what you wanted that night? In my office after your date?" he demanded, one hand yanking the neck of my tank down, baring my breasts, while the other taunted me by stroking back and forth from that hungry bundle of nerves to my opening. Back and forth in a torturous rhythm.

"Yes," I breathed against his mouth, pausing long enough to nip at his lower lip, his jaw. "I wanted you to fuck my mouth. To watch me make you come. To have your cock in my mouth when you say my name."

The noise he made, a deep, pained rumble, was inhuman, and it awoke something primal inside me.

"Did you use my underwear that night?" I asked the question I'd been dying to know the answer to.

"Yes." He kissed me hard, all gentleness abandoned. Our teeth clashed, and his hands gripped my hair, my hips, my breasts, as if they couldn't decide where to settle. "I fucked myself with your panties wrapped around my fist."

I made a very unsexy squeaking noise.

"I came on your wet spot and kept coming."

I was so light-headed I was afraid I'd pass out before he made me come again.

"Look down," he ordered.

I did as I was told. And watched as he fed the tip of his erection into my body. We were connected, joined. I could feel my muscles fluttering around his crown, trying to draw more of him inside. The veins on his shaft stood out rigid and angry, like what he was doing to me was an act of violence rather than beauty.

He growled, low in his throat.

I felt dirty, decadent, depraved. And I wanted more.

"Lean the fuck back," he said.

I dropped back to my elbows, my body on display for him now, my breasts suspended by the neckline of the useless tank, nipples budded and hard. My breath coming in short rasps.

"Watch me fuck you, Ally. Watch me take you and make you mine."

He unhooked my legs from his waist and placed my feet on

the edge of the counter. The only thing holding me in place was his erection. Coincidentally, it was also the only thing anchoring me to the gravitational plane.

"Stop talking. Start fucking." I gasped the words out around clenched teeth. I needed more of him. All of him.

"Are you ready for me, baby?"

"Dominic, please!"

With the plea still ringing in the air, I watched in fascination as he drove his thick length into me.

Pleasure. Pain. Otherworldly sensations of fullness and completion. All lighting up my nerves and sending jumbled messages to my brain. This was everything. He was *everything*. Nothing else existed beyond this man, this room.

If I had ever had any sexual hang-ups, Dominic's groan of satisfaction would have untied them. I wanted all he could give me. I wanted him to know and worship every single inch of me.

He pulled out before I wanted him to and then thrust back into me before I was ready. The clench of his jaw, the pulsing at the base of his throat, was catnip to me. My body was driving Dominic Russo wild. I was driving Dominic Russo wild.

"I want to go slow," he rasped. "To savor you. I want you to come on my fucking mouth, Ally. I want to spend hours just worshipping your tits. But I can't. Stop. Fucking. You." Every word of his confession was emphasized by a faster, harder thrust. A return to my body, to me.

I wasn't sure if I was going to die from the dirty talk or the looming orgasm first.

"Don't you dare stop," I hissed. "Don't ever stop."

He dipped his head and sucked a nipple into his mouth. I felt the pulls of it echo in the muscles that surrounded and gripped his erection.

I moaned or sighed or made some kind of barnyard animal

noise, and apparently it shattered any resolve he had. He released my nipple with a pop and slammed into me, burying himself to the hilt. He was thrusting wildly, and all I could do was curl my fingers around the edge of the counter and hang on tight.

My inner walls did the same thing to his shaft, closing around it in an early warning system. *Danger! Orgasm imminent!* He already recognized the signs. This man already knew me well enough to understand that I was seconds away from detonation.

He gritted his teeth and continued fucking his way in and out of me as if it were his life's mission, as if we were in a race to the top. While his dick ruined me for all future sex partners forever, his hand gripped my breast and squeezed. Then it slipped under me, where his fingers probed and stroked that forbidden ring of muscle between my cheeks.

I definitely should have been worried about work surface sanitization. I should have been overanalyzing how he knew I was that kind of girl. I should have been wondering if I needed an extra-strength birth control pill to fight off what was surely super sperm.

But I wasn't. I was bucking my hips against him greedily, begging for more.

"I want to touch you everywhere," he rasped. Sweat dotted his brow and dampened his shirt. "I don't want there to be an inch of you I don't know."

His finger pressed against me again, and I felt a new throbbing, a new emptiness waiting to be filled.

"Do it."

He brought his finger to his mouth and laved it with his tongue. I couldn't wait to get that tongue on me at some point before we both came to our senses. Rearing up, I sank my nails into his shoulders. Our lips met in a fierce kiss as his finger breached me. One finger. One kiss. And we were both out of control.

"Need. More," he insisted. The angle was too shallow. There was more he had to give me. More that I was ready for.

With one arm, he plucked me off the counter and slammed my back against the cold steel of the refrigerator. He powered into me once, twice, three times, his finger flexing inside me. And it still wasn't enough.

Down to the floor we went. He came up on his knees, bracing his hands on my thighs and pushing them up and out. I was spread wide for him like a shameless banquet of carnal need. That dirty, evil gleam was back in those beautiful blue eyes.

His finger returned, and he watched me through hooded eyes as he slid it all the way inside me. There was a satisfying fullness everywhere, and my muscles were celebrating by clamping down.

"Dom, I think I'm going to—"

"I know you are. I can feel you." Our breaths came in sharp pants as his uncontrolled thrusts destroyed us both. Cold tile bit at my back, while hot, hard man labored over me, into me. Again and again, he slammed into me, making my breasts tremble.

It was probably too hard. I would probably be walking like John Wayne tomorrow thanks to the aggressive ministrations of Dominic's dick. And I was so here for it.

My orgasm was shimmering on the edges of reality, slowly, slowly becoming a real, tangible thing. I could feel myself flutter around his cock, his finger. Implosion was guaranteed. These were for sure going to be my last few moments on this earth.

And then he slammed inside me and held for a beat. I *felt*

the first spurt of his orgasm in a place so deep inside me it was uncharted territory. That pulse, that unholy grunt of pleasure so sharp it was almost pain, sent me hurtling into the abyss. I clamped down on him like his cock was a mechanical bull on Wasted Wednesday.

My walls met the next volley of his release greedily, closing down on him hard. Beat for beat. Thrust for thrust. Wave for wave. We matched each other. Opening and closing. Coming and drowning together.

He drove into me one last time and held there while our releases mixed and mingled inside me as the waves gentled, then slowed, then finally, finally stopped.

51

DOMINIC

"Dom?"

My name from her mouth was a croak. "Mmm?" I nuzzled into her hair.

"I need something," she whispered.

Oh God. If she was going to ask me to go again, there was a very good chance I would die. I already wasn't sure if my dick was ever going to work again after the last round. There was a possibility that my heart would give out too.

I considered myself to be rather excellent in bed. But three times in one night was asking a lot of my midforties prowess. Even for a superhero. Four would quite possibly break something important.

"What do you need, baby?"

"An ice pack."

Relieved, I laughed weakly. "Oh, thank God. I thought you were going to ask for another round. Something I won't be physically capable of until I've had at least two IV bags of fluids."

Her laugh turned into a yawn. "I'm sticky. And sweaty," she murmured into my pillow.

We'd finally made it to the bed. And made good use of it too.

But my superhuman sex powers were officially depleted.

"I literally poured my entire water content into you. I'm basically human beef jerky right now."

"Thank you for your sacrifice," she teased.

I lifted my head and rolled her toward me. Her pretty pink nipples were hypnotizing, and my idiotic dick that had no concept of consequences like chafing or possible failure to launch stirred at the sight of them peeking out from my white, rumpled sheets.

Down, boy.

"I'll get you an ice pack and some water," I promised her, brushing a kiss to her forehead and one to her cheek. I threw in a nibble at her neck for good measure.

She breathed out a laugh, and I decided it was the best noise I'd ever heard in this house.

"We're so stupid," she said.

"In what way?" I asked, giving in to temptation and bestowing a long lick on the nipple closest to me.

She gave a full-body tremble against me. "We could have been doing this for weeks now." Her fingers stroked into my hair.

"Yeah, except you had to be stubborn," I reminded her, leaning over to give her other breast the same treatment.

My moronic cock was already at half-mast again.

"Me?" She snorted. "By the way, I'm still not quitting."

"We have a lot to figure out," I said to her breasts.

She sat up and hit me with a pillow. "Dominic Russo! You can't make me quit."

Obligingly playful—a description that never once in my entire life applied to me—I pinned her to the mattress.

I didn't want to think about the consequences of tonight. I wanted to live in this space where there was only now…and Ally's perfect, perky breasts rubbing against my chest. But there were things that needed to be settled. Now.

"How are you hard?" she demanded with what I deemed an appropriate amount of wonder.

"I'm not really," I scoffed modestly.

"You're hard enough," she said, staring down between us to where my cock rested against her belly.

"You need an ice pack. I need a gallon of electrolytes. And we need to talk."

She pouted. "Isn't it a million o'clock right now?"

It was after three in the morning.

"We can sleep later. First, I'm taking you home."

Her face fell, and the bastard I was preened like a rooster when I realized she misunderstood what I was saying and was disappointed at the prospect of not spending the night with me.

"To get your things. You're staying here tonight."

"Dom, my things are in New Jersey. By the time we get them and get back, it'll be time for work."

"We're both working from home tomorrow. My home."

"Is my face really that bad?" she joked.

I leaned in, the picture of seriousness. "It is." She whacked me in the head with the pillow again, and I grinned. "And speaking of faces, there's no way on this planet that we could go into that office without what we just did written all over ours."

"You think another day will erase the orgasm scoreboard etched on your pretty face?" she teased, squeezing my cheeks in her hand until my mouth did that ridiculous duck-lip thing.

"We may have to take off the rest of the year," I muttered through her fingers.

Her laugh untied knots in my chest that I didn't know I had.

And I knew I wasn't going back to before.

Before tonight.

Before I saw the bruises on her face.

Before I knew what Ally felt like from the inside out.

Before she could laugh naked under me.

I wasn't physically capable of it.

With extreme male reluctance, I crawled off her, hooking her ankles and dragging her toward the edge of the bed. "Come on, Maleficent. Let's find you some pants."

A middle of the night road trip with Ally bundled into another pair of my sweatpants and Brownie wedged onto her lap seemed otherworldly. She unabashedly sat on a bag of frozen lima beans I'd found in my freezer while I guzzled my second sports drink.

"Sex in our forties is supposed to be even better," she mused, stroking Brownie's head and staring out the window. "But I'm not sure I'll survive to see the end of thirty-nine."

"When is your birthday?" I asked, already knowing the answer thanks to the HR file I'd memorized. Maybe it was a test to see if the unveiling of Ally Morales began and ended with sex.

"May."

"How does Maleficent plan to celebrate forty?" I wanted to know everything there was to know about this woman.

She wrinkled her nose. "All celebrations are on hold until Dad's situation is settled."

I brought her fingers to my mouth and kissed her knuckles. "Then what?"

"So far, the only thing I've come up with is a mango margarita on a beach that requires a passport. I want to sit in the sun and stare out at an ocean so blue it doesn't seem real. And I don't want to have to worry about if I can afford to tip the bartender."

I approved of the plan. Especially if it involved Ally in a bikini and me in the lounge chair next to her.

I held her hand as she directed me, first to an all-night convenience store for surprisingly decent green tea and an armload of snacks to stave off the hunger caused by our sex marathon and then on to her father's house.

It was still dark when I swung into the skinny driveway, but I breathed a sigh of relief. Google Street View hadn't lied. The neighborhood was not terrible, and the house itself looked… comfortable.

"Brownie should probably wait in the car," she said, unbuckling her seat belt.

I was immediately suspicious. "Why?"

"It's a bit of a construction zone inside. I don't want him to step on a nail or something." She hopped out of the car and carefully closed the door in my dog's face.

Brownie looked crestfallen for all of two seconds before he remembered it was an unholy hour in the middle of the night and curled up and went to sleep behind the wheel.

"Is it me, or is it colder here in Jersey?" I asked, following her up the walkway.

"I'll keep you warm, big guy," she said with an exaggerated wink.

I gave her ass a slap. And then immediately shifted gears into preparing a safety lecture with some significant yelling when she opened the front door without unlocking it first.

That lecture was put on the back burner when I followed her inside.

"What the… Tell me you don't actually live here."

What I assumed had been a living room at some point was a tidy ruin.

"It's not that bad," Ally said with a roll of her brown eyes. It wasn't really her fault that she wasn't taking this seriously. Basking in the glow of the impressive number of orgasms that I'd personally delivered, she hadn't noticed how pissed off I really was. "Just watch your step," she cautioned.

"There's a hole in your ceiling." It was the first of many, many problems I had with the room.

There was a gaping hole in the ceiling. The plywood floor was water-stained in a six-foot radius. The carpet had been removed at some point, but the strips of tacks were still in place, offering a nice dance with tetanus to anyone who ventured too close.

The spot against the wall where I assumed a TV had once been was bare, the drywall behind it stained and bowed. Capped wires hung out of a hole.

"It used to be a lot worse," she said cheerfully. "There used to be a bathtub right there."

She pointed to the spot.

It was freezing in the house. I blinked at the thermostat reading. Fifty-two fucking degrees.

"It happened right before Dad was diagnosed. He forgot he left the faucet running. It overflowed and ran all night. The tub fell through the floor. It wrecked the entire bathroom and part of the hallway and bedroom upstairs. Down here, well, you can see. The worst was the piano," she said sadly, gesturing toward the ruined instrument. "My father loves music. We used to play together, make up silly songs. Just the two of us. On his good days, we used to joke that he couldn't have done more damage if he tried."

"Why are you living like this?" I asked.

"You don't really want to hear yet another Morales family story of woe," she said lightly, but I could hear the note of strain in her voice.

Oh, but I did. I pinned her with my gaze.

"Geez. Fine. So my mother stealing my father's savings was just the first problem."

I needed to move, so I wandered around the room while she talked. I paused at the piano.

"No shit," I spat. I was so fucking angry that the woman I'd spent my evenings lusting after from my warm, cushy Upper West Side town house had been living here. Like *this*.

She picked up a box of drywall screws and put it on an end table.

I stopped pacing and leaned against the wall.

"Once upon a time, I had savings too," she sighed.

I waited, not trusting myself to keep the anger roiling beneath the surface contained.

"After I moved back, I hired a contractor. A contractor who came in twenty percent below the other bids. I thought I was being smart with my money, but..." She waved her hand around the room. "It was the worst thing I could have done. He took the check and ran. Twenty thousand dollars."

I swore ripely. Besides touching Ally again, my second priority was to find this contractor and punch him in his face until he had no teeth left.

"Yeah, pretty much my sentiments," she agreed. "With my savings gone, I cashed in my retirement savings to cover the nursing home. That's all gone now too."

"I want the contractor's name and contact information. Your mother's too," I said.

"Good luck with that. The business number is disconnected, and the Facebook page is nothing but posts from people demanding their money back. My mother is out of the country building schools or planting crops. Anyway, the rest of my savings went to the nursing home. Again, astronomically expensive, but my father deserves the best care I can get him, and I'm not letting him go back to the other place."

I'd heard enough. I was going to hunt that fucking contractor and her thieving, holier-than-thou mother down and wring them dry until every cent they owed Ally was paid back.

"Get your things. You're not staying here anymore."

"Dom. You're overreacting."

"It's fucking freezing in here! There's a fucking hole in your fucking ceiling. If you take one step to the left, you're going to end up with dirty fucking nails in your foot." I was yelling now, and I wasn't sure I'd ever be able to stop.

"Look, I know it's not the Four Seasons," she snapped.

"The Four Seasons? This isn't even a burned-out hull of a roach motel frequented by toothless prostitutes and meth-addicted johns. You're not staying here."

She drilled a finger into my chest. "Breaking news, Dom. You don't get to tell me what to do."

I felt physically ill. Thinking about all those nights I'd been fantasizing about her in my big, warm bed. In my comfortable home with food in the fridge and heat and money. And she'd been *here*. I thought about the balance of the trust fund I'd touched once. The one that could have saved her from all this.

"Ally, don't fight me on this. You're not spending another night under this Swiss cheese roof."

"It's not that bad."

"If a building inspector showed up right now, he'd rule this place uninhabitable. You're not staying. Pack your shit. Now."

"Just because we had sex doesn't give you any right to tell me what to do."

I dragged her a step away from the tack strip she was standing too close to. I was so angry the edges of my vision were going red. "Listen to me, Ally. I don't care if this is inappropriate or high-handed or controlling. You aren't staying here. I'm not fucking around. And you're not winning this one."

"I know you've never had to deal with not having money, but staying someplace better involves rent money. A lot of it. And the more money I pay out to expenses like that, the less I have for my dad."

I closed my eyes. Clenching my jaw, I tried to count backward from twenty. I was so fucking pissed at her, at myself, at the assholes who screwed her over, that I didn't trust myself to speak.

"Dom—"

"You *matter* to me, Ally. Do you get that? I *care* about you. And yet you insist on not taking what I can offer you. I need you safe. I need you warm and happy and fed and rested. Goddammit, Ally. You are killing me with this stupid pride."

She was staring up at me wide-eyed and dazed.

"You can't make me leave you here. You have to understand that, Ally."

"Why are you so mad?" she whispered.

"Why? Because I live in a three-bedroom town house with all the heat and food and fucking solid floors I could ever want. And this whole time, you've been *here*. Your front door doesn't even lock."

"Don't push your privileged guilt off on me. I never asked for—"

"Anything. You never asked for any fucking thing. I can make all your problems go away. I can fix all this, and you won't let me!" I needed to take a step back. I needed some space for this helpless rage that was clawing its way up my throat. But I didn't want to not be touching her.

"Why would I let you help me?" She looked genuinely confused, and I couldn't blame her. I'd done nothing but send mixed signals. "This is my problem, Dom. My responsibility."

I dropped my forehead to hers. "Let me fix this, Ally."

She looked stricken. "No! Dominic, you've done nothing but tell me we can't be together. That you aren't going to let yourself want me. I respected that. Why can't you respect this?"

I didn't care if she had a point. It was all different now. *We* were different. "I was lying to myself. To you. You know damn well that tonight changed everything."

Those golden-brown eyes were wide and scared. Good. It was about time she got scared about something. "What do you mean 'everything'?"

"Everything, Ally. Every fucking thing."

"So the sex was good. That doesn't mean we're—"

"In a relationship. That's exactly what it means."

"Oh no you don't, Dominic Russo. You can't boss me into a relationship. I don't have time. I don't *want* to be in a relationship!"

"Well, tough shit. Because we're in one."

"This is *not h*ow relationships work! You don't just tell someone you're in a relationship. That's why restraining orders exist!"

She looked panicky. And I was glad because I didn't want to be the only one with this sick, terrified feeling in my gut.

"Fine. Be my girlfriend."

Her eyebrows skyrocketed up her forehead. "What?"

"Be my girlfriend. Date me. Be in a fucking relationship with me, Ally."

She opened her mouth, and the only thing that came out was a squeak. Not exactly a reaction that stroked the ego.

"You… I…can't…" A language barrier had apparently sprung up between us.

"Where's your bedroom?" I demanded.

Her gaze flicked toward the stairs, and I charged up them. Ally was hot on my heels. "Be careful of the floor up there. I haven't replaced it yet," she said, grabbing my arm as I stepped onto the rotted landing.

I didn't give in to the need to take her by the shoulders and shake her. Instead I shrugged her off and stepped into a tiny, drafty bedroom. The twin bed was made with three cheap comforters. A pair of sweatpants—my sweatpants—a hooded sweatshirt—again mine—and a long-sleeve T-shirt were neatly folded next to the pillows. She slept in layers huddled under cheap-ass blankets just to stay warm.

I felt physically ill.

"What are you doing?" she demanded when I moved to the doll-size closet and started pulling clothing out of it.

"Packing."

She yanked a skirt out of my hands. "Knock it off, Dom. You're starting to piss me off."

"You'll stay with me," I decided.

She hit me with the skirt. "Excuse me! I'm not moving in with you!" She looked horrified.

"I have spare rooms. You can take one of them."

"You have lost your damn mind. I am not living in your house!"

"Fine. Then I'm staying here with you." I abandoned the clothes I'd piled up on her bed and started for the stairs. I'd pack a bag for me and Brownie and make a few calls. A contractor and an all-night locksmith to start.

She ran after me. "You can't stay here!"

I rounded on her, and she came to an abrupt stop on the step above mine. "Get it through your stubborn fucking head, Ally. If you're staying here, then so am I."

"I'm handling this. I don't need you."

"What you need is to realize that you're in over your head and that I am not just willing to help, I am begging to help you."

The panic was still there in those sweet brown eyes. "Dominic, I can't afford to owe you anything more."

Overwhelmed, I dragged her into my arms. "Baby, listen to me. The way you felt about your dad living in that shithole is exactly how I feel about you living here. This isn't a favor to pay back. This is purely selfish on my part. I can't live with you staying here."

"You've already done more than I can ever thank you for. This job, this salary, literally saved my dad. And I don't know if I'm ever going to be able to repay you for that." Her voice broke, and I couldn't take it any more than I could take the image of her huddled up under the covers while I texted her from my warm, safe town house.

I held on tight.

"I promised my Dad that I would handle this. That he'd never be a burden. I can't let him down. He'd be humiliated."

I pressed her face to my chest. "Oh, Ally. How do you think he would feel if he saw you living like this? If he knew how hard you were working and how little you were eating? You tell me what would be worse for him."

"He's never going to know," she said firmly.

"So if you're not going to tell him that, why do you have to tell him if I help?"

Ha! I had her there. It was her own pride getting in the way right now, not her father's.

"I…"

Clearly she didn't know what to say in the face of my flawless male logic.

"You're not in this alone anymore, Ally. I get that this feels like just another curveball coming from me. I do. And I'm fucking sorry for that. But I'm on your team, whether you want me or not. And you are not staying here alone ever again."

"Knock knock!" The cheery, heavily accented call came from the open front door.

I grabbed Ally and tucked her behind my back to face the pre–crack of dawn threat.

The woman couldn't have been more than five feet tall. She was roundish and oldish with a bright, nosy smile. There was a blue casserole dish in her hands. "I heard lots of yelling and came to investigate."

"Mrs. Grosu, it's 4:30 in the morning." Ally choked the words out.

"Yes. It is. And you're having a fight with a very handsome man. I'm hoping for a lovers' quarrel, but even handsome cat burglars deserve love."

"No lovers' quarrel," Ally insisted, trying to get around me on the stairs. "I'm sorry we woke you."

"Nonsense!" The woman beamed. "It's always the perfect time for French toast casserole. Now, introduce me to your handsome, loud friend."

Together, we trooped down the stairs, and when Ally tried to put some distance between us, I dragged her into my side.

"Mrs. Grosu, this is my—"

"Boyfriend," I finished for her.

"Boss," she said.

We glared at each other. One of us was going to win this. And it wasn't going to be Ally.

"What happened to your face?" Mrs. Grosu asked.

52

DOMINIC

We took Brownie next door to Mrs. Grosu's warm, cozy bungalow and ate French toast casserole while she updated us on what sounded like an entire army of children and grandchildren.

I took advantage of Ally's exhaustion and helped her pack two days' worth of clothes—a compromise that I magnanimously agreed to—before driving us back into the city that was just beginning to wake up.

It had been a long fucking night, but I was energized. For the first time since I'd stepped into my father's role at *Label*, I felt confident in what I needed to do.

While Ally got Brownie his breakfast, I warmed up the kettle and fired off a text to my mother.

Me: Need to talk. It's important. My house?

Mom: You really know how to strike fear in a mother's

heart before 7 in the morning. Is Brownie okay? Are you okay?

Me: Sorry. Brownie and I are both fine. Everything is fine. Just need to talk.

Mom: I can be there by 8. But I want breakfast if you're determined to deliver bad news.

I winced.

Ally yawned and bent down to peer under the kitchen sink.

"What are you doing?" I asked, admiring the view of her ass in my sweats. It felt like a claim staked.

"Looking for some kind of cleaner. Aha!" Triumphantly, she produced a bottle.

I watched as she grabbed the paper towels and liberally sprayed the spot where only hours ago, we'd fucked like horny teenagers.

For some reason, it struck me as funny, and I laughed.

Ally raised an eyebrow in my direction. Brownie lifted his head out of his bowl and stared at me, head cocked. Had I never laughed in front of my dog before? Was I really that soulless?

"What?" Ally asked, wiping down the countertop. "Sooner or later, someone is going to make a sandwich here."

I took the bottle and the towels from her. "Go upstairs and shower."

"Bossy," she complained, yawning again. "Can't we just go to bed?"

"Not yet. My mom is coming over."

"Oh!" Her eyes widened as it sunk in. "Wait, you're telling Dalessandra that we had sex?"

I laughed again at the horror on her face. It had been a hell of a lot more than sex, and we both knew it.

"My father kept a lot of things from her."

"But it was just—"

I put my hand over her mouth. "If you try to say that last night was 'just sex,' I am going to work very hard to prove you very wrong."

She pulled my hand away and poked me in the chest. "Excuse me. Don't you think this is a conversation *we* should have before we include your mother, our *boss*?"

The woman seemed really hung up on the hierarchy. She also had a practically infinitesimal point. "Fine. Ally, last night changed everything for us, and I'm not willing to return to a strictly professional relationship."

"There are miles between a strictly professional relationship and dating, Dom."

"Not in this case there aren't. Are we together?"

"What about the policy?"

"Forget everything else right now. Forget the policy. My mother. Your father. Forget that hovel in New Jersey."

She rolled her eyes.

"Forget everything else except you and me. Right here. Right now." Pulling her into me felt so fucking right after all those weeks I'd wasted pushing her away. "Are we together?"

She studied me quietly. There was a war brewing behind those whiskey eyes.

"We can make this work. All of it. I promise you that. I just need you to say the words, Maleficent."

She bit her lip as her fingers worried little circles into my biceps. I was asking her to trust me when I hadn't ever given her a reason to. But I needed her to have faith in me.

"Give me a minute," she said.

I dipped my head and traced my tongue over her earlobe. "Think about last night, Ally. That was real. We're real. We can make this work. If you want to."

"But how?"

I shook my head. "The how doesn't matter right now. What matters is if you want this. If you want us." On cue, my very smart dog wedged his face between us.

I was holding on to her too tight. I could feel her balanced on that ledge, and long seconds ticked by without me knowing which way Ally would lean. My Ally. She didn't really have a choice. Neither did I. And I think we both knew it.

"When you say 'this,' what do you mean?" she asked.

"Us. Together."

"Monogamous?"

I glared at her. "Yes. So don't even think of that asshole Christian James again."

"Both of us. Monogamous," she repeated.

"Of course."

"What else?" she pressed.

"Ally, I don't fucking know. We'll figure it out. We both want to continue having sex with each other and only each other, correct?"

"That's not exactly romantic," she pointed out.

"Yeah, well, I'm not really a hearts and flowers kind of guy." I was more of a "fuck her in a dark corner until she screamed my name" kind of guy.

"This is crazy," she breathed.

"It is."

"And irresponsible and stupid, and we're both probably just drunk on sex."

"Life-changing, counter-defacing sex," I pointed out.

Her lips trembled, then lifted. "I'm probably going to regret this."

I held my breath and squeezed her arms. *Say it.*

"But I'm in. Let's give this disaster waiting to happen a shot."

Relief and something brighter, warmer, happier, lit me up

from the inside. I picked her up and spun us around. Ally's arms came around my neck and held tight.

"This is insane," she laughed.

It was. And for the first time in my life, the insane choice felt like the right one.

Forty-five minutes later, my mother arrived in a subtle cloud of Chanel No. 5 and oversize sunglasses.

I took her coat while she showered her granddog with attention. "I still can't believe you got a dog," she said, straightening back into her elegant and proper posture.

"I'm an excellent dog dad," I pointed out, opening the door and ushering her through.

"Of course you are," she said, patting my cheek. "I'm just surprised you committed. It's a good thing you haven't felt compelled to commit to everything you've ever French-kissed."

"About that."

My mother stopped in her tracks in the kitchen doorway.

"Hi." Ally waved guiltily with a spatula from her sentry at the stove.

"Ah," Mom said and turned back to me. Her expression was unreadable. But I wasn't picking up on any hostile vibes. *Yet.* "Hello, Ally," she said.

"Mom, have a seat," I said, pushing her toward the table Ally had set in the dining room while I cooked.

She sat, and I gestured for Ally to do the same. I took the pan off the heat and scooped eggs and spinach onto plates with sliced tomatoes.

Carrying the plates into the dining area, I felt remarkably calm for what I was about to do, and that told me everything I needed to know. It was time for new priorities.

I took the chair next to Ally's and picked up my tea.

"Mom. I'm resigning."

53

ALLY

My fork hit the plate with a resounding clatter.

"You're what?" Dalessandra and I said together.

Dominic placed a hand over mine, but his attention was on his mother.

"As of last night, Ally and I are in a relationship. You're the first to know. Well, besides a Romanian woman who broke into Ally's house."

I felt like I was having an out-of-body experience. I was floating up toward the ceiling and looking down at this scene with a distinct feeling of *what the fuck?* I imagined people who were hit by buses felt the same kind of detached bemusement as they shuffled off this mortal coil.

"You are not resigning," I said a few decibels louder than I intended.

Brownie trotted into the room, Dominic's underwear dangling out of his mouth.

"I am," Dominic insisted. "Ally will stay on in her current position for whoever you appoint to take my place until Greta comes back. If Greta chooses to leave or retire, Ally can continue on in the position permanently. If Greta prefers to stay, I want you to find Ally a suitable placement with the salary she has currently."

"You can't just make decisions like that without consulting me," I choked, valiantly trying to wrench my hand free of his so I could smack him upside the head.

"Or me," Dalessandra agreed. She was handling it better than I was, slicing up a dainty portion of tomato and egg.

"You hardheaded, bossy, alpha—Brownie, put those down!" The dog shot me a guilty look and ran out of the room, underwear flapping. "This is not how a relationship works. You don't just make all the decisions and expect me to happily go along with them!"

"Ally is absolutely correct," she said, picking up her tea.

"This is the only way this works," he insisted. "I'm not willing to put you through another scandal. Or drag Ally's name through the mud."

"A consensual relationship between two people who care very much for each other is not a scandal," she said.

"It's still fodder. There will be rumors. People will say things," Dominic pointed out.

"Of course they'll say things," I snapped. "You can't control people's reactions."

They were both ignoring me, and I wondered if perhaps I really had ceased to exist. Maybe a bus had plowed through Dominic's town house, and I was the last to know.

"I do not accept your resignation," Dalessandra told him.

"You're not fucking firing Ally," he said.

"Of course not," she agreed.

"Can either of you two see me? Am I invisible?" I yanked my hand free from his grip, but Dominic grabbed my thigh under the table and held me in place.

"First of all, how serious are you? Is this just sex, or is it more serious?" Dalessandra asked.

"Once again, this is a conversation that should be had with *me* first, not your mother or our *boss*." I was screeching.

"We had the conversation. We're together."

"Darling, if you're not willing to put up with a few bloviating windbags and their blind speculation, then I have to wonder just how serious you are about this relationship," Dalessandra said.

"We're serious enough. End of story," he said calmly. "I'll announce my resignation today."

"No, you fucking won't, you egotistical jackass," I snapped.

"You'll do no such thing," Dalessandra insisted much more politely. "I suppose keeping this quiet is not an option?"

"There isn't going to be a relationship to keep quiet about in a minute," I said through clenched teeth.

It would be my shortest relationship on record.

"I'm not hiding this," Dominic said quietly. "I don't think I could even if you asked me."

Okay, coming from Dominic Russo, *maybe* that was kind of a swoony thing to say. It wasn't a declaration of love, but it was real. These feelings felt real.

But still.

Dalessandra nodded. "Well, that settles that."

I fought his hand off my thigh and stood. "Look, Russos. I am not a minion. I am a human person with feelings and opinions and decision-making capabilities."

"Your decision-making capabilities have you living in a water-damaged icebox," Dominic said.

Oh, if he wanted a fight, I was happy, *thrilled*, to wade in swinging. "Up until last night, your permanent stance was you didn't want to have anything to do with me!"

"I am trying to save you both from another scandal," he growled.

"I don't need to be saved." Dalessandra and I blinked at each other as the words came out of both our mouths in unison.

Dominic took a breath and let it out slowly. "I am offering a solution that puts all the problems to bed," he argued.

Dalessandra spoke first. "That policy was designed to protect employees from predatory power plays and the workplace from disasters like your father left us with last year." She shot me a look.

"What exactly do you suggest?" Dominic asked, annoyed.

"I suggest you disclose your relationship to human resources and the rest of *Label*'s senior management, myself included. Let us worry about how to deal with it."

"I willingly ignored the fraternization policy. How do you think they're going to deal with it? It's grounds for termination for both of us. And Ally can't afford to lose this job. If I leave, no one has to know why."

"*Everyone* will know why," I said, regaining my voice. "You think just because you didn't confirm any rumors about Paul Russo that they just went away? This is the problem. Sweeping secrets under the rug doesn't help anyone. The rumors are usually worse than the truth. People know about your father, and they're going to find out about us."

Dalessandra paled visibly.

"You think rumors are worse?" Dominic asked icily. "Are the rumors worse than my father locking an intern in a conference room and putting his hand up her skirt until she cried? She's in therapy three years later because he thought he could take what he wanted. I read every affidavit, and believe me, the rumors don't do the bastard justice."

His pissed-off vulnerability snuck up on me and gripped my heart. I reached for him, intending to put my hand on his shoulder, but he rose.

"I'm taking the dog out," he snapped and disappeared out the back with Brownie, who was still carrying his underwear around like a trophy.

An awkward silence descended.

Dalessandra took her tea to the window that overlooked Dominic's backyard. "He cares very much for you," she mused.

I snorted.

"I hope you can see beyond his high-handed actions," she continued. "There is no one in this world I would rather have on my side than my son. He's fiercely loyal, protective."

I'd seen both those sides of him.

"I hope you don't see him trying to resign as him choosing me over you," I said. The bonds between parents and their children shouldn't be so fragile.

She turned to face me, a smile playing on her lips. "Darling, I think this is the first time that Dominic chose himself. I'm ecstatic."

I joined her at the window. "I don't want him to have to walk away from *Label*. Not for me," I told her.

"I have a potential solution in mind that I will present to the powers that be."

"Are you firing me?" I'd understand. I'd caused a lot of unnecessary drama for an admin. And I'd seduced my boss in direct disregard of company policy.

"No." She laughed. "But if you're open to being reassigned within the company—at your current salary level, of course—I believe we can minimize the fuss."

A flicker of hope lit inside me. "As long as I don't report directly to Dominic?"

"Precisely."

I blew out a breath and nodded vigorously. "That would be great."

"I don't know if they'll allow it. We could have been destroyed by what Paul did, and this might stir up memories among the staff. There will still be talk and speculation. There is always interest in any woman Dominic dates, but this situation is rather salacious," she said, choosing her words carefully.

"I can handle it," I assured her. "It's better to be honest about it anyway. Makes whispering about it harder."

"I suppose we'll find out," she said quietly. "Not everyone can face the whispers."

Something tickled at me. Some of her previous comments gelled into something nebulous. Dalessandra was hinting at something.

"I think the Russos have paid enough penance, don't you?"

She glanced my way and raised a questioning eyebrow.

"I mean, you both have worked hard to clean up your ex-husband's mess and to ensure it doesn't happen again."

"We've made strides," she agreed. "But I'm not convinced it's enough."

"If anyone owes a debt, it's Paul. He committed the crime, but it seems like you and Dominic are the ones who paid the price."

"My son doesn't deserve to carry the burden of his father's past mistakes."

"Maybe you should start thinking about the future instead of the past," I suggested.

She gave me a quizzical look and then turned back to the window.

We watched Dominic pick up a tennis ball and toss it across the frozen yard for the joyful dog to chase.

"Would you have let him hide it? If that was what he wanted to do?" I asked her.

She sighed. "I'd told myself I was done lying for the Russo men. But Dominic is not his father."

"He most definitely is not," I agreed. "He didn't start this, Dalessandra. I want you to know that. He didn't pursue me or strong-arm me into it. If anything, I did the convincing."

"I would do anything to protect my son's happiness. I have a good feeling about you and him, but…" She turned to face me again, holding eye contact so there was no mistaking her message. "Dominic is a wonderful man with a very soft heart hidden under layers of armor, and if you hurt him or take advantage of him or play on his insecurities, I will be very disappointed in you. And angry."

I didn't mean to smile, but I was. "I'm glad you love him. And I promise you I'll do my very best to protect that soft heart he tries to hide. He's a good man. You raised a good man."

She nodded her approval. "Good. Then we'll protect him together."

"Team Dominic," I agreed. "Unless he insists on continuing to boss me around. There's no hierarchy outside the office."

"You be sure to remind him of that," she said with another smile. "So, shall we chat about what happened to your lovely face?"

54

DOMINIC

When I had burned off enough of my anger with the derpy Brownie and the disgusting, sodden ball of slobber he loved so dearly, I went back inside.

And found the two most important women in my life looking awfully smug.

"What?"

"Nothing, darling," Mom said, rising from her chair. "I've got to get to the office. Get me a disclosure notice today, and I'll present it. You both should stay home for the day. You look like you could use the rest." She said the last with a raised eyebrow.

I walked her to the front door. "I'm sorry about this," I said as I helped her into her coat.

She turned around and patted my cheek. "Really? Because I'm not. Not in the least."

"You don't have to say that. I know this puts you in a shitty position. I know it looks like a repeat of everything you already went through."

"Dominic, my only son is head over heels in love with a woman who challenges him and makes him smile. I'm happy for you."

My guts did a cartwheel and didn't stick the landing. "Hang on. No one said anything about love," I argued, feeling the icy licks of panic.

She grinned. "You're a good, stubborn man who will hopefully get out of his own way someday. Trust your mother on this. You've never looked at another woman the way you look at Ally."

There were a lot of feelings I had for Ally that I'd never experienced before. Not the least of which was an unholy obsession with her naked body. But I wasn't inclined to share that with my mother.

"This is very new. I wouldn't go throwing labels around," I said dryly.

"It's an awful lot to go through for a woman you just kind of like. Enjoy your day off, darling."

She left on a smug, finger-wiggling wave, and I closed the door after her.

Love? I didn't understand how the woman who had been systematically humiliated by her husband for decades could still believe in such ridiculous notions. And if she knew I'd played a part in it, I doubted she'd be able to love me back.

With absolutely nothing settled like it would have been had they let me commit to the obvious solution, I returned to the kitchen.

Ally was doing the dishes and carrying on a one-sided conversation with Brownie. Fat snowflakes were falling faster outside the windows. A cozy, domestic scene. One that took place in homes across the country, around the world. But never here.

Something weird and uncomfortably warm bloomed in the center of my chest.

My first instinct was to squash it, and I went with it. I wasn't going to fall prey to some adorable domesticity. Not when I was annoyed with her.

"Do you want to fight first or nap first?" I demanded gruffly.

Ally looked up from the dishwasher and crossed her arms. "How about an abbreviated fight and then nap?" she suggested. "We can finish up fighting when we're better rested."

"Lady's choice." I stepped around the island but kept my distance.

She nodded. "If this whatever this is is going to work anywhere besides the bedroom—"

"Relationship, Ally. Say the damn word."

Her glare was withering. "Relationship," she said in a caustic tone that made me want to kiss her until she shut the hell up. "I need to feel like an equal partner. Which means I want my fair share of the decision-making, and I don't want to be beholden to you financially."

"That sounds not completely stupid." It was fair. It made sense. But it left out the how.

"Gee, thanks. Your approval means the world to me," she said, heavy on the sarcasm, slowly closing the distance between us. "Dominic, you're not my winning lottery ticket. This can't be based on you being some kind of benefactor to poor little old me."

She probably didn't mean it in the way I took it, but I was looking to stay pissed off. "I'm so sorry you don't think I'm a prize," I snapped.

"Stop deliberately misunderstanding me," she said. "You know damn well I meant that I don't consider you to be my very own ATM. I don't want your money. I want you. I want an us. And for there to be an us, I want a say."

Okay, so maybe that appeased me a little bit.

"Fine. How the hell do you propose we actually make that happen?"

She stepped into me, and I wasn't certain that she *wasn't* going to try to knee me in the nuts. "Oh, look who's suddenly interested in *how*," she said.

When she moved, I flinched, and a smug smile spread across her face just a second before she slipped her arms around my waist. I was used to the bickering, the banter, but this physical affection was...different. Plus, I'd been in fear for my balls.

"Don't be an ass." I wrapped her up and tucked her head under my chin. "How do normal people do this? Who's in charge of what? How do they assume debts or keep assets separate without pissing each other off?"

Ally sighed against me. "I know you're trying to be a smart-ass right now, but to be honest, I don't really know how the dynamics of a long-term relationship work. Neither one of us has a solid example from childhood. Maybe it depends on the people in it having an ongoing conversation?"

"Fine. We're conversing. What do you want a say in?"

"Everything that affects me that doesn't involve your money," she shot back.

"Ally, I don't want my...*you* lying awake at night trying to figure out if you need to skip meals to make ends meet." I wanted to take care of her. I wanted to take her worries and concerns and problems and solve every last one of them so she could focus all her attention on me. And Brownie of course. I wasn't a completely selfish monster.

She was going to argue with me again, but I was suddenly too tired to fight it out.

"Look, can we figure this out later?" I asked. I didn't want her drawing lines when I wasn't thinking clearly enough to redraw them properly.

She would live here. She would have anything and everything she needed. No one would ever take advantage of her or lay a hand on her ever again. End of fucking story. I was her Prince Fucking Charming.

"Okay. But only because I'm so tired I'm seeing two of you." She sighed.

"Come on," I said, taking her arm and leading her up the stairs.

Brownie bolted ahead of us.

"We're just sleeping, right?" Ally asked as we turned into the bedroom.

"Just sleeping," I agreed, dragging my shirt over my head. "Naked sleeping."

"How's your hydration?" she asked, pulling off her sweatshirt to reveal the stars of all future fantasies for me, her bare breasts.

"Great. Totally rehydrated," I lied. "How's the soreness?"

"Hardly feel a thing," she fibbed. I could tell it wasn't the truth because her neck flared red like a beacon.

I took off my pants, my cock already flying like a flag.

"Just sleep," I promised, watching as she removed her leggings and underwear. We stared at each other, naked and maybe even a little vulnerable, from opposite sides of the bed.

The linens were an unholy mess from our gymnastics mere hours ago. So much had changed so quickly, and there was so much more to come.

But I wouldn't break that to her now. She'd been through enough for one day...or twelve hours.

For now, I would settle for holding her while I worked out what needed to happen next.

We slipped under the blankets, Brownie making himself comfortable at our feet. And when Ally hesitated, I made the decision for her, pulling her against me. Her back to my chest. My face to her hair.

She hissed out a breath and an honest to God giggle when her ass wiggled against my hard-on.

"Just sleep," I promised her again.

"I won't be sore forever," she hinted.

"Shh," I ordered, not ready to test my own chivalry or hydration levels.

She settled against me, sighed, and was fast asleep within minutes.

Having her in my arms, in my bed, felt foreign. Familiar. Right. Wrong. And everything in between.

We slept for three hours.

And when I woke with her round, soft ass pressed against my erection, I thanked my lucky stars. When she rolled over and looked at me with sleepy eyes and "please" on her lips, I promised my soul to whatever deity had delivered her to my bed. And when I slipped inside her slowly, sweetly, when she sighed out my name, I wondered if maybe I'd finally been forgiven for my own sins.

One thing I knew for sure when I felt her start to surrender was that I was going to fix everything for her. Whether she wanted me to or not.

55

ALLY

I was officially living in an alternate universe.

Not only had I spent the night in Dominic Russo's bed—and surprisingly snuggly arms—now I was riding with him to work. The streets had been cleared of yesterday's modest snowfall, leaving the pavement clean and wet.

A new start. A blank canvas.

It looked as though there would be one for us too. We'd been summoned.

By his mother.

And I wasn't sure if that was a good or very, very bad thing. HR and management could easily decide to fire us both.

Or just one of us. And I already knew which one of us that would be.

Just because *Label* had made strides since Paul Russo's reign of terror didn't mean that the son of the editor in chief would be judged on the same level as a lowly admin. Especially not one who admittedly pursued and seduced her boss…while coated in body glitter and shame in a strip club.

Technically, on paper, I was a Malina.

A thought that made my skin crawl.

I leaned forward to check my makeup in the mirror. With the swelling down, the bruising had been easier to hide under a thick coat of concealer and a spunky side part.

"What's wrong?" Dominic asked from the driver's seat. The only outward sign of his nerves was the frenetic, silent tapping of his thumb on the wheel.

"Nothing at all. Just feel like I'm marching toward a firing squad."

"You're not going to get shot," he assured me.

"Not that kind of firing squad. Like a 'you're no longer employed, pack your shit' firing squad."

Eyes on the road, he took my hand, squeezed it. "Stop worrying," he insisted.

"Of course. Why didn't I think of that? You're so handsome and smart," I said, heavy on the eyelash-batting sarcasm.

"Hey, I could have easily fixed this," he reminded me.

"Your solution was to quit your job. On what planet was that even an acceptable option?"

"On the planet where I want to be able to get you naked guilt-free more than I want that job."

My lady parts performed a discombobulating quiver. My vagina was fangirling over Dominic Russo.

"I wouldn't ask you to do that. You *like* working there," I pointed out.

He shot me a skeptical side-eye. "What makes you say that?"

"I think you're a lot more comfortable at *Label* than you realize," I pointed out. "You've never once complained about fashion being boring or unnecessary or shallow. If anything, I think you have an appreciation for it. You clearly enjoy working with your mother and Linus. And I've seen your face when you get the final mock-ups for the issue."

He grunted rather than admitting I was right.

"Besides, you're a Russo. You and Dalessandra are building a legacy. I'm the one who has no idea what I'll do once things are more settled with Dad."

"You'll stay here." He said it in that annoyingly confident way as if he'd already made the decision for me.

"I haven't decided," I sniffed primly as he pulled into the parking garage.

"Yes, you have. You're not setting your father up in a nursing home and then moving away."

Smug Smarty-Pants had me there, and he knew it.

He swung into a parking spot, and we sat in silence for a beat.

"I don't like it when you worry," he said.

It was an oddly sweet sentiment coming from him. I opened my mouth to tell him that, but he cut me off.

"Especially not when there's an obvious solution."

The tiny cartoon hearts orbiting my head popped like balloons. "Are you trying to annoy me?" I asked.

"I'm pointing out that by ignoring my solution, you're setting yourself up for unnecessary discomfort. No matter what, people will talk."

I shifted on the heated leather seat to face him. "Dom, of course people are going to talk. Trying to avoid being a topic of conversation is a pretty lame way to live life. Sometimes, accepting the discomfort is how good things are earned."

"I don't want you to be uncomfortable. Or scared. Or hurt. I *want* to protect you from all that. I *can* protect you from all that. You're just too damn stubborn to see the light."

Bizarrely, those little cartoon hearts reappeared.

"Dom, as much as you want to, you can't protect me from everything. And if people want to gossip and speculate about us or our sex life or what I'm going to do after I definitely get fired, let them. I'm not going to lie and hide things in hopes that Malina won't be hissing insults behind my back."

Or more likely to my face.

"I want this to be worth it to you," he said, staring straight through the windshield.

"Are you talking to me or that concrete pillar?"

He gave an exaggerated eye roll. "Don't be a smart-ass."

"Why stop now?" I said, feeling marginally more cheerful.

"Just don't worry about this thing today. Whatever they decide, we'll figure out a way that I can still see you naked and you can still pay your bills."

"And they say romance is dead," I said airily.

He grabbed my face in his hands and kissed me hard. "We'll make this work," he promised.

And I believed him.

Ruth stood behind the reception desk looking flushed and terrified when Dominic ushered me through the office door. I'd texted her and Gola a heads-up this morning.

> **Me:** So, I have news, and I might be fired. Don't say anything yet. I'll spill as soon as I can unless I'm being escorted out by building security.

Ruth's eyes were twice their normal size. "Dalessandra is ready for you in your office, Mr. Ru—Dominic," she squeaked. She pushed a drink carrier in our direction. "I ordered you a tea and a coffee."

Dominic paused, a puzzled frown on his lips. "Uh, thank you, Ruth. That was…nice of you."

Ruth gave what looked like a little curtsy and then turned bright red.

Dominic cleared his throat and picked up the tray. "Are you ready?" he asked me.

"As I'll ever be," I said grimly.

He turned and started down the hall.

"Thanks for the drinks," I whispered to Ruth.

"I can't believe I curtsied! He's just so hot it makes me stupid."

"Preaching to the choir, my friend."

"Good luck in there. Drinks tonight after dance?" she said.

No matter what happened in Dalessandra's office, I was going to need a sweaty dance class and alcohol. "Yeah. Sounds good. I'll text you."

We found Dalessandra seated on the white silk sofa next to the head of HR, a woman with deeply etched frown lines bracketing her mouth. Clearly Jasmine had snapped her photo ID too. In it, she had one eye closed and something resembling a snarl twisting her mouth.

"Good morning, Dominic, Ally," Dalessandra said, putting her teacup down on the oval glass coffee table. "Please, have a seat." She gestured toward the white leather chairs across from her and Lady McFrowny.

"Morning," Dominic said, sounding about as friendly as a pissed-off wolverine.

"I believe you two know Candace from HR," Dalessandra continued.

I actually didn't know her but didn't feel like it was a good time to bring that up.

There wasn't a hint of what kind of shoe was about to fall

on me. Was it a steel-toed boot designed to smash me into the carpet? Or perhaps a designer stiletto that would skewer me.

"Hi." I croaked out a forced greeting.

Dominic sent me a *what the fuck* look, then took my hand and squeezed. Hard. Whether it was a good idea to rub our physical affection in HR Lady's face, I wasn't sure. But the contact calmed me. We were in this together.

Dalessandra's lips quirked.

"I'll just go ahead and put you two out of your misery," Candace announced, peeling what looked like legal contracts out of a folder.

"Am I fired?"

"Christ," Dominic muttered under his breath, rolling his eyes.

"No one is fired," Candace said dryly, sliding the pair of contracts toward us.

I reached for mine, my sweaty fingers leaving smudges on the pristine glass beneath. I skimmed over the first page looking for words like "termination" and "pack your shit" and "security is being called."

"Since you two managed this budding relationship in a professional manner, the HR department is not opposed to allowing it to continue with a few caveats."

Dominic squeezed my hand hard. *Professional manner?* He must not have mentioned me watching him masturbate in his office after-hours or me giving him a lap dance in his disclosure document.

"Which are?" he asked crisply.

"Ally will be transferred out of her current position and into a new placement at her current level of pay and benefits but further removed from your direct management."

"Is that really necessary?" he asked, looking annoyed.

"It's quite necessary," she insisted.

I was busy scanning my document for the pertinent information. Graphics. I was being transferred to the graphics department. I was going to work for one of the premier publications in the world as a graphic designer, *and* I got to keep my hot boyfriend.

"I accept," I said quickly.

All three of them looked at me, eyebrows raised.

A laugh bubbled up in my throat, and I covered it by choking on my coffee.

Dalessandra looked amused.

"In that case, Dominic, you'll be assigned a new assistant until Greta returns," Candace continued, peering over her glasses at him. "You and Ms. Morales will be expected to maintain a professional demeanor at all times during work hours." Her gaze lingered on our linked hands. When I made a move to pull away, he merely tightened his grip.

"We're not interested in creating any workplace drama," Dominic said smoothly. "We are both serious about this relationship. I'm confident we can continue to do our jobs without allowing our personal lives to interfere."

"Yeah. That," I said, nodding effusively.

Dominic's mouth quirked, and I knew he was going to tease me mercilessly for this student-principal interaction.

"Then I'd suggest that you speak as little as possible about this situation. We certainly don't want to set a precedent that makes the rest of the staff feel like the rules are up for debate."

They'd given us everything we could have wanted, but it still felt like a censure.

And I wasn't cut out to be anyone's secret girlfriend. I wasn't going to lie to my friends just to make human resources more comfortable. There had been more than enough secrets kept within these walls. I was already shaking my head when Dominic met my eyes. He sighed.

"Ally and I would both prefer to be up-front about this with our coworkers. We're not interested in keeping secrets."

Anymore. The word he hadn't said hung in the air between us, shimmering like a neon sign that I hoped Dalessandra and Candace couldn't see lest they start questioning us about the particulars of our relationship.

They shared a look.

"While our preference is that our employees keep their private lives private, perhaps a simple statement acknowledging the relationship and the reassignment will head off any unnecessary speculation," Dalessandra suggested.

Dominic looked my way again, and I nodded vigorously.

"Fine," he grumbled. "I'll draft a statement and run it by HR."

"Good enough for me," Candace said. "Now, if you two will just sign those contracts stating you won't let this relationship interfere with your working environment, we can all get back to work."

I got the feeling Candace was annoyed that my silly love life was dragging her away from employee reprimands and benefits paperwork.

Hastily, I scrawled my signature on the contract, trying not to worry about words like "terminated" or "breach of contract" or "If for any reason you feel you are unable to adhere to the terms of this contract, please alert a human resources representative immediately."

Dominic signed his contract without any outward reaction.

"Shall we all get back to our days?" Dalessandra asked with a smile.

56

EVERYONE

Gola: Girl, why am I Dominic Russo's new acting assistant? Did you spell something out in his breakfast burrito?

Ruth: The entire office is whispering right now! Most popular rumors: Ally punched Dominic in the face. Dominic told his mother that it was him or you, she chose you, and now he's packing.

Gola: Can confirm that Boss Man is NOT packing. Repeat. Not packing. Also, he knows my name.

Ruth: Video footage from the admin pool shows Malina sharpening her claws in anticipation of a new hunt.

Gola: I'm concerned. There hasn't been an Ally sighting on this floor since she left Dalessandra's office.

Ruth: You don't think she's dead in a ditch somewhere, do you? Did Malina finally snap?

Gola: ALLY, WHERE ARE YOU? DO YOU NEED ASSISTANCE?

Ruth: I'll check the stairwells.

Gola: I'll check my old stomping grounds…a.k.a. the 42nd floor.

Ruth: Ally sighting report! Sources confirm she just took a desk in the graphics department!

Gola: Is she happy? Crying? Does she look like she's being held against her will?

Ruth: Stand by for confirmation…

Ally: You guys! I lost my phone in my meager box of possessions that I've packed and unpacked four times since I started here. Everything is fine. I've been reassigned because…*going through a tunnel*

Gola: ?

Ruth: Don't you do the fade away thing on us! We will hunt you down in graphics and make you spill everything!

Ally: Hehe. I was just messing with you. Ladies, I'd like you two to be the first to know that Dominic Russo and I are…

Gola: Going to jail?

Ruth: Being fired for embezzlement?

Gola: Donating your paychecks to a worthy cause?

Ruth: Moving to Kentucky to start a bourbon distillery?

Ally: Dating.

Ally: OMG! Ruth, was that you screaming?

Ruth: Oops. You heard that? I got your text in the stairwell. It was more of a squeal.

Gola: Dominic just came out and asked me if I was okay because I choked on my green juice when I read your text. He almost tried to clear my airway.

Then he told me I should probably start calling him Dominic.

Ruth: Now we really need to go for drinks tonight.

Gola: Drinks after dance? Count me in.

Dominic: I take it you told your girls?

Ally: I wanted to give Gola and Ruth a heads-up. Why?

Dominic: I nearly had to give Gola the Heimlich maneuver.

Ally: Did you by chance also hear a terrifying shriek in the stairwell? That was Ruth.

Dominic: Dominic and Ally, nearly killing friends with good news since today.

Harry: Been too long. Drinks. Tonight.

Dominic: Not sure. Got a lot going on.

Harry: I have two girls under four who just got into Mommy's $200 lipstick and used it to draw on our fancy bed linens. I am the one with a lot going on.

Dominic: How fancy?

Harry: Something about organic silkworms and monks.

Dominic: Ouch.

Harry: So drinks. You're coming.

Dominic: Maybe. What time? And can I bring someone?

Harry: If this someone identifies as female and your

primary goal is to get/keep her in bed, I'll bring Del. She can make sure this isn't another Elena.

Dominic: Joke's on you, loser. Del's already met her.

Harry: Name?

Dominic: Ally.

Harry: Hold please.

Harry: Del says and I quote "I knew it. I knew it. I knew it. I KNEW HE WAS AFTER HER. Your wife is the smartest woman in the world. Suck it."

Dominic: You two are what the annoying kids call #relationshipgoals.

Harry: Please tell me this woman isn't under the age of 30 and that's why you're dusting off your pound signs. Because if I'm bringing my wife out and getting her too drunk to notice our murder duvet I don't want to have to listen to her complain about grown men who insist on dating women young enough to be their daughters.

Dominic: She's 39. That would have made me five years old when she was born.

Harry: Standing ovation gif. Wiping tears of gratitude gif.

Dominic: You know there are actual ways to send gifs instead of just explaining them.

Harry: Leave me alone. I'm old, and my kids are still too young to show me how to install a gif keyboard on my phone.

Dominic sent his standby middle finger selfie.

Harry: That's the spirit.

To: Label NY Headquarters Staff
From: Dominic Russo

Subject: HR Policy 135 Sections B-D

Ally Morales and I have entered into a romantic relationship. To avoid any potential workplace favoritism or friction, Ms. Morales has been transferred to the graphics department. No questions or opinions will be entertained.

Sincerely,
Dominic Russo, Creative Director

Ally: Nice subject line, boss. Only one of my new coworkers opened the email so far. She spun around in her chair so fast, she knocked over an entire bowl of ramen.
Dominic: Good god. Not another poor person.
Ally: Not poor people ramen. Fancy ramen. It's a whole thing now.
Dominic: Adding this to my list of things I wish I didn't know.
Ally: Your crotchety-ness is adorable.
Dominic: Let's come back to my crotch, which is recovering nicely from its overuse. But first, can you go for drinks tonight after your dance class?
Ally: Yes. But only if you don't mind going with Ruth

and Gola. Uh-oh. Hang on. More spinning. And now some loud whispering. Did your email insinuate that I was deaf?

Dominic: My email insinuated that everyone should mind their own damn business and leave us the hell alone. I suppose your friends are fine if you don't mind Harry and Delaney joining us.

Ally: Look at us doing the boyfriend-girlfriend thing. What's next? Potluck suppers and coed baby showers?

Dominic: I am going to vehemently hope not. Oh, whatever you do don't mention lipstick or bed linens to Delaney.

Ally: I don't even want the context. This will be more fun.

Dominic: Let's go out to lunch. I want to touch you without a few hundred people watching.

Ally: Count me in. They're all staring at me and eating popcorn.

Dominic: Want me to come down there and give them something to stare at?

Ally: The part of me that saw you naked for twelve straight hours wants to say yes. But maybe we should at least give the HR guidelines a try for a full two hours before we ruin everything?

Dominic: Setting my timer for two hours and one minute.

Ally

I ducked down to the cafeteria for coffee and to get a break from the stares of my new coworkers.

I was just browsing the spectacular pyramid of pastries that I was absolutely not going to buy when a snide presence threw its evil shadow over me.

"Well, if it isn't Dominic's new toy," Malina said snidely.

She was dressed in an ice-blue pantsuit with a V neck that went almost to her belly button.

"Lovely as always to see you, Malina." I sighed.

"How did you do it?"

"How did I do what?" I asked wearily. I should have stayed upstairs. At least the graphics department was too afraid to ask me any direct questions.

"How did you convince Dominic Russo to put his job on the line for *you*?" The emphasis made it clear that Malina didn't think I was worth putting anything on the line.

"That's personal. And this is work. I'm not discussing my personal relationship with you. Also, we're not friends. At this point, I'd rather befriend Missie's tarantula than you." Copywriter Missie had a pet tarantula that she'd named Hercules.

"You think you have what it takes to keep a man like Dominic Russo?"

I actually had no idea what it would take and whether I had it.

"Did you ever have it checked?" I asked.

"What checked?"

"The thing that crawled up your skinny ass and died."

"The weak never understand," she scoffed.

"The weak?" I laughed. Seriously, someone had seen *Mean Girls* one too many times.

She looked me up and down. "The weak. The pathetic. The ones who show up where they don't belong. You don't belong on Christian James's arm any more than you belong in Dominic Russo's bed."

"Who are you talking to, Mal? Me or you?" I shot back.

She bared her teeth at me. I realized the woman before me had years of practice in being a domineering bully. I shuddered when I thought of High School Prom Queen Malina.

"You think you're so special," she hissed.

"We're *all* special," I said, exasperated. "That's the point. Me being special doesn't make you less special. You being a douche to all of humanity factors in though."

"Fuck you, Ally."

"No, fuck you, Malina. We're not in some *Hunger Games* competition for male attention," I spat out. "Don't you think you're worth more than being some rich dick's trophy lay?" I mean, at this point, I wasn't sure she was. There didn't seem to be a human being under all those layers of contouring and fillers.

"Now who are you trying to convince?" she shot back. "You follow Dominic around like a cat in heat."

Ouch. That one hurt.

"You need to stop acting like men are some precious commodity and go find your soul somewhere. Because you are a truly horrible person, and right now, I don't know if there is anyone on this entire island who would be sad if you got hit by a bus tonight."

"Are you threatening me?" Her eyes narrowed to slits.

I rolled my eyes. "No, you idiot. I'm not threatening to steal a city bus and run you over with it. I'm trying to warn you. You're young and smart and beautiful, and you are wasting it all on being a raging asshole. Do you really want to be on the receiving end of an alimony check from someone like Paul Russo? A man who used you and saw you as nothing more than an accessory? Or do you want to live and love and find some scrap of happiness or whatever your vampire equivalent is?"

I didn't have the energy to dodge the slap. Plus I'd just caught a glimpse of a cheese Danish that was calling my name and kind of missed the diva-worthy windup. The shithead caught me on my preexisting bruises.

"That's the only shot you get at me or anyone else I care about, Malina. So take your flat ass and your bony elbows home and think long and hard about what you want in this life," I hissed.

She looked like she was thinking about hitting me again, and I looked for a nearby chair to hit her in the face with if necessary. But then the beautiful, soulless blond whirled away from me and stormed toward the lobby.

I felt sorry for her. I mean, I totally hated her guts also. But somehow, me dating Dominic Russo had cracked this woman's fragile sense of purpose. It wasn't love she had for him. It was designs of a grander life. And in her twisted, malnourished mind, I'd taken that opportunity away from her.

"Damn, girl. That looked like it hurt," the cashier called to me. "You want a free ice cream?"

"I really do."

"Take your pick, honey. That one is a rattlesnake."

"How do you feel about being my witness if she tries to sue me or get me fired?"

"Happy to." The woman nodded. "Take two ice creams," she insisted. "You can put one on your face."

57

ALLY

Dance class passed in a sweaty blur of thumping beats, high heart rates, and good spirits. My little class seemed to expand every week. The windows were steamed, faces glowed, and dancers of all ages and sizes high-fived on their way out the door.

"That was amazing," Gola announced, patting her face with a towel.

"Yeah. Uh-huh. Tell us everything," Ruth said, grabbing me by the front of my sweaty tank.

"Motion seconded," Missie said between swigs of water.

"There isn't much to tell," I lied.

"Bullshit," Ruth coughed into her hand.

"Have you had sex?" Missie wanted to know.

"I'm not answering that."

"Question: Does naked Dominic Russo have the same brain-melting potency or a higher dosage than fully clothed Dominic Russo?" Ruth asked.

"Definitely not answering that."

"How did he ask you out? Was it super romantic?" Gola wondered.

"That one I'll answer. I believe he *told* me that we were officially dating and that if I had any concerns, too bad, because we were seeing this through."

"That's totally romantic!" Missie crooned.

We shrugged into coats and scarves and headed the two blocks north to the designated bar. On the walk, I deflected questions like a ninja.

"Did you guys hear that Malina got into a fight with someone in the cafeteria this afternoon?" Ruth asked, staring at her phone.

I decided to keep my mouth shut.

"I heard she came back to the admin pool crying and just walked out," Gola said.

"I heard someone hit her in the face with a cafeteria tray and called her a stupid asshole."

"I don't think that's what happened," I interjected.

My friends continued to entertain themselves by asking more ridiculous questions and ignoring my even more ridiculous answers.

Is he a tiger in the sheets?

Who puts a tiger in their sheets?

How did it happen?

I went to a voodoo priestess and cast a love spell on him.

Are you in love?

How about we figure out if we like each other first?

Do you just run around yelling at each other all the time?

Okay. That one I could answer honestly. *Yes.*

I got my revenge when I opened the door to the bar, a cool speakeasy kind of vibe with an entire wall dedicated to just bourbons. Warmth and laughter spilled out, and Gola rushed in. But she stopped short just inside the door, and Ruth walked into her back. It was a three-body pileup when they all realized Dominic Russo was waiting at the bar.

It looked like Dominic had brought along a few extra friends too. In addition to Harry and Delaney, there were three other suited stock-broker types each vying to tell a better punchline.

"You Sneaky McSneakerson," Gola hissed in my ear. "I survived a whole day with the man as my boss, and now you expect me to have a drink with him?"

"Yup," I answered. But my attention was on Dominic.

He abandoned the conversation he was having with Delaney and a guy with a Garfield the cat tie and crossed to me. It was a magnetic force that drew us together, one that I thought should have dulled a little since we'd finally given in to temptation.

His gaze traveled the length of my body, pausing in what I now knew were his favorite places. The curve of my hips, the hint of skin between my pants and cropped sweatshirt. My breasts, even though they were secured and smushed by a sports bra.

I returned the survey. Slate-gray slacks that were just loose enough to fall short of the adjective "indecent." A navy tie that I intended to wrap around my fist at my earliest convenience. His sleeves were rolled up, and his hair, that lovely brownish-blond mess of it, was effortlessly styled. I wanted to mess it up while reminding myself that this man was mine.

We met in the middle, our posses at our backs, eyeing each other with interest.

"Looks like you brought backup," I said softly. But it came out kind of breathlessly because all I could do was think about how much I wanted his mouth on mine. He'd given me one hell of a kiss when he'd dropped me off for class. Hands roaming, teeth nipping. Dark, delicious promises of things to come.

And I wanted more promises out of him.

He leaned in, and my heart rate returned to post-"Uptown Funk" choreography levels. But he merely grazed his lips over my temple. I heard one or two of the girls let out a swoony sigh behind me.

"Five minutes, and then we abandon these people so I can fuck you in the car," he whispered in my ear.

"An hour," I countered.

Those blue eyes narrowed on me. "Thirty minutes, and you take your underwear off in the restroom so we don't waste any time later."

I licked my lips, and he followed the motion. "Deal."

His expression softened, lips lifted. "Look at us negotiating."

"And they say relationships are hard," I joked.

"Five minutes to lose the underwear," he reminded me. "Now, let's make a horrible mistake and introduce our friends."

It took a few minutes of everyone staring at Dominic and me like we were alien overlords sent to enslave the human race before they all lightened up. Dominic included.

He was lighter, happier around his friends. There was an easy camaraderie between him and his old coworkers. I liked seeing him like this, and from the telltale glances Gola, Ruth, and Missie were exchanging, they did too.

I was reacquainted with Harry and Delaney, who had already had an impressive amount of wine to drink.

Dominic's friend Mike with the Garfield tie seemed to take a liking to the petite Missie. Ruth dove into an argument about bourbon barrel aging with one of the other financial types. Gola's new boyfriend showed up, and I watched their sweet, nervous greeting with joy.

Dominic was deep in discussion with one of his former coworkers about very boring-sounding reports when he subtly tapped his watch without even looking at me.

I grinned. If he wanted to play a private little game, I was more than willing to kick his ass at it. I excused myself from Gola and her boyfriend and followed the service hallway to a short flight of stairs with signs for the restrooms. I found the ladies' room tucked away on the second floor just outside a darkened private dining room.

Inside, I successfully shimmied out of my workout tights and underwear before taking a picture of my pretty pink thong and attaching it to a text.

Me: Mission accomplished.

I sent a second picture, this one of... Well, let's just say it was what my underwear had been covering.

I smirked to myself as I got dressed again, imagining Dominic's face when he saw the texts.

Still feeling awfully proud of myself, I slipped out of the restroom. And found myself crushed between Dominic's pelvis and the wall.

He was ragingly hard. I could feel his unyielding erection pressed against the softness of my belly. More promises.

He kissed me like it was the only thing he'd had on his mind for years. Hungry. Demanding. Desperate.

"Give them to me, Ally." His voice was a filthy, carnal growl. And it couldn't have turned me on more than if he'd said it completely naked with his cock pointing at me.

Breathing heavily, I reached into the pocket of my sweatshirt and handed over my underwear.

Pinning me with his gaze, he brought the crumpled, cheap

pink lace to his nose. My jaw fell open, and once again, I found myself questioning whether I was about to wake up from a coma in a hospital room somewhere.

God, I hoped it wasn't going to be right this second. Because Dominic had plans for me.

He half dragged, half carried me through the doorway of the dark dining room and then spun me around to face the wall.

My heart was in my throat. My mouth was dry with need. All I wanted in this entire world was this man. Nothing else existed when he touched me like this.

"I can't not touch you, Ally," he groaned in my ear, nipping at the lobe as he shoved his hand down the front of my pants.

I braced my palms on the wall as he leaned his weight into me.

"Yes." It came out as a hiccup. Because the very bad man slid two very nice fingers deep inside me, and I forgot how to do unnecessary things like breathe. "Dominic."

He pumped his fingers into me over and over again as my greedy flesh clamped down on him. My legs, now officially some sort of jelly, started to tremble.

"I want you, Dom. I want you inside me."

"Fuck, baby."

I didn't know what I was saying, and I sure as hell didn't think he'd actually *do* anything about it, but then he was pulling those lovely fingers out of me and shoving my pants down to midthigh. I still thought he was kidding, until I heard his fucking zipper.

"Dom!" I hissed.

"You asked, sweetheart. And I'm giving it to you. I live to give you what you want, Ally." He growled the words against my neck as he bent his knees and lined up that satin-smooth crown with my center. "Hold still," he ordered.

I went stock-still and held my breath for good measure. He gave one short, sharp thrust and sank into me. The angle allowed for only shallow penetration, but holy hell, was it good enough for me. Apparently for Dominic too, because he brought one hand to my belly and the other under my sweatshirt to dip into my sports bra.

He teased me with shallow thrusts while tugging at my nipple.

"I love that you want me this badly." He grunted his confession in my ear. "You're always so wet, like you've been thinking about me as much as I think about you."

"I do," I promised.

I did. I would have been willing to bet more.

His thrusts were coming faster now. Short, jerky motions that turned me on to no end. There was no real satisfaction for me in this position, but I knew Dominic would always take care of me.

"I want to come, Ally. Will you let me?" he rasped.

"Yes," I hissed.

It was all he needed. He moved, releasing my breast and pressing me against the wall, bracing his forearm against my shoulders. He pulled out of me, and I felt the slick, wet slide. I couldn't tell what he was doing with his free hand. But then I felt the synthetic lace against my ass and knew.

Dominic Russo had my thong wrapped around his hand while he fucked his fist.

My knees went out, but he held me pinned to the wall.

"I'm going to make you come so hard tonight, Ally. My Ally," he crooned in my ear. The sound of hard, mean strokes on flesh turned me into a ball of need.

I was living out a dark fantasy that had wreaked havoc on my imagination ever since that night I found him in the washroom. This was what I'd wanted then.

"Ally." He groaned, low and guttural, sliding the head of his cock through my folds.

He came.

Hard.

I felt the first hot burst of it up against my clit, and then he was fucking his way between my ass cheeks, ending at that greedy bundle of nerves. Once, twice, and out of nowhere, my own impossible orgasm took me hostage.

He kept right on nudging my clitoris, kept right on coming. Branding me from front to back with his seed.

Whatever didn't get soaked up by my underwear coated my slit, dampened my thighs.

"Baby," he said, and I felt the final volley of his orgasm explode against that tight ring of muscle between my cheeks.

It was dirty, hedonistic, and downright wrong. I freaking loved it.

"I couldn't wait," he panted, making no move to pull back from me. His dick was wedged between my thighs, and he was still making tiny, gentle thrusts.

"Me neither."

This was a new, interesting version of the walk of shame for me: returning to friends we'd abandoned mere minutes ago with dirty, sweaty lust written all over our faces. Even the historically and heroically unreadable Dominic couldn't hide his smile.

Conversation came to a screeching halt when we returned to our group. Someone had ordered a few bottles of wine, and everyone paused mid sample to stare at us.

"I told you you should have let me come back down first," I whispered out of the side of my mouth.

"Baby, not on your life. You're not getting five steps from me before I make you come again," he intoned back.

"How was the bathroom?" Harry asked with a knowing grin.

"Ally, what are you planning for Dominic's birthday next month?" Delaney asked, listing dangerously to the left on her barstool. "Have you convinced him to have a party?"

"Your birthday!" I turned to him, visions of birthday cakes dancing in my head.

"No. Absolutely not," he said emphatically.

"No what?"

"No birthday."

"Russo here is afraid of getting old," his friend Kevin chimed in.

"But he just keeps getting better looking," Missie said, the wine loosening her tongue a bit. "If I were him, I'd be celebrating every year as a sexy milestone."

"How long were we up there? They're all shit-faced," I whispered to Dominic.

"Delaney, I've been meaning to ask you where you got your bed linens," Dominic said.

Harry shot him a dirty look as Delaney's hands fluttered to her chest. "I found the most amazing duvets and sheets," she began.

"Middle finger GIF," Harry coughed into his hand.

58

DOMINIC

"You've got a little spackle right here," Ally said, gently scraping a finger over my neck just below the ear.

It wasn't meant to be a come-on, but my dick—as it did with most things related to Ally—took it as such.

"Why are you looking at me like that?" she asked with suspicion.

"No reason," I lied, giving Brownie's leash a tug so he'd get his face out of the neighbor's flower bed. "Where are we going again?"

"Ice cream," she said, cheerfully taking my free hand and pulling me down the sidewalk.

"Who goes for ice cream in the middle of winter?" I asked gruffly. We'd spent five straight hours drywalling the bathroom in her father's house because the only help she would accept from me was from my own two hands and not my bank account.

I could have hired someone, a crew of someones, and it

would have been done while I went down on my girlfriend. But no, Ally "Do It Yourself" Morales drew the line at the wallet. So instead of spending our precious weekend naked and in bed like I wanted to, we did our best impression of HGTV weekend warriors.

Turns out I wasn't half bad at drywall. However, I still would have preferred Plan A. The naked in bed thing.

"It's in the midthirties. This is practically a heat wave," she said, flashing a grin up at me. "Consider it a celebration of surviving the fallout."

We'd made it through the first week after the relationship announcement. The last few days consisted mostly of conversations cutting off midsentence when I entered the room and me wondering when the whiplash workers' comp claims would start pouring in from people pretending not to look at us.

But we were officially dating and both still employed. Besides the home improvement eating into our quality naked time, everything was going well.

Ally certainly wasn't complaining. She loved her new position, and she was a great addition to the graphics department. Not that I was checking up on her.

Okay, so I was checking up on her. I wanted to make sure no one was saying or doing anything to her that would hurt her or piss me off.

There had been a few items about us in the gossip blogs. Someone had leaked the office-wide memo, and it had been shared far and wide. But there hadn't been any real fuss.

Yet.

It would come. It always did. And when it did, it wouldn't be a warm and fuzzy "we wish them the best."

Ally stopped on the sidewalk.

"This doesn't look like an ice cream shop," I observed,

checking out the three-story brick house behind the iron fence and neatly trimmed hedgerow.

"It's not," she said. "This is the big house on the corner."

"I can see that."

She hugged herself, and I stepped closer to block the wind.

"When I was growing up, I always dreamed of living here. I'd put the Christmas tree there," she said, pointing at a wide wall of glass on the front. "And the piano over there in that window on the north side."

"You've given this a lot of thought."

She grinned. "I've been obsessed with this place since I was eleven."

Right around the time her mother left. I guessed it wasn't a coincidence.

"What is it you like about it?" Brownie joined us in our real estate perusal and gave the fence a good sniffing.

"I think it was the life that went on inside it. There were kids who lived here who were a few years older than me. They had a mom and a dad and each other. A basketball hoop in the driveway. Lemonade stands in the summer. It just always looked idyllic. Still does. Their kids are grown. Now it's the grandkids playing basketball. They have dinner parties here and Christmas mornings." She shrugged. "It's stupid. I know."

"It's not stupid," I told her, taking her hand again. I'd known that kind of longing too. Not that I'd admit it. For siblings. For parents who were around and not fighting or ignoring each other in stony silence. For a family to belong to.

We started walking again, but I noticed she kept her gaze on the house until we crossed the street.

"Do you still play the piano?"

"Not really. If Dad's having a good day, I'll sit with him, but I haven't practiced in forever. Did you ever play?"

I shook my head. "I was into baseball," I said.

"I bet your butt looked really cute in those uniform pants," she teased.

"My butt looks good in all pants," I insisted.

"Speaking of birthdays—"

"We were not."

"We are now," she said, guiding me down the block toward the ice cream sign. "What's with the birthday hating?"

I rolled my eyes. "I don't hate birthdays." Just my own.

"Just your own," she said, apparently reading my mind.

"It's just another day," I insisted.

"It's just the anniversary of you surviving another entire year on this planet. It's a celebration of being here. Didn't you love birthday parties when you were a kid?"

"Growing up, it wasn't so much of a celebration as just one more day for my father to either disappoint me or pit himself against me in a competition."

She stopped outside the cheerily painted shop with a hand-lettered sign in the window promising homemade hot chocolate. "That's terrible."

"Ally, I'll be forty-five. I don't need or want a celebration. I don't like receiving gifts. If there's something I want, I buy it for myself. My worst nightmare is a bunch of people who have better things to do singing 'Happy Birthday' to me."

"But, Dom—"

I shook my head. "Stop looking at me with pity eyes." Her brown eyes were wide and sad for a privileged kid she'd never known.

"Can I please do something for you for your birthday? Please?"

She was not going to let me say no. And letting her do something for me would make her happy, which would make me happy. This was one of those stupid compromises she'd been talking about.

"Fine," I said. "One thing. One small, inexpensive thing."

"Yes!" She threw her arms around my neck and pressed a noisy kiss to my cheek.

I realized I'd be willing to say yes to a lot of things if it always got that reaction out of her.

"No singing," I warned her.

"No singing," she agreed.

"And no spending money on me."

"Excuse me, why are you allowed to make that a rule, and I'm the one with a dozen pairs of La Perla thongs that magically appeared in her drawer?"

"Because I have money to spend, and I'll take great pleasure in taking those thongs off you. Consider them a birthday gift for me."

"Well, consider this," she said, reaching for the door. "I'm wearing one of your birthday gifts right now."

That night, I made dinner while Ally worked on her laptop at the island with a glass of wine. It was a nice, normal scene that I was still having trouble adjusting to.

"How's Gola working out?" she asked.

"We're getting along reasonably well. She doesn't yell at me as often as her predecessor." Work had been going well. In an unforeseen consequence of announcing my relationship, the women of *Label*—with a few notable exceptions—had seemed to finally embrace me as human. Nina from advertising had actually told me a joke when we'd both arrived early for a meeting. And I'd actually laughed.

"Har har," she said. "Have you heard from Greta?"

I sighed and threw a pinch of fresh herbs on top of the pasta I'd just plated. "Greta has decided to officially retire." I still wasn't ready to think about my life without her. I didn't deal well with change. Especially change that I had no control over.

"Apparently sending her off on a European jaunt backfired," Ally said, giving me a look over the rim of her wineglass.

"Or maybe I still got what I was after." She grinned at me, and I slid her plate to her. "In here or at the table?"

"Uh-oh. Hang on," she said, squinting at her screen.

"What?"

"Faith just sent this to me." She turned the laptop so I could see. "It's about us."

It was a popular fashion gossip vlog run by a woman I considered to be an obnoxious pain in the ass. "Don't waste your time with it."

"Too late. Already playing."

"Rumor on the catwalk has it that serial model dater Dominic Russo is finally settling down with a dancer he just met. Inside sources say Russo was so infatuated with her 'moves' he created a position just for her in his mother's fashion empire."

"That lying little twerp! She makes me sound like a stripper," Ally said indignantly.

"Well—"

"Do not finish that sentence if you want to continue not breathing out of your neck," she said, wielding her fork.

"This is why we don't watch this garbage," I told her, making a move to close the screen.

She swatted my hand away instead.

"Most of you will remember Russo's scorching hot affair with model Elena Ostrovsky, a Russian beauty known for her Calvin Klein contract."

Oh. Shit.

Ally slowly turned to face me. "Did you forget to tell me something?"

I took a hasty step back and put my hands up. "First of all, it was not a scorching hot affair. It was more like a series of lukewarm—"

"You mean to tell me you had a relationship with the cover girl of the May issue? And I'm just now hearing about it?"

"When you say relationship—"

She cracked a grin. "Relax, Charming. I'm just messing with you. You dated models. I know this. They're disgustingly beautiful. It's not news. Holy crap. Is she, like, a million feet tall?" She peered at the screen as the idiot vlogger plastered image after image of me with Elena during our short but unsatisfying relationship.

"We weren't serious," I insisted. At least not serious enough for me to feel anything but seriously pissed off when I'd found out exactly what she'd been up to.

The last picture was one from New York Fashion Week two years ago. I was towing her by the hand through a crush of photographers outside a restaurant. I was scowling. She was smiling smugly. I'd had a reason to scowl. The paparazzi had an uncanny way of finding out where we were every time we went out. I didn't like having cameras shoved in my face and questions hurled at me, but Elena didn't seem to mind.

It was only a week or two later that I'd found out she was the reason they always knew where we were. That she'd been using me to grow her followers and, in turn, increase her visibility. She'd been the last person in a very long line who'd used me.

"This is a story about us, and they're running more pictures of you with Elena, the long-legged gazelle. Oh, wait, here I am," she said, cheering up.

It was my turn to get annoyed.

"Ally Morales is the mystery woman widely photographed with designer Christian James. So the question is: Is this real love, or will Delena find their way back together again? Cast your vote below—"

"Delena? Ew. Barf. Hey!" Ally said when I slammed the lid of the laptop closed.

"No more garbage gossip. It's time for dinner."

"Fine. I just have to do one thing first," she said, opening her laptop again.

"What?"

"I'm writing that vlogger a strongly worded email and attaching some naked pictures of us," she said, brown eyes sparkling. "Oh, and we need a celebrity couple name. How do you like the sound of Alominic?"

I sighed. "Eat your pasta, weirdo."

59

DOMINIC

The morning of my forty-fifth birthday on this revolving circus began with my naked girlfriend rolling on top of me and fucking me until I went blind and lost the power of speech. It was what I considered to be the best birthday gift I'd ever received to date.

Apparently, Ally was just getting started. She insisted we stop for "birthday tea" on the way into the office. Then she gave me an entirely inappropriate birthday kiss just outside the office doors.

I'd actually gone a little weak in the knees when she walked away. Chalking it up to more dehydration, I watched that sexy ass sway in the curve-hugging Dior skirt I'd snuck into her side of the closet.

Gola was waiting outside my office with a smile and a goddamn birthday cupcake. It had an actual candle in it.

I was oddly touched and covered the moment by threatening to fire her if she sang one bar of "Happy Birthday."

A month or two ago, that threat would have had every woman—and several of the men—in a twenty-foot radius running for cover. Now, Gola laughed and reminded me that I had birthday lunch plans with Ally.

What the hell were birthday lunch plans?

Food truck ramen. That was what. Maybe it was holding Ally's hand on the three-block walk. Or maybe it was listening to her talk about the graphics she was designing for a June piece on espadrilles. Maybe it was that nudge of spring I could almost smell on the air. April was coming.

Whatever it was, I felt almost…light.

She squinted up at me. "What's happening with your face right now?"

It was probably having an allergic reaction to the ramen. I reached up to touch my cheek, and she snickered.

I got the joke.

What was happening with my face was that I was sitting on a low wall with a woman I'd brought to orgasm with my tongue before most people had opened their eyes for the day. A woman who was doing her damnedest to make my stupid birthday special.

I, Dominic Russo, was smiling.

That odd facial contortion stayed with me as we walked back to the office. As I brushed a kiss over Ally's lips, once, twice on the sidewalk in front of the building.

Her hat—a felt, emerald-green trench I'd snuck out of a photo shoot for her—made her brown eyes even warmer.

"You're beautiful."

Her cheeks pinked up, and I didn't think it had anything to do with the wind. There was a stirring in my chest. That odd, heartburn-y glow rose up again. I realized I'd be content to stand right here with Ally Morales looking up at me just like that for the rest of the day. The week. Hell, I'd free up all of April if it meant I could keep feeling like this.

"Dominic."

God, would there ever be a time when my name on her lips wasn't a fucking shot of adrenaline?

"Ally."

"When you look at me like that, it makes me dizzy," she confessed.

"Good," I said. I didn't want to be the only one off-balance here. This was something…different, almost comforting. Something apart from the lust-fueled obsession I'd gotten used to. I hoped to hell I wasn't just imagining it.

That afternoon, Linus dropped off a very nice bottle of whiskey tied with a black bow. My meeting with the online content team was kicked off with fancy teas and muffins. Even Shayla had muttered a "Happy birthday" before insisting that we were going in the wrong direction with a sidebar on bucket bags.

My mother sent me a huge arrangement of showy white flowers, a ridiculous gold paper party hat—which made me roll my eyes—and a very nice Armani jacket that I didn't mind at all. She was out of the office all day working with designers and coordinators for the upcoming gala in May. It was one of the biggest nights in New York fashion every year, and as always, my attendance was expected.

I wondered if Ally would like to go and how creatively she'd commit to the theme. Or, more accurately, how creatively she'd make me commit to the theme.

And then I realized how quickly I'd begun making plans that revolved around her. It was less of a battle every night to get her to stay. She had things at my place, space in my closet. I'd insisted that she start doing her laundry at my place so I wouldn't have to miss out on a few hours with her every weekend.

We had routines now. Early morning and late night walks around the block with Brownie. Naked Sunday brunch. I knew where all the hardware stores within a five-mile radius of her father's house were because we spent so much of our weekends in them.

It was disconcerting to wake up one day and find myself… well, here. Making plans for two instead of one. Looking forward to sharing things like beds and weekends and closet space. I'd dated before, but I'd never gotten this deep, this fast. I'd never made space in my home for a woman before. Change was happening, and I didn't know how I felt about it.

Did I like it, or did it terrify me? Should I start applying the brakes?

After all, we hadn't talked future. Not really. Ally was just trying to survive the next few months. Things would be different when the house was sold. When her father's situation was secure. When she had choices and the resources to make them.

Would she choose me when she didn't have to rely on me for a roof? For good cheeses and nights out and clothing not previously owned by half the city?

Did I want her, or did I want to be needed?

There it was. That little icy finger of doubt that I'd been waiting for. I'd learned over and over again to be careful. To not give too much of myself. Because it never seemed like it was enough. That was why I did things anonymously. Like Buddy's wife's physical therapy. Buddy didn't know it was me, which meant he couldn't ask me for more.

When would Ally start asking for more?

A text popped up on my phone.

Ally: Getting to know you birthday edition. Gun to your head. If you had to choose between vanilla cake with chocolate icing or a chocolate cake with peanut butter icing, what would you choose?

And there it was again. That stupid smile on my face.

Me: I thought I told you not to use the v-word in my presence?

I let myself into the foyer, leaving the cold night at my back. I'd stayed late for a generally useless conference call with the West Coast. All I wanted was a quiet night with my dog and my lady. Ally had promised me a home-cooked birthday dinner and one present to unwrap.

Brownie trotted up to me.

"Hey, buddy. What are you doing out here?" I leaned down to give him a good scruffing and found he was wearing a sparkly green bow tie. "Let me guess. A birthday bow tie?"

Brownie jumped up and licked my face from chin to hairline.

"Really have to call that trainer." I sighed, leading the way into the house.

It was dark inside, but something smelled good. Like home-cooked meal good.

"Maleficent?" I called out.

The lights—all of them—came on in a flash.

"Surprise!"

"Jesus H. Christ," I groaned. I *hated* surprises.

My kitchen was full of people. Harry and Delaney were there with their girls—who were currently shrieking "Happy birthday, Uncle Dominic" at the top of their lungs. Linus, his wife, and their three kids wore matching all-black outfits and were blowing the hell out of those obnoxious noisemaker things. Gola and Ruth were pouring champagne.

My neighbors, Sascha and Elton, waved from the stove where they were dishing out bowls of something. Jace was hugging Brownie and letting the dog eat his face. My mother, who was supposed to be on a plane right now, beamed at me from where she sat at the island, a gin martini in front of her. Her longtime best friend, Simone, was beside her. They were laughing. Ally's New Jersey neighbors Mrs. Grosu and Mr. Mohammad were lighting candles on a chocolate cake.

I counted four guys from my old office lingering near the alcohol, typical for them.

Ally's best friend, Faith, was playing DJ in the corner with my wireless speakers. And Christian Fucking James was lurking near the cheese tray.

Every single one of them wore a ridiculous gold party hat just like the one my mother had sent me.

And then there was Ally.

Front and center in the black Valentino dress I'd snuck into the closet just two days ago. It hugged her breasts and waist before flaring out into a short, flirty skirt. I'd intended for her to wear it for me with the express purpose of me taking it off her, which would unfortunately have to wait until I could get these people out of my house. Her party hat was askew on top of those thick, loose curls that I loved. But it was her smile that hit me the hardest.

She was bone-deep happy. And it was just for me. It was all for me.

She danced over to me and threw her arms around my neck. "Happy birthday, Charming," she whispered in my ear. "Were you surprised?"

Surprised didn't even begin to describe the feelings I was having. "Appalled," I told her. "Why the hell is Christian James in my house? I hate that guy."

"You only think you hate him," she teased. "I have an ulterior motive there. Don't you worry your pretty little birthday head about it."

"Potluck? Really?" I teased, noting the mismatched dishes and trays on the island.

She beamed up at me for remembering our little inside joke. "Potluck food and alcohol. No presents. And the only thing you get to unwrap tonight is me, and I'm not wearing anything under this dress."

"You're in huge amounts of trouble," I warned her.

"You can punish me later," she promised, pulling back and raising on tiptoe to kiss me on the mouth.

It wasn't enough. It was never enough. "Don't think I won't."

60

ALLY

The music was on, the lights were low, and the kids and Brownie divided their time being glued to the living room TV upstairs watching one of the movies Delaney thoughtfully brought and racing downstairs to sneak snacks.

The adults claimed the kitchen and dining room as our territory. Plates of food were passed, drinks poured, and a dozen conversations were happening at the same time.

The smile on Dominic's face while he chatted with Mrs. Grosu and Harry made every hour of sneaky subterfuge absolutely worth it.

"Miracle of miracles," Dalessandra said, sidling up to me in the kitchen. "You managed to surprise Dominic, *and* he looks like he might actually be enjoying himself."

I liked seeing Dalessandra slip out of her role of indomitable boss.

"I couldn't have done it without you and your last-minute, urgent conference call," I reminded her.

"Introduce me to your miracle worker," Simone insisted, slipping in next to Dalessandra. She was lovely. Born to a Chinese father and Nigerian mother nearly seventy years ago, Simone either had incredible genes or a very good doctor on standby. Her glossy ebony hair hung in a curtain that just brushed her shoulders. A model since sixteen, she managed to make the simple white silk blouse and slim black pants look effortlessly chic.

I was the teensiest bit starstruck.

"Simone, meet Ally. Ally, meet Simone, my oldest, dearest friend."

"Thank you for coming, Simone."

"I wouldn't have missed it. I've known Dominic since he was a little boy, and I'm very fond of him," she said, eyeing me over the rim of the pink fizzy cocktail Faith had mixed up.

"I am too," I admitted, locking eyes with the man across the room where he was pouring a whiskey and smirking at something Elton was saying.

"Ladies." Christian joined our little circle. Simone gave him the same appreciative once-over that all women did.

Dominic's eyes narrowed across the room, and I sent him a little wink.

"Christian, I'm so glad you could come tonight," I said. "Have you met my friend Faith yet?"

Dalessandra and Simone shared a sly look.

"I have not," Christian said.

"She's the stunning, Gwen Stefani-esque woman currently telling children that Santa Claus isn't real," I said, leading the way to my friend, who was telling Linus's kids a story that had them transfixed. "Excuse me, guys. Mind if I borrow this lady for a minute?"

"Aww," they pouted.

"Here's five bucks each," Faith said, opening her wallet.

"Yay!" The kids forgot all about Faith and dashed off with their earnings.

"Faith, this is Christian. Christian, this is Faith. You two have a lot in common. You both spend a lot of time around mostly naked, beautiful people for a living."

Christian raised an eyebrow. "Model?"

"Strip club owner. Plastic surgeon?" she shot back.

"Designer."

"Faith has no intentions of settling down and no tolerance for sweeping judgments on her lifestyle. Christian here has zero time to devote to an actual relationship because he's in love with his business. I thought you two should meet."

"Tell me more about strip club owning," Christian insisted, leading Faith in the direction of the bar by the elbow.

Mission accomplished. If those two beautiful people didn't decide to take their bodies on a strings-free test drive, then there was something very wrong with the world.

"When can we kick everyone out?" The gruff voice was accompanied by a nibble at the spot where my neck met my shoulder.

I turned and looped my arms around Dominic's neck. His tie was loosened. He'd ditched his shoes at some point, and he had a cinnamon butterscotch cookie in his hand.

"It's your birthday, Charming," I said saucily. "We can fake food poisoning at any time."

The music changed to a Frank Sinatra favorite, and I felt us begin to sway to the beat.

"Am I still in trouble?" I asked.

There was an eruption of laughter behind us as Mr. Mohammad finally reached a punchline. Brownie ran past us with a kid's sock in his mouth. Several someones drank a toast to someone named Dave behind us. The back door opened, bringing just a hint of sweet cigar smoke into the room.

"Of course. Just because this is a moderately not horrible experience doesn't mean you've escaped punishment," Dominic said, running the tip of his nose around the shell of my ear.

A delighted shiver worked its way up my spine. "I really like you, Dom. A lot." Smitten and dizzy. That was exactly how I felt.

His eyes, those denim-blue eyes, roamed my face intently.

"I just thought you should know," I said, starting to feel embarrassed.

He gathered me tighter to him and danced me in a little circle. "I really like you too, Ally." His voice was rough and raspy. And I thought I detected just the slightest hint of emotion in it.

With the snick of the lock on the front door behind our last guest, my charming, civilized Dominic turned into an animal. He shoved me against the wall. "I wanted to do this all night," he growled into my hair as he ground his erection against my ass.

"Yes," I breathed.

"Do you know how many pieces of furniture I've bent you over, how many walls I've fucked you against in my fantasies?"

"Tell me."

But he was too busy biting and nipping his way down the back of my neck.

One hand roughly shoved its way into the top of my dress and palmed my breast.

Pushing away from the wall, I turned in his arms and spun us so his back was against the wall.

"What are you doing?" he asked gruffly as I unbuckled his belt.

"Just reenacting a little fantasy of my own," I whispered. I let my teeth graze his jaw and then pushed back, slowly sinking to my knees.

"Fuck," he hissed.

"Take out your dick, Dom, and tell me what you want me to do."

If his jaw got any tighter, enamel would shatter, bone would crack. Oh, how I loved pushing the birthday boy's buttons.

"Ally." There was a warning in the way he said my name. I decided to ignore the warning.

I waited where I was on my knees, the neckline of my dress clinging precariously to my breasts, my hair a mess from his hands. I knew exactly what kind of picture I was painting for him.

"Come here," he said gruffly.

I crawled to him, savoring the flare of his nostrils, the white-knuckled grip he kept on his control. The sound of his zipper was like music to my ears.

I stopped in front of him and watched as he fisted his shaft at the root. I licked my lips.

"Taste it," he ordered.

Dutifully, I took that hot, velvety crown into my mouth and ran my tongue in a circle.

He hissed out a breath and shoved a hand into my hair.

"You make such a beautiful fucking picture right now, Ally."

As a reward, I took a little more of him into my mouth.

His head hit the wall behind him. I hoped not hard enough for a concussion. I hummed my pleasure against his flesh.

I could taste him. Could feel the pulse of blood beneath his skin with my tongue. He fed another inch into my mouth and held my head still with his hand in my hair.

The guttural growl that rose up from his chest had me squeezing my thighs together to relieve some of the pressure that was building there. This wasn't my life, I decided. Any minute now, I was going to wake up in a ditch somewhere after having been hit by a bus and not know how powerful it felt to have Dominic Russo's cock in my mouth.

But until then, I was going to savor every damn second of this.

I slid my mouth over him as far down as I could go without choking. My lips brushed his fingers.

"Ally," he rasped again. I reveled in hearing my name. If it had been hot hearing him hiss out my name while pleasuring himself in secret, this was a five-alarm inferno, and I was getting burned.

I rocked forward and back, laving his shaft, the blunt crown, that sensitive slit with my tongue. He was gritting out dirty promises and praise while I sucked his cock. The fabric of my dress was teasing my nipples, making them beg for more.

The noises we both made were inhuman, and if Brownie hadn't been passed out upside down on the couch, he would have been growling at the door to the foyer.

I wanted him inside me. I wanted to pull his hair and bite his neck. I wanted to come. But more than all that combined, I wanted to taste him.

"You need to slow down," he warned, his voice unsteady as I rocked faster, sucked harder.

But I wasn't slowing down, and I sure as hell wasn't stopping.

I felt the tremor that started in his legs as I took him deeper into my mouth. His hands slapped against the wall, and I grabbed the base of his shaft, moving fingers and mouth together in long, wet strokes.

"Baby, you're going to make me—"

He didn't get the rest of the words out because he was coming. Loudly, exuberantly pouring what felt like an entire fucking protein shake directly down my throat. *Oh my God.* I was drowning. And he just. Kept. Coming.

He was sliding down the wall, still coming. I was still valiantly trying not to die as my eyes watered and my mouth overflowed.

We ended up in a tangle on the floor, the tile cooling heated skin, muscles still shaking. Dominic stroked a hand over my hip.

"I think I pulled a hamstring," he whispered.

"I think you impregnated my lungs."

"This is my best birthday ever," he said, his chest still heaving.

"Birthday blow job for the win," I said, sucking in a breath of jizz-free air.

"I'm going to need ten minutes, some ibuprofen, a glass of water, and then I'm going to return the favor," he promised.

61

ALLY

Dominic: I am so bored I might set this place on fire just to stay awake.
Me: Poor baby, in beautiful sunny Los Angeles surrounded by beautiful people wearing beautiful clothes.
Dominic: What are you wearing?

I laughed.

And caught the side-eye Nelson sent me from behind the wheel.

I held up my phone. "Dominic from LA. He's grouchy."

Nelson's mouth twitched under his mustache. Dominic had assigned him to Driving Miss Ally duty while he was gone. We were on our way home from my evening dance class that Nelson had politely declined to attend and instead had waited in a coffee shop one block down.

Me: A parka. You're missing out on the cold snap to end all cold snaps.

It was a frigid Friday night, and Dominic had been gone for four days for LA's Fashion Week. I didn't think it would be a big deal. Six days away? Pfft. No problem. I had plenty to keep me occupied. And I hadn't had the guy in my life for so long that I was used to having him around. Right?

Big fat wrong-o, buddy.

I missed him aggressively, obsessively. I made tea every morning just because the smell reminded me of him. Every night before I left work, I walked up to Dominic's office and sat behind his desk because it felt like he'd walk through the door any minute. Hell, the practically inconsolable Brownie and I were both sleeping in Dominic's T-shirts. Me because I missed him and Brownie because it was hilarious.

In an effort to keep my mind off how much I'd missed him, I'd smuggled Brownie into my dad's nursing home, having him pose as a therapy dog. A therapy dog that ate a nurse's roast beef sandwich when she wasn't looking. I unashamedly blamed it on Mrs. Kramer, a known snack thief. I'd even gone with Faith to a video shoot for the online content team that Christian invited us to at his studio. Sparks were definitely flying between club owner and designer, both of whom seemed to be playing a little hard to get.

But none of it made me miss Dominic less.

Dominic: I wish I was there to keep you warm.

I sighed and fought the urge to clutch my phone to my heart.

The only things that made Dominic's absence almost tolerable were his hourly texts describing every detail of the trip.

Fashion Week was a dream for some. For Dominic Russo, it was a nightmare. Endless shows, after-parties, and wardrobe changes. Red carpets everywhere. People whose names he was expected to remember *and* be impressed with.

Me: Question. Do you miss me or your vests more?

He hadn't packed a single vest. For which I was eternally grateful.

So *of course* I'd entertained myself—and tortured him—by trying on his vest collection and sending him selfies while wearing nothing else but a glossy coat of lipstick. Checking all the photos and video footage to see if he had a visible erection from one of the pictures was my new favorite game.

Speaking of photos, Dominic hadn't been photographed with his arms around any of the bevies of stunning models flooding the city. In fact, in every photo, he had a camera-thrilling scowl and both hands in his pockets. I hadn't asked him not to hug beautiful women, but he'd refrained anyway.

I was starting to think the man liked me. Really, really liked me.

Of course, just to make sure I wasn't feeling totally confident, there had been a handful of mentions of Dominic flying solo with the speculation that our relationship was on the rocks. The jabs felt almost personal, but I tried not to read too much into it.

My phone buzzed again.

Dominic: You in my vests. Next year you're coming with me.

I felt a thrill rush through me that had nothing to do with the seat warmer.

Were we really talking about next year? Was I okay with that? I checked in with several of my organs. Yep. Most of them reported back with resounding hell yeses. My brain was a little more pragmatic. There were a lot of things still up in the air. I was still behind on the bills. The renovations were stalled until Dominic came home since the man forbade me from going over there alone. It was one little carpet tack puncture and a tetanus shot. Dominic acted like I'd been held up at gunpoint.

But it was only a matter of time until the house was done and on the market and… Okay. I was overthinking. We hadn't defined what this was other than "a relationship," and we certainly hadn't talked about anything relating to the future.

Me: Count on it. I miss you.
Dominic: Good.

I woke early the next morning with Brownie's warm furry body cuddled into my side and a figure looming over us both.

The dog and I were epic sleep partners. It took a lot to drag us from our slumber.

My confused screech and subsequent flailing to free myself of blankets and pillows roused Brownie, who grumbled lazily and did not leap into attack dog mode.

The laugh was soft and undeniably familiar.

"Dominic?"

He leaned down and pressed a kiss to my mouth. I didn't care about morning breath or the fact that we were squishing Brownie. I just wanted to pull the man into bed.

"How? When? I thought you were staying for two more days? What time is it? Is everything okay?"

"So many questions," he teased, running a hand down my side to squeeze my hip.

"Wait a minute. What day is it? Did Brownie and I accidentally sleep for two days?"

"It's obscenely early Saturday morning. I took a red-eye. You have fifteen minutes to pack."

"Pack?" I croaked.

This was a dream. One I was going to be really, really disappointed to wake up from.

"Pack," he repeated with a grin. He looked tired too. "I'm whisking you away for the weekend."

Brownie wriggled his way in between us and showed Dominic his expectant belly.

"You too, buddy," Dominic said, giving the dog the required pats.

I sat up. "Oh, my God. You're really here. This is really happening!"

He laughed, and I threw my arms around him, raining kisses on his face and neck.

"Baby, I may never say these words again, but I really need you to get out of bed."

I bounced on my knees, full of adrenaline. "Where are we going?"

"Stop asking questions. Stop jiggling," he said to my breasts. "And start packing."

My breasts and I quit jiggling and started packing. "Pack warm" was the only hint he gave me. On the other side of the bed, Dominic exchanged fashion-forward suits for warmer, cozier items. The sexy eye banging we were giving each other made me hope our destination involved a short ride and a very big bed.

Between it being somewhere around zero o'clock in the

morning and the fact that I hadn't had this man's penis inside my body in five days, I was probably packing completely useless garbage. But I didn't care. I was spending an entire weekend away with the man I l—iked. *Liked.*

Packed, zipped, and still eye banging, we hauled our bags downstairs, and Dominic went to work packing Brownie's food and treats that—God forbid—we didn't give him at precisely 7:00 p.m. every night.

"Can you grab the book I left in the den?" he asked me.

I should have been suspicious. His tone was a little too casual, and when was the last time he'd read in the den? It was usually on the couch while I pinned home improvement projects to my Dad's house board.

But I wasn't thinking about any of that when I practically skipped into the small front room.

"Oh my God." I stopped in my tracks. Brownie dashed into the room in front of me, nose to the ground, checking out the new smells. The couch and chair were missing. And in their place was a stunning, brand-new upright piano.

"Dom?"

His hands came to my shoulders, his chin to the top of my head.

"I know it's not your dad's," he said while my mouth continued to open and close like a guppy. "The guy I brought out to the house took one look at that one and said it couldn't be saved. But this model is supposed to be good."

Oh boy. The piano was blurring in front of me. Everything was blurring in front of me. Nope. No. No. No. I was not a crier. I was a silent sufferer.

"Do you like it?" he asked softly.

The man bought me a piano. A very shiny, expensive piano. Just because I had good memories of my dad's.

I nodded very slowly. “How did you get it in here?”

I heard the smile in his voice. “You and Brownie can sleep through anything apparently. Including early morning piano deliveries.”

My heart physically hurt with happiness.

I turned away from the piano and into Dominic’s arms.

“I love…it. I love it.”

He cupped my face and kissed me so gently it made me go a little weak in the knees.

“I missed you this week,” he whispered.

“Good,” I said.

62

ALLY

The cabin or chalet or whatever wealthy people called their mountain getaways was tucked halfway up a ski slope in snowy Connecticut.

Smoke puffed cheerfully through a stone chimney. Dark green cedar shakes and caramel-toned wood accents gave the exterior a luxury gingerbread vibe.

"Do you ski?" Dominic asked, turning off the engine and reaching for my hand.

Sheepishly, I shook my head. "Never been." Even living in Colorado, I'd never actually gotten out on a ski slope. Mostly because I was more of a spiked hot chocolate and fuzzy socks by the fire kind of gal and less of a "Hey, let's hurl ourselves down the side of a cliff on slippery toothpicks" one.

"Good," he said, brushing a kiss over my knuckles. "Then we can spend the whole weekend in front of the fire."

Swoon.

Yup. I was falling in some serious like here.

Brownie, not wanting to be left out, shoved his face between the seats and slurped at our joined hands.

"We really need to call that dog trainer." Dominic sighed.

"When we get back," I promised.

We piled out of the SUV and trooped up onto the porch.

"This is my mother's place," he explained, opening the front door. Brownie rocketed inside to sniff everything. "By the way, we both have Monday off too. I cleared it with your supervisor. And the nursing home is happy to provide updates. If your dad is having a good day, they'll arrange a video chat."

I shook my head. Dominic the handler. "You know how I feel about being left out of decisions," I began.

"But?" He gave me a wolfish look as he pulled me into the living space. It had Dalessandra's stamp all over it. A modern kitchen with quartz and steel that opened into a dining space with a table that could easily seat twelve. The focal point of the two-story living room was the towering stone fireplace. The furniture was deep and overstuffed. There were colorful throws and pillows everywhere.

"But in this case, I might be okay with it," I said.

"If you're still on the fence, allow me to convince you." He led me into the bedroom off the living space. Floor-to-ceiling windows overlooked spectacular snowy mountain peaks and miles of forest. There was another fireplace in here and a grand four-poster bed buried under mounds of winter-white linens and pillows.

The bathroom door was open, and I caught a glimpse of marble floors, thick towels, and a huge freestanding tub in hammered copper.

"Wow," I whispered.

Dominic yawned mightily. "I'm going to shower off the

plane ride. Make yourself comfortable and be ready to spend the weekend making up for the last week. I had the staff stock frozen peas and Gatorade." He added the last with a wink.

My heart did that annoying tip-tap thing again, and I waited until I heard the water turn on in the shower before hurling myself onto the snowy peak of bed linens. It took me five minutes in my best impression of a gopher to dig my way under the covers.

Settled under forty pounds of luxury, I pulled out my phone.

Me: How is this my life?

I attached a picture of this room with a view.

Faith: Girl, you soak that up. Also, my view isn't so bad either.

She attached a picture as well. One of shirtless Christian James smiling lazily at her.

I did a little boogie on the mattress.

Me: I knew it. I knew you two would set the bed on fire.

Faith: And my office. And the back seat of his car. Oh, and his studio after you left the shoot Wednesday.

Me: I'm really happy for you.

Faith: Don't make it weird. We're just enjoying each other's nudity.

Me: Don't rule out non-naked fun with the guy.

Faith: We'll see. Meantime, Mr. James is crooking his sexy AF finger at me. Gotta go rock his world.

Me: Make good choices!

Faith: I think you and I are both past that.

It was true. I hadn't had any intentions of starting an actual relationship with anyone, let alone my grumpy boss, yet here I was. In an "I missed you so I flew across the country and whisked you away to a luxurious mountain retreat" situation.

We probably needed to talk.

Things felt like they'd gotten serious without our noticing. I yawned and rolled over, snuggling up against a pillow that was probably stuffed with organic geese feathers and gold dust.

I was dozing when Dominic came back into the room, fresh from a hot shower.

I let him pull me against his naked body and wrap his arms around me. This was where I belonged.

"Just want to hold you for a minute," he yawned.

And that was the last thing I remembered.

"I can't believe we slept the entire weekend," I said, leaning back against the headrest and admiring Dominic's now well-rested profile as he drove us home.

"It wasn't the *entire* weekend. There was sex and some food too," he said wryly. "Next time, I'll make sure we're rested and hydrated for the trip."

Dominic had gotten a pretty hilarious muscle cramp in his hip on his last orgasm, but he'd heroically powered through it to screw me into the mattress...and oblivion.

Next time. There was that flutter in my chest again.

"Are you kidding? It was perfection. How many people get to have a napcation?"

He took a conference call on the way home, and I listened while his team wheeled and dealed and made decisions that would affect how women around the world would look at raffia jewelry and raincoats.

"You're starting to enjoy it," I pointed out when he disconnected the call.

He shot me a side-eye look. "What?"

"You just listened to your team's opinions, made a series of decisions, and didn't have a crisis of confidence."

He made a noncommittal noise, and I noticed his thumb was tapping on the steering wheel.

"Aren't we going back to your place?" I asked with a frown as he drove past the exit.

"I wanted to swing by your dad's house and check out the progress," he said.

I snorted. "I wouldn't call it progress so much as chaos. Seriously, who knew home renovations could be such a pain in the ass?"

"Literally anyone who has ever attempted to do it themselves," he said dryly.

"Har har. Well, don't get your hopes up. It kind of looks a little worse than it did when you left. But it's part of the process," I said confidently. "I was a little overconfident, thinking I could have it all done by the end of next month. But hopefully I can put in some more nights and weekends and get it ready to list in June."

Tap. Tap. Tap.

He didn't seem inclined to talk, so I used the quiet to mentally start a list of projects that still needed to be finished… or started. Ugh.

He pulled onto my dad's street, and I stretched. Maybe since it was Monday afternoon, I could talk Dominic into spending a few hours here and helping me figure out where I went wrong with the tile on the tub wall.

I had just settled on the best bribe—blow jobs, always blow jobs—when he pulled into the driveway.

I frowned. "Do the porch posts look different to you?" I asked, squinting through the windshield. They looked cleaner. Whiter. The windows seemed shinier too. Had I been vandalized by a mad cleaner?

Dominic was suspiciously quiet and avoided the question by letting Brownie out of the back seat.

I stepped up onto the porch and realized the top step hadn't squeaked like it had spent the last ten years doing. It was definitely cleaner. The paint on the door wasn't peeling anymore either.

"What did you do?" I demanded, narrowing my eyes on his stoic face.

I pulled my keys out of my bag, but the key didn't fit the lock.

"Try this one." He held up a shiny new key.

"Dominic Russo." I had a lot of feelings sliding around in my guts. All I knew for sure was that he was in huge trouble. And so was I.

I took the key from him and inserted it into the lock. The knob was new too. Oil-rubbed bronze. It matched the new porch lights flanking the door.

"Oh, God. What did you do?" I moaned.

It smelled of new paint and fresh carpet. The bare plywood and those carpet tacks were gone. In its place was a pretty cherry hardwood that looked as if it could have been original. The ceiling was patched to perfection. I couldn't even tell where the hole had been. The wall was repaired. Pristine drywall painted a warm gold.

The ruined piano was gone. In its place were two overstuffed chairs tucked into the alcove.

I brought my fingers to my mouth and did a slow circle.

It was like home again, only better. Cleaner. Brighter. Updated. Like the memories and pain of the past year had been erased from the bones of the house.

"There are new countertops and a new sink in the kitchen," Dominic said, his thumb tapping out a beat against his thigh. "They put in a new water heater too."

Speechless, I looked up the stairs. They'd been recovered in a soft beige carpet.

"Go on." He nodded toward the second floor.

I took the stairs slowly, reveling in the smooth banister under my hand, the spindles that no longer wobbled. Nothing squeaked, and the landing no longer felt spongy under my feet. More fresh carpet here.

The bathroom looked like it was straight out of a magazine with a reclaimed wood vanity, large circular mirror, and a glass tile tub surround. The walls were a pretty gray that played off the new tile floor.

I couldn't breathe. My chest hurt.

The bedrooms were empty, and for a second, I felt dizzy with the realization that soon, very soon, my childhood home would be gone. Its walls would absorb someone else's memories, host someone else's Christmas mornings.

My father and I no longer lived here. And only one of us would get to keep the memories.

"I had everything up here moved into storage so you could go through it and decide what you want to keep," Dominic said behind me. "They also made some cosmetic updates to the master bathroom."

"How?" I whispered.

"I called in a crew. It took them four days."

It would have taken me four hundred. And he knew it.

I turned to him, and his face softened. "Don't do that, baby," he said, thumbing away the tears that rolled hot down my cheeks. "Please don't cry. If I'd asked, you would have said no."

He was damn right I would have said no. I'd have clung to

my plan. My timeline. My budget. And in doing so, I would have continued to endanger my father's future.

"I know you're behind on your dad's bills again. This moves up your timeline and gets you out of the red now rather than a few months down the road."

"I don't even know what to say."

"If you're mad, say it. I can take it," he said, dragging me into his chest and holding me hard against him. "I have several well-thought-out arguments planned."

I pulled back and cupped his face in my hands. "I'll pay you back. Every dime," I croaked.

He rolled his eyes, letting me know exactly what he thought of that idea.

"Shut up," he said, his voice thick with emotion.

"You really did this for me?" I asked, my voice so tight the words came out as a squeak.

He nodded.

"I don't know if I can ever—"

"Forgive me?" he guessed.

I shook my head. "Thank you. I don't know if there's a way to say a big enough, loud enough thank-you. This is everything. And I'm totally mad at you. And a whole lot of other things. I never expected anything like this, Dom."

"I don't want a thank-you. I wanted you to have your life back."

"You gave me a lot more than that," I breathed. My throat was so damn tight, like I'd swallowed a swarm of hornets. "I love...that you did this. Even though I'm also really mad. No one has ever done anything like this for me. This is huge. Thank—"

But he was covering my mouth with his and kissing the words away.

63

DOMINIC

"Don't forget your meeting with the real estate agent Friday," I reminded Ally, closing my menu and setting it aside.

We'd snuck out of the office for lunch today.

She bounced in her chair to a beat only she could hear. "I'm so excited and nervous I don't know if I'll survive that long. What if it appraises for more than I thought? What if it's less? What if the market crashed, and it's worthless? What if the buyers are horrible people and want to use the basement as a killing ground for their serial murder business?"

I gave her an exasperated look. "There's a lot that goes on in that brain of yours," I observed.

She gave me a very deliberate once-over and sank her teeth into her lower lip. "You have no idea."

I grinned when her foot slid up my ankle under the table. "Did you pick out any sheet music yet?" I asked. She'd been on the hunt for a few of her father's favorite pieces to play.

"As a matter of fact, I did. I downloaded a couple of songs, and they all look a whole lot more complicated than I thought they'd be."

"Most things are," I mused.

We ordered our meals, and when the server left, Ally leaned forward. "So I never got the chance to tell you about Christian's shoot for *Label*'s YouTube channel while you were gone."

I went from admiring the way her eyes sparkled to being vaguely annoyed. "I really don't like you spending time with that guy," I told her.

"Dominic Russo, you went to LA and hung out with some of the world's most beautiful models at after-parties. Do you hear me complaining?"

"Yes. Yes, I do. Right now."

"Christian and I are friends. And you better get used to him being around because—"

"Dominic!"

The voice, the familiar tone of it, had my blood going to ice.

He looked the same. Distinguished in Armani, his full head of silver hair ruthlessly kempt in the same style he'd had my entire life. Paul Russo was nothing if not consistent, whether it was with his appearance or his disgusting appetites for things that didn't belong to him.

He had the audacity to pull up a chair and offer his hand to Ally. His black onyx pinkie ring winked ominously.

"You must be Ally. I've heard a lot about you."

I felt her watching me, and when she made a move to accept his hand, I took it instead. This man wasn't touching her. I wouldn't let him put those fingerprints on her.

"What do you want, Dad?" I demanded coolly, my gaze never leaving Ally's face.

Her eyes widened, but she said nothing.

"Always in a rush," he laughed in a facsimile of fatherly affection that wasn't fooling anyone. "All right, my boy. I'll cut to the chase."

"You do that."

Ally squeezed my hand.

"I need a little something to tide me over until the divorce settlement," he said. "You know your mother. She's dragging this out just to annoy me. I need a few hundred thousand."

Ally's eyes went wide.

"Salary from *Indulgence* not cutting it?"

My father's charm cooled. *Indulgence* was a respected publication. But it was no *Label*. We both knew it.

"That's neither here nor there," he insisted.

The only time things mattered, the only time the world was supposed to care, was when Paul Russo was winning.

"I tell you what, Dad. I'll give you the money."

Ally's eyebrows winged up.

My father looked surprised, then smug. "I appreciate that, Son."

"I'm not finished. I'll give you the money when you pay Mom and me back for the cash settlements *we* paid to *your* victims."

Our joined hands were vibrating, and I didn't know if it was Ally's fear or my rage.

"Oh, please. We both know those girls were just looking to make a quick buck—"

I rose so quickly my chair nearly overturned. "I'll show you out," I said coldly. "It's time for you to go."

He rose and straightened his jacket. He gave Ally another appraising look. "If you ever get tired of Dominic—"

I clamped a hand on his shoulder and walked him out of

the restaurant, barely resisting the urge to throw him into the planter at the entrance.

"I don't need an escort," he complained. "I need money."

"I don't give a fuck about your needs. You stay away from Mom. You stay away from me. And you stay the fuck away from Ally, or you will regret that you ever called me son."

"I don't appreciate threats," he sneered.

"This isn't a threat. This is a promise. Remember that the only reason you still have a job in this industry is because Mom and I kept our mouths shut about your pathological inability to understand consent. And I'm getting very tired of keeping secrets."

"Everyone has indiscretions. Look at you fucking a secretary. You can't escape your blood, boy."

An icy rage squeezed my chest. I wanted to physically hurt him. To make him feel just a degree of the pain he'd caused others.

"Indiscretions? Try assaults," I spat out. "We paid your victims for the suffering you caused. And if you think you're getting another dime from Mom, I will personally see to it that every single one of your victims files criminal charges and civil suits against you. I won't rest until the world knows that you are nothing but a disgusting piece of trash."

"Don't be so naive, Dominic," he snarled. "They aren't innocent victims in all this. Women are attracted to power, to what you can provide for them. What has that girl in there gotten out of you? A few pretty baubles? Some couture in her closet? Did she make it look like it was your idea? Wake up, Son. We're all just using each other."

"Stay away from us," I said again, not wanting his words to penetrate my brain, but they were already burrowing in and releasing their poison. "I'm not protecting you anymore. I'll burn down the family name if I have to."

"You'd better rethink that strategy, my boy. I can do quite a bit of damage to your mother. You think I was the only one who strayed? That I was the only one with predilections?"

I was shaking my head. "I don't believe a word that comes out of your lying mouth."

He leaned in, and I could smell scotch on his breath. Because of course he'd already started indulging. Paul Russo didn't know how not to. "Your mother, those girls, that secretary in there? They're the liars, and you're just the fool who fell for the lies."

I did what I'd wanted to for so long. I hauled back and hit the man squarely in the face. His nose made a crunching noise that wasn't nearly as satisfying as I'd hoped.

"You're the damn liar," I said, standing over him wishing I could keep hitting him until he felt a shred of the pain he'd inflicted.

"Is there a problem here?" A doorman hustled over from his post and helped my father to his feet, shooting me wary looks.

"Not anymore," I said.

My father took a step toward me, holding a linen handkerchief under his bleeding nose.

"Believe this, Dominic. If you don't get me what I want, I'll be forced to remind you just how important I still am to you and your mother."

"Try it, old man," I said, daring him.

The doorman was debating whether to get in between us. Passersby were giving us a wide berth. That was the thing about normal people. They could sense evil. And between my father and me, there was a vortex of it swirling.

"You've made your bed," he said. "I gave you a chance. Next time your father asks for something, you'll remember this."

"You were never a father to me."

"What a coincidence. You were always a disappointment to me."

He strode away, coat billowing in the wind, looking like the villain he was.

I was so angry I was shaking.

"Dom?"

Ally. How much had she seen? How much of him had she seen in me?

"I don't want to talk about it," I insisted, refusing to look at her. I didn't want her anywhere near this. Anywhere near the feelings that my father brought out in me. I didn't want to taint her.

She reached for my hand and squeezed it. But I pulled out of her grasp.

"Dominic, listen to me. You're nothing like him," she said quietly.

"I said I don't want to discuss it," I snapped, blindly looking over her head. I couldn't look her in the eye. She'd seen us side by side. There was no way to deny the similarities.

"Let's go back inside," she said.

I followed her, careful not to touch her. And when we sat, I ordered a drink. A double.

If it was good enough for him, it was good enough for me.

64

ALLY

I decided to give Dominic some space that night. Sometimes time and space were the only things that could heal the hurt. So I used my time in my second favorite way. I ran my dance class through a challenging routine that left them all sweaty and gasping by the end. But we'd rocked it, and everyone, myself included, left grinning.

It was the last class of the night, and rather than hurrying home to Dominic as had become my habit, I cued up a new playlist.

The song started. And I let my hips and shoulders find the driving beat.

Dancing helped me physically move through the things that were bothering me. Like the fact that Dominic felt comfortable sweeping into my life and solving all my problems for me but wouldn't or couldn't share his own problems.

Yeah, okay. So there was the typical "I don't want to talk about it" guy thing that seemed to come encoded in the Y chromosome. But his vault preset was something different. His "I don't want to talk about it" came with a side of "I don't trust you."

I was hurt.

More importantly, I was worried.

I knew as well as anyone what scars parents could leave on children. But I also wasn't in the position to start a conversation about the future. Not yet.

Spinning around, I kicked high to the right. I danced and moved and crawled my way through the song and then another and another until my shirt was soaked in sweat and my muscles sang.

I kept going until I felt loose and strong. Until I felt happy again.

I took that happy home with me. The door to Dominic's office on the second floor was closed, so I headed up to the bedroom and showered. Brownie was nowhere to be found, which meant he was probably staring lovingly at his grumpy dad.

The door was still closed when I came down in my robe, so I warmed up some dinner and ate alone in the kitchen. I gave it another ten minutes before I couldn't take it anymore.

I knocked and then opened the door on his terse, "Yeah?"

He looked troubled. Brownie was sprawled at his feet, eyes mournful.

"Dom?" I paused in the doorway.

He looked up, and I saw the brightening in his eyes.

He patted his desk, and I crossed the room to him. I stepped between his open legs, and he dropped his forehead to my stomach, his fingers toying with the belt of my robe.

The knuckles on his right hand were split and bruised, but I knew it was his heart that had taken the most damage.

"Can I do anything for you?" I asked softly.

He looked up at me. His eyes and that shadow of a smile were sad. "Yeah."

"Tell me."

He gripped my hips and lifted me onto his desk. "You can ask me for something."

"Anything in particular?"

"I want you to ask me for something only I can give you. Something you need. I want you to need me."

If I'd had a shot at Paul Russo, I wouldn't stop until his face looked like ground beef. Then I'd wax his entire head, toss a stick of dynamite down his pants, and kick him off a pier into shark-infested waters.

"What's that look mean?" he asked, his smile warming now.

"You probably don't want to know."

His hands slipped inside the robe and skimmed up my outer thighs. That tiny, butterfly-light touch sent my attention-whore lady parts into a tizzy.

What could I ask of him? Something that didn't involve nudity and borderline filthy orgasms.

"Will you take me out to dinner tomorrow?" I asked softly.

He looked up at me, surprised. "Of course." Dominic slid his hands up and over my hips, parting the robe. He leaned in and pressed a kiss to the top of one thigh. "I was hoping for more," he admitted.

More? The man had given me a job, a piano, a finished house, a future that didn't involve me working myself into an early grave. What more was there to ask for?

I shifted, letting him open the robe the rest of the way.

Bored, Brownie tip-tapped out of the room and down the stairs.

Dominic's eyes were glued to the apex of my thighs, and I

watched, almost hypnotized, as he took two fingers and lazily slid them through my folds. I shuddered out a breath.

"I want you to need me, Ally. I don't care if its money or sex or a date to your cousin's wedding this summer. Ask me for something. Let me give you something."

His breath was hot on my thighs. Those long strokes of his fingertips were making my body buzz, my blood simmer.

"Come meet my dad?" I asked weakly.

His gaze flickered to mine, abandoning its vigil on my sex.

"You want me to?" His fingers found my already slick opening and pressed ever so gently.

Did I?

"Yes."

"I'd like that," he said. His eyes held mine as those glorious fingers dipped into me. I watched him watch me as he crooked them inside me. My grip on his desk was white-knuckled.

"This weekend?" I managed to squeak out the words.

"Yes."

His tongue flicked out over the curve of my hipbone, electrifying me and making me wish it was my clit he circled.

"You're wet," he breathed, staring again at where his fingers were moving inside me.

"Your fault," I whispered.

"Ask me for this," he said gruffly, scratching his stubble against the sensitive skin of my inner thighs as his fingers worked rhythmically.

"Dominic?"

"Yes, baby?"

"Will you make me come? Please?" The please was barely a whisper.

"Anything for you, Ally. Do you hear me?"

I nodded, but I wasn't thinking about his words. I was

thinking about how much I didn't like that he'd pulled his fingers out of me. But his hands were on my hips now, sliding me onto the edge of the desk.

"Lean back," he ordered.

I collapsed back ungracefully on my elbows and watched him spread my legs wide.

He gave a grunt of satisfaction. I knew what he was seeing. Swollen, pink flesh slick with arousal.

"You always need me like this," he said.

It was true. I'd handed over all responsibilities for my sexual satisfaction to my boss. I had no interest in—

My thoughts were interrupted when his tongue darted out and tickled that needy bundle of nerves.

It was like I'd just discovered my body came with a Sex Now button. And Dominic was the only person in the world who knew how to push it.

"I dreamed about you like this. Spread out for me. Open. Needing me." He said between long, languid strokes of his tongue. He licked me from clit to center and back again. Over and over again.

I gulped, unable to respond. I had definitely fallen off a train platform, hitting my head, and the last three months of my life were a hallucination. Any second now, I was going to be plowed into by a subway train.

Yet here I was, on his desk, Dominic's face pressed between my legs. Every time I tried to close my legs to protect myself, he forced them wider. It was a game that I loved losing.

I brazenly fucked his face and felt no shame.

His fingers found me again. Two slid into me and pulled out. Then it was three. And when they crooked just the slightest, my head fell back.

He was growling against my pussy, fucking me with his

tongue and fingers, and I was a blithering mess, melting on paperwork that hopefully wasn't important.

The first ripple caught me by surprise. I was so close to coming already. The man was a maestro. An expert. A damn magician, producing orgasms with a casual flick of his wrist.

He groaned, tongue pausing its delicate assault.

"Don't come," he ordered.

"Uh, then you better stop what you're doing right now," I gasped.

He stood, his desk chair slamming into the shelves behind his desk. He held me pinned to the desk with one hand on the center of my chest. The other he used to free his massive erection from his pants.

I hadn't failed biology. I knew how dicks worked. But Dominic's seemed to grow thicker and longer every time it got near me.

"I want to feel you come on my cock. I want to feel those greedy squeezes when you fucking come, baby."

Yep. Definitely almost dead in a train station. Real people didn't talk like that. Real people weren't desperate to get inside me. To fuck their way into my body.

But Dominic was.

His jaw was clenched as he fisted the shaft. Stroking himself, fucking his own hand, he brought the crown to where I needed him most.

He slid it in the same path his tongue had traveled. Back and forth, through my wet folds. My clit was tapping out an SOS, my core aching with emptiness.

He was leaking precum like it was a competitive sport. And I. Was. Here. For. It.

On the next slick slide, he kept going, the tip of his dick parting my ass cheeks, pausing to tease me at that opening.

"Not without lube, buddy." I shuddered the words out. The fact that he wanted to touch me everywhere made me excited about being touched everywhere. "And remember, I get my shot at you."

"Fuck, Ally," he groaned.

"Yes," I agreed. "Fuck Ally. Now."

He hinged forward, lining up the blunt head of his cock with my entrance. He bit my nipple, and I shivered.

"I love your tits, baby."

"Love them with your cock in me."

He was fully clothed. His pants were undone only far enough to get his cock out to play.

I loved it. I loved that he wanted me this fiercely.

Without warning, without the finesse I'd barely had time to grow accustomed to, Dominic thrust into me, holding my legs open at the knees. I really, really needed to work on my hip flexibility.

His groan was long and victorious. I spent another ten or twenty seconds arching off the desk in a silent scream of ecstasy. "I'm not going to last long. Not with you squeezing the life out of me with that pretty pink pussy," he warned.

"Shut the fuck up and fuck me, Dom."

He pumped into me without regard to items falling off his desk and crashing to the floor. "That's my girl. I feel you fighting it."

It was true. I was running away from the orgasm just so I could greedily be fucked a little longer.

But Dominic wasn't having any of it. He pinned my hips to the desk and rutted into me. "Come. Now."

I opened my mouth to tell him that it doesn't work that way. That a woman doesn't just magically come on command because a hot guy tells her to. But I was too busy writhing under him as he ground against me, driving me straight off the edge of the cliff and into a nuclear detonation. I felt it in my toes, the roots of my hair. My entire being quivered and clenched and came.

He was there. He was with me. Pumping into me, coming so hard he was grunting gutturally on every wet thrust that wrenched more from him.

I'd never felt anything like it. Not before him. The storm breaking. The clouds parting as we jumped together into the abyss.

65

DOMINIC

I waited until I'd been able to lock down on my emotions surrounding my father's spontaneous little blackmail demand before doing what had to be done. It was late Friday, and my mother's assistants had gone home for the night.

"Come in," she called a beat after my perfunctory knock.

I found her on the couch, shoes kicked off under the glass coffee table, bare feet tucked under Simone's leg next to her. They were drinking what smelled like very expensive tequila.

I had the distinct impression that I'd just interrupted something.

"Dominic, darling. Come join us," my mother said wearily. "Help yourself to a glass." I knew that look. And I knew what always caused that look. Or more specifically who.

Simone gave me a sympathetic smile. A warning that this was indeed bad.

"What did that bastard do now?" I asked, taking a glass from the well-stocked bar cart my mother kept in the corner.

Simone took my glass and poured generously. "Not him this time," she said.

"I just got off the phone with Elena's attorney," Mom said.

Incredulous, I frowned. "Why?"

"It seems she is no longer interested in being featured on the May cover," my mother said with a complete lack of the emotions I knew swirled beneath her implacable surface.

"We've already started the first print run," I said, gripping my glass.

"After she threatened a lawsuit, the print run has been paused until we can explore our options," Mom said.

"This is bullshit. This is just another stupid publicity ploy." I'd never told my mother about why I'd ended things with Elena, and she'd never asked. We didn't tend to share things unless there was no other way around it. Like my father's firing and their divorce.

"She signed the releases. Legally, you can proceed," Simone said.

"I'm not inclined to put someone on my cover who doesn't recognize what an honor it is to be there. Doing so would give her the prestige of the cover *and* the platform to complain about how big, bad Dalessandra Russo wouldn't let her change her mind."

My mother twirled the emerald on her middle finger.

"Did she give any indication that she was going to back out at the last second?" I asked. Something was niggling at me in the back of my head.

"Not at all. In fact, she sent me a card with an excessive number of exclamation points two days ago thanking me for the opportunity."

I pinched the bridge of my nose. That niggling was getting harder and harder to ignore.

I swore and sipped the tequila. Its smooth burn was a welcome relief from the tightness in my throat.

"I'll talk to her," I said.

My mother's eyebrows winged up. "Wasn't your parting a little…dramatic?"

"Not for me," I said coolly.

The two women shared a look.

"I'll talk to her," I repeated. "In the meantime, start thinking about a Plan B. Who deserves that cover?" If I was right, no amount of talking was going to put Elena back on that cover.

She still lived in the same building, a swanky location with units that faced Central Park. The *Label* cover could have earned her a penthouse a few blocks north, and Elena knew it. The woman was calculating and focused. She wouldn't have just walked away from the cover story she'd fucked her way into my bed two years ago to get.

I lucked out and caught the door as a woman with two huge dogs with rhinestone leashes exited. I paused to give them dignified pats before taking the elevator to the fourth floor. It was a case of déjà vu, walking down the sunny, yellow hallway to 4C. The last time I'd been here, she'd answered the door in another man's shirt.

But it had barely mattered then, and it certainly didn't matter now.

I knocked.

This time, she opened the door in a cloud of fragrance and her own clothes. Elena Ostrovsky was a beautiful woman, and she knew it. People had been telling her so since she was fourteen years old. She tended to get nervous if they went too long without reminding her.

For an afternoon at home, her hair was done in thick, lustrous curls and swept to the side in a low tail. Her eyes were painted in coppers and bronzes. I'd never seen her without makeup. We'd never spent a full night together, and it was only now that I found that strange.

"Dominic." I didn't like the way my name sounded from her lips. "I'm so glad you're here."

"Are you?" I asked.

"Come in," she said, stepping away from the door and opening it wider. She was wearing red leather pants, an oversize, sheer black blouse, and gold studded stilettos. Just a quiet day around the house.

"Am I interrupting?" It was half dig and half legitimate concern.

"No, no! Of course not," she insisted, either ignoring the insult or not remembering that it had been a very valid question last time.

I didn't know. Because I didn't know her.

I stepped inside. The furniture was different, I noted. Upgraded from my last visit. White couch. White chairs. One thing that was the same was the Wall of Elena. Framed headshots, magazine covers, shots from the runway and red carpets. Every picture had been cropped and edited so it was just her.

When we were dating, I'd found it "interesting" when she'd added a photo of the two of us during New York Fashion Week and then cropped everything except my arm out of it. I thought of the box of Ally's framed photos she'd brought home from her father's things in the storage unit. Candids in mismatched frames of all the people she loved the most in life. Not a glamour shot to be found.

"You can guess why I'm here," I said, shoving my hands in my pockets.

Elena gave me her prettiest pout. "You aren't here because you miss me?"

"No. The cover, Elena."

She pranced over to the low sofa and sat, crossing one knee over the other, stretching her arms over the back. Posing. "I don't want to do it anymore." But the lie didn't quite reach her eyes.

"Yes. You do. You've always wanted that cover. It's why you started dating me."

She rolled her eyes. "Always with the same song and dance." She reached for the pack of cigarettes she had on the table.

"I guess that's why you changed partners in the middle of the dance."

"Dominic, that was ages ago," she said, lighting a skinny cigarette. "Let's forget all that." She patted the couch next to her.

I ignored the invitation.

I didn't like being here. I didn't like being around her. The stark contrasts between her and Ally, my past and my present, were dizzying.

"The cover," I repeated. "What's your game?"

She looked away again and brushed a hand over a furry pillow, fingers plucking at the ivory tufts. "I changed my mind," she said less emphatically.

"You changed your mind, or someone changed your mind?"

"What does it matter?"

"We can still run your cover, your story. You signed the releases," I warned her. "This isn't going to look good for you, reneging on a deal with Dalessandra Russo."

She flinched then. Elena already had a reputation for being difficult. She showed up late, left early, and spent most shoots complaining. Her manager and her looks were the only things keeping her gainfully employed.

"She won't do anything about it," she said, studying her nails. "She'll let me out of it and play nice."

"That doesn't sound like you, Elena. I remember you confessing that my mother was your idol when you were a teenage model doing car shows and catalog shoots. You know who that sounds like to me?"

She gave a shrug as if she couldn't care less, but those unnatural green eyes were watering.

"My father," I said.

Her eyes darted to me, wide with surprise. "You know?"

"I guessed. What did he promise you?"

She slumped against the cushion. "The cover of *Indulgence*. I can't do both."

"Why would you choose *Indulgence* over *Label*? They're not even in the same league."

"It's a good opportunity," she parroted.

"Says my father who landed a job with them, and now he's poaching content from *Label*. I repeat, why are you doing this?"

She worried her lower lip between her teeth hard enough that I was concerned the filler would leak out. "He has something of mine," she said.

"Christ." I shoved my hand through my hair. "What?"

"A tape," she answered in a tiny voice.

"What kind of tape?"

"What kind of tape do you think? A sex tape."

I sighed. "Elena, come on. You know better than that." I knew her manager personally, a no-nonsense woman who schooled her charges in all the ways the world could chew them up and spit them out if they weren't very smart and very cynical.

"I didn't know. I didn't know he made one."

"That's illegal."

"I can't prove it, and he knows it," she said, fat tears finally fighting their way past the jungle of lashes.

"How did my father get the tape? Did someone sell it to him?" Maybe I could finally find a way to hang Paul Russo. Blackmailing family was one thing, but this was an entirely new low.

She shook her head.

"You don't know?"

She took a shuddery breath. "He made it."

66

DOMINIC

My mother was still in the office when I got back. She'd gathered the troops in her office. Linus, Irvin, and Shayla were joined by a handful of editors. There were cartons of Thai food and bottles of wine on every flat surface. People paced and slumped and threw out ideas while my mother twirled her reading glasses by the arm and shot them down one by one. Irvin was kicked back in a chair, his phone glued to his hand.

"Mom? A minute." I hooked my thumb over my shoulder, not wanting to air our dirty Russo laundry in front of everyone else.

She picked up her tea and followed me into the hall.

"Come on, people, focus," Linus said, clapping his hands as we stepped out. "We have seventy-two hours to come up with a plan, shoot it, and write the goddamn story."

"Did you talk to Elena?" Mom asked.

I nodded. "We have bigger problems than an egotistical model."

"What?"

"More like who. Elena has committed to do the *Indulgence* May cover."

"That's ridiculous. Their circulation is barely sixty percent of ours."

"She's being blackmailed into it."

She closed her eyes and blew out a breath. "Paul."

"It seems he's blackmailing her with a sex tape."

My mother's eyes opened. "That's rather low even for him."

"It gets worse. He has the tape because he made it."

"Made it as in…"

"He had a year-long affair with Elena, which happened to overlap both your marriage to him and my relationship with her."

It had been my father's shirt she'd been wearing when I showed up at her apartment two years ago.

My mother looked down at the teacup in her hand for a long beat, then hurled it against the wall. Conversation in the room cut off. It looked as if we Russos were starting to have trouble controlling our tempers.

"Is everyone okay?" Linus asked slowly, approaching with caution.

Mom gave him the circle-the-wagons smile. "Everything is fine. Just dropped my tea. It's time for something harder anyway."

"Mom."

She held up an index finger, effectively shushing me. Russos didn't discuss things. We certainly didn't admit to being betrayed. And we definitely didn't show weakness.

"Come inside, Dominic. We'll figure out what direction we should go in."

On a sigh, I followed her inside and pulled out my phone.

Me: It's going to be a late night. I'm with my mother in an emergency strategy session over the May cover story.

Ally: Elena? I am officially staying up for an update. I'll put your dinner in the fridge and take Brownie for his walk. Let me know if you need anything.

Maybe I should tell her. Secrets only seemed to fester.

I grabbed a carton of drunken noodles and settled in with the rest of the team.

An hour later, we were still nowhere near a solution.

Linus sat up from where he reclined on the couch. "I've got it! Why don't we put Ally on the cover? It seems her star is rising," he joked.

My mother relaxed with a laugh. "It *was* a striking photo," she agreed.

"What photo?" I demanded.

"Christian James's Instagram," Linus said, fingers flying over his phone screen. "I can't believe you didn't see it yet." He slid the phone to me.

I felt my heart clumsily miss a beat as a chill settled in my chest. "What is this?" I asked, glaring at the photo.

"You didn't know about it?" my mother asked.

"I had no idea," I said, feeling the knife twist in me. Betrayal was the theme of the day. How many times could a man have his legs swept out from under him before he didn't get back up? "I need to take care of something," I said, abruptly rising.

"You look comfortable," I said, my tone too bland for her to pick up on the anger I was choking on.

Ally looked up from her cocoon on my couch and grinned. "Your fault for having such comfy furniture," she teased. "Want to bring your dinner in here and snuggle while you fill me in on all the gossip?"

This charade of affection turned my stomach.

I tossed my phone in her lap.

She picked it up, grinned. And that knife in my guts twisted again.

"Wow. I don't look half bad."

"Care to explain?" I asked, my tone deceptively mild. I wanted her to lie to me so I could call her on it. Because there were only two reasons why she'd be in Christian James's photo on a bed, in an unzipped dress staring at the camera as if it were a lover. As if it were me.

"Well, I can't explain all of it yet," she said. "Because it's a surprise. But this is what I was telling you about Wednesday at lunch. Faith and I went to his studio for that shoot."

"Are you fucking him or using me?" I asked, my throat raw.

Ally blinked, and I watched the color slowly drain from her face.

Good. I wanted her to hurt like I hurt.

She took a breath and let it out. "You're stressed and exhausted. I'm going to give you one free pass. But, Dom, you don't get to make accusations like that," she said quietly.

"Oh, I don't get to ask why you were in his bed, half-dressed? So which is it? Fucking him or fucking me over?"

She unwound herself from the blanket and came to her feet. "Nothing happened," she said icily. "Where is this even coming from?"

"Insta-fucking-gram. That's where. Seems you're becoming quite popular."

"There is nothing going on between me and Christian. We're friends. He did me a favor, and I did one for him."

"Was the favor posing half-naked on a bed or fucking him?"

Ally wasn't the kind of girl to bitch-slap someone. And thanks to my red tunnel vision, I didn't even see her fist fly until it connected with my face.

The new pain was a welcome relief from the wound inside me.

"How dare you," she hissed.

I grabbed her wrist and hauled her against me.

Her breath caught as our bodies collided, and I hated myself for going stone fucking hard against her. My dick had zero self-respect. I wasn't so sure about the rest of me.

"Why were you even alone with him in a room with a bed?" The idea of her and that charming, slimy son of a bitch on a bed together ripped me apart from the inside. Even if he was just taking pictures of her.

"Do you realize how ridiculous this is? I wasn't alone with him. And if you weren't so busy trying to hang me for imagined crimes, you'd notice that was the same set for the video shoot the online content team set up last week. I was on set."

She was trying to tug her arm out of my grip, but her free hand was curled into my shirt, holding me against her. I felt a trickle of blood at the corner of my mouth, and my tongue darted out to taste it. Ally's eyes followed the movement. Her lower lip trembled, and I wanted to sink my teeth into it. I wanted to kiss her until she hurt the way I hurt.

Forget my parents—we were the fucked-up ones using a fight as foreplay.

I let her go and took a deliberate step away.

"Do you honestly believe I would cheat on you? That you mean so little to me that I'd be willing to throw it all away?" she asked.

Thinking wasn't really happening for me right now. I was too busy feeling a thousand different knife edges of emotions. But did I really believe Ally would have let someone else touch her when we were so…connected?

"No," I rasped. Her shoulders relaxed for a moment. "But it certainly raised your profile." I spat out the accusation, astounded that once again, I'd fallen for it. Only this time, it hurt. It really fucking hurt.

"My *profile*? Have you lost your mind? I don't have a profile! I'm Dominic Russo's girlfriend, and I wore a nice dress in front of a couple of cameras once."

"You'll have plenty of opportunities now, thanks to this little pseudo-celebrity stunt."

"I hope you were nicer to your model ex about her chosen profession," Ally shot back.

"Don't ever mention her to me again," I snapped. She'd pushed exactly the right button to remind me of what I'd wanted to forget.

I felt sick and empty and like it wasn't worth the effort to stand anymore. I leaned back against the wall and slid down it.

I stared at the ceiling, picturing the room above us. My bed. Our bed.

It was where we started. Where we were at our best. The center of our fucking relationship. But that didn't prepare me for this. I was shaking. Physically shaking.

"Dom?" Her voice was more gentle than I deserved, and she was kneeling in front of me. She should have been kicking me, throwing things, not looking me in the eye.

"He fucked her. While I was dating her."

"Who?"

"My father," I spat out. "We were never serious. Elena and me. She was using me for the attention. She'd tip off paparazzi when we were out. I found out, and when I went to confront her, she answered the door in another man's shirt. He was still there, and I didn't care enough to find out who."

"It was your dad?" Ally asked slowly.

"He always loved to take things from me. Always a competition."

She laid a hand on my shoulder and squeezed. "Your father is a sick bastard."

"You don't know the half of it. He made a tape. A sex tape. That's why she backed out of the issue. He threatened to release it. Her reputation would have taken a hit." Meanwhile his legend would only grow. The sixty-eight-year-old man fucking models forty years his junior.

"She told you?" Ally asked.

I nodded. "I went to see her. I was pissed. I thought she was doing it for attention. And she told me. Then she begged me to help her. Asked me to take her out, be seen with her so people would be talking about us instead of her. She thought no one would believe there was a sex tape if I was willing to be with her again."

She wanted to use me again. That was what they all wanted. And no matter how much I gave, it was never enough.

"I don't know who I'm more mad at right now. You, your father, or Elena. And believe me, that's saying something," Ally said.

"I guess I have a type," I said bitterly.

She pinned me with her gaze, daring me to say the words that were setting my tongue on fire.

"Users," I said.

The hand on my shoulder fisted and then released me entirely. "Uh-huh. So you accuse me of cheating on you, and when that doesn't stick, you go right on down the list to I'm a user? Guess what? You win. I'm more pissed at you."

"It's not really your fault," I assured her. She hadn't forced me to give her anything. She'd just made it easy, fun even.

"Dominic, I'm giving you a chance to shut the hell up. I know you're hurt. I know you're reeling. But I don't know if I can forgive you for what you've already said."

I didn't need forgiveness. I didn't want it. I was the one who'd been wronged.

"Is that what you were doing? All those gifts were tests to see if I'd accept them?" she asked.

"You took them. You don't even put up a fight over staying here anymore. You've stayed here every night for weeks."

"Because you asked me to!"

"Or is it because it works better for you? You get a nice warm place to stay that doesn't require you to get up at the ass crack of dawn for a commute. Is that why you were finally willing to introduce me to your father? Were you hoping I'd walk in there and magnanimously decide to pay off his debt?" The words were spilling from my mouth like I had no fucking control. I used to have control. Before her.

She sank back as if I'd actually struck her.

"I'm such a fucking idiot," I murmured to myself.

"Yeah. No argument there," Ally said. Her teeth were chattering, and she was hugging herself. "You can't take these things back, you know."

"The gifts are yours to keep."

"No, you ass. What you're saying. You can't take any of this back. You can't erase any of this. You're accusing me of using you. You don't get to have a bad day and try to hurt me because of it. That's not what a relationship is. I don't deserve this."

I was starting to waver. Starting to doubt my righteous anger. That only made me recommit myself to it. I'd been blinded by sex. It was just sex. Maybe we'd been using each other. Me for her body and her for everything else I could offer her.

What kind of a fucked-up foundation was that?

We were doomed from the beginning.

"You should go," I told her. "You can get your things tomorrow after I leave for work."

67

DOMINIC

It was not a good day. I spent the entire night haunted by Ally's tearstained face, the hurt in those soft brown eyes, the shake in her hands.

"I don't know if I can forgive you for this."

In the light of ugly gray morning, I wasn't feeling as self-righteous or confident in my decision to protect myself.

My desk phone rang.

"What?"

"What did you do to Ally?" my mother demanded in my ear.

I'd arrived at work only to find my assistant had called in sick and someone had waved a magic wand taking me from Dominic back to Mr. Russo.

"Good morning, Mother. I'm fine. How are you?"

"I'm not happy."

"Everything is fine. Consider it business as usual."

"Ally sent me her resignation this morning, effective immediately."

"Maybe she was just tired of working here," I said wearily. She didn't really need this job anymore. Not with the house ready to be put on the market.

"What did you do, Dominic Michael?"

"What makes you think it was me?"

"Because I know you. I know your baggage."

"Where do you think that baggage came from?" I asked uncharitably.

"Darling, you're forty-five years old. That excuse stopped working sometime in your early twenties when you became an adult responsible for your own choices."

The woman had a point. An annoying, infinitesimal one.

"It was a private matter. I didn't ask her to quit. I would have been willing to continue working together."

"Dominic, I say this with love. You're being an unconscionable fool." She disconnected with a sharp click.

It was official. Every woman in the building, including my own mother, hated my guts.

Nina from advertising had to be physically restrained in the elevator this morning. I got off on the thirty-third floor and took the stairs only to walk straight into Missie the copywriter, who took one look at me and burst into tears.

I took my lunch in the cafeteria, and hoards of people turned their backs on me as I walked past their tables. Linus returned my "good afternoon" with a roll of his eyes and a middle finger. Even Buddy couldn't look me in the eye. Buddy. The nicest human being in the world thought I was Satan. He'd picked up his brown-bag lunch the second I pulled out a chair at his table. "Have a nice day," he whispered as he left.

It was time things were back to normal. Normal was familiar. Comfortable.

I was single again.

My home was my own again.

And I could go back to business as usual.

I stabbed my chicken with a violent jab of the fork and grimly ate my lunch alone.

Christian James, the cocky son of a bitch, strutted into my office like a rooster. Or a peacock. Whichever fowl was more annoying.

He tossed a dark brown garment bag over the back of my visitor's chair.

"The only reason I'm giving this to you is because it'll make you feel like shit," he announced.

"I doubt there's anything you could do that would make me feel anything," I said, ignoring him and returning to the stupid fucking article that I couldn't focus on writing because everything in the world was wrong.

"Big man hiding behind his desk. I guess you're braver when you're yelling accusations at a woman half your size," he snapped.

"Be very careful, James," I enunciated coldly, forgetting about the document on my monitor.

His laugh was cold, mirthless. "You never deserved her."

"I'd like to remind you that *Label* and the Russo family have been one of your most generous backers. That backing can easily be taken away."

If I'd expected him to back down and apologize, I was mistaken.

"Fuck you, man. That's your problem. You think everyone is out to use you, to get something out of you. Did it ever occur to you that Ally loved you?"

Loved.

Loved.

Loved.

My heart echoed the word sluggishly.

"Some people are incapable of love." I was a blasé motherfucker.

"Yeah, and I'm looking at one of them. I can't believe she cared about you. You really had her fooled, you know? You're a fucking emotionless iceberg."

"And you're the guy who fucked my girlfriend. Congratulations to you both."

"Stand the fuck up."

I put my reading glasses back on and went back to looking at my monitor. "Get out of my office, James. I have real work to do."

"Stand up and make me."

I had a good thirty pounds on the man, but he was ten years younger. I wasn't certain he couldn't beat me to a pulp.

"It was a trade, by the way. I made her what's in the bag, and she did a little promotion for me. There was no sex, and you're the dumbest motherfucker on the planet if you believe that she'd do that to you. I don't know if you're deflecting your own sins or what—"

"I never so much as looked at another woman," I growled, yanking off my glasses. This idiot needed to leave my office. Immediately.

"Oh, does it piss you off when someone accuses you of something you didn't do?"

"Fuck off, James. I'm losing my patience."

"You've lost your damn mind. She's a great girl, and I'm going to do everything I can to convince her to run in the other direction when you realize what a huge mistake you made and try to crawl back."

"In the meantime, you can talk her into your own bed," I said flippantly.

"Okay. My turn!" Faith, Ally's friend, stormed into my office. She wore hot-pink leather leggings and some kind of woolly, white cropped sweater. Her hair was pulled up on top of her head in one sleek ponytail.

"I've got this, babe," Christian said, instantly softening.

Faith paused to cup the man's face in her hand. "I don't want you to break your gorgeous, talented hands on this steaming piece of shit's face."

"Can I help you?" I asked dryly.

She glared at me and casually strolled around my desk. I turned my chair to meet her but refused to stand.

She gave me a terrifying smile and cracked me right across the face with her open palm. Ally didn't bitch-slap, but Faith did it like it was an Olympic sport and she was a gold medalist.

My ear rang like a school bell.

"You hurt my friend, and I want to murder you for it. I want to reach into your chest, rip your pathetic excuse of a heart out, and drop-kick it across the Hudson, you stupid son of a bitch. I don't care what baggage you come with. That's no excuse for treating one of the nicest, most beautiful souls in the world like garbage," she hissed in my face.

"Okay, babe. Let's get you out of here before this coward calls security," Christian said, towing Faith away from me.

"I'll meet you out front," she said, stopping to kiss the man hard on the mouth and then give me the most violent middle finger I'd ever received on her way out.

Christian watched her go with the eyes of a man half in love.

Fuck.

I'd forgotten what Ally had said at my birthday party.

Invisible knives inserted themselves into my gut.

"Well, it's been fun. I hope you're real happy with yourself, man," he said, turning his attention back to me.

"It's been delightful," I snarled.

"Everyone has baggage, Russo. Most of us are just smart enough not to hurl full-size suitcases at the people we love." He patted the garment bag. "Here's your custom fucking vest Ally asked me to make for you. Hope it doesn't even come close to making up for losing the girl."

My world was starting to close in on me. The walls of my office loomed closer and closer. Had I really thrown away something real, or was I justified in my distrust?

She wasn't Elena. She hated artifice. Ally taught women to dance and love their bodies. She created beauty with color and design. She inspired kindness and generosity in everyone—myself included. She put her entire life on hold to clean up someone else's mess.

And I wasn't my father.

No, I chose to hurt people in other ways.

The realization was crashing over me like a brick wall when a new email popped into my box. Ally Morales.

I clicked it before I was even conscious of grabbing the mouse.

Subject: Itemized remittance sheet

The message itself was blank, but attached was a spreadsheet with estimates of food, utilities, gas, the storage unit I'd rented for her father's furniture, and the entire renovation bill from her father's house. There was a notation at the bottom. First payment $50.

Because she no longer had a job thanks to me. She had

nothing until the house went on the market and sold. Even then, the money went to the nursing home.

I swore under my breath. I was an asshole. Lower than low. Ally Morales was worse off having met me.

I jumped up, intending to get my coat. I'd made a very big mistake, and I wasn't sure I could live with myself now.

There was another knock at my door.

"Go away," I snarled.

But the knocker was either feeling brave, or they'd underestimated how much I wanted to punch someone.

Malina the Man-Eater stepped into my office.

"Not now, Malina," I snapped. I didn't have time to fend off another one of my father's ex-lovers.

"This is important," she said.

I doubted that very much. But when I looked at her, really looked at her, I realized there was something off. For one, she was wearing jeans. For two, she didn't have any makeup on. She looked softer, younger, less angry.

"What is it?" I asked.

"Well, first of all, I quit."

"Why are you telling me?"

"Just go with it. It's this whole full-circle moment for me. I turned down the job your father offered me at *Indulgence* this morning."

That caught my interest.

"He offered you a job, you turned it down, and now you're quitting this job?"

She nodded. "It's been brought to my attention that I don't have the healthiest priorities." She cleared her throat. "I'm leaving New York. But I wanted you to know some things first. Things I'm not proud of."

I closed my eyes. "Malina, you don't need to walk me

through your personal life. I know you and my father were… involved."

"It's not that. Or only that. I fed him information after he left. Things about *Label* and…" Her gaze shifted to the ceiling. "About your mother."

I doubted there was much about my mother that an admin could uncover that my father wouldn't have already known.

"Okay," I said slowly.

"I wasn't the only one still friendly with him," she said.

"Who else?" I asked.

"Irvin. We had a few dinners, the three of us. Your father promised him managing editor at *Indulgence*. Also, Irvin wasn't dipping his pen in the company ink, if you know what I mean. But that doesn't mean he was innocent."

"What are you saying, Malina?"

She looked uncomfortable. "I don't think it's my story to tell," she said finally.

Exasperation was my new permanent company. "Whose story is it?" I asked.

"Start with Gola and Shayla," she suggested. "And talk to your mother. Tell her Paul knows, and he's going to use it against her."

68

ALLY

I left my key and my work phone and laptop on Dominic's foyer table. Every gift he'd ever given me stayed right where it was. The only thing that actually hurt to leave was the glossy black piano I'd only just begun to acquaint myself with.

And Brownie. My sweet, sweet boy who was currently chewing on the strap of my gym bag. "Come here, buddy," I said, kneeling down and hugging his warm, furry body. Excited, he half tackled me to the ground, and a good six inches of tongue went down my ear canal. "I'm gonna miss you so much," I whispered into his soft fur. "You be the best doggy in the world and miss me and don't chew on that piano, okay?"

His tail thumped happily against my gym bag, and I wondered if he would actually fit inside the bag. I could say he got out while I was leaving… But then Dominic would be all alone again. And as much as he deserved it, I couldn't take his Brownie from him.

One last kiss on the head, one last accidental mouthful of dog tongue, and I picked up my bag and walked out.

The blinding pop of sunshine wrenched a humorless laugh from me. It was almost fifty degrees today, but I was cold and dead as winter on the inside. I should have seen it coming. I should never have gotten involved.

There were a lot of things I should have done. I pondered each and every one of them at great length during my train ride.

I felt my numbness starting to crack, felt the thrum of pain, real pain, beneath the icy surface. As a defensive measure, I cranked my Men Are Big Stupid Shitheads playlist. I needed to get through the next two hours of my life as a functioning human being before I could give in to the tidal wave of really shitty feelings that was threatening to crush me.

"Just hang in there," I whispered to myself.

It must not have been a whisper, because the woman next to me shot me the side-eye.

"Sorry," I mouthed.

"Don't you be sorry. Men are dirtbags," she said.

I closed my eyes. I was going back home to Jersey. Or back to my father's house. I guess I didn't really have a home.

Home had been my father's house. Then Dominic's. Nothing had been mine since I'd moved back.

Maybe it was time I remedied that. I had a lot of freaking decisions to make...after my impending breakdown.

The meeting with the real estate agent went well. Better than well. Even though I was a broken shell of a human being who just couldn't quite keep my shit together.

I got teary-eyed showing him the bathroom where Dominic had helped me level the vanity. Because of course everyone got sentimental over *bathrooms*.

The agent was a cute guy in his early thirties, and when he

told me what price he thought we should list the house at, I burst into tears and hugged him. He'd patted me awkwardly on the back and then announced loudly that he needed to go meet his girlfriend for lunch.

When he left and I was all alone in the house that no longer felt like home, I got antsy. I took advantage of the warm weather and walked to the nursing home. I found my father in a chair in the lounge staring out the window.

But when I told him about the house, he called me my mother's name and asked if I'd seen his term papers.

I left feeling abandoned by the two men I loved the most.

And that was why it hurt so, so much. That devastation simmering beneath the surface just waiting to erupt.

I loved Dominic Russo.

And he'd cast me aside like I was nothing. Thank God I'd been too chicken to tell him I loved him.

I reached for a lifeline.

Me: I know I swore I'd never say these words again, but I think I need tequila.

Faith: I. Am. Here. For. This.

She arrived an hour later with a bottle of much better stuff than what we'd nearly gone blind on last time.

"My boyfriend yelled at your boyfriend, and then I slapped him in the face, and it was pretty fucking hot," Faith said, stepping inside and closing the door.

I chose to ignore the latter part of that statement for now. "Your boyfriend? Wait a second. What happened to 'we're just having mind-blowing sex,' 'we're too different to be serious'?"

"Look, I'm not here to rub your face in my new awesome relationship. I'm here to get you shit-faced."

I nodded somberly. "But just because I'm sad doesn't mean I can't also be happy for you. Are you happy? Do you like him?"

She reached for my hand and squeezed. "I'm happy. I like him. He's gorgeous shirtless. Now, how are you? Are you ready to talk?" she asked, pulling the stopper out of the tequila.

Ah, the sound of bad decisions.

I shook my head. Maybe there was something to be said about keeping the bad stuff inside. I'd trusted Dominic with so much. With my fears, my secrets, my heart.

And look what had happened.

"The real estate guy is going to list the house on Monday. In the meantime, I need to find gainful employment."

"Christian said you were doing some branding work for him? But I think he said it with his shirt off, so I wasn't listening very closely."

I nodded. "It was the other half of our deal for Dom—the vest." His name used to mean so many other things. Its definition, my association with the arrangement of those seven letters, was irrevocably changed.

"Christian said the concepts were really good."

I shrugged. Apparently getting your heart stomped on made it hard to care about anything.

"Do you want to go on a revenge spree? Maybe drive by his house and set his bushes on fire? Rub some dog shit all over his Range Rover? We could get all the girls from the office together and make shirts that say Domidick."

I should have laughed, but the cracks couldn't hold back the hurt anymore. *Thanks, tequila.*

"I really loved him, Faith. Like really. A lot."

She pushed the emergency box of tissues at me and pushed my hair off my forehead. "I know, babe. I know," she said grimly.

69

DOMINIC

As if to prove what an asshole I was, Christian's new Instagram post was a picture of Ally and Faith, both in couture, laughing and lounging on those same rumpled sheets. It was followed by a picture of Christian and Faith in a lip-lock.

I was a champion asshole, and I'd spent one too many hours last night listening to people who should have felt comfortable talking to me in the first place. But apparently I didn't encourage open communication and honesty. My attitude convinced people that I didn't care about them and left them to deal with things on their own.

I'd spent an uncomfortable hour with Shayla, followed by a trip to HR to get Gola's home address. For the second time, I'd shown up unannounced on a woman's doorstep to ask her tough questions about abuses of power and trust.

I was still turning it all over in my head when my mother summoned me to her office to talk about cover stories.

"We can't get Amalia," she was saying. "She's on location shooting some music video for six days. So that's out." She sat perfectly still, staring up at the whiteboard someone had wheeled into her office. Ideas for the cover were listed out in order of potential. Over half of them were crossed out.

"Mom," I said wearily. "I can't talk to you about stories. I don't know anything about stories. You know what I do know? Secrets. I know how to hide the dark, dirty truth. How to be ashamed of it."

"Oh, lord. Dominic, I really don't need you having some sort of existential crisis right now," Mom sighed. "We have an issue to discuss."

She was talking about the magazine.

"Actually, we have several issues to discuss," I countered, leaning back and shoving a hand through my hair.

Issues.

Stories.

Secrets.

Ally.

I sat up a little straighter, thinking it through. I heaved myself out of the chair and crossed to the board. "Secrets and stories," I said and picked up the eraser.

"What's gotten into you? Are you having a breakdown right now?"

"Probably," I said, starting to erase the list.

"Dominic!" Mom appeared at my side as I scrawled the words *secrets* and *stories* at the top of the spot I'd just cleared.

"We foster secrets. We encourage people to keep secrets and hide things, and this is what happens. Everything rots from the inside."

"What are you talking about?"

"Dad. Irvin—who I'm firing in twenty minutes if you want in on that. Me. You. Simone."

Mom went still again.

"We've all kept secrets," I said. "But what happens if we stop keeping them? What happens if we tell our stories?"

———

Twenty minutes later, I was back in my office with calls in to HR, the magazine's general counsel, and the family attorney. Mom was working her magic on her favorite designers and photographers. There was a new energy, an excitement. But I could only watch from the outside.

My cell phone buzzed, and I pounced, hoping that something had happened and Ally had magically forgiven me.

Harry: Del just texted. She read that you dumped Ally for being pregnant with another man's baby.

Me: Tell Del not to read that shit.

Harry: So you didn't dump her? I can tell my wife to stop sobbing into her bottle of merlot?

Me: Ally and I decided we were no longer a good idea.

Harry: Mainlining wine gif.

Harry: WTF gif with a really pissed off face.

Harry: Are you fucking with me right now?

My phone rang. I knew it had been too optimistic, hoping that Harry would give up and leave me alone.

"Man. Seriously?"

It sounded like he was ringside at a professional wrestling event.

"Where are you?"

"At home. Why?"

"You don't hear that noise? What is it? Banshees? Someone running kittens through a wood chipper?"

"Oh, that," he said dismissively. "That's the girls. They're either mad or happy. Can't really tell just from the sound. The screaming is pretty much the same." There was another blood curdling shriek on his end. "Oh, good. They're happy," he said. "Lay it out for me, man. Don't go all Vault on me."

"Vault?"

"That's your mean, behind-your-back nickname bestowed upon you by the lovely and never-wrong Delaney," he explained.

Harry had once lost a bet with Delaney. The stakes had been he had to refer to her at least once a day as "The lovely and never-wrong Delaney."

I sighed audibly.

"Every guy has one," he continued. "Mine's Pretends to Be Listening. And don't insult either of our admittedly limited intelligences by asking me to explain why you're Vault and I'm Pretends to Be Listening. Just tell me what you did, and I'll tell you how to fix it. Or get Delaney involved if it's a bad fuckup."

Oh, it was a bad fuckup. An unrecoverable one.

"I don't think even Delaney could fix this," I admitted.

"That bad, huh?" he asked.

"Think about the worst thing you've ever done to your wife," I advised him.

"Uh-huh. Okay. Got it."

"Then make it ten times worse."

Harry let out a low whistle. "That's bad. Did you accidentally cut off one of her limbs?"

"Worse."

"Okay. I'm with you, brother. We've all done really stupid fucking shit. Lay it on me."

I thought about everything. About my mother, my father. About Ally and the women my father victimized and used. About Elena and Gola and Harry and Delaney. About that jackass Christian and Faith. About how I'd never once confided in Harry, my best friend.

So I told him everything. From my father's gruesome predilections to my breakup with Elena to my epic, unforgivable fuckup.

"You fucking asshole," he said without heat when I'd finally finished.

"I know," I agreed. "I'm a monster. Just a different kind from my father."

"No, idiot. You should have had this conversation with me or someone a year ago."

"You have to admit, it was the worst possible thing I could have done."

"Not the worst. You could have cheated on her in her own bed, and when she walked in on you, you could have chopped off one or two of her limbs. Or you could have accidentally nudged her grandmother with your car eight years ago so everyone in the family had to spend Thanksgiving in the emergency department."

"That last one sounds a little specific for fictionalized moral lessons."

"Yeah, so I accidentally hit Delaney's grandma with the car. To be fair, the woman hated me, and I swear she jumped behind me at the last second. That woman would have been willing to break a femur to make a point. Anyway, she was fine, and Delaney and I recovered. You can too."

"I abandoned her, Harry. Not only did I live up to the example her shitty mother set, I accused Ally of using me."

Harry sighed. "Look, the point of a relationship isn't hiding your stupid wounds and flaws. It's about showing them to someone and letting them still love you. You were able to hurt her because she let you in."

"Is that supposed to be good news?"

"I think so, but now I'm having flashbacks to Granny Mabel lying on the asphalt. I'm going to have to call in the big guns."

I pinched the bridge of my nose while my best friend conferenced in his wife.

"You stupid motherfucking guy." Delaney didn't mince words.

"Already acknowledged, Del," Harry said, stepping in. "How does he fix it?"

"Fix it? The man stuck his fingers in her open wound and rooted around in there. He conned her into caring about him, trusting him, and then he abandoned her just like her mother did."

Fuck.

"You want someone you can trust with your nightmares, not just your dreams. She showed you her nightmare, and you walked," Delaney continued.

"Babe, focus. How does he make it right?"

"Listen, I don't know about Ally, but there wouldn't be any fixing this for me."

"So what you're saying is this is worse than Granny Mabel."

"Harry, honey, you could have backed over Granny Mabel six times, and this is still worse."

My desk phone had incoming calls. Several of them. "This has been really helpful, guys. I've got to go."

There was a knock at my door, and Irvin sauntered in.

"What can I do for you, my boy?" he asked.

"Irvin, you're fired."

70

DOMINIC

To: Ally
From: Dominic
Subject: I'm so sorry.

Fun Fact: I'm terrible at apologizing.

The words "I'm sorry" didn't mean anything when I was growing up. They just meant "I wish I hadn't gotten caught." Or "I'll do it again."

I realize it's pathetic to be 45 and still not know how to say those two little words. But I'm sorry, Ally. I'm so permanently, painfully, unforgivably sorry. I don't deserve your forgiveness. But that doesn't stop me from hoping for it.

Yours Always Even Though I Don't Deserve You,
Dominic

To: Ally
From: Dominic
Subject: Getting to know me

I've only recently learned that my nickname is the Vault. I don't trust easily. I don't share easily. And in an incredible dent to my male pride, apparently I'm always waiting to be taken advantage of. All this should have come up in the "getting to know you" stage. Which we skipped over because I was too focused on the "getting you naked."

Not that I regret that part of it.

But I did you a disservice, Ally. I gave you things, but I didn't share. I forced your secrets into the open while refusing to tell mine. It was never an even exchange. You always gave more.

And for that, and so many other things, I'm sorry.

Love,
Dom

To: Ally
From: Dominic
Subject: Getting to know me

I can't stand the smell of hummus. It makes me gag.

Love,
Dom

To: Ally
From: Dominic
Subject: Getting to know me

Adding to the hate list.

I hate not knowing what's going on in your life, in your day. Instead of knowing how your dance class went or what you had for lunch or even where you're working now, my knowledge of you is limited to the fact that I lost the right to know anything new.

I hate that your birthday is coming up and I don't have any right to be a part of it.

I hate that you're not here to ask me how far I am in *Pride and Prejudice*. I finished it, by the way, and then watched one of the movies.

I hate not being able to ask you who your favorite on-screen Mr. Darcy is.

I hate that I ruined us just as you were fixing me. I'm doing something good. Really good here. Mom too. And it would never have happened if it weren't for you. I hate that I can't share it with you.

I hate that I let old bad ruin new good.

I hate finding pieces of you around the house. They remind me that not only will you not be walking through the door, but I'm the reason you won't.

I hate that $50 you send me every week. And I know that's why you're sending it. I don't want your money. I just want you. And I hate that that's how you felt about me and I didn't see it.

Love,
Dom

To: Ally
From: Dominic
Subject: Getting to know me

I can't breathe without you. Nothing makes sense anymore. I'm an asshole without you. Ask Gola. She's #TeamAlly. Along with everyone else in this building.

Buddy finally felt bad enough to eat lunch with me. He told me that you introduced his wife to Christian and that she's consulting on some of his adaptive designs. That's just like you. Connecting people.

Sometimes I feel like I'm holding my breath all day just waiting for someone to say your name around me. I don't ever want a life without your name in it.

Love,
Dom

To: Ally
From: Dominic
Subject: Getting to know me

I took a page out of your book with Brownie. He misses you almost as much as I do. So I dressed him up in the sweatshirt you left behind. Picture attached. I had a few drinks with Elton—who confirmed my dumbass diagnosis—on the deck last night. I may have had one too many, and I tried to wear your Halston to bed. I got it stuck over my head and shoulders, and for a few seconds, I thought I was going to suffocate and die.

By the way, I owe you a new dress on top of everything else I owe you.

I know what you brought to my life. I know nothing I gave you could ever compare. But I'm going to fix that.

In the meantime, Brownie and I are still hoping you'll walk back into our lives. He doesn't know that I don't deserve you. Please don't tell him.

Love,
Dom

To: Ally
From: Dominic
Subject: Getting to know me

The first time I saw you—before you yelled at me and sagely said "Fuck You" with pepperoni—I was infatuated with your hair. I called you Sex Hair in my head because I wanted to put my hands in your hair while I kissed you.

Love,
Dom

To: Ally
From: Dominic
Subject: Getting to know me

When I was a freshman in college, my roommate lied and said he didn't have a place to go for Christmas break so I would invite him home with me and he could attend my parents' annual New Year's bash. Think models, champagne, caviar, fireworks. He snuck twenty of his closest asshole friends into the party, and I had to break his friend's nose when he wouldn't let a seventeen-year-old model out of a bedroom.

Elena dated me thinking I could make her a household name, and when tipping off the paparazzi every time we went out didn't work, she started sleeping with my father.

My mother knew I was honor bound to our family and used that to make me walk away from a career that fit me to clean up a mess my father had made.

You never once used me. Never once asked me for anything. And I threw my baggage in your face because I thought I had no idea what a healthy relationship looks like. Harry and Delaney have since informed me differently.

Love,
Dom

To: Ally
From: Dominic
Subject: Getting to know me

I lay in bed last night thinking about all the things I miss about you. Here's the Top 10 out of infinity.

10. The way you're dead to the world when you sleep. A marching band could parade by and you wouldn't even hear the tubas.
9. The way you play the piano (badly but with charming enthusiasm).
8. Your horrible taste in ice cream.
7. Your optimism. I've never been around someone who always believed that things would work out. I hope I didn't break that, because your hopeful heart is the most beautiful thing I've ever known.
6. The way you spell things with pepperoni.
5. Your breasts. Let's be honest. You wouldn't believe this list if they didn't make the Top 5.
4. The way you dance. The way you teach others to dance. The way you're always moving to a beat.
3. The way you say my name in any mood. Sleepy. Hungry. Annoyed. Wanting. I miss it so much sometimes I think I can still hear you calling my name.
2. How you not only conned me into adopting a dog but taught me how to make a home for him.
1. Your heart.

Love,
Dom

To: Ally
From: Dominic
Subject: Getting to know me

I will make this right. Also, I've decided that I'll continue to email you daily for the rest of my life. If you have a problem with that, I encourage you to tell me. Please. Say something. Anything.

Love,
Dom

To: Ally
From: Dominic
Subject: Getting to know me

When I was a senior in high school, I had a girlfriend who dated me just to meet my mother in hopes that she'd be discovered as a model. My mother didn't discover her. But my father did.

I walked in on them in the garage the day before my eighteenth birthday. Dad was "showing her the car they'd bought me." He had her backed into a corner with his hand up her shirt.

At the time, I thought she was as much to blame as he was. I made it so much worse by blaming her. I know better now. I wanted to reach out to her last year.

After my father was forcibly removed. After reading the affidavits of his victims. After I paid for his crimes from the trust fund he'd set up for me that I'd never touched.

I finally understood the damage that he and I had inflicted on a seventeen-year-old girl. But I didn't reach out. I didn't think I could handle hearing her story because I was still keeping secrets.

It wasn't the first time I'd walked in on my father and someone who wasn't my mother. The first time, I was thirteen. He was with a neighbor's wife on the brand-new couch my mother had ordered from Milan.

He explained that if I told Mom, I would be ruining our family. That if I kept his secret, we'd all stay together. He promised that he'd make amends and he'd never make that mistake again. At the time, I thought he meant he wouldn't cheat again. I didn't realize it then, but he meant he'd never make the mistake of getting caught again.

If I had gone to Mom when it happened the first time, my father wouldn't have been at *Label* to harass and assault those women. If I had told his secret, none of this would have happened. I've never told anyone that, Ally. You're the first. I wish it was a happier, healthier secret. But a wise, angry woman told me that sharing the good stuff is worthless if you're not willing to share the bad.

So here's the bad: I am the reason my father was in a position to prey on and violate women. And I can't forgive myself for that.

Love,
Dom

71

ALLY

As March gave way to April, as winter mellowed into spring, Dominic's emails kept coming. Every night, there was a new one despite the fact that I'd never once responded. And every night, I read them all over again from the couch I'd moved back into my dad's house from storage.

Call me a glutton for punishment. A masochist. A broken-hearted idiot. Take your pick.

My shattered heart bled for the boy who'd been charged with keeping a family together. But the man he'd grown into had done the aforementioned shattering. And while Dominic didn't know much about sharing, I didn't know much about forgiving.

I certainly hadn't forgiven my mother for abandoning us, not to mention taking away my father's financial security. I hadn't forgiven the contractor for stealing my money. I hadn't forgiven Front Desk Deena for taking joy in threatening me with my father's eviction.

I didn't know how to forgive. I knew how to move on. And that was what I was doing.

The only communication Dominic received from me was a weekly check of whatever I could spare to go toward my debt to him. The bastard never cashed them.

Everything sucked. Every single thing.

In so many ways, I was back to the beginning. Back to BD: Before Dominic. I was back to waitressing and bartending gigs and avoiding Front Desk Deena. The only thing different was now I knew what it felt like to have Dominic Russo smile at me. Fuck me. Hold me.

It was a colossal, cosmic joke.

The nursing home came into view ahead, and I did my best to shove down my negativity. Dad didn't deserve a visit from Gloomy Gail, spreader of depression and angst.

The side door was open—thank the gods of debt collector avoidance and health-care workers who sneak outside for smoke breaks—so I let myself in and headed toward the memory ward.

Braden was on the phone at the desk and buzzed me in.

I waved and made a move for the hallway, but he stopped me with a finger in the air. "Yeah, she just walked in."

Crap. Had Front Desk Deena spotted my surreptitious building breach? I made a frantic slashing motion over my throat. I didn't have the money owed or the energy required for the woman.

Braden's toothy grin confused me. "Yep. No problem," he said before hanging up.

"What?" I asked, grimly girding my loins for whatever shoe was about to drop on me.

"Relax," he said. "It's good. Really good."

Yeah. I wasn't falling for that.

"Oh, gee. Look at the time. I have to go," I said,

pantomiming a watch check on my naked wrist. My neck flared up as I pivoted for the door.

But there was a small crowd of people in scrubs coming through the door and blocking my exit. I already knew my dad's window didn't open far enough for a body—safety feature—plus it opened to the inside courtyard, and these were not my wall-scaling shoes.

I was trapped.

A nurse in pink heart scrubs handed me a Congratulations balloon. One with a French braid and librarian glasses shoved a cheery bunch of carnations at me. They were all smiling.

Clearly, they had mistaken me for someone else.

"Ally Morales," nursing supervisor Sandy said, stepping to the front of the little smile mob.

Okay. That was definitely my name.

"On behalf of everyone at Goodwin Childers Nursing Home—"

"Except for Deena," someone coughed from the back.

"We'd like to congratulate you on being the first recipient of the Lady George Administration Memory Care Grant."

She handed me a letter, and over the excited buzz, I managed to skim the gist of it.

Congratulations…the first recipient of the Lady George Administration Memory Care Grant… Delighted to inform you that your father's long-term care expenses… covered in full for the next twelve months…

A piece of paper fluttered to the ground, and I bent to pick it up. It was a receipt for twelve months of care.

I couldn't breathe, so I stayed where I was, head to knees, and sucked in air.

"How did this happen?" I wheezed.

"The foundation contacted us. We submitted your name for their approval process. And you won, Ally!"

Dad's care was guaranteed for twelve months. That meant…*everything*.

I gave up on the whole breathing and standing thing and sank to the floor as an entire nursing staff cried with me.

Once I recovered a tiny bit of my dignity, after I hugged and wiped my nose on every single staff member there, I spent a joyful hour with Dad. He didn't recognize me, but he was in a good mood and telling stories about his daughter Ally.

When he started asking what time his piano student was arriving, I decided it was time to head home to get ready for my serving shift.

My steps were lighter than they had been an hour ago. But as relieved as I felt over the unexpected answer to my prayers, my heart still ached.

I missed Dominic. And I hated that. It reminded me of how much I'd missed my mother that first year after she'd left. When I'd still had hope. I'd never really stopped missing the idea of having a mother. But every time the pang arose, it brought with it a bigger, meaner twinge of self-recrimination.

How could I miss someone who had so carelessly hurt me?

I was so busy feeling like crap that I almost walked right by the big house on the corner without my usual daydreaming. And today, I didn't feel like daydreaming. I didn't know if I even believed in happily ever afters like the walls of that house held.

As if to add insult to injury, an older couple appeared in the front window. They were locked in one hell of an embrace that didn't look even remotely grandparent-y.

Okay, fine. So happily ever afters existed. Just not for me. The jokester who said it was better to have loved and lost than never to have loved at all was a real jerk as far as I was concerned.

I turned my back on the happy scene and started down the block when my phone clunk-clanked inside my pocket.

I could just make out my real estate agent's name on the dimly lit screen.

"Bill, hey," I said.

"We've got a full-priced cash offer on the table, Ally," Bill said in an excited rush.

I stopped in my tracks and shook my head to quiet the ringing in my ears. I was dreaming this whole day. I was going to wake up on my stupid twin bed and be devastated any moment now. "I'm sorry. Could you repeat that?"

"Full-priced cash offer," he said. "They want to close by the end of the week. I know it's short notice, but—"

"Accept it. Oh my God. Accept it!" I said, dancing a circle on the sidewalk. Then I froze, a terrible thought stealing into my brain. "Wait a minute. Tell me the buyer isn't Dominic Russo."

"Who? No. It's not even a person. It's a trust. The buyer's agent said the buyer fell in love with the house."

"They did?" I whispered.

"Actually the email said fell in love in the house, but that was a typo. So you're going to need to start packing."

There wasn't much to pack. A couch and a gym bag of dance clothes and work uniforms. The extent of my earthly possessions. But it was better to start fresh without a lot of baggage.

72

ALLY

Things kept happening. Good things.

On Tuesday, the Foxwood police contacted me to tell me my weasel of a contractor had been arrested for fraud, theft, and some other charges that sounded like general douchery. Apparently I hadn't been the only client he'd skipped out on.

The detective wasn't confident that I'd get my money back, but she had recovered my father's pocket watch that the guy had helped himself to.

On Thursday, I got an email from a design firm in Manhattan. They'd seen my work in *Label* and somehow got a direct line to Dalessandra, who sang my praises. They wanted to know if I was interested in a job doing design work.

Friday was bittersweet goodness. The closing on my father's house went off without a hitch. The buyers signed over power of attorney to their agent, so I didn't get to meet them. Over a sun-dappled oak table, I traded keys for a check that would not only keep my father in Goodwin Childers for the next several years but would rebuild some of my own savings and clear my debt to Dominic.

I swung by the bank and deposited the check before anyone could change their minds. Then I wrote out a check for every dime that I owed Dominic Russo, dropped it in the mail, and treated myself to a Lyft to Mrs. Grosu's. I was staying in her guest room for a few days until I could figure out my next move.

I was also hoping to get a glimpse of the new buyers next door.

Halfway to Mrs. Grosu's in a spotless Prius, my phone gave one actual ring and then a half-hearted vibration. It was a *Label* office number. I hesitated. I'd ignored all calls for the last month, afraid it would be Dominic. Afraid it wouldn't be.

I was so tired of being afraid. I was so tired of missing him.

"Hello?"

"Ally, it's Jasmine from HR," the caller announced briskly.

Grumpy Jasmine, bad picture taker.

"Hi," I said.

"I'm calling about where to send your last paycheck."

I was too sad, too depressed, to get excited about money I'd forgotten about.

"Oh, sure," I said and rattled off Mrs. Grosu's address.

"Great," she said. "By the way, I have some information you might find interesting."

I doubted that very much.

"Actually, Jasmine, I don't think—"

"I received a call from this cute junior peon in accounting named Mickey, who I make out with sometimes."

"Uh." Grumpy Jasmine had just officially broken my brain.

"He was talking about this audit of the credit card statements or some other boring stuff that I usually don't hear because I'm too busy staring at his biceps."

Apparently she was into the arm porn.

"Anyway, he mentioned that there was this weirdness because the creative director kept buying food for the admin pool."

"The creative director?" I said slowly.

"In January, Dominic started buying food for the admins almost every day."

"Wait. Wasn't that, like, a thing? Like a thing that they did before…"

Before what? Before me? Before me and my poor ass with my expired salads and rationed leftovers started showing up for work?

"Nope. It started the day after your hire date."

I felt like I needed to sit down.

Okay, so Dominic paid for some food. Big deal. That didn't make up for him not trusting me.

"And then there's the phone and laptop," Jasmine continued.

Oh, shit.

"What about the phone and the laptop?"

"Did you ever notice other new hires weren't getting free tech?"

Yes. "Not really."

My neck started to flare up.

"There was no record of the purchase. So I checked with Gola, who handles some of Dominic's personal bills. He bought them out of pocket and had IT set them up for you."

I thought of Buddy and his wife. How they still didn't know that Dominic Russo was their secret health insurance Santa.

"I don't understand," I began.

"Look, maybe I'm just a romantic at heart," she said.

I doubted that very much.

"The guy screwed up. Big time. But numbers don't lie. He clearly cares about you. Anyway, I'm totally coming to dance this week. See you there!"

"Yeah. See you," I said lamely.

Something occurred to me, and I couldn't get it to un-occur.

Almost every good thing that had happened to me since January had been at the hands of Dominic Russo. The food. The phone and laptop that I desperately needed. The job. The renovations. The closetful of couture. The freaking piano.

It was a pattern. A consistent one. Dominic recognizing a need and quietly filling it.

I was not a lucky person. I didn't win on scratch-offs. It was more fun for me to set dollars on fire than to put them in slot machines that never paid off. And I sure as hell didn't win grants that I didn't know about.

I dug into my backpack in a frantic search. I finally found it at the bottom under a banana and last month's issue of *Label*.

The letter from the foundation.

Lady George Administration Memory Care Grant.

Lady. As in Faith's club, Club Ladies and Gentlemen, where he'd first touched me.

"Please, no," I whispered.

George. George's Pizza, where we'd first met. My stomach dropped.

Administration. The admin pool. Where I'd fallen in love with him.

No. No. No. My head didn't want to believe it. But my heart, that stupid forgiving traitor, was fluttering with idiotic hope.

I dialed the nursing home. "Sandy in the office, please?"

I waited impatiently while the transfer went through.

"This is Sandy," she answered brightly.

"Oh, thank God. It's Ally Morales. I have a very important question."

"Yes, *of course*, Mr. Swanson. I'm happy to help."

"Is Deena there?" I guessed.

"Absolutely. That's confirmed."

"I'll keep this short. Did Dominic Russo have anything to do with the grant for my dad?"

"Uhhhh…" Sandy's nonanswer was damning. "I don't think I have that information currently," she said in a voice two octaves higher than normal.

"Sandy, are you lying to me or Deena right now?"

"Sometimes both options are viable," she said.

"Has Dominic Russo visited my father?" I asked.

"Well, with HIPAA, I'm afraid I can't answer that," she said lamely.

"Oh my God." I rolled my eyes. "Call me when Deena goes for her blood of children break."

I put my head between my knees and tried not to barf everywhere.

"You okay back there?" the driver asked nervously.

"Fine," I lied. "Absolutely fine."

I sat back up and grabbed the sale paperwork out of my bag. The buyer's entity was listed front and center.

Alominic Trust.

I made a half groan, half whine.

The driver swerved to the side of the road. "Lady, please don't barf in my car."

73

ALLY

"Hey, Als. Table three just got here. You can grab his order," Jorge said over the whoosh of the exhaust fan when I walked in the back door for my Saturday shift.

In my opinion, Jorge's Wood-Fired Pizza was better than George's. Jorge was a jolly kind of guy who actually liked both people and pizza. The tips were decent. The pizza was way better. And I got a free meal and as many bathroom breaks as I needed with every shift.

Plus, the pizzeria was located an easy walk from Dad's nursing home.

"Sure," I said, pasting a smile on my face. I was still reeling from yesterday's revelations. In Mrs. Grosu's pink and yellow guest room, I'd added up the cost of twelve months of long-term care.

If I was going to pay Dominic back, I would have to start selling internal organs.

I still didn't know what I was going to do. I needed to talk to him, but I didn't know if I could survive seeing him.

His email last night had been short and oh so sweet.

To: Ally
From: Dominic
Subject: Getting to know me

I'm never getting over you, Ally. And I'm not going to try. My heart was yours from the pepperoni on.

Love,
Dom

My mind on pepperoni, I clocked in and then pushed through the swinging door into the dining room. It was a busy Saturday afternoon. Half the booths were already full. The other server waved to me while she keyed in an order.

But I didn't wave back.

Because I couldn't stop staring at table three.

Those blue eyes pulled me across the checkered tile floor like an industrial magnet.

Dominic Russo, looking more casual than I'd ever seen him in jeans, a sweatshirt, and a ball cap, was staring at me. So sad, so hopeful.

My feet stopped in front of him, and my heart did its best to climb out of my throat.

I *missed* him. My body physically ached for him. The sound of his voice, the furrow of his brow, the smell of him after a shower, the heat from his body that always thawed me.

"Ally," he rasped, then cleared his throat.

"Hi, Dom," I said lamely. I wanted to break down and

cry. I wanted to climb into his lap and let him hold me and convince me that everything was going to be fine now. I wanted him to make it all better. Somehow.

His gaze roamed me from head to toe as if he couldn't quite believe I was here.

Remembering where I was, I pulled my notepad out of my apron and swallowed hard. "Do you know what you want?"

He glanced down at the unopened menu and then back up at me. "I was thinking I could go for a pepperoni pizza."

Ouch. Direct hit on the ol' ticker.

I put the pad back. "Sure. Is there anything else you want?"

He rested his hand on the edge of the green Formica table. His pinkie was an inch from where my hand hung at my side. But sometimes an inch might as well be a mile, and I didn't know how to cross it. I didn't know how to ask him for what I needed. Because I didn't know what I needed.

"There are a lot of things I want," he said softly. His hopeful gaze found mine and held it. His pinkie flexed, and for one glorious, perfect second, it brushed mine. My body lit up like a Christmas tree.

I loved him. So damn much. And he'd hurt me so damn badly. And I didn't know what I needed from him.

I took a self-preserving step backward. "It's so good to see you," I said, addressing my sneakers. "I'll put your order in."

He was looking at me with so much *feeling* it was making me dizzy. His thumb tapped out a silent beat on the table. And the familiarity of it took my breath away. My heart squeezed like it did on days when my dad recognized me.

Maybe it was as simple as that. Loving someone, forgiving someone. Maybe it was about showing up and being strong enough to take the hurt.

He nodded and looked down at the table. "Thanks," he said quietly.

I flew into the kitchen.

"Jorge, I need a pepperoni on the fly, and I need to put the toppings on myself," I announced.

My boss shrugged and shoved a naked pie at me. "Suit yourself, Als."

It was the longest three minutes of my life, waiting for the pizza oven to work its magic.

I almost burnt the shit out of my hand getting the pizza out of the oven and onto a tray.

"Calm down before you get hurt," Jorge admonished.

"I already got hurt. But it's okay because I love him!"

Jorge said something about "crazy women" under his breath. But I was too busy sprinting for the dining room.

Once again, I stopped in my tracks when I saw table three.

He was gone.

I did a quick scan of the restaurant, but my body already knew Dominic Russo was gone. In his place was a thick manilla envelope under a crisp twenty-dollar bill. I dumped the pizza on the table, sat, and tore open the envelope.

A certified check from one Dr. Claudia Morales fluttered out and onto my lap. My mother had written my father a check for the exact amount that she'd snuck out of his savings. There was a second check to me for an amount that made me blink. In the memo field, it said "for expenses incurred."

"Oh my God," I breathed.

"Honey, are you okay over there?" A woman across the restaurant asked. "You look like you're having a fit."

I shook my head silently.

"You're not okay, or you're not having a fit?" she pressed. More customers were turning to stare at me.

"I'm not okay. It's not a fit. It's love."

She nodded sagely. "You're in love with that fine man who was sitting there all broody and beautiful?"

"Yeah."

Next on the stack was the deed for dad's house. Attached to it was a handwritten note.

Ally,

It's yours. No one can ever take your memories from you.

Love,
Dom

"Damn you, Dom," I whispered on a half sob.

Next came a report from what looked like some kind of private investigator.

Subject: Deena Smith, Goodwin Childers Nursing Home

I turned the pages, skimming quickly. It looked like an investigation into unorthodox and illegal collection tactics. Attached was a formal complaint to the state accusing Front Desk Deena of using harassment and intimidation tactics to coerce families into paying the debts of loved ones even when there was no financial responsibility.

There was a newspaper clipping beneath it. A short paragraph in the police blotter mentioning a nursing home employee under investigation for intimidating families of patients to earn large bonuses for on-time collections. The employee had been suspended without pay.

Well, that explained all the damn jewelry.

"That doesn't look like any kind of jewelry or flowers," the woman called over, craning her neck to see what I was looking at.

The last thing in the envelope was an advance copy of *Label*'s May issue.

Dalessandra, looking strong and fierce, stood with four other women on the cover next to the headline "No More Secrets: Survivors Share Their Stories."

"Oh. My. God."

"Well, what is it?"

"A magazine," I said.

"Huh. Guy thinks you want to do a little light reading? You sure there's no diamond ring in there?"

I flipped through the magazine to the spread. Dalessandra and each of the other four women had written essays. There was a breathtaking, full-page picture of Dalessandra and her friend Simone…in an embrace?

"I'm tired of keeping secrets. I'm in love with Simone. We've been in a relationship for years."

"Holy. Shit," I breathed.

I scanned to the bottom.

Editor's Note: Paul Russo was fired from *Label*. He is currently employed by another magazine. At the time, *Label* made the mistake of choosing not to enforce his noncompete and requiring Russo's harassment victims to sign nondisclosure agreements in return for cash settlements. We have since reversed our stance on both issues. Victims will never again be silenced in our offices. On a related issue, managing editor Irvin Harvey has been fired for violating our harassment policy. Dominic Russo will take on the role of managing editor while beauty editor Shayla Bruno steps into the creative director position.

I wanted to read every word.

But first, I wanted to give Dominic his pizza.

"I need a box," I announced to the dining room.

"Yeah. A ring box," the lady at table eight harrumphed.

"A pizza box. Did anyone see which way he went?"

Every woman in the restaurant pointed to the right.

Table two dumped their leftovers onto the bare table and handed me their box.

"Thanks!" I said, shoving my masterpiece inside.

"Go get him before someone else does," the woman said.

I hit the door at a run, pizza box firmly clutched in my hands.

"Dominic Russo!" I yelled at the top of my lungs. But I didn't see his familiar frame anywhere.

He'd left minutes ago. He could have driven away by now. Out of my life again.

I kept running. Kept looking.

"I didn't know Jorge's delivered," a guy in coveralls said as I sprinted past.

"We don't," I called over my shoulder.

I charged across the street to the next block, my heart racing. Where was he? He couldn't be gone. Not now.

I saw the cluster of people, the blue bus stop sign at the end of the block, and stumbled.

Could it be? Would he be there?

I took off again, my heart in my throat.

The sunshine was bright and warm on my face. It felt like hope. Like love.

And there he was. Sitting on a glossy green bench against

a fence behind the bus stop. He was hinged forward, hands hanging between his knees, eyes on the ground.

"You forgot your pizza," I wheezed out.

He tensed and looked up at me, an expression of hope so pure it stitched together every tear in my heart.

"Ally." He was on his feet, reaching for me.

"Oh, hey, Jorge's delivers," a woman in a bright yellow jacket said to her neighbor.

"Man, I could go for a slice of pepperoni right now," her neighbor said.

"Here." I thrust the pizza at Dominic.

"Baby, I don't want a pizza. I want you," he said dryly. "I want to tell you how fucking sorry I am for everything. I want to make it up to you. I want to demand another chance."

"You want this pizza," I insisted, shaking the box.

"Listen, honey, if he doesn't want it, I'll take it," the guy called from the bus bench.

"Remember when you told me that if I wanted anything in the world, I just had to ask you?"

Dominic nodded, looking at me very seriously. "What do you want, Ally?"

"I want you to open this pizza. Please."

Reluctantly, he released his grip on my wrists and took the box from me.

He lifted the lid, and for a moment, I wondered if the pepperonis had gotten sloshed around during my sprint. But then I saw him clench his jaw and swallow hard, and I knew my little message was intact.

He looked up at me, blue eyes burning with intensity. "I don't have my reading glasses on me. Can you read it for me?"

Jorge's pepperonis were huge. Dominic knew exactly what they spelled.

But he wanted me to say the words.

We stood there, a pizza box between us.

I wet my lips and took one last breath before the plunge.

"It says 'I Love You'—well, 'I Heart U,' but you get the gist."

The pizza box was sailing in the direction of the bus stop, and I was flying through the air, landing exactly where I belonged. In Dominic Russo's arms.

"Woo! Free sidewalk pizza!" someone hooted.

But I was too busy being kissed.

He rained kisses over my cheeks, forehead, and chin. And finally, finally, Dominic's mouth was on mine.

He tugged on my hair, pulling my head back, a move so familiar and so missed, I teared up.

"I love you, Ally."

"You guys got any Jorge's garlic bread you wanna throw over here? I won't complain."

Dominic rolled his eyes. "If you give me a minute here, I'll buy you all everything on Jorge's menu."

"Deal!"

I laughed for the first time in what felt like forever.

"Say it again, Maleficent. Please?" Dominic begged.

"I love you, Charming. I'm ready for our happily ever after."

He picked me up right off the ground and twirled me around to the hoots and hollers of our little audience.

I wrapped my arms around him tight enough that he'd never escape. "You Russos keep changing my life at bus stops."

Epilogue

Ally

What are you doing?"

"Shh. Don't distract me with your near nakedness. I'm trying to see if my straw is long enough to reach the bottom of the glass without sitting up," I told him.

But it was too late, I was distracted. Because the breathtaking view of sugary white sand and turquoise waters was already eclipsed by Dominic Russo in package-showcasing swim trunks and dark sunglasses.

I loved the intense man in vests, but the relaxed, sunscreened, island tan version was possibly even more appealing.

"It's your birthday, Ally. I'll order you mango margaritas all day long if it means you never have to see the bottom of your glass."

"Are you trying to get me drunk, Mr. Russo?" I peered over my sunglasses and batted my lashes at him.

He grinned wickedly.

"I think it's time to reapply," he said, holding up the bottle of sunscreen.

"Last 'application,' you spent ten minutes rubbing my breasts, and I got a sunburn everywhere else."

"I promise to pay equal attention to every inch of your beautiful body," he said lecherously.

I felt a quickening between my legs and took a second to pinch myself. Nope. Not dreaming. Not in a coma somewhere. Not hallucinating after an unfortunate bus accident. This. Was. My. Life.

"Are you ready for your birthday present?" he asked.

I laughed. "I thought this trip was my present. And the bikini wardrobe. And the candlelight dinner." Not to mention last night's hamstring-pulling sex for dessert. We were both still limping.

"Oh, baby, I'm just getting started," he said devilishly.

My heart rate kicked up a few hundred notches. Because giving made him so happy. And I had no freaking clue how he was going to feel about what I had to give him.

"Vacation agrees with you, Mr. Managing Editor," I teased.

He abandoned his chair and crowded onto mine. "No work talk," he said sternly.

With Irvin Harvey's unceremonious firing for being a prejudiced bastard, Dominic had stepped into the vacant position and promoted Shayla to creative director. Everyone was happy.

"I love you," I said. Sometimes the words bubbled up and couldn't be contained. And Dominic's face did what it always did when I felt compelled to tell him. It softened as if he too couldn't believe this was his life.

"I love hearing you say that," he said smugly.

Since our reconciliation, we'd played an intense game of getting to know you…outside the bedroom. It was an ongoing conversation. Just like our relationship was an ongoing negotiation. Revelations had been both big and small. Like Dominic's confession that he'd built his life around wanting to outdo his father on every battlefield.

Considering that the man was suspended from *Indulgence* for harassment and facing civil lawsuits and criminal charges, I reminded Dominic that he'd already won.

I hoped to sweet baby cheeses that my little revelation today would give him one more place to win…and not send him into a downward spiral.

He hooked a finger in the string between my breasts. "Are you ready for another drink?" he asked me, his voice husky.

I nodded and bit my lip, ready to take the plunge. "Make sure it's a virgin margarita though, okay?"

He cocked his head. Then took off his sunglasses, his gaze more intense than the Canouan sun.

"Ally?"

I took his hand and slid it over my stomach. "So I know we didn't plan this," I said, the words tumbling out. "And I know liking kids is a lot different from actually having them and raising them and turning them into not terrible human beings. And I know that I'm freaking forty now. But I'm healthy and in good shape, and I think I can do this. I mean, I hope I can do this."

The waiter, in a polo shirt the same blue as the ocean, arrived with a silver tray and a smile.

"Are you two ready for something special?" he asked.

"Uh, hang on a second," Dominic said, his hand still flat on my stomach. "Ally, are you saying… Are we…"

"I'm pregnant. You're going to be a dad. And please don't freak out in a bad way because I really, really need you to be happy about this because I am scared shitless."

"Pregnant? Like with a baby?"

I nodded, suddenly wishing I could drink alcohol. Copious amounts of it.

"Are you okay?" I whispered. He looked like he was going into shock.

"Pregnant," he said again.

"With a baby," I repeated in case he'd missed that part.

He covered his eyes with one hand.

"Oh God. Dom? Charming? Are you okay?" I scrambled into a higher seated position and dragged his hand away from his eyes.

His damp eyes.

"I'm going to be a daddy."

And here came my waterworks like a faucet opening.

I nodded, tears squirting from my eyeballs. "Yeah. You're going to be a daddy," I whispered.

He grabbed me and picked me up off the lounger. I wrapped my legs around his waist and held on tight.

"You're not mad?" I clarified, cupping his face in my hands.

"Mad? I'm floored. And terrified. And excited. And worried. And so fucking happy, Ally. We're gonna have a family."

A family.

Yep. Now I was audibly sobbing. These freaking hormones were turning me into a lunatic.

"Excuse me, *ass*. You were supposed to signal us so we could witness the proposal!"

Startled, I whipped off my sunglasses. "Faith? Christian?"

My best friend and her "see where things go" guy were standing at the foot of my abandoned lounger, looking annoyed.

"I didn't propose yet," Dominic growled.

"Propose?" I shrieked, trying to climb down my very handsome baby daddy.

"Oops," Christian said, flashing his dimples.

"If you didn't propose, what's all this?" Faith demanded. And then her mouth formed a perfect O. "Holy shit. Are you *pregnant*?" she screamed.

I could only nod and cry some more.

"Oh my God!"

She reached for me, and I grabbed her arm. "I know!"

Dominic cleared his throat. "Ladies, I still have this little bit of business to take care of."

Faith released me and snuggled into Christian's side, making a zipped lips gesture. "By all means."

"Thanks," he said dryly. He sank down on the lounger, settling me in his lap.

"Ally Maleficent Morales, will you marry me?"

He reached past me and produced a velvet jewelers' box.

I was nodding vigorously.

"Don't you want to see the ring first?" he whispered, a smile playing on his lips.

I shook my head violently.

"But you're saying yes?"

"Yes!" It burst free. "Yes. Yes. Yes."

And then I was laughing because I felt his erection twitch under me.

"Not my fault. Usually we're doing something else when you say that," he whispered in my ear.

"I love you, Dom."

"I love you, Ally. So fucking much."

"We're getting married," I said.

"And having a baby," he added.

We grinned at each other. His cock moved again.

"Can I hug them yet?" Faith asked Christian.

After a series of hugs and questions, a round of virgin

mango margaritas, and a quickie in the villa's kitchen, Dominic Russo finally slid a beautiful diamond ring on my finger.

"I'm going to need to start lifting weights on the right so I don't bulk up on just one side," I said, sighing dreamily as the very large solitaire caught the light.

Dominic's hand was on my belly again. As he leaned back against the kitchen cabinets, I noticed a smile I'd never seen before on his lips. Contentment.

"Do you want to call your mom and Simone?" I asked.

His smile widened. "Of course."

"Can we call my dad?" I asked. "I mean, he might not understand, but I really want him to be part of this," I said.

"Of course. But first, there's something you should see," he said, reaching for his phone in his discarded swim trunks. "Your dad gave his blessing," He opened a photo.

"Oh. Dom," I breathed.

It was a selfie of Dominic and Dad. My dad was grinning and holding the open ring box.

"I went every day and asked him until it was a good day," Dominic said softly.

And I was back to nodding and crying again.

"This hormone thing," he said, gently wiping the tears from my face with his thumbs. "How long does it last?"

"I guess we'll find out," I sobbed.

Bonus Epilogue

ALLY

One year-ish later...

"What are you doing? Breaking and entering?" I asked, readjusting Maya's blanket like any obsessive new mom concerned about the effects of pollen, suffocation, sun, and fifty-degree temperatures on my perfect child.

"It's not breaking and entering if you have a key," my husband said smugly, opening the front door of the massive brick house with a flourish.

"Dominic Russo, why do you have a key to the big house on the corner?" I hissed.

Brownie tapped out an anxious beat with his toenails on the brick porch.

He'd *said* he was taking our little family for a drive.

I'd been delighted when we left Manhattan's skyline behind us and crossed the river into my old stomping grounds. We'd cruised past my childhood home, now the home of a nonprofit community center for adults with memory disorders. I'd missed the grand opening because I'd been in labor with Little Miss Hey I'm Coming Three Weeks Early.

There was a sturdy fence around the yard—now a small but colorful flower garden—and rocking chairs on the front porch. Two of the chairs were occupied. I waved and the chairs' occupants waved back.

Dominic had then delighted both me and Brownie by stopping at our favorite ice cream place, where our little family sat in the sunshine and devoured our cones.

Now, we were about to be arrested for trespassing at the house I'd loved since I was a kid.

"What are we doing here? Why do you have a key? Where are the people?" I asked.

"So many questions," my husband said, dropping a kiss to my forehead and repeating the gesture with our daughter's wrinkled brow before taking the carrier from me.

There was a softness about him now. An ease, as if the knots of hate and guilt had untied themselves, leaving behind only love.

"Dom? What did you do?" I whispered, stepping inside.

The house was empty. As in furniture-less rooms, bare walls, every sound echoing off the hardwood floors.

I turned to face him. He was unbuckling Maya from her seat, then cradling her against his chest.

He'd been a rock through both pregnancy and labor, as expected. And when our little girl arrived, screaming her way into the world, my beautiful husband had cradled her in one arm, dropped his head to mine, and cried.

My heart broke and glued itself back together ten times stronger in that moment. Because Dominic Russo finally realized that the love he had in that big, soft heart of his would never allow him to turn out like his own father.

Our daughter's arrival was the evidence he'd been waiting for his whole life.

I may have sobbed so hard that the doctors considered sedating me. True story.

A week earlier, Gola and the admin pool threw Dominic a surprise baby shower. Greta came out of retirement to attend. Dalessandra and Simone showed up in the hospital room with a six-foot-tall stuffed giraffe and a flower arrangement worth more than my first car. After snuggling their beautiful baby granddaughter, they broke into our house with a team of designers and handy people to finish painting the walls and arranging the ridiculously expensive nursery furniture.

Our daughter was perfect.

Not just because she looked a whole lot like me or because she had Dominic's fierce frown. And also not just because I was filled with all the motherly hormones that rendered me incapable of murdering my own child because she was only sleeping in what felt like fifteen-minute increments.

Part of it was that she was no longer physically attached to my body, and it was really nice to get back some autonomy. Pregnancy and I had not agreed with each other. Any woman who tells you pregnancy is the full expression of womanhood is a dirty liar or selling stretch mark cream.

Orgasms, ladies, are the full expression of womanhood. Have as many as you possibly can. But get your own Dominic Russo. This one's all mine.

But I digress.

So there I was, standing in the foyer of every dream I'd ever had, afraid to hope.

Because this man had already given me so much.

The look he gave me was so raw and real I almost couldn't take it.

And when I looked past him, I spotted a very familiar musical instrument alone in a swath of light from the stained-glass bay window.

I crossed to the piano and ran my fingers over the keys. "You already bought it, didn't you?" I whispered.

Dominic, hands on our baby's feet, leaned against an empty built-in bookcase. "Maybe. That depends on how much trouble I'm going to be in."

"Oh, Dom." I shook my head, eyes glistening. I'd cried a lot the last few months. Hormones and whatnot. But this feeling was something altogether different.

"It needs some updates. Especially the kitchen. There's five bedrooms. Three bathrooms. An office off the back with room enough for both of us when I work from home," he said. "And the third floor is one big room. I thought maybe we could turn it into a studio for you."

"I love you so damn much."

"You're not mad?" he ventured.

"I'm a whole lot of things right now." And I was. A vibrating mess of feelings that threatened to swamp me.

He gave a little shrug. "It was your dream."

That was the only reason he needed to make it happen.

I shook my head, digging my nails into my palms because this beautiful, perfect man deserved a reprieve from crazy wife tears. "Not this house. You. You are my dream."

"Ally." It sounded like a caress.

"Put the baby down, Dom."

His smile was sly and sexy. "Why?"

"Because I'm going to thank you properly."

Minutes later—hey, we're still figuring our way through

postbaby sex, okay?—I rested my head on Dominic's stomach and stared up at the plaster ceiling. Our plaster ceiling. Maya babbled in her car seat next to our discarded pile of pants and shoes.

"What are we going to do with all this space?" I asked him.

His fingers lazily combed through my hair. "Fill it."

A little less than ten years later...

"If you two don't get out from under my feet, I'm going to lock you in the backyard," I threatened sternly.

The big house, *our* big house, had been filled all right. Right now, it was two dogs doing the filling in the kitchen. But the rest of our home was art and furniture, music and friends, family and children.

No, people, I didn't have triplets at forty-one. After that pregnancy, I wasn't delusional enough to beg Dominic to put more babies in me.

Luckily, I didn't have to. Because our former next-door neighbors in Manhattan, the Vargas family, had a solution. It turns out Elton and Sascha's adopted son, Jace, had a brother and sister who had entered foster care. It was also right around that time that they fell in love with a house on our block. So our kids, all four of them in total, got to grow up together.

Our big house contained not just a family of five but two dogs—Brownie and Cookie—a pet rabbit, and seven goldfish. *Crap. Make that six.* These walls held memories. Of Christmas mornings and spontaneous weeknight dinners that ran way too late, resulting in school drop-off hangovers. Of me going back to the professional life I loved, building my own small graphic design company, and teaching dance as often as possible.

Of tears and heartbreak. Big and small. My father was gone, and I still missed him every day. I wished that he could be at our table with our loud, loving brood. I wished that he could have been in the audience during Jack's drum solo at last night's high school band concert. But Mr. Mohammad, Mrs. Grosu, and Dalessandra and Simone had been there.

In small ways, Dad was still here. Just like my childhood, there was always music at home. Only my kids got to see their mom and dad dancing to it in the kitchen between soccer practice and black-tie galas. Jack and I took over the Morales family tradition of screaming at the TV during Mets games. Maya was following in my footsteps in dance. Dominic and I weren't quite sure where her equal love of martial arts came from, but we were down with it.

I heard the music and tiptoed closer.

Dominic and our fourteen-year-old daughter, Reese, were side by side on the piano bench, talking quietly and playing around with a tune. Watching Dominic with our kids was a balm. Building new memories with a family of my own was the best way I could think of to honor my own dad.

Dominic played a riff and bumped shoulders with Reese when she answered it. I pressed my fingers to my lips. The teenage hormones were strong with this one. I remembered the angst and misery of fourteen and prayed to the goddesses of puberty that they would be kind to our girl.

So far, she was hanging in there.

"Dad, I know," Reese sighed dramatically. "Consent. Consequences. Birth control. Jeez. Between you and Mom, I'm basically a walking encyclopedia on sex."

"It's a big deal," he told her. "And it's entirely up to you."

"I'm fourteen. Boys my age are gross."

It was true. Fourteen-year-old boys were gross.

"Your mom and I just want you to be prepared. Everything that happens to your body should be your decision."

"Oh my God, Daaaaad. I have more respect for my body than the rest of the girls in my class combined," she assured him. "Can we please talk about literally anything else?"

Respect your body and everyone else's. Our kids weren't required to hug anyone they didn't want to. Jack and his brother, Jace, had been given the "anything other than an enthusiastic yes is a no" lecture on everything from hand-holding on up. Our girls, well, you just witnessed the outcome of a years-long education on body autonomy.

They knew vaguely of Paul Russo. That they had a grandfather out there who wasn't a part of their lives. And not just because he went to jail. Our kids understood that blood didn't make a family.

"How's your friend Chloe doing with the divorce?" Dominic asked, changing the subject.

"She's okay," Reese said, changing the classical tune to a pop song. Dominic followed her.

My husband took parenting seriously. He knew our kids' friends, knew their parents, knew who was spending what night at whose house. He knew which kid hated raspberries (Maya, the little weirdo) and who needed more space when they were upset (me and Reese).

Happy that we were raising kids with boundaries, I ducked back into the kitchen and checked the cookies. Cinnamon butterscotch were Dominic's favorite, and Sascha had given me her recipe. We'd have a full house tonight. We always did on Dominic's birthday. It was tradition.

So was the new black dress I'd found tucked away in my closet.

This one was a form-hugging Valentino. I couldn't wait to

put it on. And I already knew that Dominic couldn't wait to take it off.

"Mom! Can I have a cookie?" Nine-year-old Maya exploded in from the backyard, her cheeks pink from the March cold.

"How did you know they were done?" I teased, swiping a hand through her tangled curls.

"Brownie came outside eating one," she said.

"Damn that dog," I said, noticing the missing one on the very edge of the tray.

"If Brownie gets one, I should get one," she insisted.

"Mom! Are the cookies done?" Jack trooped inside, Jace on his heels. They both had skateboards under their arms. At fifteen, Jack was pretty much over spontaneous shows of parental affection. So when he rested his head on my shoulder, I wisely decided not to yell at him for the grass stains and hole in the knee of his new jeans.

My kids were making memories too, and sometimes that involved falling down and ruining nice things.

That was the very reason we had moved the completely ridiculous $8,000 white silk sofa Dalessandra and Simone had gotten me for my last birthday into the office. We could have nice things. They just couldn't be in rooms where children and dogs were allowed.

"Did someone say cookies?" Reese sauntered into the kitchen. I opened the fridge and handed her a fizzy water, her grandmothers' doing.

She gave me a smile, a real one, and a spontaneous peck on the cheek.

The kids and dogs crowded around the island, helping themselves to warm cookies right off the racks, bickering for the most part good-naturedly. There was only one thing missing. I snagged a cookie and ducked out of the kitchen.

I found Dominic behind his desk in our office. He was in sweatpants and a T-shirt that showed off his unfairly fine form. His hair had started to go gray, and I was obsessed with the deepening crinkles in the corners of his eyes. Fifty-five looked good on the man.

"Happy birthday, Charming," I said, sliding the pocket doors closed behind me and wandering around his desk.

"Do you have something for me?" he asked devilishly. I produced the cookie from behind my back, and he laughed.

"What's so funny?" I asked.

He shook his head and pulled me between his legs. "Nothing."

"Do you want your cookie or not?"

"I'd rather have you," he said, rising from his chair and pinning me between his desk and the very inappropriate hard-on trying to escape his pants. "Tell me you locked the door," he said, nuzzling into the side of my neck.

"Mr. Managing Editor. Here? Now?" I asked, my voice embarrassingly breathy. "What about later?"

"Later is later," he said, slipping one hand under the hem of my sweater. "The kids are distracted by cookies."

"That only gives us four-ish minutes before they start fighting," I reminded him, shivering as his fingers dipped under the cup of my bra to capture my already-pebbled nipple.

"Then I guess we'd better work fast," he said, giving a tug.

"Fast is good," I breathed, yanking the waistband of his sweats down and grabbing his shaft with enthusiasm.

"Floor or desk?" He groaned, shoving my sweater up and bra down.

"Desk?" It came out as a hiss because he'd just sucked a nipple into his mouth.

"Quiet," he ordered, biting down.

"Gah. Bossy!" I whispered.

He growled and spun me around so I was bent over his desk. My leggings were dragged down my legs, my feet kicked wider. But the hand that coasted over my hip and thigh was gentle, reverent.

"Hold on," he said, his voice rough.

Obligingly, I curled my fingers around the opposite lip of the desk.

The throbbing between my legs intensified as I felt Dominic trace the wet head of his cock down the cleft of my ass.

I let out a needy, desperate groan.

He slapped me on the ass. "Didn't I say quiet?"

Every damn time was a seduction, a master class in pleasure. No matter when or where or how long we had, it was always, always perfect.

A dog barked. A kid yelled, "I'm gonna tell Mom!"

But I was suddenly extremely confident in their conflict resolution abilities.

Besides, Dominic Russo was sliding his cock into me inch by gorgeous inch and telling me how much he fucking loved me.

AUTHOR'S NOTE

Dear Reader,

This book came from two places—me wondering what the heck an office romance would look like after the #MeToo movement got everyone talking about consent and positions of power and my obsession with *The Devil Wears Prada*. (Side rant: Don't get me started on how mad I get at Andy's friends for being all grabby hands for her fancy fashion gifts and then acting like jerks about how hard she works.)

Setting my ire aside, I love a grumpy hero who is trying to do the right thing and a sunshiny heroine who is convinced she doesn't need any help. And I *especially* love it when they don't like each other. I had so much fun writing this slow burn and their wicked banter.

I hope you loved Dominic and Ally (and Brownie) as much as I did. If you did, please feel free to leave a gushing review raving about my literary genius on Amazon or BookBub. Don't want to miss a new book? Sign up for my rarely annoying, almost always entertaining newsletter on my website.

Thanks for reading! I think you're wonderful!

Xoxo,
Lucy Score

Wondering What to Read Next?

Check out my blue-collar Brooklyn babe and the Manhattan bachelor rich guy who have to work together to rescue a groom and save a wedding in *The Worst Best Man*.

Read it in Kindle, audio, and paperback.

ACKNOWLEDGMENTS

Without the following people (and things), I would not be able to deliver quality entertainment to you. Please rise and applaud the following:

Kari March Designs for BOTH amazing covers for this book.

Jessica Snyder, Amanda Eden, and Dawn Harer for their editorial eyeballs.

Binge Readers Anonymous for their refusal to accept any other title than Grumpy Grump Face.

Jelly Krimpets.

Everyone on Team Lucy for taking enough off my plate that I can continue to spend ridiculous amounts of time imagining up characters and writing their stories.

My secret street team for being the best cheerleaders ever.

Single-stream recycling.

Every single person who stepped up to keep our world spinning during the COVID-19 pandemic. You are our real-life heroes, and we applaud you.

Mr. Lucy for being my very own grumpy hero with a caretaking complex. I love you so much.

ABOUT THE AUTHOR

Lucy Score is a *Wall Street Journal* and #1 Amazon bestselling author. She grew up in a literary family who insisted that the dinner table was for reading and earned a degree in journalism. She writes full-time from the Pennsylvania home she and Mr. Lucy share with their obnoxious cat, Cleo. When not spending hours crafting heartbreaker heroes and kick-ass heroines, Lucy can be found on the couch, in the kitchen, or at the gym. She hopes to someday write from a sailboat, oceanfront condo, or tropical island with reliable Wi-Fi.

Sign up for her newsletter and stay up on all the latest Lucy book news.

You can also follow her here:

Website: lucyscore.com
Facebook: lucyscorewrites
Instagram: @scorelucy
BookBub: bookbub.com/authors/lucy-score
Binge Books: bingebooks.com/author/lucy-score
Readers Group: facebook.com/groups/BingeReadersAnonymous

Things We Never Got Over

Welcome to Knockemout, Virginia

Knox Morgan doesn't tolerate drama, especially in the form of a stranded runaway bride.

Naomi Witt is on the run. Not just from her fiancé and a church full of well-wishers, but from her entire life. Although if you ask her, Naomi's riding to the rescue of her estranged hot mess of a twin, Tina, to Knockemout, a rough-around-the-edges town where disputes are settled the old-fashioned way...with fists and beer. Usually in that order.

Too bad for Naomi, her evil twin hasn't changed at all. After helping herself to Naomi's car and cash, Tina leaves behind something unexpected: the niece Naomi didn't know she had. Now she's a guardian to an eleven-year-old-going-on-thirty with no car, no money, and no plan.

There's a reason this bearded, bad-boy barber doesn't get involved with high-maintenance women, especially not Type-A romantic ones. But since Naomi's life imploded right in front of him, the least Knox can do is help her out of her jam. And just as soon as she stops getting into new trouble, he can leave her alone and get back to his quiet, solitary life.

At least, that's the plan.